Life is sweet with

Jenny
COLGAN

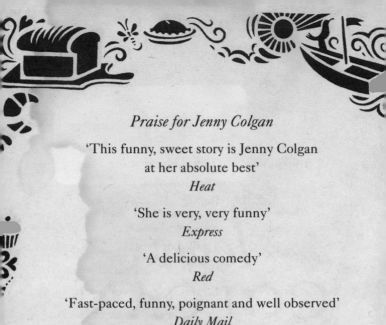

'A smart, witty love story'
Observer

'Full of laugh-out-loud observations ...
utterly unputdownable'
Woman

'A fabulously sweet concoction of warmth, wit and
lip-smacking childhood treats'
Candis

'A chick-lit writer with a difference ... never scared to try
something different, Colgan always pulls it off'
Image

'A Colgan novel is like listening to your best pal, souped
up on vino, spilling the latest gossip – entertaining,
dramatic and frequently hilarious'
Daily Record

'An entertaining read'
Sunday Express

'Part-chick lit, part-food
porn ... this is full on
fun for foodies'
Bella

Jenny COLGAN

Little Beach Street Bakery

sphere

SPHERE

First published in Great Britain in 2014 by Sphere

A CIP catalogue record for this book
is available from the British Library.

ISBN 978-0-7515-5592-9

Typeset in Caslon by M Rules
Printed and bound in Great Britain by
Clays Ltd, St Ives plc

Papers used by Sphere are from well-managed forests
and other responsible sources.

MIX
Paper from
responsible sources
FSC® C104740

Sphere
An imprint of
Little, Brown Book Group
100 Victoria Embankment
London EC4Y 0DY

An Hachette UK Company
www.hachette.co.uk

www.littlebrown.co.uk

To Anna-Marie Fourie, my dear first reader, and far too distant friend, who knows what it is like to wait for someone to come home from the sea.

Little Beach Street Bakery

I wish I was a fisherman
Tumbling on the seas
Far away from dry land
And its bitter memories
Casting out my sweet line
With abandonment and love
No ceiling bearing down on me
'Cept the starry sky above
With light in my head
You in my arms
Woohoo!

The Waterboys, 'Fisherman's Blues'

Rise up rise up you fine young men
The ship she sails in the morn
Whether it's windy, whether it's cold, or
    whether there's a deadly storm

'Sir Patrick Spens',
*c.*14th century, traditional

Chapter One

Years later, when she was an old lady, and many miles away, Polly would find it hard to explain that that was how they had lived back then. That some days they could cross to the mainland in a car, but some days they had to take the boat. Sometimes they were cut off for a long time and nobody would quite know when or how; the tidal charts could only track the tides, not the weather.

'But wasn't it awful?' Judith would ask. 'Knowing you were cut off?'

And Polly would think back to the way the sun had glinted off the water, when it wasn't receding, and the light would change and the water would glow pink, rose, violet in the setting sun over to the west, and you knew another day was going past and you weren't going anywhere.

'Actually, it wasn't,' she'd say. 'It was lovely. You just had to snuggle down, settle in. It was only you and everyone else on the Mount. Make sure everything was high up, and if the power was still on, that was nice, but if it wasn't, well, you'd manage that too. You could see the candles glowing in all the little windows. It was cosy.'

'It sounds about a hundred years ago.'

Polly smiled. 'I know. But it wasn't that long ago, not really . . . It feels like nothing to me. If there's a corner where you plant your heart, it's always with you.

'But of course that all came much later. To begin with, it *was* awful.'

2014
Polly leafed through the paperwork they had given her in the shiny folder with the picture of a lighthouse on the front. It was, she noticed, a pretty picture. She was trying incredibly hard to look on the bright side.

And the two men in the room were nice. Nicer than they had to be; so nice, in fact, that they made Polly feel oddly worse instead of better. She felt sorry, rather than angry or defiant.

They were sitting in the back room of the little two-room office in the converted railway station that she and Chris had been so proud of. It was dinky and charming, with an old non-working fireplace in what had once upon a time been the waiting room.

Now both rooms were a mess: files pulled out, computers lugged around, papers strewn everywhere. The very nice men from the bank were patiently going through all of them. Chris was sitting there sullenly, looking like a five-year-old deprived of a favourite toy. Polly was dashing around trying to be helpful, and every so often he would shoot her a

2

sarcastic look, which she knew meant 'Why are you being so helpful to these people who are trying to destroy us?', and even though she supposed he had a point, she couldn't help herself.

It also occurred to Polly later that the bank employed these people to be nice for exactly that reason: to encourage helpful behaviour, avoid confrontation, stop fights. This made her sad, both for herself and Chris, and for these nice men, whose job day to day was witnessing other people's misery. It wasn't their fault. Chris thought it was, of course.

'So,' said the older of the two men, who wore a turban and had small neat glasses perched on the end of his nose. 'The normal form is that bankruptcy procedures come before the circuit court. You don't both have to go; just one of the directors needs to actually be there.'

Polly winced at the word 'bankruptcy'. It sounded so final, so serious. Something that happened to silly pop stars and celebrities. Not to hard-working people like them.

Chris snorted sarcastically. 'You can do that,' he said to Polly. 'You love all that busy bee stuff.'

The younger man looked sympathetically at Chris. 'We realise this is very difficult.'

'How?' said Chris. 'Have you ever gone bankrupt?'

Polly glanced back down at the pretty lighthouse, but it wasn't really working any more. She tried to think of something else. She found herself admiring the lovely drawings from Chris's portfolio they'd hung on the wall when they'd first moved there, seven years earlier, both of them in their mid-twenties, full of optimism for launching a graphic

3

design firm. They had started out well, with some of Chris's clients from his old job, and Polly had worked ceaselessly on the business management side, drumming up new contacts, networking relentlessly, selling to businesses all over Plymouth, where they lived, and as far away as Exeter and Truro.

They had invested in a flat on a new-build development near the waterfront in Plymouth, very minimalist and modern, and had gone to all the right restaurants and bars, to be seen and to do business. It had worked well – for a time. They had felt themselves quite the up-and-comers, loved saying they ran their own business. But then came the 2008 banking crisis, and new technology in computers was making it easier than ever to manipulate images, do your own artwork. With firms cutting back on outside commissions, advertising and freelances, loading more and more on to their own staff, graphic design, as Chris pointed out, went horribly downhill. It got done. Just less and less by them.

Polly had worked her fingers to the bone. She had never stopped pitching, closing, discounting; doing anything to get the sales for her talented other half. Chris, on the other hand, had withdrawn completely, blaming the world for not wanting his wonderful artwork and hand-crafted lettering. He had become sullen and uncommunicative, which Polly had tried to counter by maintaining a positive attitude. It had been pretty tough to keep that up.

Although Polly would never, ever admit it, barely to herself, the fact that the day had finally come – long after she had implored him to wind up the business and find a job elsewhere, and he had accused her of disloyalty and plotting

4

against him – was something of a relief. It was unpleasant, awful; so shaming, even if lots of people they used to barhop with in the trendy centre of Plymouth were going through – or knew people who had been through – the same thing. Polly's mother didn't understand at all; she saw it as something akin to prison. They were going to have to put the house on the market, start over. But having Mr Gardner and Mr Bassi here from the bank at least seemed to mean that something was getting sorted out, something was happening. The last two years had been so miserable and defeating, professionally and personally. Their relationship had been put on hold really; they were more like two people who grudgingly shared a flat. Polly felt wrung out.

She looked at Chris. New lines were etched on his face that she'd not really noticed before. It had been a while, she realised, since she'd really looked at him properly. Towards the end, it had felt that even glancing up when he came back from the office – she always left first, while he would stay, going over their few commissions again and again and again, as if sheer perfectionism might change the inevitable – carried a note of accusation, of blame, so she had kept her head down.

The weird thing was, had it been only their personal lives coming apart, then everyone they knew would have been full of sympathy and help and advice and reassurance. But a failing business ... people were too scared to say anything. They all kept their distance, and didn't probe too much, even Polly's fearless best friend Kerensa.

Perhaps it was because the fear – of penury, of losing the life you had worked so hard for – was too deep, too strong, and everyone thought their situation might be infectious. Perhaps it was because people didn't really realise. Perhaps the pair of them had kept the facade up too successfully for too long: looking cheery; putting joint meals on the credit card and holding their breath when it was time for it to go through the machine; hand-made birthday gifts – thank goodness Polly could bake, that was useful; hanging on to the flashy black Mazda, though that would have to go now, of course. Polly didn't care about the car. She did care about Chris. Or she had. In the last year or so, she hadn't seen the Chris she knew at all. The sweet, funny man who had been so shy and awkward when they'd got together, then blossomed when he'd started up his own graphic design consultancy. Polly had supported him all the way. They were a team. She'd proved it too; come to work for the business. Put in her life savings (which after the mortgage hadn't been much), fought and fought for custom, charmed and chased and exhausted herself in every conceivable way.

That made it worse, of course. When he'd finally come home that fateful night, a cold cold spring, though it felt more like never-ending winter, and sat down, and she'd looked at him, really looked at him, and he'd said, grimly, 'It's over.'

Local newspapers were closing, so they didn't need advertising, so they didn't need layout or design . . . and businesses didn't really need flyers any more, or they did but they designed them themselves on the web and printed them out at home. Everyone was a designer now, and a photographer, and everything else Chris had once done so well, with so much care and attention to detail. It wasn't really the recession, although that hadn't helped. It was that the world

6

had changed. He might as well have been trying to sell pagers, or cassette tapes.

It had been months since they'd last made love, but she'd woken often in the early hours to find him lying wide awake beside her, desperately doing sums in his head or just letting misery and anxiety churn around inside him. And she'd tried to find the right words to help, but nothing had.

'No, that won't work,' he'd bark to her every suggestion, from wedding stationery to school yearbooks. Or, 'It's pointless.' He'd become more and more obstructive, until working together was almost intolerable, and because he didn't like any of Polly's ideas for the business, and they had almost nothing coming in, Polly had less and less to do. She'd let him leave first in the morning so he could go for a run; my only form of stress release, he'd said, at which she'd bitten her tongue to stop herself pointing out that any time she suggested anything – a walk, a stroll down to the harbour, a picnic, things that cost nothing – he'd snarl back at her that it was useless and he couldn't be bothered.

Polly had tried to get him to a GP, but that was a waste of time too. He simply wouldn't admit that there was anything wrong – with him, with them, with anything. It was just a slump; it would be all right. Then he came across her looking on a jobs website and that had been the catalyst. The row they'd had that night had nearly blown the roof off, and it had all come tumbling out: how much money he'd borrowed, how much worse the situation was than he'd ever let on to Polly. She'd stared at him open-mouthed.

A week later – a silent, agonising week – he'd slumped in, sat down and looked her straight in the face.

'It's over.'

And now here they were in the wreckage of their business with the very nice Mr Gardner and Mr Bassi, and every happy dream and plan they'd come up with in the days when they thought they could do anything . . . every piece of paperwork she'd watched him sign as they popped the champagne, christened the desk in the lovely little office, goggled at their ad in the Yellow Pages . . . all of it was gone, into a world that really didn't care how hard they'd worked or how much they'd wanted it or any of those reality-show clichés that actually were completely irrelevant in the scheme of things. It was over. All the pictures of lighthouses in the world couldn't change that.

Chapter Two

'Here are the things I have,' said Polly, walking through the town, the chill spring wind catching her. She was desperately trying to gear herself up and count her blessings; she had a summit with her best friend and didn't want to be in tears when she met her.

'I am healthy. I am well, apart from the dodgy ankle that I twisted dancing in that bar, which served me right. I have my own faculties. I have lost my money in a business, but people lose more all the time. I haven't been in any natural disasters. My family are all well. Annoying, but well. My relationship ... people go through far worse. Far worse. It's not like we have to divorce—'

'What are you doing?' said Kerensa, loudly. Even though she was tottering on really high heels, she still moved as fast as Polly did in her Converses and had caught up with her on her own way home from her management consulting job. 'Your lips are moving. Are you actually going properly crazy? Because you know ...'

'What?'

'Might be a strategy. Disability living allowance?'

'KERENSA!' said Polly. 'You are awful. And no, I was counting my blessings, if you must know. I'd got to "don't have to get divorced."'

Kerensa pulled a face that would probably have expressed doubt if she hadn't had so much Botox that it was often difficult to tell quite what she was feeling, although she would then immediately explain at high volume.

'Good Lord, seriously? What else was there? Two arms, two legs?'

'I thought we were meant to be meeting so you could cheer me up.'

Kerensa held up the clanking bag from the wine shop.

'We most certainly are. So go on, how far did you get? Once you'd discounted homeless, jobless, all that.'

They had stopped outside Kerensa's immaculate Plymouth town house, which had two little orange trees either side of the polished red door with the brass knocker.

'Actually, I'm not so sure I do want to come over,' said Polly, but she didn't really mean it. This was Kerensa's way; she always confronted life head-on. Something Polly should have done a little more of in the last year or so, she knew, as the business went down the tubes and Chris became ever more unreachable. She had asked Kerensa for professional advice only once, when they'd had a bit to drink at a Christmas party years ago, and Kerensa had told her that what they were doing was risky and then had begged her not to ask again. Polly had convinced herself that all businesses were risky and the subject had never been mentioned since.

'Well, you're here now, and I'm not eating all these Pringles by myself,' said Kerensa cheerfully, taking out her key on its Tiffany fob.

'You never eat Pringles,' grumbled Polly. 'You put them all out, then you go, "Oh, I had a gigantic lunch that I'm pretending about, please eat these Pringles, I can't keep them, they'll go off." Which they don't, by the way.'

'Well, if you stay, you can eke them out in the manner of your choosing, rather than guzzle them down like a starving vole.'

Before Polly could say anything, Kerensa put up her hands.

'Just stay for tonight.'

'OK,' said Polly.

Polly closed her eyes when she said it, but there it was, set out by Mr Gardner and Mr Bassi: the bank was going to take the flat. When she had told her mother, her mother had basically responded like she'd had a child then sold it. That was why she tried not to confide in her mother more often than was strictly necessary.

'So. I am trying to look on the bright side of this.'

'Of being homeless?'

'Shut up. I am just going to need a place of my own.'

Kerensa tried to wrinkle her brow, then looked at the light dusting of Pringle crumbs Polly had left on the BoConcept sofa.

'Just you?'

Polly bit her lip. 'We're not breaking up. It's just … I'm not sure the two of us, kicking about in a tiny horrible rental …'

11

She took a deep breath and a large slug of wine.

'He said he wants to go back to his mum's for a bit. Just until ?... until we get ourselves a bit straight, do you know what I mean? Then we can see how the land lies.'

Polly was doing her best to pretend this was the result of a calm, logical decision-making process rather than tempestuous fights and sulking.

'I mean, it'll be good ... a bit of a change.'

Kerensa nodded sympathetically.

'Until the flat sells ... I mean, I have nothing. If it fetches more than we're expecting, that might clear the debts, but ...'

'But you're not counting on it?'

'The way my luck is at the moment,' said Polly, 'I probably will get a tiny bit of money back, and as I leave the bank after picking it up, a bolt of lightning will come out of the sky and set it on fire. Then a piano will fall on my head and knock me down a manhole.'

Kerensa patted her hand.

'How's Chris doing?'

Polly shrugged. 'About the same. They were very nice, the receiver guys. You know, considering.'

'What a horrible job.'

'It's a job,' said Polly. 'I'm quite impressed by that at the moment.'

'Are you looking?'

'Yes,' said Polly. 'I am overqualified and far too old for every single job on earth. Plus nobody seems to pay for entry-level jobs any more. Plus I really need an address.'

Kerensa said instantly, 'You know you can live here.'

Polly looked round at the immaculate, pristine single

woman's lair. Kerensa had her pick of men – a result of an extremely fit body, expensive clothes and an incredibly snotty attitude – but had never been remotely interested in settling down with anyone. She was like a pedigree cat, thought Polly gloomily, whereas she, Polly, was more like a big, friendly, messy dog. Maybe a springer spaniel; she had long strawberry-blonde hair and small features.

'I would rather sleep in a bin than risk our friendship sharing a place again.'

'We had a great time living together!' said Kerensa.

'We did not!' retorted Polly. 'You went out every weekend with those braying bellends with boats and you never did the washing-up!'

'Well, one, I asked you to come with us every weekend.'

'And I didn't go because they were bellends.'

Kerensa shrugged.

'And two, I never washed up because I never ate anything. You were the one trailing flour and yeast everywhere.'

Polly's baking hobby had never quite left her. Kerensa actually believed that carbs were poison and genuinely thought she was allergic to gluten. It was amazing they were as good friends as they were.

'Still, not a chance,' said Polly, looking sad. 'But God, I don't think I could move in with a bunch of twenty-somethings and pretend to get down with the kids.'

She had turned thirty-two earlier in the year. She wondered, briefly, if one of the tiny upsides of being a bankrupt would be having a good excuse to stop buying wedding and christening presents for absolutely everybody she knew.

Kerensa smiled. 'You totally could. You could go clubbing.'

'Oh God.'

'Stay up all night talking about the meaning of life and smoking dope.'

'Oh Christ.'

'Go camping at musical festivals.'

'Seriously,' said Polly. 'I'm in despair already and you're rubbing salt. Rub rub rub. Mmm. Salt.'

Kerensa handed over the Pringles tube with a practised air of weariness.

'Well, carry on staying with me, I've told you.'

'On your zillion-dollar sofa in your one-bedroom apartment for an unspecified amount of time?' said Polly. 'Thank you, it's kind of you to ask, but I'm going to look online. For me, by myself. It'll be ... cool.'

Kerensa and Polly pored over the laptop in silence. Polly was scrolling through the list of flats within the budget set by the bank. It was not an edifying sight. In fact, rents seemed to have gone crazy. It was awful.

'That's a cupboard,' said Kerensa periodically. 'That one doesn't have any windows. Why would they take a picture of the stained wall? What's the other wall like? I know that street from when I dated that ambulanceman. It's the local bottling blackspot. People get bottled.'

'There's nothing,' said Polly, panicking. She'd had no idea, not really, that their mortgage was so low and rentals were so high. 'There's absolutely nothing.'

'What about an "executive flatshare"?'

'They're incredibly expensive, and you have to pay for

satellite television and probably share with some weirdo who keeps weights in his room.'

As she scrolled further down, Polly grew more and more worried. She didn't know quite how low her standards could go, but the more she looked at it, the more she realised she had to be on her own. However much she was trying to keep up appearances with Kerensa and Chris and her mum, something truly awful had happened and it wasn't going to go away, not for a long time. The thought of herself crying quietly in her bedroom surrounded by partying young things was desperate at best, utterly tragic at worst. She needed to retreat, get her bounce back. She was not instantly going to start dressing ten years younger and talking about boy bands. Or go back to her mum, who loved her and would do anything for her, but who would also undoubtedly sigh, and make sorrowful enquiries about Chris and talk about other people's grandchildren and . . . No. Their relationship was all right, but she doubted it was quite up to this.

So then. What?

Chapter Three

The next morning, Kerensa was up and out the door shortly after six, off to do British Military Fitness in a nearby park, even though it was March and rain was bouncing off the windows. She invited Polly, of course, but Polly groaned and turned over. She had a mild hangover and the taste of Pringles in her mouth.

Once Kerensa had gone, Polly made coffee, then tidied up as much as she could in the tiny, immaculate space. It was no good, though: her overnight bag was still cluttering the place up, and she didn't know how Kerensa got the cushions to sit upright, because she certainly couldn't. She picked up her coffee and spilt a little on the very expensive rug, and cursed. No. This wouldn't do.

She fired up the laptop again. The jobs page could wait for a moment; right now, she needed somewhere to live.

More slowly this time, she went through every single place to rent in Plymouth in her price range. They were all either hideous, or in areas she wouldn't feel safe getting to without a car. Page after page scrolled by until she reached the end. That was it. Nothing else. There was not one place she would even consider going to see, never mind living in.

Many of her friends, not just Kerensa, had offered her a spare room or a sofa to kip on, but she couldn't bear that either – the 'Are you okays?' and the concerned murmuring. And most of them were married now anyway; were hitting the baby stage. A couple of her girlfriends she suspected would quite like her there to help with childcare from time to time, but she absolutely couldn't bear the thought of that: tiptoeing around trying not to outstay her welcome, like some kind of maiden aunt combined with unpaid help.

Once upon a time, in her twenties, way back, she had thought that she and Chris would be married by now, settled; Chris making lots of money, her with her baby ... and here she was.

Ugh, she had to stop thinking like this. She could drown in self-pity, or she could keep pushing on. On a whim, she broadened her search to take in the entire country. Wow. If she could move to Wales, she could live in loads of places. Nice places, too. Or the highlands of Scotland. Or rural Northern Ireland. Or the Peak District. She didn't strictly know where the Peak District was, but at least there were loads of places she could move with no money and no connections and no Pringle-offering friends and no jobs ... Hmm, maybe not.

She narrowed her search back down, asked for all of the south-west, and that was when she saw it.

It was a name she hadn't even thought of in years. They

must have gone there on a school trip; everybody did. Mount Polbearne. She was amazed anyone still lived there.

She studied the little thumbnail. It wasn't much; it differed from the hundreds of other pictures she had scrolled past in that it had been taken from the outside rather than the inside, and showed a little window in a gabled roof, the paint peeling from the frame, the roof tiles serrated and ancient-looking. 'Unusual location', said the blurb, which usually meant 'unspeakable skip'. She clicked on it nevertheless, taking a big slug of cold coffee.

Mount Polbearne, well well. It was a tidal island, she remembered that. They'd gone by coach, and there was a cobbled causeway that connected the island to the mainland, bristling with terrifying signs warning you of the dangers of driving across it as the tide came in, or sailing over it when it had. They had squealed excitedly when the water had surged up across the cobbles, then thought they would all be drowned. There were the remains of old trees by the side of the causeway that used to be on land and weren't any more, and a bit of a ruined castle at the top of the island, along with a gift shop where she and Kerensa had bought oversized strawberry-flavoured lollipops. But surely nobody *lived* there. Half the time you couldn't even leave. You certainly couldn't commute.

There was another picture on the website. The building looked practically derelict. It had a wonky roof, and two of the windows she'd seen in the first picture were dirty and opened outwards. Downstairs was the black maw of a deserted shop. Obviously being perched out at sea was hitting it hard. Also Polly wondered if a buried causeway was quite as exciting for tourists as it used to be. These days they all wanted surfing beaches and theme parks and expensive fish restaurants. Cornwall had changed a lot.

There was one thing that did catch her eye, though: the place had two rooms, plus a little bathroom. Not a bedsit, not a flat share: a flat. Within her budget. Not only that, but the first room, the front room, was rather large: twenty feet by twenty-five. The front room in their Plymouth flat certainly wasn't that big; it was small and narrow, with built-in spotlit mirrors at each end to create an illusion of space. She wondered briefly how high up the flat was, under the eaves like that. And if downstairs was deserted, it meant there would be nobody else in the building – except for the rats. Hmm. Then the last picture caught her eye. It was the view out of the front windows, taken from inside.

Beyond the window was . . . nothing. Just a straight stretch into outer space, or, as it revealed itself to be on closer examination, the sea. The picture had been taken on a day when the sea and the sky were the same shade of grey and blended into one another. It was a great big expanse on which nothing was written. Polly stared at the picture for a long time, fascinated. It looked exactly how she felt: hollowed out, empty. But also strangely calming. Like it was all right that there was a lot of grey in the world; grey was how it was. When she looked out of the window of their executive apartment, what she saw was lots of other people, just like them, getting into their Audis and BMWs, and cooking things in woks, except their businesses hadn't failed and they appeared to be still talking to one another. Looking out of the window was stressful in itself. But this . . . this was something else.

She Google-Earthed Mount Polbearne and was surprised to see that yes, there were a few streets of cobbled houses leading down from a ruined church on the top of the hill. The streets wound their way down to a little harbour, at right angles to the causeway, where a handful of fishing boats were visible. It obviously hadn't been gentrified yet, unlike so much of Cornwall; in the unfashionable part of the county and far from the motorway, it had escaped attention. But it was only fifty miles from Plymouth, so she could still nip back for things . . .

With slightly wobbly fingers, she clicked on the 'Contact estate agent' button.

Chapter Four

'I think the thing to do now,' said Kerensa, who was wearing a ridiculous blazer with gold buttons that nevertheless managed to look quite chic on her, 'is marry someone with money. This is not going to happen in this hole, I can tell you that for nothing.'

'Thanks as usual,' said Polly. She was wearing black. Normally she never wore black; it didn't suit her strawberry-blonde hair and pale skin and made her look short. It was as if she'd kind of forgotten how to go about her normal life, without a job, or her other half, or a set of car keys jangling.

'You really need to stay near a big city,' said Kerensa. 'Dress with a bit of style. Hook someone.'

'Is that what you're trying to do?'

'Please,' said Kerensa, rolling her eyes, and Polly looked out of the window quickly, before Kerensa started singing Beyoncé songs.

It was a grey, overcast Saturday and they had limped out of Plymouth, confused by the satnav and all the narrow, windswept roads it wanted them to take. Finally they decided that if they kept the sea on their left they would get there eventually, and so it had proved.

There was a car park by the causeway, and a daily tide table, which they had both neglected to check before they set out, so they lingered round the car park and studied the island in the distance. Finally Kerensa said it.

'Looks ... windy.'

It was true: Mount Polbearne had a windblown, tumble-down look to it. The waves were worryingly high; it seemed unlikely that this place was, as the sign promised, going to be accessible in twenty minutes. It looked like something out of the past; as though they were staring at something forgotten, the ruined castle looming over the just visible streets.

'It looks romantic,' said Polly, hopefully.

'I wonder if they still do wrecking,' said Kerensa. 'And marry their cousins.'

'It's not far out of town,' said Polly.

Kerensa looked at her watch. 'Well, that very much depends, doesn't it? What if I have a terrible martini accident and you can't get to my house because it's all watery? And you don't even have a car! Look around!'

It was a desolate spot, just narrow country lanes leading away from the little car park.

'I don't see a bus service, do you? How are you going to get to Plymouth? Horse and cart?'

Polly's heart sank. But the previous day she had gone out, under Kerensa's orders, to look at a couple of flat shares closer to home. Both of them had been unspeakably filthy, popu-lated by twenty-somethings, with sinks full of washing-up and fridges with notes pinned to shelves and the smell of unwashed duvets and old bicycles in the communal hallways. She hadn't cried till after Kerensa had gone to bed.

'It would only be for a bit,' she said hopefully. 'Until the flat sells.'

'The flat that's exactly like the other fifteen thousand overpriced Plymouth executive waterside apartments built in the last ten years?'

Polly's brow furrowed. Chris had always seen himself as a man with an eye for a good investment; she remembered his excitement. 'It's got a gym in the basement, Pol!' (He'd used it once.) 'It's got fingerprint entry!' (Always broken.) What it didn't have – a garden, space for a nursery – was never commented on.

'Let's just take a quick look,' she said.

The water slooshed back from the causeway incredibly quickly, like it was revealing a magic road. Very carefully they drove across, parking in the car park on the other side, which today was empty of vehicles – too early for holidaymakers, Polly surmised, and pretty chilly – except for a grey Vauxhall Astra, out of which emerged an overweight young man wearing an extremely cheap suit and a bright red tie. Even though he'd been sitting in a car, he seemed out of breath.

'Oi oi!' he said in a surprisingly jocular tone. 'Are you our city girls?'

Kerensa sniffed. 'Does he mean Plymouth?' she said. Even though Kerensa had been born and raised in Plymouth, she liked to pretend that really she was more at home in London, Paris or New York.

'Ssh,' said Polly.

'This must be a small town if you think Plymouth is

23

Vegas,' said Kerensa, stepping out of the car and immediately having to extract a stiletto from between two cobbles.

The portly man got closer. In fact, he was more of a boy. It struck Polly how young he was. That implied that she *wasn't* young, but she totally was, she told herself. Totally. There was a huge grin plastered on his face. Polly thought that if he'd been born in a different era, now would have been the time for him to pull out a massive spotted hanky and dab his forehead with it.

'Lance Hardington,' he said, offering a ferociously strong handshake and staring deep into their eyes. He'd obviously been on some kind of training course. Kerensa was stifling a grin. Anyone less like a Lance it was hard to imagine.

'Nice to meet you, Lance,' she purred, making the boy's red face even redder.

'Don't start,' said Polly sotto voce as they set off behind him. For a chubby man, he moved at quite a clip.

'Oh, I'm only having fun,' said Kerensa.

'You'll terrify him.'

'That's fun for me.'

Lance turned round, waggling his eyebrows at them in a way that obviously meant *hurry up, time is money and you clearly have far too much of one and hardly any of the other*. He made a show of checking his iPhone, but Polly took her time and looked around her. It was actually rather pleasant to be here, in this little place, away from the noise and traffic of Plymouth. They were standing by a jetty next to the causeway, on the far side of the town, which curved around a bay to their left, facing out to sea. Overhead, the castle – more of a ruin, really, its crumbling walls full of holes and covered in moss – overlooked the higgledy-piggledy collection of weather-beaten houses, made of old Cornish slate and sandstone, often with peeling window frames. There were very few cars; Polly guessed, correctly, that the locals generally left them on the mainland and walked across the causeway.

The narrow lanes meandered all the way down to the little harbour on their left, where the masts of fishing boats rattled and tinkled in the wind and the waves lapped the stones of the old harbour wall. On the waterfront there was a chip shop, a slightly bedraggled-looking souvenir store and an old inn, which still had a water butt outside for horses, and what looked like a stable yard. It was resolutely shut. At the far end of the harbour Polly registered a tall lighthouse striped in black and white, its paint peeling off. It looked unloved.

'Up and coming,' sniffed Lance.

Kerensa looked around suspiciously. 'Why hasn't it upped and come already, then?' she said. 'Everywhere else has.'

'It's good to get in on the bottom rung,' said Lance quickly.

'But it's rained constantly here for about five years,' said Kerensa. 'I think the bottom rung has gone.'

'The real benefit of Mount Polbearne,' said Lance, swiftly changing tack, 'is how unspoiled it is. So quiet, no problems with traffic. Total peace and tranquillity.'

Kerensa sniffed. 'Do you live here?'

Lance was completely unfazeable.

'No, but I'd LOVE to.'

'Total peace and tranquillity,' murmured Polly, wondering if this might not be just what she needed.

Lance set off along the harbour front and they trotted

25

obediently behind him. There was water pooled among the cobbles, which were littered with brightly coloured fishing flies, netting and something that might have been guts. Kerensa made a face.

'Stay with me,' she hissed. 'For ever. Somewhere with coffee shops and Zara.'

'I've really had to change my recent views on what constitutes "for ever",' said Polly.

Lance finally drew up in front of the last house on the shabby little parade. His fake smile grew even more fake as he stood back. The two women regarded the building in front of them. Polly fought her first inclination, which was to turn and run.

'There must be a mistake,' said Kerensa.

'No,' said Lance, looking suddenly like a guilty schoolboy. 'This is it.'

'This should be condemned, not up for rent.'

Suddenly the reason why the flat had larger-than-average floor space for the money had become very apparent. The building was small and narrow, made of dirty grey stone. The ground floor had one large arched window, cracked in several places and unutterably filthy. Through it could just about be made out the murky shapes of large machinery, untouched for years.

'So what was it?' said Kerensa. 'A fire?'

'Oh no!' said Lance heartily. 'Just general . . .' His voice trailed off as he tried not to say 'neglect'.

He darted down the side of the building, the roof of which tilted crazily. There was a little wooden door in the side that you had to bow your head to get through, and he took out a large brass key and unlocked it. The hinges squeaked painfully.

'Had many people wanting to see it?' asked Kerensa, her heels clicking on the flagstones. Lance ignored her.

Inside there was nothing but pitch black and a faintly musty smell. Lance used his iPhone as a torch until he found a swinging lead and pulled it. An old-fashioned low-wattage bulb, festooned with dust, buzzed noisily into life, revealing a set of rickety wooden stairs.

'And this meets all health and safety requirements for renters, does it?' continued Kerensa, as if they were swanning round a Sandbanks penthouse. Lance muttered something inaudible and led them up the stairs, Polly coming up next, a little too close to his well-fed bottom. Her heart sank. This was impossible; it was barely safe.

Another key, fumbled for, turned the Yale of a second door at the top of the stairs. Polly crossed her fingers for the very last chance of a 'ta-dah!' as she stepped into the room.

They were all silent.

Well. It was big. There was that, Polly told herself. They were standing at the back of a large loft with a sloping roof through which she could see chinks of daylight. The floor was made of bare polished planks. At the very back, the roof was high, with exposed rafters. Set against the plain brick wall was a table with two mismatched chairs, looking incongruously small, next to a blackened wood-burning stove. On the far side, there was a little corridor leading left, evidently to the bedroom and bathroom, which were housed in a brick extension round the back. Down one wall of the main room was the bare minimum of horrible old melamine kitchen

27

units, and one odd thing: a huge iron oven. Lance saw her eyeing it up.

'They couldn't shift it,' he said. 'Bugger knows how they got it up here. I mean, um, charming period feature.'

At the front of the room, where the roof sloped down towards the windows, there was a nasty ratty old sofa covered in cracks. Polly approached carefully; every floorboard creaked.

'This place is falling into the sea,' said Kerensa crossly. 'Get many rats, do you?'

'No,' said Lance, looking crestfallen. It had obviously been the company challenge to offload this place. At that very moment there was an enormous shrieking noise. All three of them jumped. Polly jerked her head up. Through a missing tile, she could see an enormous seagull having a shout. The noise was absolutely deafening.

'So, just rats with wings,' said Kerensa.

Polly didn't hear her; she was moving forward to the windows. Crouching down, she could see their flaking paint; take in the fact that they were single-glazed, with various cracks in the glass. She would freeze. It was colder inside than it was outside.

She peered out through the dirty, salt-encrusted glass. She was higher than the masts of the boats and could see past the harbour wall, with its bobbing buoys and line of chattering seagulls, right out to sea. There was a break in the low-hanging cloud, and the sun had broken through and was glancing off the distant tip of a white-topped wave, making it glisten and dance in the light. She found herself with a hint of a smile on her lips.

'Polly! POLLY!'

Polly turned round, aware that she hadn't heard what Kerensa had been saying.

'Come on, I'll take you home. We'll stop somewhere on the way for a nice glass of white wine, not that I'm sure Polbearne isn't festooned with chic little bars and restaurants. The chippy, for a start.'

Lance's chubby cheeks started to sag.

'Why doesn't the owner do it up?' Kerensa said. 'No one is ever ever going to rent it like this.'

'I told her,' said Lance mournfully. 'No one would buy it, either. It's a total pain in the behind.'

'Oh great, a crazy person's house covered in holes, with rats in the basement,' said Kerensa. 'Thank you SO much for your time. Come on, Polly.'

Polly took one last, slightly wistful glance at the sea.

'You know,' she said. 'Beggars can't be choosers.'

'You are kidding,' said Kerensa. 'Your family would sue me after you died here.'

'I'll tell them not to,' said Polly. She turned round to face her friend.

Kerensa eyed her carefully. Polly might be soft on the outside, but inside, somewhere, she knew, there was a tough streak. The same streak that had made her fight for her business and her relationship even when it was completely obvious to the rest of the world that all was lost.

'I have to live somewhere.'

'Polly. Sweets. This is a hole at the end of the world.'

'Maybe,' said Polly, 'that's exactly where I want to be right now.'

'Excellent,' said Lance, pinkening up again as he added, 'I mean, I am so sorry for ... um, well, I think ...'

Polly put him out of his misery.

'I'd need a very short lease,' she said.

Lance put his hands up, as if this could be arranged.

'And the roof ...'

'Uh huh?'

'No daylight through the roof. I think that seems reasonable.'

'Hmm.'

'And what if ...' she said carefully. 'What about ...' And she named a figure half of what the property was advertised for.

Lance looked like a five-year-old who needed to go to the toilet. 'Er, I'm sure that wouldn't ... I mean, I'd have to talk to head office ... I mean, negotiation ...'

Kerensa looked furiously at Polly. 'You're not serious?'

Polly related her dispiriting trawl through Plymouth's less salubrious flat shares. 'I can't do anything else.'

'You can't do *this*! It's a disaster!'

'I'm renting, not sticking my life savings in it. Just for a little while ... Summer's coming.'

'Summer's coming,' repeated Lance.

'Summer will probably skip Britain this year,' said Kerensa. 'This place is a deathtrap.'

Polly had a set to her mouth Kerensa had seen before; it meant she was basically unbudgeable on the issue.

'Let's go and have lunch and discuss it,' said Kerensa in desperation.

As the three of them stood there, the seagull dropped a

substantial poo through the hole in the roof. Kerensa wrinkled her nose.

'Where's a good lunch place round here?'

Lance pulled his collar a little anxiously.

'Er ... Plymouth?'

Chapter Five

They had to wait thirty-five minutes for the tide to go out far enough for them to get back across the causeway. Polly spent the entire time humming to distract herself from Kerensa, who had come up with another ninety-five reasons why she couldn't possibly move to Polbearne. Funnily enough, they only seemed to make her more determined.

'Stop it!' said Kerensa, scowling at her, after pointing out that there weren't any taxis on the island.

'Stop what?' said Polly, looking innocent.

'Stop deciding to do it! It's crazy.'

'I'm not deciding anything.'

'You so are. I can see your lips twitching. You look happy for the first time in about a year, even though it is a TERRIBLE mistake.'

Polly half smiled as she thought about everything that had happened.

'At least this time it's *my* terrible mistake,' she said.

Kerensa was working – all her friends were working – the day Polly moved. She knew that they would have helped, but, feeling a bit defiant, that was kind of how she liked it.

She didn't want the ignominy, the feeling that she was having to give up her life: her central heating and her flat-screen TV; her interest-only mortgage, her successful progression up the career ladder, her handsome, fit boyfriend, etc., etc., blah, blah. She felt she had 'FAILURE' branded right across her forehead; that the boxes she was sending to storage should be stamped 'ALL MY HOPES AND DREAMS, BOXED UP AND PUT AWAY FOR EVER', and she didn't want to sit in a van discussing it.

Most things were going to storage: good clothes (they'd get damp), books (would warp; nowhere to put them), jewellery (could fall through cracks in floor), photos and memorabilia (made her too miserable to look at anything cheerful). She was taking her most waterproof clothing, a bed, and, even though it was a horrible mark of her hubris, their very expensive, super-designed sofa.com sofa, in layers of the softest pale grey. It would get ruined where she was going, but she had chosen it – well, they had chosen it together, but it was mostly her – and she absolutely loved it; its comfort, its luxury. She couldn't, she absolutely couldn't sit on the ratty moist brown rattan one that was there already. She couldn't think of a single way to get the old one out and the new one in, but she'd figure it out when she got there.

Chris had come by whilst she was packing up; nice Mr Bassi had also come to make sure she wasn't taking anything the bank could possibly sell back, but even he let her get away with the sofa.

'Getting rid of this should help,' Chris said. 'Make it look nice and minimalist for selling. And I feel good that you're taking the sofa, even though obviously we should have shared it.'

Polly had just carried on packing the two last, most valuable items: the coffee machine and her big mixer for making bread. She loved to bake, and had done so more and more often in the last year or so, whilst Chris was hiding away at weekends. Then he'd come home and complain about carbs, so she'd end up eating most of her experiments herself. Anyway, those things were hers, and Mr Bassi kindly let her take them. She wasn't so bothered that she was leaving behind the huge framed Muhammad Ali posters, and the stupidly expensive surround-sound system that Chris had expected her to chip in for even though it was wildly overpriced, far too loud for the flat, and the subject of extremely long and boring lectures on its myriad qualities every time somebody new came to visit.

'Do you need a hand to get it out to the van?'

She nodded, too sad and tired to even think of being sarcastic.

They got the sofa to the lift in silence, both of them thinking back to a couple of years ago, when the men from the delivery company had arrived to set it up, and Chris had teased her over how excited she was, given that it was only a bloody sofa, then asked the men if they would have bought such a boring colour, and one of them had said no, he had white leather at home, and Chris had said, see, that was funky.

Once it was safely in the van Polly had hired, they looked at each other, not knowing what to say. Polly's commitment to trying to be as sunny and upbeat as possible suddenly deserted her. She was on her way, completely alone, to an utterly strange destination, against the advice of everyone she knew, leaving the only life she'd known for seven years. The enormity of it all weighed her down.

'Thanks,' she managed, trying to think of something less trivial, less useless to say about everything they'd been through together.

'Pol . . .' said Chris.

'Mm?'

'I'm really . . . Well, you know.'

'I *don't* know,' she said, her heart racing. She didn't know how much he felt the sadness of what had happened to them both, and all their hopes and dreams. Certainly he'd never once talked about it. He had withdrawn so thoroughly, she worried about him.

He looked at her, those narrow blue eyes she'd once found so attractive. She steeled herself not to cry.

'Well, I am,' he mumbled.

Polly leant forward. 'You are what, sweetie?'

'Oh Pol, don't make me . . .'

'I think you might feel better if you do.'

She held her ground. There was a long silence. Then, finally:

'I'm sorry. About everything. I know it wasn't your fault.'

'Thank you,' she said. 'I'm sorry too. I'm sorry we couldn't make it work. I don't think either of us could have worked any harder.'

'No,' said Chris, holding her gaze at last. 'No, we couldn't have.'

And they had, oddly, shaken hands.

35

As she drove away from the crowded streets of Plymouth and hit the open A roads through the downs, the sun was shining in the rear-view mirror and Polly tried to feel she was moving into the future.

'We'll be okay, sofa,' she said, glancing behind her.

'Oh Christ,' she realised, 'I'm the kind of woman who talks to sofas.'

It was after lunch when she finally arrived on the island. She'd had to wait an hour this time for the causeway to open. She was absolutely, she realised, going to have to get organised with the timetables; this was really inconvenient.

As she waited, she bit into the petrol-station sandwich she'd bought on the way. It was disgusting. One thing Polly took very seriously was her bread, and this was no good at all. While she ate, she gazed out of the window at Mount Polbearne. There were comforting-looking lights dotted here and there, their reflections shimmering in the water. From this distance you couldn't see that things were a little dilapidated.

At last the causeway cleared fully. Very carefully and tentatively, sure that one slip would lead her to a watery grave, she drove the van across and turned left at the car park, taking it straight to her brand-new front door – or, rightfully speaking, side door. One thing about moving to a tiny deserted nothing of a place was that she could park anywhere; there were no meters, or even lines on the road. She fumbled for the large keys Lance had handed her when she'd signed the contract (for, in the end, about five pence more than the discount she'd demanded; she had to leave him with some pride after all), and climbed out of the van. She had hired the vehicle for a few days – enough time to find someone to lug the bed upstairs, she thought – but for now she took only the absolute bare essentials. Although as these included her coffee machine, carrying everything was not that easy a job.

As she opened the side door, she looked at the downstairs shop on Beach Street. It creeped her out a little bit. Who knew what malevolent creatures might be lurking there ... She gave herself a little shake. It was only a bakery, she realised, recognising one of the shapes as an oven. The place had probably failed once it became clear that in the hierarchy of beautiful little coastal towns in the south-west of England that people wanted to visit whilst eating a sausage roll, Mount Polbearne came in at about number 5,000, and people were too nervous about the causeway flooding over to hang about for long anyway.

The island had seemed pretty cheerless before, even with Kerensa's bracing presence. But now, in the wet wind of a cold spring day, with nobody else around, it felt utterly desolate. The sea, which Polly had hoped would provide something relaxing and comforting to look at, was grey and choppy and angry-looking, and made her feel nothing but slightly chilled. Sighing, she put down her bags (and the coffee machine) on the stone step outside the faded wooden door, which had obviously once been green, and fumbled for the heavy key. The door swung open, creaking, and immediately banged back in the strong wind. Her pile of books was starting to flap ominously. She pushed the coffee machine in to hold the door open and went back to the van to retrieve her suitcase and a selection of black plastic bin bags. Thirty-two was, she felt, a little old to still be banging on with black plastic bin bags. She should probably have a full set of luggage that matched. Not Louis Vuitton or anything like that, but . . . Well. Something more than a wheelie case seemingly designed to bump down the aisle of a plane against people's ankles. And she had a sports bag of Chris's. It wasn't, she reflected, much to come away with.

The rest was boxes of bits and pieces, many more than she'd hoped. She'd started to heave them out of the van when she heard a rattling noise behind her. She glanced around, nearly toppling over a box, to see that the pile of books she'd put down by the door had been caught by a stray gust of wind and had actually taken off, pushed up, up by the force of the breeze.

'AARGH!' shouted Polly. Most of her books had gone into storage, but she had kept back a few; a very specific few. When she was feeling down in the dumps, she wanted comfort, and comforting reading, and she'd decided that the present situation called for a binge. So she'd held back her childhood books, the dusty old eighties editions she'd read so often the covers were falling off. Inside each jacket was her name and address, carefully printed: 'Polly Waterford, age 11, 78 Elder Avenue, Plymouth, England, Europe, the world, the solar system, the galaxy, the universe.'

There went *Anne of Green Gables*. And *What Katy Did at School*. *Vet in a Spin* was flipping merrily over the cobbles, along with *The Dark is Rising* and *Daddy-Long-Legs*, and *Marianne Dreams* . . .

'Noooo!' yelled Polly, dropping her box and charging after them at full pelt. She couldn't bear to lose them.

The books danced in the grey air as if taunting her, and headed straight for the harbour wall. Polly made a desperate lunge and managed to grab *Good Wives*, but *Alice in Wonderland* spun blithely over the wall and into the grey emptiness beyond.

'Oh,' said Polly, crushed beyond compare. 'Oh.'

The other books thankfully landed before they reached the sea, and she grabbed them up and hugged them close to her, then sank down on the cold stones and, uncaring, feeling this the final straw after what had been really an awful bloody lot of straw, burst into tears.

Her father had given her that book. He had loved it when he was a child and had read it to her and explained the bits she didn't understand, and even though it was cheap and old and easily replaceable, it wasn't, because it had been his. When he had died of a heart attack when Polly was twenty, she had been furious; with him, and with the world, who broadly treated her as an adult who didn't need as much support as if she'd been a child.

Polly felt snot coming out of her nose, and wiped it on her jacket, so upset and impervious did she feel. There was no one around for miles, nobody who gave a damn for at least forty, so she didn't care who saw her or what she looked like. She was alone, she was miserable, she was freezing and a bit wet, and she had lost her dad's book. And how could she be heard above the wind anyway?

Eventually her howling was interrupted by a noise she could barely hear above the waves and the weather. It sounded, oddly enough, like a cough. She stopped, swallowed unprettily and listened. The cough came again.

Polly sat bolt upright and peered around. Behind her, standing on the wall to the left, she spied, to her horror, five men. They were wearing sou'westers with bright yellow dungarees.

'Er, excuse me,' said the first one in a Cornish accent as thick as clotted cream. They were all shuffling and looking embarrassed. Polly jumped to her feet.

'Yes?' she said, as if she hadn't just been caught sitting outside bawling her head off like a two-year-old.

'Um, is this yours?'

The first man, who had a brown beard, red cheeks and creases round his blue eyes, held up her copy of *Alice in Wonderland*. He looked at her hands, which were still gripping her other books.

Polly gave a quick, sharp nod. 'Yes ... yes, thank you.'

He stepped forward to hand it to her. Polly put out her arms, realised immediately that she had a big snot stain on her sleeve and, in the embarrassment, dropped the rest of the books on the ground.

They all bent down together to pick them up.

'Big reader, are you?' said the man.

'Er ... kind of,' Polly managed, her cheeks flushed bright scarlet. 'Where ...'

'It came down on our boat, dinnit?' said the man, and Polly turned her head to look at the line of fishing boats clanking in the harbour. They were brightly painted green and red, with nets piled high on their bows and a scrubbed,

40

rough-and-ready look to them. The nearest one was called *Trochilus*.

'We thought it were books from heaven, din't we, lads? Like, a new library idea.'

The other men chuckled and shuffled.

'It's . . .' Polly tried to pull herself together and not seem too weird and tearful. She just about had the rest of her books in a pile now. 'It's very good.'

The man squinted at it.

'I mostly read . . . well, I like books about war.'

'Any specific war? Or wars in general?' asked Polly, genuinely interested. He was incredibly tall, but his face was gentle.

'Well, I reckon . . . just about any war will do.'

'Borrow it,' said Polly suddenly. Something that had seemed so precious only moments before had become, by light of its extraordinary resurrection, something to be shared. 'See if you like it. There isn't any war. But there is some chess,' she added doubtfully.

The man looked at it.

'Well, I will then,' he said. 'Get pretty long, them nights.' He nodded at the boat.

'I didn't know fishing boats went out at night,' Polly said. The other men, still loitering and listening in, laughed.

'I'll tell you a secret,' said the first man, straight-faced. 'We like to catch the fish when they're sleeping.'

'Is that true?' said Polly, forgetting to be miserable for a second.

The man smiled. 'So you normally walk about our town throwing books?' he asked.

41

'Oh ... no,' said Polly, flustered again. 'No. I've just moved here.'

'Why would you move *here*?' said youngest of the men, who had bright pink cheeks, but the tall man – who must have been the captain – shushed him.

'Welcome to Mount Polbearne then,' he said. His eyes followed hers up to the van and the pile of boxes. 'You're not ... you're not moving into Mrs Manse's old place?'

'Um, the one on the corner?' said Polly.

'Aye, that'll be right.' The captain looked at it.

'It's haunted, that place,' said the young man with the pink cheeks.

'Ssh,' said the captain. 'Don't be ridiculous.'

'I don't believe in that kind of thing,' said Polly stiffly.

'Well that's lucky,' said the captain. 'For you, anyway. Ghosts never come if you pretend you don't believe in them. Hello. I'm Tarnie.'

'Polly,' said Polly, wiping her face fiercely.

'Well, thanks for the book,' said Tarnie. He looked over at the van parked across the road, with the sofa clearly visible poking out of the back. 'Can we do anything for you in return?'

'No, no, I'm fine,' said Polly quickly.

'You lifting that sofa up by yourself?'

'Oh, that,' said Polly. 'Um. I hadn't quite ... I hadn't ...'

'Come on, lads,' said Tarnie.

With a will, the men heaved the sofa out of the van, and, with some swearing and bother, managed to lug both it and the bed upstairs.

Tarnie let out a low whistle as he looked around the flat.

42

'You're living here?' he said.

It looked, if possible, even worse than before. There was dust everywhere, rafters creaking, tiles shifting here and there.

'It's just temporary,' said Polly in a rush, not wanting to have to explain her entire life.

'It certainly is,' said one of the men, who Tarnie introduced as Jayden, and they all laughed again.

Polly looked around. 'I ... I think ... Well, with a bit of work ...'

'And a bulldozer.'

'That'll do, Jayden,' said Tarnie and the lad fell silent straight away.

Polly glanced about. 'I'd love to offer you a cup of tea ...'

The men looked hopeful.

'But I don't even know if the water's on.'

'And you lot have got bilges to rinse,' said Tarnie.

There was a collective groan.

'Come on.'

'Um, can I use your loo?' asked one of them.

'Of course,' said Polly.

'Oi, don't start that,' said Tarnie. Polly looked confused. 'Once one starts, they'll all want to,' he explained.

'I really don't mind,' said Polly.

'We don't have one, you see.'

Polly blinked, and Tarnie looked a little embarrassed.

'So, er, see you around,' he said, holding up the book.

'Thanks,' said Polly. 'Thanks so much ... for bringing it back and helping me and ...'

'Don't mention it,' said Tarnie, looking a little pink. 'Can't bear to see a lady in distress.'

43

One of the young fishermen made a 'woo' noise and the captain swung round with a fierce look.

'Right, you shower. OUT!'

After they'd gone, Polly hauled up the last few bags. She took out her sheets and covered the sofa with them, then investigated the large box of industrial cleaning products that Kerensa had given her as a parting gift.

'You work with these for forty minutes,' she'd said fussily, and you'll realise how absolutely terrible your life is now. Then you'll turn round and come straight back home.'

Polly grinned and checked the water – it was running, thank goodness, and the boiler made a very reassuring whooshing noise when she turned the hot tap – then realised that after her long drive and her cry, she was absolutely starving. Something to eat first, then she'd hit the bleach. It would be like hitting the beach, she figured. Just many, many times worse.

The weather hadn't really cleared up, so she put on her thickest jacket and a hat. She desperately needed a cup of coffee, even though the fishermen helping her had made her feel slightly less chilled inside than she had before.

She took the cobbled road that led upwards and curled round into what she supposed must be the main street. There was a little newsagent's that also sold shrimping nets and buckets and spades, all of which looked dusty and neglected; a bar with a fishing net hanging outside, and a beer garden; a butcher's, a greengrocer's and a hardware shop. There was a van down by the harbour that had a sign outside indicating that it sold fresh fish, but it was shut; and a little minimart-style shop that appeared to sell everything – she popped in there for some milk for her coffee, and some soup for later. Next door to that was a bakery, with some rather gummy-looking unidentifiable cakes in the front window, and a dusty wedding cake that Polly wasn't entirely convinced was real.

Emboldened by the first locals she'd met, she decided to venture inside. After all, if this was going to be where she was buying her bread ...

Polly was very specific about bread. She loved it. She had loved it in fashion and out of fashion; as a child, as an adult. It was her favourite part of going to a restaurant. She loved it toasted or as it was; she loved bagels, and cheese on toast, and *pain d'épices*, and twisted Italian plaits. She loved artisan sourdough that cost six pounds for a tiny loaf, and she loved sliced white that moulded and soaked up the juices of a bacon sandwich.

She had started making her own bread at college, and it had become a fully fledged hobby when she and Chris had got the flat; she would spend her Saturdays kneading and pulling it, leaving it to rise. Then one day about a year ago, for his health he'd decided on no more bread; he was allergic to gluten. Given that he had been eating the stuff for thirty-four years with no negative effects whatsoever, this had seemed unlikely, but Polly had bitten her tongue and stopped making it.

For now, though, what was she going to have to eat? Some

nice local ... Well, what was local? she wondered. Maybe a cheese scone?

'Hello,' she said cheerfully. She had always felt a huge affinity with bakers. Their commitment to early mornings; warm, strongly scented yeast; feeding the hungry. It had always seemed a noble profession to her. When they had gone on holiday to France once, she had driven Chris nearly demented by wanting to visit *boulangeries* just as he wanted to visit vineyards; to feel the difference between the various grains and local specialities.

Behind the counter was, Polly saw, a woman who absolutely resembled her own products. If Polly had been feeling less foreign and strange, she might have found it amusing. The woman looked like a bun. She was completely circular in her flour-dusted white apron. Her face was utterly round too, folds of skin overlapping her hairnet, doughy cheeks hanging down. Her hair – very long, and streaked with grey – was tied back in a bun too. She resembled nothing more than an enormous brioche. Polly was inclined to like her.

'What do you want?' said the woman shortly, looking very bored and glancing at her watch.

'Ooh, let me take a second,' said Polly. 'I'm new here. What do you have?'

The woman rolled her eyes and simply nodded at the wall, where in badly spelled scrawl was a list: pan, sliced pan, pasty, cheese toastie, ham toastie, cheese and ham toastie, cheese, ham and pineapple toastie – hmm, exotic, thought Polly – fancy cakes, tea cakes, Welsh cakes and scones. As far as she could tell, there was only one sort of bread. There wasn't, now she came to think of it, much of a smell of baking in the air; more a kind of slightly stale, starchy aura that might even be coming from the woman herself.

'Um, toastie, please,' said Polly. The petrol-station sandwich seemed a long time ago. She looked round. There was nowhere to sit and eat, and apart from a few dusty cans of Fanta, nothing to drink either.

The woman grunted as if this was a huge chore, and barked, 'Cheese, cheese an' ham, cheese an' ham an' pineapple?' at her.

'Um, the last one, please,' said Polly, wondering if she'd inadvertently done something offensive. But the sandwiches were cheap.

The woman sighed heavily and turned round.

'Got to warm up toaster.'

Polly glanced at it. It was blackened and looked utterly filthy. She was beginning to regret the entire enterprise. Those friendly fishermen had made her feel fleetingly optimistic about her new home, but this was bringing her down again.

She glanced around awkwardly. The cabinets could do with a bit of a clean, too. The woman lugged her huge bulk over to one and picked up a soggy-looking pre-prepared sandwich, which she slapped into the toaster. Polly speedily changed her mind as to how hungry she was.

'So, I've just moved here,' she said brightly, trying to do her best. A positive mental attitude, that was what she needed. 'It seems really nice! I was in Plymouth before.'

The woman stared at her rudely. 'Right. So you're here to push up our property prices, keeping local people out?'

'No!' said Polly, surprised. 'Ha. No, it's not like that at all. I'm ... er, I'm taking some time out.' She was trying this phrase out on people, and almost everyone got what she was aiming at and didn't enquire too much further. 'Then, you know, I'm going to start looking for a job.'

The woman sniffed and checked the toaster. 'Well you won't find one of those. Nothing for incomers to do round here. We're not one of your pretty-pretty towns, you know. We're for our own folk here.'

Polly raised her eyebrows at this, but simply took her sandwich, paid, and said goodbye. The woman didn't answer until she was nearly at the door.

'But you can still pay the rent?'

Polly turned back, surprised.

'I'm Mrs Manse,' said the woman, huffily. 'I'm your land-lady.'

Polly took the sandwich down to the other side of the harbour, away from her own place and the boats, and closer to the causeway. The wind was still blowing, but the wall provided some shelter. There was scarcely anyone about. To her right she saw a fishing boat chugging noisily out to sea, thick black smoke coming from its little funnel, a flash of yellow overalls visible on the bow. She took a bite of her sandwich. It was cheap, nasty, horrible bread, plasticky cheese, tinned pineapple. Somehow, it was also rather comforting.

Mrs Manse hadn't said any more after that, but she hadn't had to, reflected Polly rather glumly. That chilly warning had been enough.

48

She gazed out to sea, pulling her coat around her to keep herself warm. She needed a plan. Okay, positive thinking. So it was going to be hard to get a job that required her to turn up on the mainland at the same time every day, because of the tides. Yes, everyone had told her that and she had chosen to ignore it, but surely she'd figure something out.

In retrospect, she realised that she'd kind of imagined herself somewhere round here – she had accountancy skills, marketing experience, maybe a little local solicitor or something would take her on till she got going again. But now that she'd seen the town, that seemed a little less likely. Okay, a lot less likely.

Well, she had to be realistic about it. Maybe she'd let herself get carried away by the romance of living on a tidal island. But it was a short lease. She would find a job in town and move back. Of course she would. And until then she would use the peace and quiet to help her recover. That was the plan, remember? To slow down, chill out. Take deep breaths of salty sea air. Panic wasn't going to help.

She finished up her lunch and gave the rest to the seagulls, who made a huge racket dive-bombing to the greasy bread.

Well. She was going to take things one day at a time. Once she'd thought years ahead, and look where that had got her. All her business plans and life schedules had come to absolutely nothing. You never knew what was behind the next door. But she knew what was behind her own new front door – a horrible mess that needed cleaning up pronto.

She smiled when she saw that Kerensa had put a ridiculous pair of rubber gloves with fake fur at the wrists in the box for her, as well as, at the bottom, a little bottle of ready-made gin and tonic, with a note round the top saying 'Drink Me'. Polly went to work with a will, scrubbing the horrible old kitchenette units thoroughly and swearing to herself. Couldn't that woman at least have put laminate veneer on them?

The bathroom had a grimy white suite that she guiltily attacked with powerful stain removers. At least there was a bath, she thought. One apartment she'd looked at had had a shower unit with a bed on top. Life when you were skint came down to taking your pleasures where you could find them, she decided.

The floor of the little bathroom, with its roof hanger for drying clothes, was filthy old rutted linoleum, but three rounds of scrubbing revealed a perfectly serviceable black and white pattern, and the frosted glass cleaned up to let in some of the afternoon light. The bedroom was small, but quiet and calm, and again she scrubbed the window, taking down the nets then cursing when she realised that of course she didn't have a washing machine.

It wasn't that her parents had been wealthy – in fact, she couldn't have gone back to her mum's even if she'd wanted to, as her mum lived on a tiny fixed income in a one-bedroom flat on a housing estate in Rochester – but she had never, ever, even as a student, lived in a house that didn't have a washing machine.

I am not going to cry, she told herself, wondering if Mr Bassi and Mr Gardner had made away with their smart Bosch yet. I shall make a pile and find a launderette like plenty of people do all the time. Every day. I'll pretend I'm on *EastEnders* or something. It'll be great. GREAT.

She continued into the main room, feeling herself grow warmer with the exertion – which was a good thing – and as she leant out at an extremely dangerous angle to wash her filthy, salt-stained front windows, she noticed the clouds slowing down and the rain falling on one stretch of the ocean far away, like its own personal patch. She gazed out on to her new landscape and wondered: choppy waters? Calm seas?

She boiled the kettle and poured hot water into her favourite Scrabble mug. The mug had cost seven pounds. Suddenly that seemed like a ridiculous amount to spend on a mug. Had she even noticed? Had her life changed so very much? There was a small weekly amount forthcoming from the receivers, so she wouldn't starve – very small, barely better than benefits – and it was possible that they might make a little money from the flat after everyone had been paid off. Maybe. It probably wasn't worth counting on. For the last few months Chris hadn't even let her see the accounts. It had come as a shock to realise how bad things really were. She should have insisted. Oh, she should have done a lot of things.

Polly dragged out an old-fashioned armchair she'd found in the bedroom – it was squashy and old, upholstered in a turquoise fabric, but actually not as tasteless as the other sparse furnishings – and placed it by the front-facing windows, which were swung wide open to dry. Then she sat down and put her legs up on the window ledge. From that angle she couldn't see anything except sea and sky; she practically felt like she was flying. She sipped her coffee, breathing in the salty air and watching the waves, trying to time her breathing as they rolled in and out, in and out. Before long, she was in the deepest, calmest sleep she'd known for months.

Chapter Six

A positive attitude, Polly discovered, was a lot easier to fake at five o'clock in the afternoon than the early hours of the morning. She'd woken, chilled, then found it hard to get back to sleep, to stop the negative thoughts from creeping back.

And the flat was cold. As well as the wood-burner, which she wasn't at all sure how to use, there was an exceedingly dangerous-looking black stove, so she'd turned that on, then, stupidly, gone and checked the meter, which, sure enough, was whizzing round and round at the speed of light. So she'd pulled a sweatshirt on over her pyjamas, wishing she hadn't put her dressing gown into storage – what was she thinking? – and snuck under the lightweight breathable duvet that had been perfect for a small, modern, centrally heated apartment but wasn't nearly adequate here, as the wind whistled through the last remaining holes in the roof and she could hear the waves thundering on the shingle below. She thought longingly of the soft fluffy white duvet they'd used for visitors, or, increasingly, on the nights they'd slept apart because of Chris's tossing and turning.

The strange noises were unnerving. At one point she dropped off and dreamt that she was down a hole and water was lapping at her; that she was being pulled under the water. Then, suddenly, she heard a bang and a scream.

Completely disorientated, she sat bolt upright, her heart thudding in her chest. Where was she? What was that? Where was Chris? Oh GOD, someone had broken in. News had got around of the lone female moving into town, into a house that wasn't even vaguely secure. It was a posse. It was a crazy town where they sacrificed people. It was ...

Gradually she got a grip on herself for long enough to check her phone. She cursed when she saw it: 2.30, the very dead of night. It was completely freezing in the flat, and pitch dark: the harbour street lights were few and far between, and beyond was just complete blackness. Suddenly, bright light flooded in underneath the bedroom door and she nearly screamed herself before realising that it must be the beam from the lighthouse on the point coming through the front windows. She realised she was trembling and gathered the duvet around her. She didn't have a bedside light yet. She was going to have to fumble across the room in the dark. Or maybe wait till the lighthouse beam swept past again. She strained her ears but could hear nothing. It must have been a bad dream. A bad dream, that was all, something to do with the lighthouse ...

This time when the scream came it sounded even closer.

'OhSHITohSHITohSHITohSHIT,' said Polly to herself, fighting a desire to stick her head underneath the duvet. Her heart was pounding like it wanted to leap out of her chest. It occurred to her that a gang of bloodthirsty pitchfork-wielding locals would be unlikely to scream at her, but that didn't really help. What was it that the fishermen had said about ghosts?

'He ... hello ...' she called out tentatively into the dark. There was a kind of whimpering noise.

Oh God. Maybe there'd been an accident outside. Maybe someone – a child? – had been thrown from a car. Grasping her phone, she waited till the lighthouse swept its beam over her once again, then scuttled across the room to the main light switch. Flicking it on, she felt a tiny bit calmer, but only till the next yelp hit her ears.

'All right, all right, I'm coming,' she said, pulling on another jumper. Why hadn't she brought a torch? Because the more she thought about it, the more sure she was that the noise was coming from downstairs. From the dark and dusty abandoned shop below. She wondered where the entrance was, then remembered a doorway leading off the stairs. It would be locked, though ... She should probably phone the police right away. Yes, that was what she would do.

The cry that came was so lonesome and desolate, she steeled herself and headed down the stairs towards the door. Lance had given her a huge bunch of keys – when she'd asked why she needed so many, he'd shrugged and said he didn't know, he was only a trainee – and she fumbled with them as she went.

Sure enough, the second Yale worked. She shook the warped old door hard and it popped open. She let it swing into the room beyond, holding her breath. She realised she was shaking.

'Hello?'

No reply, but there was movement.

'Hello?' she said again. She glanced to the right. There was light coming in through one of the broken panes in the shop door. As she let her eyes adjust to the gloom, it occurred to her that it might be a cat or a dog – or a troll or a zombie, her subconscious added. She told her subconscious to shut it.

'Hello!'

She hoped it wasn't something that would bite her. On the other hand, she couldn't wait for the police – she guessed there wasn't a police station anywhere near here – whilst there was an animal in pain. She took a deep breath and stepped into the room.

There was the musty, dusty, heavy smell of a neglected space, and large shapes that must be counters and, in the corner, huge ovens. She could hear a funny kind of snuffling noise but there was no more screaming.

'It's all right, it's all right,' she said, peering around the shapes, terrified of what she might find. 'It's only me,' she added, which was obviously a totally stupid thing to say under the circumstances. If it was a gigantic mutant spider with lots of little spider babies, for example, she was going to stomp on them all, so being *only me* wasn't exactly any use.

Finally, near the front, just behind a glass cabinet, she felt the snuffling grow closer. Holding her breath, she crouched down.

'Oh!' she said. 'Oh dear me.'

Down in the corner was a tiny bird with black and white plumage and a huge yellow and orange beak. As Polly knelt next to it, it let rip with another overwhelming screech. It was a huge noise to come out of such a little creature.

'What happened to you?' she said. She could feel the bird's little body trembling, and she tried to stretch her arms out in as unthreatening a way as possible. 'Ssh, ssh.'

She could see from the light from the street that the bird's wing was all twisted. It looked broken. She wondered what had happened, and then realised that it must have accidentally flown into the glass in the dark, and the glass must have been sufficiently weak to break. It had probably had a nasty bump on the head too, poor thing.

'Come here, come here.'

The bird tried to flap away, but instantly squawked in pain and stopped. Continuing to make soothing noises, Polly gently picked up the little creature. She was temporarily worried she was going to give it a heart attack; she could feel its heart beating incredibly quickly in its chest.

'It's okay, it's okay,' she said. 'You know, I was absolutely more scared than you.'

She looked at the little thing.

'Well, okay, maybe not quite as scared as you, but it was close.'

She glanced at the window. That would have to wait. She'd put some cardboard on it tomorrow, or tell the agents. Suddenly she was relieved she hadn't phoned 999. Explaining that she had a poorly bird on her hands probably wouldn't have gone down too well.

'Well,' she said, looking at it, 'I don't know much about puffins – I don't know anything about puffins actually. I had no idea you could even fly – but I think you'd better come upstairs with me.'

Compared to the eerie deserted shop, upstairs, with the lights blazing and her familiar sofa and bed, seemed almost homely. She popped the kettle on out of habit, not feeling the least bit sleepy now, and pinned up a spare sheet over the front window to block out the sweeping lighthouse beam. Then she wrapped a towel round the puffin – his feathers were dense and soft; he must be a baby – and googled on her phone 'how to fix a bird's broken wing'. It suggested gauze tape, but since she only had packing tape from the move, that would have to do. The bird had stopped trying to flap itself free and was regarding her with its deep black eyes instead.

She taped the wing to its body, then cut some air holes in one of her packing boxes.

'Bed,' she said. 'Bed for you.'

The website suggested cat food, which she also had none of, but she did have an emergency tin of tuna in her supplies box. She put a small dish of that and a saucer of water in front of the bird, who tried to waddle forward to inspect it, and promptly fell over.

Polly carefully righted him again. He looked at the two dishes, glanced at her fearfully – Polly found herself saying, 'It's all right, it's fine' – and then he started pecking at the fish. Polly found herself smiling as she watched him eat –

partly out of relief at all the horrible things that could have gone bump in the night but hadn't.

'Okay,' she said, after the bird seemed to have tired of the food. 'I guess you're going to be my flatmate for the night.'

She'd take him to the vet tomorrow – there must be somewhere that dealt with this kind of thing – but for now, she'd try him in the box. She put the towel underneath him – 'Basically, bird,' she told him, 'you're wearing a nappy, right? And no hopping on my sofa' – and the box on top. She expected him to grumble at that, but he didn't; perhaps it was a bit like a nest. Instead he fluttered a little, then went quiet.

Polly got back into bed, with the duvet doubled over and the rest of her towels on top of it. To her surprise, she fell asleep straight away, and didn't stir till the seagulls started to bark at the return of the fishing boats on a bright and sunny April morning.

Chapter Seven

'The good thing,' said Polly the next morning as the little bird pecked away at the remains of the tuna, 'is that I'm not going to get very attached to you or start giving you a name or anything.'

The puffin attempted another wobble, but fell over again. She helped him up. 'No matter how amusing you think you are,' she said. The puffin cawed a little.

'I know. When you're better, I'll set you free and you can fly off and find your mummy and daddy, okay? Scout's honour.'

She sighed. 'I will say this for you, puffin. Talking to a bird is definitely a step up from talking to a sofa.'

As she drank her coffee, she watched the men unloading the fish on the harbour. There were people around the crates staring in and poking and prodding, and a man had already set up a little bench and was gutting the fish and selling some straight off a boat. Polly watched him, fascinated. He was so quick with the knife it was almost impossible to follow his fingers; he slit and gutted the fish like lightning. Several vans were parked up with the names of famous Cornish fish restaurants on the sides. So this was how it was done, she thought. She should probably head down and buy some; it seemed unlikely she'd get fresher. And perhaps the little puffin would like some too . . .

The men coming off the boats looked tired. It must be a long night, she thought, realising as she considered it that she'd never given the life of a fisherman the least thought at all. She was tired too. She went over to unpack one of the food boxes she'd brought. She'd cleared out the store cupboards at the flat in Plymouth. Once upon a time she wouldn't have bothered to keep a mostly empty tin of salt, and two little packets of yeast.

The oven was absolutely black with filth – Polly sighed and mentally assigned herself another two hours' hard labour – and was the old-fashioned kind that required a long match and a steady hand until the flame caught at the back. But the gas hissed reassuringly, startling the puffin, who had been practising walking with his bound-up wing, his claws clacking on the wooden floorboards. Polly glanced at her watch.

'You know,' she said, 'I'm going to do it. Then I'll take you to the vet.'

The puffin tilted his head at her.

'Sorry,' she said. 'I didn't say vet.'

She clicked the kettle on to heat the water for the yeast, then moved the table by the chimney breast over to the kitchenette, to at least give herself the illusion of having a worktop. She shook some flour out on to the freshly cleaned surface. The puffin bustled over to see what she was up to, trying vainly to hop upwards.

'No chance,' she said. 'You're mucky, and I don't want footprints in the flour.'

The puffin eeped a bit, so she relented and hoisted him up, running enough soapy water in the sink to cover his feet. He liked this a lot, kicking out at the bubbles and making happy noises. Polly turned the radio on, and he seemed to like that too.

'Right, you play,' she said, and picked up the bread dough in her hands. It felt sticky, which was good – the stickier the dough, the lighter the bread – but it was too sticky too work with, and she sprinkled more flour underneath it. Then she set to work kneading. She pushed and pounded, pulled the dough out then folded it back again.

As she did so, she found that something odd was happening. First, a song she loved came on the radio: 'Get Lucky'. Given how much luck she currently felt in need of, this struck her as perfect, and she turned the radio up incredibly loud. It was cheesy, but she absolutely didn't care; it made her feel good every time she heard it. Secondly, she could see, out of the newly cleaned front windows, watery spring sunshine bouncing off the waves. A brave little sailing boat, its white sail flapping in the wind, was taking a trip out of the harbour. To her left she could hear the puffin happily splashing in his little paddling pool.

Suddenly Polly felt something. As she threw, and pushed, and kneaded, it was as if an energy was leaving her body. A bad energy. She hadn't even realised how high her shoulders had been; how much tension there had been locked up in the knots behind her neck. They must have been hunched about her ears.

There had been no one, she realised, no one in months to put a hand on her neck, to say to her, *there, there, you seem so stressed*. She had spent so long trying to look after Chris; trying to keep up appearances to the rest of the world; trying not to invite pity from Kerensa and their other friends, that all her worries had stored themselves up inside her.

She stretched her arms out luxuriously, realising, as her gaze followed the little white-sailed boat bobbing out to sea, how long it had been since she had focused on anything further away than a computer screen.

And as if starting to unknot the muscles in her shoulders had caused something else to loosen too, she felt a tear plopping off the end of her nose; a great big salty tear that fell directly on to the dough.

But they weren't the frustrated, angry tears of yesterday at the harbour, raging against the world and its horrible unfairness. These were cathartic tears; unstoppable but somehow not upsetting. She let them fall, couldn't wipe them away even if she'd wanted to with her doughy hands, and tried instead to be, for once, in the moment – not regretting the way things had worked out, or panicking madly about the future, or thinking about what she could have done differently, or said to Chris, or worked on or planned for, but instead listening to the radio, which had changed now to another pop song she loved, and the splashing, and feeling the dough change and mould under her fingers as the sun sparkled on the now empty sea.

It wasn't as warm outside as the sunlight might have suggested; a harsh salty wind still blew through the town. Polly left the dough to proof in a sunny spot, cleaned herself up a little, then set out with the puffin, who was slightly grumpy, under her arm to look for a vet. The woman in the grocer's shop where she bought her milk and soup was happily a lot more polite than the woman in the bakery, and directed her to a small surgery which appeared to be shared with the doctor's. Polly panicked for a moment when she got there about how much it was going to cost; she'd heard vets were expensive. But there wasn't a lot she could do about it.

The vet was rather peremptory and busy, but he raised his head from his computer when she arrived with the box.

'Um,' she said. 'He had a bit of an accident.'

The vet, whose name was Patrick, and who secretly hated cats, looked up at this and put on his glasses. Then he looked at the woman who'd brought the box in. Tired-looking, but pretty. Her hair was strawberry blonde and soft around her shoulder blades, her eyes were unusually green, and her lips were, at the moment, being nervously bitten, but it looked like there might be a nice smile under there.

'Are you passing through?' he remarked.

'No. Yes. No,' said the woman.

'So you're not sure?'

'No. Yes. I mean ...' Polly felt flustered. She was going nuts, she told herself; she hadn't spoken to enough people recently. 'I mean, I'm renting a place here. Temporarily.'

64

Patrick frowned. 'Why would you do that?'

Polly felt quite cross. She certainly wasn't going to say 'It's all I can afford, thank you.'

'What's wrong with here?' she replied instead.

'Nothing, nothing,' sighed Patrick. 'It's just, most people who come down here prefer Rock or St Ives; you know, those places.'

'Well I'm not most people,' said Polly.

'No, I can see that,' said Patrick, glancing into the box. 'You do know this is a seabird.'

'Good Lord, really?' said Polly. 'I had it down as an armadillo.'

Patrick smiled despite himself. 'It's just that normally . . . I mean, round here we don't really suffer from a shortage of seabirds.'

'Well there's no shortage of cats either, but I'm sure it doesn't stop you treating them,' said Polly, stung.

'That is true,' said Patrick grimly, lifting the puffin out of the box. 'Come on then, little fellow.'

His gruff manner belied a very gentle touch. The puffin jumped slightly, but let himself be picked up. Patrick looked at the bandage.

'That's not a bad job,' he said, glancing up.

'Thanks,' said Polly. 'I'm glad I took that bird rescue evening class.'

Patrick looked at her. 'Do you know how many puffins there are at the sanctuary in the north?' he asked.

'No idea,' said Polly. 'I missed that week.'

'About one point four million,' said Patrick.

'Well this is the one I like,' said Polly stubbornly.

Patrick looked serious again. 'You can't keep him, you know.' He checked under the feathers. 'Yes, it is a he.'

Polly smiled. 'I knew that,' she said, tickling the puffin's ear. 'Why not? Is he protected or something?'

'No, it's just not good for him. He needs to fly and breed and grow up. He's only a puffling.'

'A what?'

'A puffling. A baby puffin.'

'Oh!' said Polly. 'That's the cutest thing I've ever heard.'

'Well, cute or not, he needs to be with his loomery.'

'His what?'

'His loomery. It's the name for a group of puffins.'

'A loomery of puffins,' said Polly. 'That's lovely. It sounds like one of those really weird independent albums my ex used to buy.'

She smiled, a touch wryly. Aha, thought Patrick. An ex. That probably explained a lot.

'Or an improbability,' he added. 'That's the other word. An improbability of puffins. But I don't like that so much; there's nothing improbable about puffins, there's billions of the damn things.'

The little puffin opened his bright orange beak and croaked. Patrick leant over to a drawer, took out some fish food and put some down for him to peck.

Polly sighed. 'So I have to give him up,' she said sadly.

'Well, no point in doing it until he's fixed,' Patrick said. 'He can't fly. Do you think you could look after him until he's better?'

'Yes!' said Polly, delighted. 'Yes, I think I could. How long will that be?'

'Two or three weeks?' said Patrick. 'He seems quite happy. Birds are much more likely to die of fright than anything else.'

'I think this puffin is pretty chilled,' said Polly.

'All right. Don't get attached, though, okay? When he's ready to fly away, you'll have to let him go.'

'Story of my life,' said Polly. 'I'll do my best.'

'Don't give him a name.'

'Okay.'

Polly stood up to go.

'How much do I owe you?'

Patrick waved his hand.

'I didn't do anything; you're the nurse. Don't worry about it.'

'Seriously?' said Polly. 'Thank you SO much.'

He was surprised at the vehemence of her gratitude. Her clothes weren't super-expensive, but they weren't that cheap either.

'Just don't make a habit of it,' he said. 'You foster a seagull, you'll know all about it.'

'Okay, fine,' said Polly, still happy. 'I don't suppose I could get him a lead, could I?'

'Absolutely not,' said Patrick, half smiling as he ushered her out of his office. There were two cats in the waiting room, hissing at one another like clawed snakes.

'Right. He'll probably want to fly off of his own accord, but if he's still around in three weeks, bring him back in.'

'Will do,' said Polly, and finally she smiled. He'd been right, thought Patrick. She did have a lovely smile. He wondered what had made it disappear.

Polly continued to feel more cheerful than she had in a while, walking up the little high street with the puffin in the box. She took the route down towards the harbour again and headed along past the boats. Tarnie's boat, the *Trochilus*, was in harbour, and she was looking at it when she ran into the man himself.

'Hello, hello,' he said as she tripped over a cobblestone and nearly stumbled into his arms. His beard brushed the top of her head. 'You're looking a bit more cheery.'

Polly winced at the memory. 'That wouldn't be difficult,' she admitted.

'That book you lent me is a bit strange,' he said, in his odd thick accent. Polly liked it.

'Oh, you've started it!'

'Not a lot to do when you're heading out to sea. Then, suddenly, a LOT to do.'

'What do you think?'

'I think whoever wrote it might have been dabbling in things he shouldn't have.'

Polly smiled. 'Interesting. I think he was just a bit peculiar.'

'More'n a bit, I'd say. Who's this, then?'

Polly glanced into the box. The bird was looking up at her expectantly, as if waiting to be introduced.

'Yes,' she said. 'I'm, er ... Fostering a puffin.'

Tarnie frowned. 'Is this like a joke someone's playing on you for being the new girl in town? You have to tell me if they're being mean to you.'

'No, no,' said Polly, and she told him the whole story.

'Well, I never heard of anyone keeping a seabird as a pet before,' said Tarnie. 'They taste pretty good though, puffins.'

'No!' said Polly. 'Ssh! I'll have to cover his ears and I'm not sure where they are.'

'He's an Icelandic grey,' said Tarnie. 'Durnt speak English.'

'Oh, okay. Don't eat puffins.'

'You eat duck, don't you?'

'This conversation is over.'

Tarnie chucked the bird under the chin. 'Well, you're obviously smitten,' he said. 'Got a name for him yet?'

'No,' said Polly dubiously. 'The vet told me not to give him one.'

'You can't just call him "the puffin". What about Pete?'

'Peter Puffin?' said Polly. 'Not sure. Sounds a bit like a newsreader. What about Muffin?'

'MUFFIN?' said Tarnie. 'I can't believe you'd inflict that on the poor thing. All the other birds will laugh their heads off at him.'

'Or think it's cool,' said Polly. 'Having an actual name, instead of "Puffin nine million and seventy-two".'

'Ha, you could call him Stud,' said Tarnie. 'Stud Puffin, get it?'

'I do,' said Polly. 'And I think it's offensive.'

Tarnie smiled and found a stone in his pocket. He turned quickly and threw it far off out to sea.

'I don't think he should have a cute name,' mused Polly. 'It'll be weird to be a named puffin. I'll give him something that will make him feel safe.'

The puffin wobbled forward in his box.

'Like Neil.'

'Neil?'

'Yes. Good solid, honest name. Neil the puffin.'

Neil shook out the feathers on his uninjured side.

'See, he likes it.'

'You're nuttier than the girl in that book,' said Tarnie.

'You're jealous of my puffin,' said Polly.

'If you say so,' said Tarnie. 'Bring him down to the boat later. I'll give him a bit of herring.'

'I will,' said Polly.

Back in the little flat, the dough had swollen up to twice its normal size. Polly kneaded it again, sat down for forty minutes – she slightly fell asleep – then woke up and lit the terrifying oven, which set itself alight with a whomping noise. She ladled the sticky mixture into a battered old blackened pot she'd found in a drawer underneath the oven. It had a suspicious patina from decades of use, but she had nothing else. Hopefully it wouldn't be poisonous. She wiped it round with olive oil to try and stop the bread sticking, and crossed her fingers. Then she took a deep breath and tackled the bathroom again. The first scrub hadn't quite got it all; she'd discovered the linoleum, but had ignored the end bit of the long, narrow room, which was carpeted.

Is there anything worse, she thought, than carpets in bathrooms? Carpets in bathrooms with loose roof tiles that let the rain in from time to time; bathrooms that have played home to a passing population of temporary renters, bachelors, bedsittees, people with no vested interest in the place at all. She glanced underneath the horrible cheap squares. The original floorboards were still there. And it wasn't a bad size for a bathroom, with another window looking up into the town. She imagined pale blue tongue and groove all down the walls; a claw-foot bath on a raised platform, so you could sit and watch the boats bob about whilst you were in the tub; some pretty shells maybe … She wrenched herself back from her silly reverie to concentrate on the matter at hand, which was a) to clean the place enough so that she didn't catch some revolting disease; b) to sort herself out and find a proper job; c) to get over … well. Deal with things. Get back on her feet. Stop embarrassing her friends by bursting into tears every time she had two glasses of wine. Find inner peace.

HAHAHA. Polly picked up a square of cheap office carpet with mysterious-looking brown stains on it, and damp newspaper from 1994, and sighed.

Still, at least there was a good smell coming from the kitchen, which overlaid the numerous less pleasant ones she was uncovering. She kept her rubber gloves on and emptied bucket after bucket of dirty water down the drain until the bathroom was, if not sparkling, at least not reminiscent of some upsetting BBC2 documentary about a substandard housing estate that was about to be hit with a wrecking ball.

Finally, she stood up and stretched. She could finally see her reflection in the mirror – she looked pink and a bit flushed. She'd run water into the sink for Neil, deciding, having checked over his feathers, that he was a very clean puffin, without too many vermin. She tried to smile at herself. It had been a while since she'd smiled properly, she thought. Two furrows seemed to have landed between her eyebrows without her noticing, as if she constantly held her face in a worried frown. Perhaps she did. She smiled again – okay, she was looking a bit mad now – then headed into the main room of her odd little home.

Inside the oven, her loaf – it was a cottage loaf, with a smaller round head on top – had risen beautifully and was a gorgeous golden brown. It smelled absolutely heavenly. She slid it out of the oven with the only oven gloves that came to hand: a horrible old mucky tea towel – she'd definitely have to start a laundry pile, she decided – and turned it upside down, tapping it lightly on the bottom. It sounded crisp and fresh.

Polly felt much more cheerful suddenly, reflecting that she had done two things that morning – well, three if you counted Neil's bandage – that had turned out well: she had cleaned the bathroom and made some bread. It probably wouldn't seem much to anybody else, she thought, but it was a big step for her.

When the bread was cool enough, she cut it into thick doorsteps and spread it with butter and a little jam she'd brought with her. Then, putting Neil back in his box – he didn't seem to mind this at all, though Polly wondered in passing if he might sit on her shoulder like a pirate's parrot, then discarded the thought as being a) ridiculous, b) messy, c) bad for Neil and d) confusing, given that her name was Polly to begin with – she headed down to the harbour.

The fishermen were mending nets in the weak afternoon sunlight and gathered round her shouting cheerful hellos, which pleased her a lot.

'What's this, then?'

'Er, I made some bread.'

'You made it? Yourself?' said Jayden.

'No, I found it in my new flat,' said Polly. 'Of course I made it. Would you like some?'

Tarnie grinned at her. 'Want some tea?'

In two ticks, there were chipped blue and white enamel cups, filled from an urn with ridiculously strong tea. Polly was given milk and two sugars without being asked. Then everyone tucked into the bread and jam, and Tarnie made good on his promise to produce some herring for Neil, so everyone was happy.

'This is fantastic,' said one of the boys. Someone else with his mouth full agreed.

'I've never had home-made bread before,' said the youngest, Kendall, the pink-cheeked boy, who could barely grow a beard.

'Really?' said Polly. 'Do you like it?'

He shrugged. 'I like anything really.'

'Don't listen to him,' said Tarnie. 'This is brilliant. It's really good. Do you know what it could do with, though?'

'You could get some of that nutter's honey for it,' said Jayden.

'That's exactly what I was thinking,' said Tarnie.

'Whose honey?'

'The only other person to move to the region in years,' said Tarnie. 'When everyone else is getting the hell out – excuse my language.'

'That's not language,' said Polly happily. She was incredibly pleased with how the bread had turned out. It didn't taste at all like when she'd made it back in Plymouth. It had a deeper, richer flavour. She wondered, slightly anxiously, if it could be anything to do with the old burned black oven and the old burned black dishes. Hmm. And the fact that she'd cried into the dough, she remembered. She flushed a little pink.

'Well it is – you're blushing,' said Tarnie.

'I'm not really,' she said. 'Who's the honey person?'

'He's weird,' said Jayden.

'He's American,' corrected Tarnie. 'That's not weird. Well, you know. It is a bit weird but it's not his fault.'

'There's an American who came here to make honey?' asked Polly.

'I think he was misinformed,' said Tarnie. 'I'm not quite sure what he thought he was coming to. But he got nine months of rain anyway. He's on the mainland.'

'Gosh,' said Polly. 'He sounds . . .'

'Loopy,' said Jayden. 'This is great. Can I have some more?'

'Can I have some more too?' said Kendall quickly, jam across his mouth like a five-year-old.

'Boys! Quieten down,' said Tarnie. He brushed at some crumbs. He wasn't in his yellow sou'wester today; he was wearing a Breton shirt and faded cut-off jeans, and his beard was trimmed.

'Uh oh,' said Jayden suddenly. He took a second piece of bread and jam from the plate and hid it behind his back.

'What?' said Polly, turning round. All the fishermen's faces had fallen and one or two of them had disappeared into the body of the boat. It was the woman from the bakery, and, of course, Polly's new landlady. Outside, oddly, she looked even larger, a round wobble of a woman, though it in no way slowed her down as she marched directly towards them. A seagull set up cawing and looking for lost crumbs, adding to the ominous atmosphere.

Tarnie ran a hand through his thick hair as the woman approached.

'Er, afternoon, Mizzus Manse.'

The woman sniffed loudly. 'Afternoon, Cornelius.'

Polly raised her eyebrows and Tarnie shot her a slightly hunted look.

Mrs Manse didn't bother saying hello to anybody else. 'What are you eating?'

'Um, just . . .'

Polly glanced down at the plate; half the loaf was still there.

'Where did you get that?'

'We're just having a little tea break, Gillian. I'm sure you understand.'

Gillian Manse's face darkened and she drew herself up sturdily.

'I tell you what I don't understand. When we're all trying to pull together and stop local businesses going under and be proper Polbearnites and have a bit of pride, I don't understand why you're going to some happy-go-lucky incomer for your bread.'

'It was just—'

'I mean, I am the only baker in town. And I know you didn't buy that from me.'

'Now, Gillian—'

'I made it,' said Polly, feeling ridiculous that she'd gone a little shaky. Who did this horrible woman think she was? She could make whatever the hell she wanted.

'You did WHAT?'

She might as well have said 'I spat in it.'

'I . . . I made the bread.'

'You. Made. The. Bread.' Gillian looked utterly insulted. 'And what's wrong with *my* bread?'

'Nothing's wrong with your bread,' said Tarnie, trying to be placatory and spreading out his hands. 'It's just that Polly here—'

'Polly,' said Gillian.

'Polly made us a snack. You know, she's new.'

'Obviously she's *new*,' sniffed Gillian. 'She's taking up space in my house. I know she's new.'

Polly stiffened as the woman turned towards her.

'People in this town get their bread from me,' Mrs Manse said menacingly.

Polly was determined not to be cowed. 'But I'm not from this town.'

'All the more reason,' said Gillian, 'for you to keep away from other people's businesses and stop trying to ruin them.'

Ordinarily Polly wasn't an easy person to intimidate, but this hit home.

'I would never,' she said quietly, 'try and ruin anyone's business.'

Mrs Manse glanced witheringly at her rough-hewn efforts.

'No, not with that you won't.'

Polly bit her lip.

'I'll be on my way,' said Mrs Manse, giving them all another dose of the bad eyes. As she manoeuvred her considerable bulk to go back along the harbour, she stopped and glanced into Polly's box. Polly winced.

'What is this?' said Gillian, eyeing up Neil, who eyed her back beadily.

'Oh yes, I'm taking on the butcher next,' said Polly in a low voice, and Tarnie couldn't help grinning.

Mrs Manse raised an eyebrow. 'It's a shame when people

arrive in town and can't fit in,' she hissed. 'But they usually move on soon enough.'

After she'd gone, and the other fishermen had re-emerged, Polly had to sit down.

'Don't worry about Gillian,' said Tarnie, uncomfortably. 'That's just her way.'

'To behave like the DEVIL?' said Polly. 'How can that be a "way"? "Oh, you know he killed all those people? Just Harold Shipman's way."'

'Aye, well. She's lived here a long time.'

'She's probably what's been holding this town back. Oh Lord, and she's my landlady. She's actually going to kick me out for baking.'

'She's scared of change really.'

'But I went to her bakery.'

'Aye, it's kind of gone downhill ...'

'It's horrible.'

'It's all she's got,' said Tarnie. 'It's hard to scratch a living round here, you know.' The look in his eyes made it clear that his words were heartfelt.

'So why's she doing her best to drive trade away?' said Polly. 'I'm never going back there ever again.'

'Neither am I,' said Jayden. 'Polly, can you make bread for us every day?'

'Yes please,' said Kendall.

'Um, your boss says not, apparently,' said Polly, giving Tarnie a look. 'Don't want to upset Mrs Manse. Although she seems pretty upset already.'

Tarnie didn't look happy. Polly decided to head off.

'Me and Neil have to get back,' she said. 'Cornelius.'

The other boys laughed at that.

'It's . . .' Tarnie looked a bit embarrassed. 'It's tricky.'

'It's not tricky,' said Polly. 'She's being like the Mafia, warning me off moving in. I tell you, that might be a good enough reason for me to break the lease.'

'No, don't do that,' said Tarnie, and for a moment there was a slightly embarrassed silence between them.

'Right, well, we'll be off,' said Polly. She looked at the plate. 'I'll get that when you've finished.'

As she walked off, Tarnie suddenly seemed to remember something and called after her. Polly turned back. He was holding up a bundle wrapped in newspaper.

'It's a cod,' he said. 'I gutted it for you. Fry it up in a bit of butter and lemon and it'll be right good.'

Neil eeped excitedly.

'It's not for you, young man,' he said. 'It's for your mistress.'

Polly took the cold package as the peace offering it was.

'Thank you,' she said. 'Have a good night.'

Tarnie looked at the great cluster of dark grey clouds that had sprung up whilst they were talking, obliterating the weak sunlight of earlier like a menacing bully.

'I don't think it's going to be a good night at all,' he said.

Although Polly still had her laptop – it was so old and huge the creditors hadn't wanted it – and some DVDs to play in it, she found that actually, as she ate the fish – which did indeed taste divine with nothing more than a little lemon and salt and pepper, cooked in the last of her olive oil – and a salad made, for the first time in years, from individual lettuce leaves rather than an expensive plastic bag, she was quite happy just to sit by the window, watching as the weather lowered and the rain started to clatter against the cobblestones and the harbour walls, and the wind made the entire house rattle and creak. She saw the fishing boats, looking tiny against the might of the flailing sea, puttering one by one out into the ocean, their lights growing feebler as they bobbed along. Soon she was no longer able to identify the *Trochilus*, as it weaved in and out of the line and into the chill and unforgiving night. She shivered and thought of the men out there in that tiny boat under the huge sky as the stars began to pop out, only to be covered again by the hastening clouds and the roaring wind.

After supper, out of nothing other than sheer mischief, she kneaded up another batch of bread and set it to rise next to Neil's cardboard nest. Then she climbed into bed and fell asleep straight away.

She didn't know what woke her this time.

Most likely it was Neil, shuffling about in his box. She sat bolt upright, the sheet she'd hung over the windows only partly keeping out the light swooshing over her then vanishing, leaving the room once more in darkness. The waves crashed against the harbour wall; it was windy out, but not stormy. Some instinct took her to the window, and she pulled the sheet aside, not entirely awake.

Outside was blackness. Seawater had spattered against the windows and the taste of salt was in the air; Polly had left the window very slightly open. She craned to see outside rather than her own sleepy reflection.

Suddenly, as the lighthouse beam flitted past, she saw it. An outline – a figure, a mere shadow – standing on the quay, staring out over the water. Not moving, not doing anything; just standing stock still.

Polly jumped, startled, dazzled by the light, which was now gone. She couldn't refocus her eyes in time, and everything was dark. Who would be out there at this time of night, standing in the dark? Chilled by the night air and the motionless figure, she waited ninety interminable seconds for the lighthouse to complete its cycle. But this time as the light came over, there was nothing and nobody there. The harbour was deserted, its dock empty of boats – the fish must still be running – the causeway invisible, Mount Polbearne an island once again, being gradually reclaimed by the sea. Polly shook her head. It must have been a trick of the light. She crawled thankfully back into her warm bed.

The next morning the entire thing had slipped from her mind like a dream.

Chapter Eight

The next day dawned chilly but sunny; the attic rooms were cold. Polly checked Neil's bandage (he hopped over towards her quite happily now, and she skritched him behind the ears) as she toasted the tiny bit of leftovers from yesterday's bread in a toaster she found out a little too late hadn't been cleaned out since the royal wedding before the last royal wedding.

It didn't, however, detract from the quality of the bread. It had a rich nuttiness, a perfectly balanced crumb, and tasted sweet and wholesome, with a quick swoosh of lovely butter melting on the top. Neil immediately left his tuna and hopped over to explore what she was eating, and she fed him some crumbs straight from her fingers.

'Even better than fish?' she said, smiling, then got up to pop in some more, and reminded herself to clean the toaster.

After breakfast, she cleared up and sat by herself looking out of the window. This was a novelty in itself. She had never really been alone, from her grotty flat shares back at college, through the shared house with Kerensa, to the years in the flat with Chris. The silence – apart from the wheeling gulls – was soft and amazing. She realised she hadn't charged her phone, or even thought about it. She probably ought to do that. But after the last few months of dodging creditors, or taking phone calls for Chris that he just couldn't deal with 'right at this moment, Pol, can't you SEE I'm busy, for Chrissakes?', and basically feeling the entire time like she was on the run from a pack of hungry wolves, the relief of it all being over, even if she'd been left with next to nothing, felt like a blessing, a moment of solace.

Of course, there was a limit to how long she could go on staying here. She had a tiny allowance and a short lease, but if one of her shoes got a hole in it, she was completely screwed. She needed a job. A real, proper job. She needed an internet connection and a computer and an updated CV and a vehicle of some sort, she guessed.

In her fantasy, there would be some little business nearby in desperate need of a local office manager who would let her work flexible hours for when the tide was high, or pay her enough so that she could move back to the mainland. Many of the prettier villages up the Cornwall and Devon coastline had attracted hi-tech start-ups whose employees liked to code all night and surf all day. But this southern inlet didn't really have the surf, or the quaintness, or the cool cafés those people liked to hang out in. Which meant she'd probably end up commuting back to Plymouth – which meant she'd need a car, though she wasn't quite sure how that would work, given that she couldn't get financing or use a credit card. Alternatively she'd have to catch the bus every day, which would take ninety minutes by the time it wound round all the local villages and she couldn't always time it against the tide. Kerensa had been right. She had been far too head-strong.

On the other hand, she thought, as she skritched Neil and waited for the new bread to bake, its fabulous scent perfuming the old building and causing the rare passer-by outside to stop and take deep sniffs, she was meant to be pausing. Regrouping, not diving into another life straight away. The irony of trying to force herself to relax made her smile.

Well. One thing at a time. And today she was going to take a walk and get to know her new surroundings.

'You can't come,' she said patiently to Neil, putting him down. 'It's getting ridiculous if I take you everywhere.'

Neil hopped back over piteously and perched himself up on her hand.

'WOW,' said Polly, genuinely delighted. 'Hello! Look at you!' He obviously wanted his feathers scratched again, and she was happy to oblige. 'You're clearly getting better, little fella.'

At this, Neil did a white poo on the floor.

'Oh Lord,' said Polly. 'I'm not sure I can leave you here either.'

She cleaned up and regarded him carefully. He cocked a beady eye at her, and when she went to use the bathroom, he followed her to the door.

'Oh my goodness, you're a lap puffin,' she said, exasperated. 'Now listen, I know you're little and you got lost and you want your mummy, but I'm not your mummy, okay?' She crouched down. 'I'm just passing through. Soon I'll leave Polbearne and you're going to fly away and never ever think of me again in your little puffling brain, okay?'

Neil put his head on one side.

'Okay, okay. All right. Just this once.'

She took a heap of paper towels and spread them on the bottom of her little rucksack, then popped him inside.

'Don't tell anyone you're here, okay?' she said. 'There's already one person in this town who appears to hate me without reason. I don't need everyone else thinking of me as the weird puffin lady.'

Neil chirruped.

Polly took the bread out of the oven, adding the last scrapings of olive oil and some salt crystals, and not making the raise too high, to give it more of a focaccia flavour. She wondered whether she could buy rosemary in this town, then discarded that idea as a) ridiculous and b) slightly over her budget. She wrapped the bread in a tea towel to keep it warm, then in a plastic bag to stop Neil pecking at it, and made an extra sandwich from yesterday's bread just in case. She also took some tap water she'd put in the freezer to chill, and a couple of local apples she'd bought the day before.

The causeway gleamed open wide this morning, the tide low. As Polly walked across, she wondered how the townspeople – once a part of the mainland – had felt when the sea had gradually started to reclaim their route out of town, having to build the road higher and higher and finally giving up altogether.

As she headed into the countryside away from the shore-line, she realised how long it had been since she'd taken a walk for a walk's sake. She had marched up and down Plymouth's shopping streets in her more solvent days, and she'd once belonged to a gym, but she'd never really been one for just . . . walking.

But out here, with her lunch in her backpack (along with a chattering puffin), marching along narrow shady country lanes with no particular plan in mind, she felt . . . not too bad. Not too bad at all. She was aware of that funny feeling in her shoulders again, then recognised it for what it was: an absence. An absence of heaviness, of tightness. They should, she thought, advertise walking as an alternative to massages.

The sun did its best to break through as she walked past fields of rape and sweet meadow grass, with the occasional friendly-looking cow and ugly-looking tractor. On one particularly sunny corner, she noticed, to her amazement, what turned out to be rosemary. She broke some off right away, delighted. Even though it was probably covered in diesel fumes, it would certainly do. She stretched her legs and straightened her back and breathed in the smells of the fields – well, the nice fields; some of them were awful – and as she passed the occasional little hamlet, she managed to stop herself from bursting into song with 'I Love to Go A-Wandering'.

She thought about Chris and wondered what he was doing right now. If he was still at his mum's, he'd be sullen, truculent; he often was there, the golden boy gone a bit wrong. He would have liked this, she thought. Then again, would he? She barely knew him any more. Anything she'd suggested in the last couple of years he'd shot down right away. The idea of a fresh, healthy country walk would have been met with scorn; the only thing he wanted to do when he wasn't working obsessively was jog and drink, rather quickly and with only one objective in mind: getting as drunk as possible, whereupon he'd become self-pitying and repetitive, needing a lot of reassurance that everything was going to be all right, then instantly falling asleep wherever he was and waking up the next day in an even filthier mood than before. And Kerensa was not a country walk kind of person at all. Mind you, Polly wouldn't have considered herself one either.

But now, the sun warming her back, Polly breathed in deeply and tried to make her brain focus on the future rather than the past. Yes, the future was a frightening place, but then where wasn't?

In this slightly contradictory frame of mind – and wishing she'd brought her old iPod; 'I Love to Go A-Wandering' was getting a bit annoying in her head now – she was about to sit down for her lunch when she saw the sign.

Fresh wild-flower honey for sale.

A string of daisies hung round the wooden sign. Ooh, thought Polly. This must be the weird American the fishermen had mentioned. Maybe she should go and introduce herself as the other stranger just arrived in town. They obviously didn't get that many, and it might help her next time Gillian Manse came round baring her teeth. It struck her that Mrs Manse would of course have a key to the flat, and this gave her the shivers. So. Reinforcements.

Normally the idea of marching up and saying hello to

someone out of the blue would have been something she'd avoid at all costs; she'd spent enough time trying to network for the business, even though she'd hated doing it. But in Plymouth she'd known lots of people, which had made things very difficult by the time she'd left. Here, on the other hand, no one had any idea of – and not that much interest in – her situation. And he might need a honey marketing person.

She looked at the sign again. Okay, so that seemed extremely unlikely. But even so . . .

She started off down the rutted path. The trees met overhead, making it dark and oddly quiet. She felt her shoes clomp on the muddy ground.

'I don't like this,' she said, after she'd been walking for twenty minutes and could see nothing apart from trees and fields stretching away in every direction. However, she didn't fancy stomping her way back through all the mud. She had just stopped, hot and thirsty, not sure whether to carry on, when she saw in the distance a very thin stream of smoke. Could that be it? She struck out towards it.

'If he isn't home, I'm going to be very irritated,' she said crossly to Neil. 'I don't even WANT honey that much.'

But she was intrigued; she wanted to try baking a honey loaf, and the more local and natural ingredients that went into it, the better she suspected it was going to be.

Quite suddenly, the trees thinned out, and Polly gasped. She was in a clearing, in front of a tiny thatched cottage that looked like something out of a fairy tale. Smoke was coming from the stone chimney, and the walls were made of grey slate, as was the path that wound through an enchanting cottage garden to the little white-painted wooden front gate.

The windows were small and mullioned, and a careless tangle of rosebuds clambered over the walls.

'Ooh,' said Polly involuntarily. It was absolutely lovely. 'I hope there's not a witch inside,' she whispered to Neil. 'I'm SURE there isn't . . .'

'Hello?' she said tentatively. There was no sign of movement, but with the smoke . . . It couldn't be a man; it had to be an old lady here, with grey hair and a long dress and a frenzied appetite for the bones of children . . . Polly told herself to stop being daft and go and ring the doorbell.

There was no bell, but there was a knocker in the shape of a bee, so at least she knew she'd come to the right place. She let it thud, the noise sounding ridiculously loud in the quiet murmur of the forest clearing, and stood back to avoid freaking out whoever came to the door.

But nobody did.

'Hello?' said Polly, louder this time. 'HELLO?'

She really didn't want to just turn round and head back again. In fact, she thought, slugging water, she was actually quite hungry now. Another half-hour tramp along such a boring track would be too much; maybe there was a way back to town through the trees.

'HELLO?'

The slate path continued around the right-hand side of the cottage, so she followed it past a well and round the back.

There a sight met her eyes. The garden broadened massively behind the cottage, a long, wide green lawn, filled with heavily scented wild flowers, leading down to the bottom of a hill, where a stream ran through straight from the forest. On both sides of the stream she saw what at first glance looked like little blunt-nosed rockets waiting to take off. Closer examination, of course, revealed them to be bee-hives. There was a hum in the air, and she took an instinctive step back, then another, as one of the rockets moved and she realised that what she had taken for another hive was in fact a person clad in an astronaut's outfit – or, rather, a beekeeper's outfit. She had to stop being so jumpy.

She was about to retreat altogether – she was slightly at the limit of her capacity for bold exploits recently – when the figure straightened up and waved a hand at her. So it had seen her. Polly sighed, and reluctantly waved back, realising she felt nervous. This was completely stupid; of course it was all right to be nervous meeting people, but she wasn't the one buried in the countryside talking to insects, right? And all she wanted was to buy a jar of honey; it wasn't as if this was going to take very long or be a surprising thing to do.

The man – it had to be a man; he was tall and had very long legs – stepped over the stream with a practised hop and marched up to her with loping strides.

'Wffgargh,' he said, holding out a hand encased in a huge white gauntlet.

'Um,' said Polly. 'Don't you normally take your hat off?'

His huge white hat covered his entire head, except for his eyes, which were hidden by thick netting. He looked like a cross between a spaceman and an extremely coy bride.

The man brushed himself down quickly, checking his arms – Polly instinctively found herself checking her arms too – then apologetically removed his hat.

'Yeah,' he said slowly. 'Yeah, I forgot. I get it in the wrong order. Not enough visitors.'

Now he was looking down sadly at his gloved hand, as if wondering whether to hold it out to be shaken again.

Polly glanced up at him. She was surprised; she'd been expecting a retired man, in his sixties probably, who'd decided to opt out of the rat race after reading a feature in an airline magazine, and who was rapidly regretting it.

This wasn't the man standing in front of her at all; this man was young and tall and broadly built, with longish yellow hair pushed back out of blue eyes. He looked slightly alarming, in fact.

'Shall we try that again?' said Polly, putting out her hand formally. 'Hello, I'm Polly.'

'Huck.'

'Excuse me?' said Polly.

'Huck.'

'Oh, that's your name.' Polly felt herself go red. She'd thought he was coughing.

'Well, my mom calls me Huckle.'

'HUCKLE?'

The man spoke in a very low drawl. Polly had known he was American, but he was obviously from the South. She wanted to hear him talk some more.

'What I really like' – he pronounced it 'rilly laack' – 'about Inglin' – Polly realised he meant England – 'is the way everyone is just so polite and welcoming all the time.'

'Sorry,' said Polly, putting her hand to her mouth. 'I was just a bit surprised, that's all. I haven't heard the name before.'

'If you don't mind, ma'am, you're the one named after a parrot.'

'Ooh, I like being called ma'am. It makes me feel like the Queen.'

Huckle smiled a slow smile. He had amazing teeth. Polly wondered if America had some kind of tooth factory for everyone when they turned thirteen, the same way her mother's class had all had their tonsils taken out at the same time.

'Well then, ma'am, what can I do for you?'

'I think I'd like some honey, obviously,' said Polly. 'But first, would you mind if I had a drink of water? I'm really hot.'

The sun had risen high in the sky and was giving out a lot more warmth than she was expecting. Normally she'd have been delighted – it had been such a dreadful winter – but now she was conscious of being very pink in the face and of sweat trickling down the back of her neck.

'Oh, sure. Water? I have some iced tea, if you'd like.'

'I don't know what that is,' said Polly, 'but I'll try it. Is it just tea you've let go cold? I do that. It's not very nice.' She realised she was babbling. She had clearly gone too long without talking to another human being.

'I don't know 'bout that. Sit yourself down there.'

He indicated a little wrought-iron table and chair set that had been placed in the middle of a cloud of daisies. It had striped cushions on the seats and looked wonderfully welcoming. Polly sank down gratefully and Huckle went into the house.

Polly looked around. It really was the most ridiculously beautiful garden. The buzzing in the air undercut the soft warmth of the sun on her face, and she found herself, with two broken nights on top of months of worry and a long walk, letting her eyelids droop, just for a moment. Just for a second …

'Yo.'

Polly jumped up, not sure where she was. She saw the tall blond man standing nearby and blinked rapidly. He had taken off his beekeeping outfit and was wearing perfectly normal Levis and a red lumberjack shirt.

'Oh my God, did I fall asleep?'

'I hope so. Either that, or it was quite a fast coma.'

Polly rubbed her eyes, hoping frantically she hadn't let her mouth fall open and drool drip out.

'How long was I . . .'

'Well, it's Tuesday,' said Huckle, and it took Polly a moment to register that he was joking.

'Here,' he said, proffering a glass. There were ice cubes clinking in it, and fresh mint floating on the top. Polly took a long swig.

'Oh, that's delicious,' she said. 'So that's iced tea?'

'Yup,' he said. 'Not as good as the stuff back home, but . . .'

He sat down companionably on the other seat. Polly remembered that she was ravenous. She considered it for a second, then decided to press on.

'Um,' she said. 'Would you like to share my lunch?'

'What, now that we've slept together?' said Huckle, with that same serious drawl.

'Ha,' said Polly. She realised that she didn't expect Americans to be sarcastic; the ones she'd met tended to tell you exactly what they were doing and why. She reached down for her bag. As she opened it, Neil waddled out, complaining.

'Hello, sweetie,' she said. 'Sorry, I shouldn't have left you in there.'

He ignored her, pecking at the plastic bag that contained lunch.

'Well, no,' said Polly. 'That's why I put it in a plastic bag.'

She glanced up. Huckle was observing her with an amused look on his face.

'What? Does this look weird?'

'Er, I'm supposed to say no, right?'

'Yes. Sorry. I guess it must look a bit odd.'

'Is he a magic puffin? Can he talk?'

'No, he's just a normal one,' said Polly.

'Oh. Disappointing.'

'I like him for who he is,' said Polly stiffly.

Huckle smiled again. 'Do you always keep a bird in a bag? Is this, like, a "thing"?'

'Nope,' said Polly, picking up Neil and displaying his bandaged wing. 'We're healing.'

'In a rucksack?'

'He likes company.'

Huck nodded and looked around. 'So, here I am, just hanging out, not getting any lunch,' he said.

Polly frowned, unwrapping the packaging.

'You know it's a British sandwich, not an American one, yes?'

She had been to New York once, with Chris. A long time ago. The quality and quantity of the food had amazed them both.

'Do you mean I'll be able to actually fit it in my mouth?'

'You have quite a big mouth,' said Polly. 'Sorry, that came out wrong. Anyway. Here.'

She tossed him the package. He took one of the enormous doorsteps and handed the bag back.

'I'd say this is not doing too badly in its efforts to be a big sandwich,' he said, then took a bite. Polly did the same. It was surprisingly pleasant to be sitting in a lovely garden drinking iced tea and eating a sandwich with an odd giant. If her aim was, she reflected, to try new things in her new life, this was definitely a successful day.

'Wow,' he said after a few seconds. 'That's good. Where did you get this bread? The only stuff I can find round here is inedible; it tastes like plastic.'

'I made it,' said Polly, pleased. 'Actually,' she remembered, 'I have something better than the sandwich. Try the focaccia first, I made it this morning.'

She unwrapped the other package and tore off some crumbs for Neil.

'In fact, wait!' She felt in her pocket for the rosemary. 'Do you have some scissors?'

'This is the worst honey-selling I've ever done,' said Huckle, but he smiled as he said it, and got up. When he returned with a pair of pinking shears, Polly clipped little bits of the herb on top of the salty loaf. It smelled sensational and tasted even better. Huckle wolfed his half in about two seconds flat.

'You are seriously good at this,' he said, looking longingly at hers.

'You can have it,' she said, 'but give some to Neil.'

'I mean it. Do you do this as a job?'

Polly laughed wryly. 'No. No, no job.'

She changed the subject.

'So what about you and honey?'

'Oh yes, let me get you some. It's a shame it doesn't go with focaccia.'

'I'm sure I can make something it will go with,' said Polly, hoping this didn't sound flirtatious.

'I'm sure you can,' said Huckle in the same slightly silly tone of voice, so she had obviously failed.

He brought out a jar from a shed by the side of the wall, and a little wooden spoon with a winder at the bottom. The jar was prettily painted and had a sketch of the cottage on it, with 'Huckle Honey' written on the side.

'Wanna taste?' he said, proffering the wooden winder. She wasn't quite sure what to do, so he took it back and showed her, shaking off most of the honey from the end so he could get it out of the jar.

'Now this is apple blossom. You plant different types of flowers, you see, so you get different types of honey. I kind of experiment, move the hives around.'

Polly licked the honey off the winder. It was absolutely sensational. It had a warm depth and heart to the flavour that she'd never tasted before; not as sweet as commercial honey, but gentler and more satisfying.

'Wow,' she said. 'That's amazing.'

'Isn't it?' His face looked animated. 'Hang on, let me get some of the orange flower.'

That was just as good: light and fruity, and a pure golden colour.

'So I don't understand,' said Polly. 'Are you putting the accent on, or did you just pitch up on your horse like a cowboy and say' – she tried to do his voice – '"Well hey, little missie, I'm a here to be a doing your honey"?'

Huckle laughed. 'No,' he said. 'It wasn't exactly like that. Are you from round here?'

'I am not,' said Polly. 'I'm from Plymouth.'

'That's only forty miles away!' said Huckle. 'Trust me, where I come from, that's local.'

'Well where I come from, it's a different world,' said Polly.

'Sure enough,' said Huckle. 'Well. Anyway. This is the old beekeeper's cottage. They've been making honey here in some form or other for getting on for two hundred years. So they knew which flowers to grow and where to keep things and so on. It was just falling into disrepair when I found it.'

'But what brought you here?' said Polly. It seemed so unlikely.

Huckle glanced at his watch. 'Ma'am, that is a bit of a long story.'

Polly waited for him to start telling it, then, when she realised he had absolutely no intention of doing so, she flushed and jumped up. She'd gatecrashed this man's house, fallen asleep in his garden, and now was patently overstaying her welcome.

'Sorry, sorry,' she said. 'I didn't mean to intrude.'

'Not at all,' he said, nonetheless getting to his feet. 'It was an honour to meet you. And Neil.'

Neil pooed on some of the daisies and tried to eat some others.

'Sorry,' said Polly. 'He's only a toddler really.'

Huckle smiled. 'It's weird, it makes me miss my dog.'

'Ha,' said Polly. 'You look like a man who'd have a dog.'

'What, like I shed hair?'

'No, just . . .'

She was going to ask what had happened to his dog, but he'd already indicated that he didn't want to talk any more, and she wasn't going to pry.

'I'd better be going.'

He walked her to the gate with three jars of honey, which he refused to take money for, on the promise that she'd bake him some bread.

'If you come to Mount Polbearne, I'm living in the house on the harbour above the old bakery,' she said shyly.

'That place?' He looked horrified. 'I thought they'd condemned it.'

'No,' said Polly. 'They've condemned me to it, that's all.' She tried to make it sound like a joke, but it came out with a little crack in her voice. Huckle looked at her for a moment.

'Well, I would say a bakery is a great place for you to be,' he said. 'That other place ... ugh.'

'I know,' said Polly. 'She's already given me the evil eye.'

'You gotta watch out for those evil eyes,' said Huckle.

'You do,' agreed Polly.

Polly mused on the strange man all the way home. No wonder the fishermen called him weird. He *was* weird. Who lived in the middle of nowhere? How could he afford to eat, giving away pots of honey like that? Why had he been so welcoming, then wanted her to leave as soon as she asked him any questions about himself? A horrifying thought struck her. Maybe he'd thought she was coming on to him. After all, he wasn't that much older than her. Oh God, surely not.

She felt her face flush from more than the sunshine. Yes, he looked nice, but the very idea ... Plus it had been years since she'd had to flirt with anyone, except the bailiff to get him off the phone. She and Chris had been together for such a long time, and they hadn't even really formally broken up, she reminded herself. She would have to make it clear to the American at the first opportunity. She tried to figure out a way to get this across without making everything worse, and couldn't. She tramped all the way home, picking up more rosemary from the fields, and popping in to the friendly little minimart that sold everything, for more bread flour. The woman there, a cheery type, looked a bit concerned when she saw Polly back again, making the same purchase.

'That's the last of the bread flour,' she said. 'I'm all out now.' She paused. 'Do you ... do you bake a lot of bread?'

Polly internally rolled her eyes.

'Why, is it dangerous?'

The woman tried to smile, but it didn't quite reach her eyes.

'Only, we have a local bakery ...'

'I've heard,' said Polly, then, feeling defiant, 'I don't like their bread, it's horrible.'

The woman glanced around, as if the evil tentacles of Gillian Manse might be everywhere.

'Oh,' she said. 'Only, I don't want to upset anyone.'

'You'll upset me if you stop stocking bread flour,' said Polly.

The woman smiled meekly. 'It comes in a job lot with the other stuff. I don't ... I'm not really supposed to order it, but it's for the tourists ... not that we get many this time of year. I mean, no one in the village would actually bake bread ...'

Polly didn't want to make enemies, given that she'd just arrived and didn't know a soul. 'How about we fill up the hole here with another type of flour,' she said. 'So you can't see it's empty.'

'What . . .' The woman was tentative. 'What kind of bread do you make?'

Polly opened her bag avoiding Neil; there was a little of the focaccia left, still moist in its tea towel, that Huckle hadn't snaffled.

'Here,' she said, passing it to the woman, who glanced around fearfully at the door, then snatched at a small bit.

'Oh my God,' she said. 'That's amazing. That tastes incredible. GOD, I miss bread.'

Polly looked round. Sure enough, the little minimart didn't sell any of the usual stacks of Mother's Pride and breakfast rolls.

'You don't . . . you don't . . .'

'You don't cross Gillian Manse in this town,' said the woman, looking fearful again. 'It's just not worth it.'

'Why is everyone so scared of her?' said Polly The woman's face turned dark and she busied herself with tidying up the Polo mints.

'I'm Muriel, by the way,' she said out of the corner of her mouth.

'Nice to meet you, Muriel. I'm Polly.'

Muriel turned back round to face her.

'Oh, she had . . . she's had a tough time of it. And it's hard to keep businesses afloat here, especially in the winter.'

Polly realised the woman must be about her own age, but she looked very weary.

'She wants everyone to stick together. The only problem is . . .'

'Her bread is so horrible.'

'Most people get used to it,' said Muriel. 'But ...' She looked sadly at Polly's tea towel.

'Okay, here's the deal,' said Polly. 'You smuggle in bread flour for me to buy and I'll cut you in on it and supply you with loaves.' Ridiculously, she glanced upwards at the CCTV. Muriel looked at the door again. They both took on an oddly conspiratorial air.

'Deal,' said Muriel in a low voice. She looked at her watch. 'This is a good time of day. After lunch but before the school rush.'

'Roger,' said Polly. 'Let's call it a loaf a week.'

Muriel pushed the bread flour towards her. 'Here. Take this on account.'

'I might need the stronger stuff,' warned Polly. 'Double 0.'

'Let's cross that bridge when we get to it,' said Muriel in a low tone.

Polly wrapped the flour tightly in a plastic bag and put it in her rucksack next to a squawking Neil. Then, remembering to grab some more milk, she sidled quietly back out on to the cobbles.

Chapter Nine

That would have been it, Polly always told herself afterwards. That would absolutely have been it. She would have seen out her twelve weeks at Mount Polbearne, handed back the keys, waved goodbye to the fishing boats and headed back to Plymouth with a few stories to tell, plenty of new bread recipes and a great big dollop of R&R under her belt – she was sleeping better than she had in years. That would have been it, if she hadn't begun to find herself in unbelievably straitened circumstances.

Before she'd left, she'd signed up at a temp agency in Plymouth, but every time she phoned them, they sounded despondent and suggested she came in. She'd been in before, though, and it had been full of glamorous students and ex-students, all of whom had amazing computer skills – she could just about manage a simple spreadsheet – and she knew she didn't stand a chance. She said she'd take anything, but the woman had explained something about zero-hours working, whereby she had to stand by whether she was working or not, and she had recoiled in horror. No. She was a professional. She would find a professional job.

That was then. Now, as the weeks went by, she was horrified to see that in the years since she'd last applied for jobs, the entire system had changed. Everything was online, for starters; no more printed-out CVs and stamps. The etiquette had changed too, and she didn't hear back from any of the jobs she'd applied for; not a letter, not even an email confirming that her application had been received. She tried calling one place, only to get through to a voicemail that was so full it wouldn't even let her leave a message.

At first she thought it was bad luck – she'd updated her CV, it looked good, professional, she'd achieved ... Well, ultimately it hadn't gone her way, but she'd worked hard. Kerensa had warned her about this. 'Don't say you ran your own business,' she'd insisted. 'They'll think you don't really want to work with them, that you'll be too much of a maverick.'

'That sounds cool,' Polly had said. 'I like the idea of being a bit of a maverick. I've always been too staid, that's my problem.'

'Hmm,' said Kerensa, who was privately more worried about Polly finding another job than she was about her finding a flat or a new man. The market was brutal out there. 'Well, any time you want me to go through your CV, let me know. I'd take a couple of years off your age too.'

'Blatantly lie?' said Polly. 'You think I should just lie all over my CV?'

'Well, you have to look at it like this,' said Kerensa. 'Everybody lies, so if you don't, you're showing a terrible naivety about the nature of the real world of work. People will adjust for lies, so if you don't lie, they're adjusting downwards from a truthful position, and that's awful. Like your doctor assuming that you're lying about how much you drink.'

Polly gave her a look.

'Just telling the truth about the world out there,' said Kerensa.

'I don't want to be in the world out there!' Polly had said with a groan. 'I want to stay in my cosy flat, running a nice little business and dreaming about me and Chris being rich and me being on *Dragons' Den* or helping Alan Sugar on *The Apprentice*!'

'You don't really dream about those kinds of things,' said Kerensa.

'Er, no,' Polly had said quickly.

Actually, recently she hadn't had many dreams at all.

And now it was getting harder and harder to ignore. Because the little money she had was incredibly hard to stretch out. It was obvious that she was baking, because you could smell it all the way down the harbour front. Tarnie had asked quietly whether, if they all chipped in, all the boats, and gave her a little bit of money every week, she would make their sandwiches. Because they didn't like Gillian's and they couldn't make their own, apparently, because they were men. And of course Muriel had her loaves, and then a man snuck by one night when she was leaving the house and said, 'Psst, are you the lady with the bread?'

It was under a street light, it took her completely by surprise and she jumped.

'Um, what if I am?' she said warily.

'I caught Muriel with some. I'm Jim Baker, I run the post office.'

'Oh,' said Polly. It occurred to her that she could get some new baking tins sent to her. This might help.

And that was how her little business started, completely illicitly. Every night she would prepare large batches, in different combinations: plain white for the boys, who were unadventurous; a poppy seed here and there; some honey and raisin which, toasted and with a scrape of local yellow butter, was absolutely heavenly. In the morning she would scuttle about delivering them, taking her payment in small amounts; small amounts she desperately needed. And the worry of applying for other jobs, or about what was coming next, started to recede a little.

Four weeks later, the sun was coming up earlier and earlier in the morning, and Polly had read everything in her library, and she knew she couldn't put it off any longer. She couldn't bear it, but it was cruel to hold on to him. It was time to take Neil's bandage off.

He'd become such a part of her life, hopping about cheerily, pecking his way through the crumbs, splashing about in the sink. Polly knew she'd been warned not to get too attached, but she couldn't help feeling this was a happy bird. He squawked cheerfully whenever she appeared, he let her ruffle his feathers and scratch behind his ears and he happily

104

sat on her knee when she finally rigged up her old laptop to watch DVDs. She put off and put off going back to the vet, but she couldn't do it for ever. This was a baby. He needed to be with his own kind, even though it was going to be a wrench.

She attempted to remove the tape herself, but he screeched loudly and hopped away from her, and she wasn't confident she could do it alone. So she made another appointment with Patrick, who had seen her around town carrying a backpack that seemed to move a suspicious amount. He'd also heard various rumours about her prowess in baking and smelled certain delicious smells when walking down by the harbour, but he had to live in this town just like everybody else, so he didn't want to bring it up directly.

His heart sank when they marched proudly into his consulting room, Neil perched happily on Polly's shoulder.

'Isn't this exactly what I told you not to do?' he said gruffly, his hand brushing his bald patch, as it always did when he was irritated.

'Um, kind of,' said Polly. There was no hint of a smile today; she looked very sad.

'I bet you've even given him a name.'

'Um,' said Polly.

Patrick stretched out a hand towards the bird. Neil tilted his head to one side and hopped a little closer to Polly's ear.

'Come on, little fella,' said Patrick. 'Come on, come with me.'

In the end, Polly held on to Neil whilst Patrick expertly clipped off the bandage. At first Neil didn't know what to do, and pecked hard at his feathers as if seeing them for the first

105

time. Then he experimentally moved his wing up and down. Patrick felt the tiny bones.

'Well, he seems to have recovered fine. Nice job. He's looking healthy too, lovely bright eyes, glossy feathers.'

Polly beamed with pride.

'Now all you have to do is throw him out of a window.'

Patrick regretted saying that.

'I'm not throwing him out of a window,' said Polly. She couldn't bear the idea of sending Neil out into the freezing cold and driving rain; the weather had changed again. She had learned too that whatever temperature the forecast said it would be on the mainland, she could take off another five degrees for Mount Polbearne.

'It's what he's meant to do,' said Patrick. 'Puffins are flock animals. He needs to be with his group, that's how they're wired. It's cruel to separate them. It's like keeping a tiger in a zoo.'

Polly nodded. 'I see. I realise that.'

Patrick softened his tone. 'Look, come on. Let's give him a little shot out of my window, okay? It's on the ground floor, so even if he doesn't manage it, he won't fall any distance.'

It was true enough: because of the steep angle of the road, there was only a couple of feet between Patrick's office window and the cobbles below. A few passers-by stopped to watch the man and woman with the little bird.

'Okay, come on, wee fella,' said Patrick gently but firmly.

'I can't watch,' said Polly, covering her eyes.

Neil perched on the old stone window ledge and looked around cautiously. He pecked at his feathers again; Polly wondered if they were itchy. A sudden shaft of sunlight illuminated the cobbled street outside. Neil hopped to the edge and looked over, then glanced round at Polly, as if seeking approval.

'Go on then,' she said. 'Go on, little man.'

Neil hopped up and down nervously. Patrick pushed him a little bit forwards and Polly winced.

'Come on,' said Patrick.

There was a long pause, and then, finally, Patrick gently tipped Neil over the edge. Polly gasped, ready to be furious with him, but the little bird, after seeming to hover in the air for a moment, ready to plummet, like something out of a cartoon, suddenly regained his momentum and flapped his wings furiously, ending up descending in a side-to-side motion before coming gently to rest.

'Yay!' said Patrick and Polly as the little puffin looked around, as if surprised at what he'd done. They gave him a round of applause, then Polly let her hands drop, sadly.

'Oh well,' she said. 'I guess that's that.'

'You know there's a puffin sanctuary on the north coast?' said Patrick.

'I know. Well, there you go then,' said Polly dejectedly.

Patrick looked at her shrewdly. 'You did well,' he said.

'I know,' said Polly.

She looked at Neil, who was vainly trying to hop back up the wall. She stretched an arm down and he jumped on to her hand, then gamely fluttered up and down to show her what he could do.

'Yes, yes, you're very clever,' she said, smiling sadly. 'Thanks, Doc.' She took out her purse.

'Actually,' said Patrick, scratching his head, 'I heard . . .'

'Mmm?'

'I heard you were ...' He glanced round. 'I heard you could get bread in?'

'Oh for goodness' sake,' said Polly. 'I'm turning into a carb-pusher.'

Patrick looked glum. 'I know, it's just ...'

'You love bread. Well, fortunately ...'

Polly reached into her bag and brought out a Tupperware box. She had figured it couldn't hurt to be prepared.

'Honey and flaxseed. Toast it with butter, I would say. It's also a very good soldier bread for boiled eggs.'

Patrick inhaled it.

'Now that,' he said, 'is sensational. Thank you.'

In the end, it was Huckle who got them found out. He literally, as they realised later, laid a trail of breadcrumbs to her door. It was early on a Saturday morning. Polly had just finished checking her emails in despair – there was nothing out there – and looking at all the jobs pages online. The only two jobs that interested her and suited her skill set were both unpaid internships. But since she couldn't afford to move back to Plymouth and she couldn't afford a car to get her there, what the heck was she meant to do?

She was looking out to sea when there was a rattle of pebbles on her front windows. She frowned – the sea sometimes splattered against them when there was a storm, but not normally on a quiet morning. She leant out. Standing there grinning broadly was Huckle, his blond hair shining in the sunlight. He looked, oddly, too big for the tiny harbour; an alien transplanted from a huge country to a small one. It didn't seem to trouble him though.

'Hey!' he said. 'You know what day it is?'

Polly pulled at her hair – she'd barely touched it that morning – and rubbed her eyes.

'Is it Huckleday?'

He grinned again, all those teeth.

'Every day is Huckleday. But also: Saturday!'

'Yes . . .'

She wished she had a weekend now. Amazing, all those Monday mornings she'd cursed getting out of bed and having to go to work, but now she would love to have those days back again. Ha, stupid contradictory life.

Huck pulled out two jars of honey from behind his back.

'On Saturday morning, you have bagels. Everyone knows that.'

'Did you bring the bagels?'

'NO!' he shouted. 'That's where you come in.'

'Did you bring coffee?'

'Nope!'

'The newspapers?'

'Nope!'

'Fresh eggs?'

He shook his head.

'I brought honey!'

Polly smiled. 'Okay,' she said. 'I guess that'll have to do.'

Bagels were tricky things, Polly knew, and she set the pot on the stove ready for boiling. Whereupon Neil, who'd been practising his new-found skills (Polly didn't think he was ready to go to the sanctuary just yet), immediately hopped and fluttered up on to the table, and from there on to the countertop, and from there up on to the edge of the pot and, triumphantly, into it, gliding along the top like a rubber duck.

'OUT of there,' said Polly, exasperated. He did this every time she put water on the stove. Not only was it a waste of water, she was worried about boiling him to death one of these days.

'I thought you and the puffin weren't serious about living together,' commented Huckle, returning after being dispatched to Muriel's little store for fresh coffee, the papers, an onion and some cream cheese. He'd popped to the fishmonger's van too, and brought back some smoked salmon and two lemons, and Polly smiled at him cheerfully.

'That's better!'

'Most people like my honey.'

'I like your honey,' said Polly. 'I like it very much. But man cannot live on honey alone. And neither can girls. Or puffins. Here, you knead this half.'

They set to work pounding and twisting the dough. Polly couldn't help but notice how muscular Huckle's forearms were, the hairs almost invisible against his lightly tanned skin.

'So,' she said. 'Bees.'

'Bees,' he agreed.

'You're ... a career bee-ist?'

'An apiarist.'

'Sure, I knew that.'

110

Polly pushed the dough hard with the flat of her hand. It rolled in a satisfying way.

'Don't overknead,' she instructed Huckle, who looked as if he might squash the dough beneath his huge palms. 'You'll make them too chewy.'

'I like 'em chewy.'

'Fine,' she said. 'You eat your half. I'll eat my half.'

'Yes, ma'am.'

'You didn't answer my question about the bees.'

'Yes. No.'

Polly glanced at him sideways.

'Are you on the lam?' she asked.

'Huh? Me? No. Not exactly.'

'When you say "not exactly", that makes me think you're absolutely on the lam. Did you shoot a man in Reno just to watch him die? You sound a bit like someone who might do that. Oh my God, I'm going to be like one of those terrible American women who write to prisoners on death row!'

Huckle smiled his slow grin.

'I didn't shoot anyone, no. The cops aren't looking for me. Purely personal reasons.'

They kneaded on in silence.

'I moved here for personal reasons too,' said Polly. 'My life went down the toilet.'

He raised an eyebrow politely, but didn't push.

'I suppose that's why everyone moves here,' she said, fishing, but all she got was the eyebrow-raise again.

'Oh God, that sounded rude,' she said. 'I mean, it's lovely and everything . . .'

'I think it's lovely,' said Huckle. 'I think it's completely beautiful.'

'What's it like where you come from?'

'Flat,' said Huckle. 'Everything is flat, and big, and there aren't many people and it goes on for miles. And lush, like a jungle. Lots of green plants that can eat you.'

'Where are you from, the rainforest?'

'Savannah, Georgia.'

'What's that like?'

'It's beautiful,' he said simply. 'In a different way. It's very old-fashioned. Has all these little garden squares.'

'In America?' said Polly. 'I thought America was all modern.'

'It is, mostly,' said Huckle. 'Atlanta is. But Savannah they just kind of forgot about. It's pretty quiet.'

'Is it hot there?'

'The summers are scorching.'

'Like it's meant to be, then,' said Polly. 'Here it's just pretty much drizzle all the time.'

'But when you do get a good day, you treasure it,' said Huckle, in a way that indicated he wasn't going to say any more. Then he smiled. 'Okay, what do I do with this?'

The dough was well and truly pounded. Polly left it to rise in a bright spot protected from Neil, and they made coffee in her recently neglected coffee machine, and opened the windows to let the sunlight in.

'You know, from the outside this place looks like it's gonna kill you,' observed Huckle, watching the dust motes play across the scrubbed wooden floorboards. 'But from in here, it's all right.'

'I know!' said Polly. 'If I had any money, I'd do more. Buy

curtains for starters,' she said. 'The lighthouse gets me every time, even through the back bedroom door. It's like living in *Close Encounters of the Third Kind*.'

'I never thought of that,' said Huckle.

'And I'd varnish the floorboards.'

Huckle looked doubtful. 'I could probably do that for you,' he said. 'But I'm not sure the floor would hold the weight of the varnish. Have you seen the way it slopes?'

'Seen it?' said Polly. 'I'm living it, thank you very much. It slopes on me every day. I keep nearly falling out of bed.'

He grinned, and Polly suddenly felt a bit strange about him thinking about her in bed. But he didn't seem in the least bit flirtatious, just courteous (and a little bit hungry). There was no point thinking like that anyway, not least because, even though they had only exchanged a few cursory text messages, she didn't feel she'd quite abandoned Chris. Still. She and Huckle were the only two strangers in town. It was natural they'd gravitate towards one another.

They got up to divide the dough.

'This is hard,' muttered Huckle, trying to stick the rings together.

'Wait till we boil them,' said Polly, putting the lid on the water pot this time and yelling at Neil every time he got too close.

The cooking, the tricky bit, was made even harder by the lack of proper utensils, and Polly burned herself slightly on the wrist trying to fish out a particularly recalcitrant bagel. Without thinking about it, Huckle took her wrist and ran it under the water way way longer than she would normally have bothered to.

113

'You can't let it deepen in,' he said. 'Even a little burn. You think they've stopped but they just go on and on. Hush.'

'Do you ever get stung by your bees?' Polly asked, curious.

'Yeah, sure,' he said nonchalantly.

'Doesn't it hurt?'

He smiled and tried to look unbothered. Then: 'It sure does,' he said. 'It hurts like merry hell.'

'You don't get used to it?'

'No,' he said. 'Man, I have to be careful. They sting you enough, you get allergic to the venom and then they can kill you.'

'A bee can kill you?'

'Happens all the time,' he said. He let her take her wrist out from under the tap, tutted at her for not having a first aid kit and showed her a yellow pen in his pocket.

'It's an EpiPen,' he said. 'In case anyone gets stung by a bee and has a bad reaction.'

'What if it's you?' she said.

'I know,' said Huckle. 'I'd have to jam it in myself. I think about that quite a lot.'

They both stared at the pen.

'Don't,' said Huckle.

'What?' said Polly, a smile playing on her lips.

'Don't think you might stick it in for fun.'

'I wasn't thinking that.'

'I bet you were.'

'Maybe a little bit. Maybe just about holding you to ransom.'

'You see an EpiPen and you want to commit a crime. That's a worrying characteristic.'

They were smiling at one another as Polly put the bagels in the oven. Ten minutes later, there was a knock on the door.

'So, we were just passing by,' said Tarnie, as Jayden shuffled about next to him.

'No you weren't,' pointed out Polly. 'You work right here.'

Tarnie smiled. 'Do you want a fish?'

'You are VERY LUCKY,' said Polly. 'Anticipating something like this. I have made twenty-four bagels, which is about two more than I can eat.'

Huckle came downstairs too to see what the commotion was. Given that it was ten o'clock on a Saturday morning, and he was wearing a crumpled linen shirt and a pair of soft old chinos with bare feet, Polly felt suddenly very much like she had to give an explanation.

'Huck just came by with some honey,' she said. 'About an hour ago. To make bagels.'

At the exact moment she said it, Huck chimed in with 'I was just passing.' This made her feel vaguely insulted that he was also so anxious to make it clear that she was someone he'd just run into, plus she rather suspected that by issuing such flagrant denials, they gave the impression that they had in fact been up to something. And why would she care what Tarnie thought anyway?

Jayden, the young fisherman, said, 'What's a bagel? Can I use your toilet? What's a bagel?'

'Jayden!' said Tarnie. 'Honestly, it's like being a school teacher.'

115

'You may use my loo,' said Polly. 'And you may all try a bagel.'

They carried the bagels – twelve onion, twelve cinnamon – plus honey, smoked salmon and cream cheese, lemon juice, knives and a coffee pot, down to the harbour's edge and all the fishermen gathered round. They looked a little confused to begin with, but took to the food with a will, crumbs spattering everywhere, the bagels perfectly crunchy on the outside and chewy on the inside. It was very easy to tell the difference between the perfect circles Polly had made and Huckle's rather apologetic shapes, which resembled a child's plasticine creations, but they tasted incredibly good all the same, and made a fine feast for a breezy spring morning.

Jayden looked up at Polly's windows.

'Have you seen the ghost yet?' he asked eagerly.

'WHAT?' said Polly, jolted. She suddenly remembered the shadowy figure she'd seen on the jetty. 'Don't be stupid.'

It had been nothing, she told herself. Just a trick of the light. Nonetheless, she felt her heart beat a little faster.

'I'm not being stupid,' said Jayden stubbornly. 'There's a harbour ghost. Everybody knows that.'

'Jayden,' said Tarnie in a warning voice. 'Shut up.'

'Well there is,' he said sulkily.

'I don't believe in ghosts,' said Polly much more confidently than she felt. Jayden didn't have to sleep up there by himself. 'What kind of non-existent ghost?'

'It's the spirit of a young woman,' said Jayden. 'She walks up and down the harbour walls, waiting for her bloke. But he never comes back, right, because he's been eaten by the fishes at the bottom of the sea. He went out fishing one day and never came home. And she just waits for him, calling like this: "Woooooo!"'

'His name was Woo?' said Polly.

'It's nonsense,' said Tarnie. 'Don't listen to him, Polly, he's basically an idiot.'

It was easy to laugh about it in the light of day, surrounded by people, especially when Jayden did an imitation of the ghost, eyes crossed, tongue hanging out. 'She killed herself,' he said. 'Threw herself into the water. But her spirit still hangs on . . .'

'So how's the fishing business?' Huckle asked Tarnie, changing the subject when he realised Polly was unsettled. Tarnie eyed him suspiciously.

'It's all right,' he said shortly.

'It's awful,' piped up Jayden, snapping out of his ghost impersonation.

Tarnie shot him a look.

'What? If we do find the fish we've got a quota, and if we don't we all go hungry. And it's cold and wet and rubbish. I wish I hadn't failed my GCSEs.'

'Did you fail your GCSEs, Jayden?' said Polly kindly. He hardly looked old enough to be shaving. 'Can't you sit them again?'

Jayden looked confused. 'You can do that?'

'Of course. Didn't you listen at school?'

'I think the answer to that's obvious,' said Tarnie. Jayden looked dismayed.

'It's not too late, you know,' said Polly gently.

'I'd never get into the blazer,' mumbled Jayden.

'I like it,' said Archie, Tarnie's second in command. He was fair and round, his cheeks ruddy from the spray and the sun. 'I like setting off into the sun going down. I like seeing the birds on the water when we know we're close to the fishing fields. I like the colour of the sky—'

One of the other men made a kissy-kissy noise.

'Oi,' said Polly. 'Shush or no more bagels for you.'

The man shut up immediately, but Archie was blushing now, his cheeks flaming, and he stopped talking.

'What about you?' Polly asked Tarnie.

Tarnie turned and stared at the sea. The watery spring sunlight danced on the waves.

'Well,' he said. 'It's what my father did. And his father. And so on. My mum always said I had salt water in my veins.'

His West Country accent deepened, and his eyes were suddenly far away.

'Archie's right,' he said. 'Sometimes when you're out there, and it's just you and the water, nothing else, and it's the middle of the night and all you can see is the stars overhead and you're out of sight of the lighthouse and you're just moving to the rhythm of something so much bigger than you . . . then yeah, it's all right.'

Polly looked at him for a second.

'Wow,' said Huckle. 'That does sound kind of cool. Can I come out with you guys one night?'

The men looked at him and laughed, but Tarnie shrugged. 'Reckon.'

'Unless you throw up,' said Jayden. 'Don't throw up on the fish. It's a bad scene.'

Huckle nodded. 'I can see how that might be a bad scene. I did sail a bit as a boy.'

The fishermen exchanged glances. They'd heard that one before.

'How did you get into the honey business, then?' asked Jayden.

Huckle shrugged. 'Well, I hated my old job—'

'What was that, jam?' said Polly, slightly peeved that he was starting to talk to them when he'd been cagey with her.

'Er, no,' he said. 'I was an ... executive.'

'A what?' said Jayden, looking confused.

'It's something you can do with GCSEs,' said Kendall. 'Mebbe.'

'Er, I don't know what those are,' said Huckle. 'But it was in an office, yes.'

'Inside?' said Jayden. 'All day? Were you ever soaking wet?'

'Almost never,' said Huckle.

'Cor,' said Jayden. 'That sounds great.'

'Well, it wasn't.'

Huckle rubbed his eyes for a moment.

'Anyway. Life takes a turn.' He clammed up again. Polly was watching him very closely.

'More money,' said Jayden, still fixated. 'That you make indoors. That sounds great.'

'I'm going to look into night classes for you,' said Polly.

'So,' said Huckle, 'I thought I'd try something else.'

'Honey,' prompted Jayden.

'No, being a cowboy,' said Huckle. 'Yes, honey.'

'Now I'm confused,' said Jayden. 'Because you sound a bit like a cowboy.'

Huckle smiled his slow smile. 'I'm not a cowboy.'

'I bet if you put the hat on you'd look like one,' said Jayden. 'Maybe I should be a cowboy.'

'Maybe you should stop talking for two minutes,' said Tarnie, and Jayden lapsed back into silence.

'But how can you do honey for a job after that?' said Polly. He made it sound so easy – exchanging one way of life for another. She alone of everyone here knew it was anything but and was wondering if she could ever have left a safe job so lightly; not without a seismic shake-up. 'I mean, does it make you any money?'

Huckle looked at her, and something in his eyes made her think he understood her own precarious position.

'Er,' he said. 'Well, I kind of . . .'

Everyone was staring at him expectantly.

'I kind of . . . I mean, the honey was very much a kind of lifestyle change, you know?'

Jayden clearly didn't understand. Then he did.

'You mean you don't have to work?' he said, eyes wide. 'Are you rich?'

Huckle went slightly pink and looked away. 'Aw, man, it's not like that,' he said, but he didn't finish the sentence and looked shy.

'Have you got a helicopter?' said Jayden. Huckle laughed.

'No,' he said.

'Damn,' said Polly. 'I should definitely have done it your way before my career change. Getting rich should have been on my to-do list.'

Now they all looked at her, and she blushed too and quickly changed the subject. 'Anyway!' she said, starting to scoop up crumbs. 'Can anyone tell me how to get a bus to the puffin sanctuary?'

'Why?' said Tarnie, but he realised why when he saw her face. 'Oh no. Not Neil?'

Neil was sitting next to Polly on the harbour wall, lazily pecking at a piece of bagel. He looked up when he heard his name.

'Apparently I am being very cruel to him and not respecting his animal rights,' said Polly sadly.

'Well, he is getting fat,' pointed out Tarnie.

'My puffin is not fat!' said Polly crossly. 'Also, he's still young. Don't talk about him like that. You could really affect his self-image.'

'Well, that would be good,' said Tarnie. 'Then he'll know he's fat and do something about it. No point ignoring the obvious.'

Polly stuck her tongue out at him. 'He is a beautiful puffin.'

'There isn't a bus,' said Jayden. 'You need to get a special coach. We went there on a school trip. It's all I remember about that entire year.'

'Was it good?' said Polly. 'Is it a nice place to be?'

'I threw up on the coach,' said Jayden.

'Ha!' said Huckle. 'Er, I mean, I'm sorry about your puffin.'

Polly stroked Neil's wings thoughtfully.

'It's okay,' she said, her voice cracking slightly. 'I'm getting good at letting go of things recently.'

Everyone went quiet, then Huckle jumped up.

'I can take you,' he said.

Tarnie looked up, as if he'd been thinking the same thing.

'Have you got a car?' Polly asked.

'Not exactly,' said Huckle.

At that precise moment, a shadow passed over the little group. Neil hopped protectively closer to Polly, who looked up, still feeling a little shaky, to be confronted by the substantial figure of Gillian Manse.

'Oh for goodness' sake,' Polly said quietly to herself.

'What's this?' said Gillian, her harsh voice echoing off the harbour walls. 'Doing picnics now, are we? I don't think that's in the lease.'

There were crumbs everywhere. The seagulls were lined up on the wall, waiting for their chance to pounce once everyone had gone. Half-eaten bagels were lying on paper napkins.

'What even IS that?' said Gillian Manse.

'It's a bagel.'

'A what?'

'A very, very famous bread product known all over the world,' said Polly, angry suddenly. 'The kind of thing any baker would know about.'

Huckle shot her a concerned look.

'Well I don't want it in this town,' said Gillian. 'Nothing wrong with a pasty.'

'There is nothing wrong with a *good* pasty,' said Polly. 'And there's nothing wrong with people in a free country baking what they like, so STOP PESTERING ME.'

Huckle patted her on the arm.

'It's all right, calm down.'

Polly turned to him. 'She's a big bully,' she whispered.

Gillian's face was stern. 'I just don't want anyone ruining my business!'

'You're ruining your own business, making such awful bread,' retorted Polly.

Tarnie stood up.

'Now, ladies . . .' he began.

'This isn't about "ladies",' said Polly, more exasperated than ever. 'It's about this witch telling me what I can and cannot do in my own damn home.'

'Well let's make sure it's not your home for much longer then,' said Gillian.

'And what's THAT supposed to mean?' shouted Polly.

'Ssh, ssh,' said Tarnie, trying to calm the situation down.

'Exactly what I said,' said Gillian. 'That place is mine. I can easily get you out of there.'

'For making a sandwich?'

'It's my lease.'

The woman was bright purple in the face, absolutely flaming with shivering fury. She looked terrifying. Suddenly all the fight went out of Polly. She just wanted to sink down and forget about everything.

Gillian bent down, picked up the last piece of bagel and hurled it straight out to sea, where it was immediately dive-bombed by a flock of squalling gulls. Then she turned and stalked away.

Polly realised she was shaking.

'She's the wickedest, most horrible . . . She's going to throw me out.'

'She won't,' said Tarnie. 'She needs the rent. She's just an old woman, trying to get by.'

'She's a horrible witch trying to drive me out of here,' said Polly. 'I can't believe you're defending her!'

Tarnie looked uncomfortable. 'I know, but—'

'She's probably the reason this place is dying, if she monsters everybody who comes to live here!'

The fishermen were starting to mutter their thanks for the food and back away.

'Oh, so now *I* look like the crazy one,' said Polly, cross. 'Well, that's just fantastic.'

Huckle smiled, but he too headed off, leaving Polly once more alone, sitting on the harbour wall. She felt ashamed; she knew she'd overreacted, that there was no point in venting her frustration on an old woman. It just felt as though every time she started to get ahead, step up a little, move on, it all came crashing back down again.

Chapter Ten

Polly couldn't sleep that night. She tossed and turned, occasionally crying a little. She couldn't believe that things had gone from bad – very bad – to worse. All she was trying to do was meet some people and make herself feel better – and baking very much did make her feel better. To meet such nastiness and resistance was just ... She would have to move back to Plymouth. She was going to be made homeless anyway; she had absolutely no doubt that that evil, nasty woman was going to make sure she was evicted. AND, it struck her, she'd probably lose her security deposit too. A chilling fear hit her that she seemed to be in freefall. She had no security; where would she end up? Living on benefits in one of Plymouth's big tower blocks, with barbed-wire fences and foul-smelling lifts and great big dogs roaming free and drug-takers in the alleyways?

Or squeezing in back with her mum in Rochester in the little overheated house she'd grown up in; her mum who had been so proud of her professional, college-educated daughter with the nice middle-class man and the nice office career and they run their own business don't you know, and they've just bought one of those spanking new waterside executive apartments and . . . It would be shameful for her mum, given all the boasting she liked to do to her friends. It would be shameful for Polly. Oh Lord.

Some anxieties were much, much worse at night and come the morning sun seem manageable; could vanish like bad dreams with the first cup of coffee, or be rationalised away into the business of the day, when the brain didn't have the chance to mull over mistakes and missed opportunities, regrets and worries for the future. Polly sensed that her problems were not the type that were going anywhere in a hurry. If only she hadn't made all that extra bread just to spite Gillian Manse and, if she were honest with herself, show off. If only she hadn't talked back to her, then the woman would have left her alone and she wouldn't be facing imminent homelessness. Oh God.

Even though it was freezing in the unheated room, she got up, carefully pulling her duvet around her, and hopped into the sitting room and over to the kettle. A hot drink would help. She would put the light on and read a book; do anything in fact to take her mind off things and stop her stupid brain from whirring. She switched on the immersion heater. It took two hours to warm up for a bath, but that was okay, she could have it in the morning if she fell asleep again. Somehow, though, she knew she wasn't going to fall asleep again. She would just have to deal with that. She had nothing to do tomorrow. Or the day after that. Or the day after that. If she had to sleep in, she could. Even Neil was out for the count, eyes shut tight in his little box. She was all alone.

Still with the duvet on, she crept to the window to look out. There wasn't much to see, but the fishing boats all being out gave her a feeling that she wasn't alone: that out there, somewhere, Tarnie, Jayden, Archie and the rest were wide awake, drinking tea too, maybe, among the silvery scales and fluttering fins of the shoal; stitching up nets, or heaving in the great piles of ice from the ice machine to keep their cargo fresh for the morning markets all the way down the coast to Penzance.

With everything else in her head, she had forgotten Jayden's silly story about the ghost woman until she actually got to the window. As the lighthouse beam swept across, her adrenalin surged, but she was feeling so exhausted and grim about things, she no longer had the energy to be actually scared by the supernatural; her real life, she reflected, was already frightening enough.

Her eyes adjusted to the dark of the harbour: the stones, the moon reflecting on the water – the night was unusually clear – a few cars parked up, the street lamps extinguished … then she saw it. She craned her neck and peered more closely, her heart threatening to erupt through her chest. There it was. A figure, in the same position, standing on the wall, stock still, staring out to sea, like a statue.

Polly's breath caught in her throat. She glanced back into the room, quickly, to reassure herself that her familiar things were still there; had not faded to some past time of long ago. Her eyes were dazzled once again, and she blinked once, twice to accustom herself to the dark. Then she steeled herself, and opened the window. The rattle seemed incredibly loud in the night-time air, but Polly didn't care; fear and anxiety were making her reckless. She leaned out, craning to see the figure.

'OI!' she shouted. 'OI!!'

The figure turned round suddenly in shock. As it did so, the great lighthouse beam swept over again, and Polly watched in horror as the figure slipped and fell, its skirts fluttering in the wind, its long hair streaming out behind it.

There was no time to think. Polly grabbed her jacket and threw it on over her pyjamas, then thrust her feet into a pair of boots before tearing out of the door, thundering down the stairs. That was not an apparition, or something she'd dreamt. There was someone out there, on this cold, blowy, scuddy night.

Down on the street, temporarily disorientated, she wished she'd brought a torch. The moon was nearly full, but the dark shapes had taken on new dimensions and she wasn't precisely sure where along the harbour wall she was headed. Finally she came upon a gap, looked down – and gasped.

There, lying in the shallow water, was the bulky shape of none other than Mrs Manse. Without the fierce bun, her hair was long; her roundness was concealed by the flowing nightdress and housecoat she was wearing. Polly knelt down next to her. She was breathing, but as the lighthouse beam swept over them, Polly saw that she was bleeding from a gash on her head. She had to get her out of the water; it was absolutely freezing.

'Gillian,' she hissed. 'Gillian! Oh my God, I am SO SORRY.'

The woman didn't stir. Polly sighed. Where the hell were five burly fishermen when she needed them? She looked up at the buildings along the front. The flats above the rest of the old shops were all empty. She needed her phone. But if she ran back to fetch it, it might be too late ... No. She would have to do this herself.

She bent down and grabbed the large woman under her arms, and heaved with all her might. Over and over again the sea tried to suck the woman back, as if demanding her. Each time, Polly swore mightily and tried to get a bit more traction. And finally, incredibly slowly, she managed to pull her, little by little, out of the waves – they were both soaking now – and towards the landing slip. She called out for help a few times, but soon gave it up as a waste of puff and energy; she just had to get on with this on her own.

The tide was starting to come in and a wave splashed her briskly on the face as she bent down to check that Gillian was still breathing. The woman's long hair was now adorned with fronds of seaweed. Polly swore as Gillian slipped from her grasp, but the woman did not wake, and Polly started to panic, thinking that her hard work might be in vain. The lighthouse beam swept past again, and she wondered if they could see her from up there. Then she remembered that there was nobody actually in there now; they were all automated these days. That was no help; bloody hell, you needed someone there to sound the alarm when stuff like this happened.

The light somehow gave her an extra burst of energy; just enough to heave Gillian on to the slip. She didn't like to think of how much bruising there was going to be, but from then on it was much easier, without the waves splashing at her and the perishing cold water lapping at her ankles.

At last she reached the top, and bent over to catch her breath. She wondered what to do. Why on earth didn't she have any of the fishermen's numbers? But then they weren't here anyway, she remembered; they were miles away from any mobile phone mast, any sign of habitation at all, out in the middle of the Irish Sea.

She glanced round the deserted town again, pulling off her jacket to cover the drenched woman. She needed help, and fast, and having to explain herself to any of the suspicious villagers would take too long.

Tearing back to the house, she charged upstairs. She turned on the kettle and grabbed some blankets for warmth, then snatched up her phone to dial 999. As she did so, she noticed the jar of honey still sitting on top of one of the meagre kitchen units. Huckle's telephone number was printed on the label.

She would call him first. He'd know what to do. She realised she was basing this supposition on absolutely nothing, but she didn't have much time. She poured boiling water into a mug, hoisted the blankets in her other arm and tore back downstairs again as fast as she could, balancing everything and dialling Huckle's number at the same time.

It rang for so long Polly started to think that maybe it was disconnected, but finally she heard the familiar drawl, slower and sleepier than ever.

'Er, yeah?'

'Huckle?'

'Yip?'

'Huckle, it's me ... Polly.'

'Oh ... yeah. Right. Sorry. Thought someone had mucked up their time zones again.'

'Huckle, I need you—'

'Um, you know I'm not really—'

'Shut up! I need you to come to Polbearne. Mrs Manse fell into the water!'

'She did what?'

'That old woman. She fell into the water.'

Polly was by now trying to take off the woman's sodden housecoat and didn't feel like prolonging the conversation.

'Huckle. Come now, I'm on the harbour.' She checked the causeway. It was still clear.

'Er, right, okay.'

She rang off, then checked Mrs Manse. She was breathing, and was starting to stir. Polly was suddenly not keen for the woman to come round to find Polly stripping her clothes off. She dialled 999. They were helpful and said they'd be about half an hour; they told her to take off Gillian's clothes and replace them with blankets, and to give her a hot drink – no alcohol – if she could sit up.

That was easier said than done. Every time Polly managed to get a blanket around her, Gillian shook it off again. She was clearly confused; she was muttering to herself and struggling to get up. Polly was having huge problems holding her.

Suddenly a throaty roar burst through the tiny town. Polly jumped up, startled. The noise was monstrous, bouncing off the old slate walls and the cobbles. Holding Mrs Manse firmly by the shoulder, she peered into the darkness, trying to see what the hell it was.

Roaring round a corner at an angle came something from the 1940s: a classic motorcycle frame in a dark burgundy colour with a small engine at the front and black spoked wheels; attached was a side car, also painted burgundy.

'What the hell?' said Polly. On top of it was perched the large figure of Huckle, and the contraption was moving at an incredible rate, its enormous roar resonating through the town. Polly finally began to see lights come on in people's bedrooms. Oh, thanks for coming when you heard me shouting my head off, she thought to herself.

Rather dramatically, like a skier coming to rest, Huckle skidded to a stop in front of her. The large round headlamp at the front of the bike blinded her, and Polly put up her hand to shield her eyes.

'Ow,' she said.

Huckle hopped off, removing his vintage black helmet and shaking out his slightly too long yellow hair.

'What is that?' said Polly. Mrs Manse was still struggling to get away.

'It's a jet ski,' said Huckle. 'Seriously, that's what you got me down here to ask?'

He turned his attention to the old woman, crouching next to her on the slipway.

'Now, what's going on with y'all?' he said, his voice slow and kind. He took Mrs Manse's lumpy body in his arms and miraculously made her seem small and light. Polly let her go with some relief and rubbed the circulation back into her arms.

Mrs Manse seemed to calm down immediately and said a few names, none of which Polly recognised.

'Have you got anything for her to drink?' said Huckle. 'Maybe we should give her a drink. Is the ambulance coming?'

'The ambulance is coming, and yes!' said Polly, feeling pleased. She handed over the mug of boiled water. Mrs Manse tasted some, then spat it out.

'I think you're on the mend,' said Huckle. 'What happened, Pol? Did you two get in another fight?'

'You're not serious?' said Polly. 'What, you think I pushed an old lady into the sea?'

'I don't know you very well.'

Polly gave him a flat stare.

'Okay, okay.'

He looked at Mrs Manse.

'So what happened?'

Polly sighed. 'Oh God, I'm going to have to explain this to the ambulance crew too, aren't I? And probably the police.'

'The police?' frowned Huckle.

'I saw her standing there – I didn't know it was her, really, she was too far away. I shouted out – I just yelled at her to see who it was. And I think I gave her a fright. She slipped.'

Polly swallowed.

'Do you think they're going to charge me with manslaughter?'

'No, I'll just sue you,' came a growling voice.

'Oh thank God,' said Polly. 'Thank God. I am SO sorry. But what were you doing out in the middle of such a wild night?'

Polly did try to explain, as the ambulancemen arrived and a little police car bumped carefully across the causeway, driven by a sleepy-looking copper with a moustache. Mrs Manse was wrapped up like a turkey in silver blankets in the back of the ambulance complaining that a body couldn't even take an innocent night-time stroll any more without being abused. Fortunately the policeman seemed disinclined to take this too seriously.

Polly felt very dubious indeed.

'She wasn't walking! She was standing right there! And I've seen her there before,' she hissed to Huckle.

'That's a nasty cut,' said the paramedic. 'I think you're a bit stunned, and I hope you haven't caught anything from being in the cold water. I think we need to take you along to the hospital for a bit.'

'I can't do that,' said Gillian regally. 'I have to open up the bakery.'

There was a silence.

'Well I can tell you THAT won't be happening in a hurry,' said the cheery paramedic.

'I have to. It's what I do.'

'And getting you better is what WE do, so I would just relax if I were you.'

'But they need the bakery.'

'And you should thank this young lady for having the presence of mind to get you out of the water and look after you without panicking. You shouldn't be dancing along slippy harbour walls at your age and in your condition,' said the paramedic. 'This could have been a lot worse.'

Gillian Manse looked at Polly. Now she didn't really look angry, just defeated and confused.

'Aye,' she said. But she didn't sound very grateful at all.

There was no point in going back to bed. Polly and Huckle drank black coffee and sat on the harbour watching the sun coming up, talking about what had happened. The chill gradually left the air and the stars blinked out, as fingers of pink started to appear across the eastern horizon. They chatted companionably in the lightening gloom. By 5.30 the sky was yellow, pink and blue, a beautiful day coming in, the sea fresh in their nostrils, the strange events of the night already falling behind them. As they watched, a little dark blob appeared on the horizon, followed by other dark blobs, and up to the harbour's edge came the gutters and the market men in their vans. The seagulls started to get more excited.

'I'll wait and tell Tarnie,' said Polly. 'He's lived here for ever. If anyone knows what was going through her mind, it's him.'

'Sure,' said Huckle, kicking his legs gently. 'Plus we need to think about breakfast.'

'Everyone will need to think about breakfast,' said Polly. 'I don't have enough bread for the entire town! What are people going to toast?'

'They'll put it in the papers,' said Huckle. 'The town with no bread. The no-carb state.'

They looked at one another.

'No,' said Polly. 'Plus, she'd do her nut. She'd never let me.'

'I thought she was only interested in saving her business,' said Huckle, swinging his long legs over the wall.

'And having me killed,' said Polly. 'Don't forget that.'

'I don't think it was personal,' said Huckle, stretching and yawning. Suddenly Polly felt a ridiculous urge to run her fingers through his thick hair. Must be lack of sleep, she thought. But there was just something so masculine about him: his size, the long muscles, the warmth of his bulk close by. She glanced down.

'I know. Just, on top of everything else that's happened to me ... it *felt* personal,' she said.

'Maybe you've lived a sheltered life,' murmured Huckle, looking at her. Her strawberry-blonde hair was tangled and blown out by the wind; it looked dramatic. Her skin was pale, but it emphasised the cute freckles on her nose.

'Not sheltered enough,' said Polly moodily. 'Anyway, I couldn't run a bakery. I bake for fun, not for a job.'

'What *do* you do for a job?' asked Huckle seriously.

Polly glanced at him, then jumped up to greet the boats coming in.

Tarnie's face was grave when he heard the news, which was already the topic of gossip and chit-chat amongst the fish traders.

'That's a bad business,' he said, his blue eyes looking downcast.

'But what ... what was she doing?' asked Polly.

'You have to get up early in a bakery,' said Jayden cheerfully. They had had a good catch, and the silvery fish caught the rays of the morning sun in their still-shining scales. They would be on the plates of Rock and St Ives and Truro by lunchtime.

'Mmm,' said Tarnie. 'I wonder ... Someone had better go to the bakery, get her bits and pieces together.'

'Has she got friends who can do that?' asked Polly.

Tarnie looked slightly awkward.

'Ah yes, well, she's always had a bit of a fiery personality, Gillian Manse.'

At this, Polly felt instantly terrible. How awful she had been, to be so angry with an old woman with no family and no friends. How spiteful to think she could come in and mess about with this woman's livelihood. She felt absolutely dreadful suddenly, guilty and desperate to make amends. It wasn't personal – Huckle had been absolutely right – and she had let herself channel her own bitterness and disappointment towards somebody else.

'Er, can I help?' she said, desperate to be useful. 'I just feel so awful about it.'

Tarnie looked at her.

'Actually, reckon you could,' he said. 'You'll know ... what a lady in a hospital bed would like, probably. I wouldn't know that.'

Polly smiled. Obviously Tarnie didn't have a girl of his own. She hadn't thought it would be hard for fishermen to find girlfriends – hadn't really thought about it at all – but she supposed the remoteness of their location, the unsociable hours ...

'Why don't you smell of fish?' she asked suddenly.

Tarnie looked bemused by the non sequitur.

'What?'

'Er, sorry, just wondered. Um, fine, of course I can do that.'

'Yes. It would be a big help,' he said. 'I could meet you at the bakery at ten, then I'll head up to the hospital.'

'When are you going to sleep?' said Polly.

Tarnie shrugged. 'Ah, I don't need much of that. Neither do you, by the sound of things.'

Polly smiled. 'Hmm.'

Tarnie started back to the boat, then turned round.

'Almond soap,' he shouted, and waved. Polly waved back.

The bakery looked dusty, unkempt, even though its owner had only been away for a few hours. It needed scrubbing down; there was a stale smell in the air. Polly sensed that goods were being left out longer than they ought to be.

'We should probably dispose of everything,' she said.

'Ha,' said Tarnie. 'I wouldn't do that. If she gets discharged tonight and comes back here, you'll know about it.'

The little flat upstairs was immaculate, much tidier and better kept than the shop. It was full of knick-knacks: little pottery statuettes and crystal horses. The carpet had a loud swirling pattern and the heavy embroidered pelmets were well dusted. A big old-fashioned television sat in one corner of the room, next to a carefully marked *Radio Times*. Polly felt claustrophobic and extremely intrusive.

'I don't like doing this,' she said.

'Mmm,' said Tarnie. 'Well, you go into her bedroom and pick up . . . stuff a lady needs.'

Polly gave him a look, but he was serious.

The bedroom was small, the bed still imprinted with Gillian's shape. She must have had problems sleeping too, thought Polly. An old-fashioned alarm clock sat on the bedside table, along with various bottles of pills. Well, that was a start. Polly scooped them all up and glanced around for a bag. She opened the built-in wardrobe and found an old suitcase. Not ideal, but better than nothing. She dug out fresh pyjamas, then, with a gulp, put out her hand to open the underwear drawer.

It was sitting quite casually on top of the piles of large flesh-coloured pants and enormous bras; why it was hidden away Polly couldn't work out for ages – it was hardly likely to be a target for thieves. Then, with a start, she realised that of course it was there for a reason: that Mrs Manse didn't like to see it all the time. Unthinkingly she picked it up. It was a framed colour photograph, with that bleached-out yellow wash that dated it to the late seventies or early eighties. It showed a dark-haired man, his face in shadow from the sun, standing next to a boy in a striped T-shirt and shorts that were slightly too small for him, with a snake belt, socks and sandals. He was beaming toothily at the camera. Both of them were holding up fish on their fishing lines. Polly stared at it. She didn't hear Tarnie enter the room until he let out a sigh.

She started and turned around.

'I wasn't prying,' she said instantly. 'It was just here, I couldn't help it.'

He nodded his head. 'That's all right, I know.' He looked around the room. 'It's already weird just being up here.'

'It is,' said Polly. She looked back at the photograph.

Tarnie's face fell.

'Who are they?' she asked gently.

Tarnie's arm went up behind his neck and he rubbed it, obviously uncomfortable.

139

'Well, that's Alf Manse,' he said, pointing at the man. 'Gillian's husband. Good man he was. Really good man.'

They both looked at the boy. Tarnie made a little noise.

'Jimmy,' he said. 'Me and him ... well, we were good friends. Same class at school – there used to be a school here. Closed now, of course. Did everything together. Wound each other up really. Pair of rascals we were. Didn't really see the point of school. We always knew we'd end up on the sea.'

Polly looked into his grave, handsome face. His dark blue eyes were focused somewhere very far away.

'Aye. We were pretty inseparable. And she was all right, Mrs Manse ... in those days.'

He fell silent. After a long moment Polly spoke.

'So what happened?'

Tarnie lowered his head.

'People don't understand ... No offence,' he said.

'Er, none taken,' said Polly.

'People don't understand how dangerous the sea is. You hear it all the time on the news – oh, the storm's passed over, it's fine,' when what they mean is, the storm's gone out to sea, but who cares.'

He rubbed his neck again.

'And it's all, oh, they're overfishing, oh, the poor fish, oh, those evil fishermen. When we're just doing what we always did, a job that is hard, pays badly and is ... It's dangerous. It's really dangerous, Polly.'

Polly bit her lip.

'I hadn't realised.'

'Aye, people don't think. They just complain about the price of their fish and chips ... We were all out that day. Jimmy was on *Calina* with his dad ... My dad was out of the game by then. And it blew up out of nowhere. Not on the forecast or anything; we got fifteen minutes' warning on the fax. Waves as high as a three-storey building, crashing down on the boats like a mountain falling on you. And no time ... there was no time. Every time you got righted and went to move, there was another one on you ... nothing but water. Your lungs get full of water just standing up; it pushes you wherever it wants you to go.'

Polly watched him. It was as if the memories were passing in front of his eyes.

'We limped back – we all lost masts, our nets were gone. Just torn away from the starboard side as if a hand had grabbed them and tugged them under.'

He turned to Polly, his expression anguished.

'It's not like we didn't look out for each other. But you've got to realise what it's like out there when the waves are thirty feet high and it's pitch black. You can't see your hand in front of your face. You can't see anything at all. You can drown without even entering the water, you understand?' His voice was fierce.

'When we got home, we could barely count up our own damage. We were all traumatised.'

'Of course you were,' said Polly.

'We didn't ... I didn't even realise the *Calina* wasn't with us. Not at first.' He swallowed.

'Oh God,' said Polly. 'Oh God, that's awful.'

Tarnie rubbed his neck furiously.

'It was a long time ago,' he said, looking at the photo again.

141

'Did they . . . did they find . . .'

'Nothing,' said Tarnie. 'Not a stick washed up. That's unusual, you know. Normally . . . normally the sea brings them home. But not this time.'

'How old were you?' asked Polly.

'Nineteen,' said Tarnie shortly.

'Oh my God,' said Polly. 'Oh my God, that's awful.'

A thought struck her.

'Oh my God,' she said again. 'She's Jayden's ghost. That's what she was doing down there.'

The horror struck Polly and she sat down.

'I saw her, you know. I saw her before. She wasn't taking a random walk along the harbour. Jayden says other people have seen her too.'

'What are you talking about?'

'She's . . . she's the ghost, Tarn. She goes down to the harbour and stares out to sea . . . I didn't know what she was doing.'

Tarnie looked at her, confused. Polly clutched the picture in her hands.

'I think she's looking out for them,' she said. 'I think she's still waiting for them to come home.'

Tarnie's face turned glum and he nodded thoughtfully.

'For a long time she wouldn't accept it,' he said slowly. 'Sent the coastguard out so often they had to stop her doing it. She just said, over and over again, "They're out there." And people felt so sorry for her. It was always hard to make ends meet, and it suddenly got a lot harder. She got a little money from the union, used it to buy the bakeries back in the days when Mount Polbearne could support two; the old bakers had seen the writing on the wall, moved to the mainland like everybody else. It's never been very good, but it's all she has, all she's ever had.'

'I feel awful,' said Polly, remembering the mean thoughts she'd had and words she'd said to someone who'd experienced worse than she could ever imagine.

'I thought . . . you would think she'd have accepted it by now,' said Tarnie, shaking his head. 'It's been nearly twenty years.'

'Did she only have the one child?' asked Polly.

'Yes,' said Tarnie. 'Just Jim. He was the apple of her eye.'

'She hasn't given up,' said Polly. 'She's still waiting for them.'

Tarnie looked round the small, confined space, at the picture she couldn't even bear to have on the wall.

'Now that is dreadful,' he said in a quiet voice.

In silence they packed up the rest of the things Polly thought Gillian might need, then Tarnie took them to the hospital along with a large box of chocolates they found in Muriel's shop. Polly waved him off feeling guiltier than ever, and vowing to make allowances from now on.

Chapter Eleven

That day, for the first time since she'd arrived, Polly started to bake with a completely clear conscience. To try to assuage her guilt over Gillian Manse, she set about making a little basket of goodies for her: sugar bread rings and brioches and pains au chocolat. It was busy, intricate work and she enjoyed it. Halfway through the afternoon, she took Neil over to the window.

'Okay, come on then,' she said sadly. Sunshine was glinting off the water, lighting up the port, and it looked beautiful outside. 'Practise flying?'

Neil eeped crossly. She put him on the rim of the window and he hopped down to the floor again, looking for crumbs.

'No more crumbs!' she said, guiltily conscious of the brioche she'd given him. 'You really are getting fat.'

She put him up on the window rim once more.

'Now I don't want to push you out,' she said. 'I've had enough of people falling off things for one day. But you really have to . . . you are really going to have to go. I have to take you back to this … Well, let's not talk about it. But you do have to go. And you have to be ready.'

Amazingly, Neil eyed her suspiciously, then flapped his wings a little. His injured wing was good as new; you'd never have been able to tell anything had ever been the matter.

'Yes!' said Polly. 'That's it! Why don't you fly out and catch a fish?'

Neil appeared to be looking at the sea quite intently. His little head tilted as the seagulls made loud throaty noises, involving themselves in some tussle or another. He moved his claws from side to side. Polly stopped flouring her surfaces and came over to watch properly. Down on the harbourside she saw the fishermen hanging out – no Tarnie – having a smoke and a chat. Jayden waved, and when he saw what she was doing, he cupped his hands out to the little bird.

'Ne-il! Ne-il!' they all chanted, to encourage him to come forward. Jayden was waving a fish head at him. Polly smiled.

'See?' she said. 'It's okay. On you go. On you go!'

She nudged him forward, very gently. Slowly at first, Neil lifted his wings, then, as gracefully as a slightly plump baby puffin can, launched himself sturdily into the air.

Polly clapped her hands together.

'Go, Neil!' she shouted. 'Go, my boy! Go!'

He got a little nervous at that and fluttered his wings slightly too fast and bent over to the right, but the fishermen urging him on made him concentrate and he glided, rather jerkily and inexpertly, straight into Jayden's hands, where a tasty piece of fish was waiting for him.

'YAY!' they all cheered.

'Yay!' echoed Polly inside the flat, grinning. 'Hang on, let me get my camera.'

She grabbed her phone, and as Jayden directed Neil back up to her window and let him go again, she took a photo of him in mid flight, the boys laughing behind him.

After that, he wanted to fly up and down for pieces of brioche and fish all afternoon. Polly reflected that this probably wasn't very good training for being released back into the wild, but consoled herself with the thought that it was good flying practice.

The brioches and pains au chocolat and sugar rings came out perfectly. Polly crept down with two baskets and left them for Tarnie, with strict instructions to share one of them with the boys and take the other to Mrs Manse in hospital. She had heard from him that they were keeping her in for a few days for observation, partly for her head and partly to check on her mental state. She was happy about this, but worried about Gillian's shop. If it wasn't cleaned up, they'd get mice, for sure. She spoke to Muriel in the grocery shop.

'I'd help,' said Muriel. 'But I work a twelve-hour shift here. I'm just not sure I'm up to it.'

'Cripes,' said Polly. Everyone around her was working so incredibly hard to keep body and soul together in this tiny place. 'I guess I'd better do it myself.'

When she let herself in the next day, the horrible smell of mould was everywhere, and she was sure she could hear the scuttle of a mouse. She took a few of the salvageable loaves away to make bread and butter pudding, which she might possibly be able to sell if she froze it – it wasn't the greatest of ideas, but it was the best she could come up with – then

146

grabbed Kerensa's box of cleaning products, rolled up her sleeves and got to work.

It quickly became apparent – unsurprisingly, thought Polly, given what a hard life Gillian had had – that the shop hadn't been properly scrubbed through for a long time. There were crumbs between the (rather nice) 1950s glass display cabinets; grime along the ceiling; spiders' webs in the storeroom where the flour was no longer kept. Polly had wondered how on earth it was possible to run a bakery single-handed, but Muriel had explained that Gillian did have someone extra during the summer, plus she had given up actually baking a long time ago, finding it cheaper and more convenient to buy her stock in from a central delivery firm. Unfortunately that central delivery firm specialised in cheap adulterated flour and nasty long-life products; they might not have cost much, but their price was reflected in their taste. If there was one thing Polly had never been able to stomach, it was bad bread – bread, the cornerstone of eating, one of the fundamentals of life! If you got that wrong, she always felt, well, then the rest of the day was going to go wrong too.

And when fashions changed and bread came to be seen as something that would make you instantly fat and unhealthy, that had only hardened her resolve. If everyone was going to have to eat less bread, it stood to reason that the bread you did get to eat had to be absolutely of the highest possible quality. Polly was as open as anyone else to the allure of the cheapest white as a covering for a fabulously crunchy, moist, salty bacon sandwich. But when it came to bread as a food in itself, this rubbish seemed to her a waste of everybody's time. Especially when the oven and the equipment was still there,

147

just waiting to be put into use. Making bread was time-consuming, but it wasn't difficult, and the end results were always, always worth it.

As she hoovered and swept and scrubbed, Polly realised that rather than hating the work, she was actually finding it quite cathartic, just as it had been cleaning the little flat; the sun gleamed through the newly washed windows, and she started to feel a little more useful. One or two people poked their heads round the door to look for bread and enquired after Mrs Manse; the news had got around town. Polly answered as truthfully as she could that Mrs Manse had had a fall and was being kept in for observation.

'So are you taking over this place?' said Jayden when he passed by at lunchtime. 'Have you not got a pasty or nothing?'

'Nothing,' said Polly. 'Sorry. Did she sell good pasties?'

'No,' said Jayden sadly. 'But you know what they say about the worst pasty you've ever had: it's still pretty good.'

'I did not know that,' said Polly.

'Why don't you start baking here?' said Jayden. 'You can bake. So . . .'

'Because,' said Polly, 'it's slightly illegal to walk into someone else's business and start working there.'

'Well what are you doing now, then?' he said.

Polly smiled. 'I'm just helping out.'

'Why don't you help out by making me a pasty?' said Jayden.

'When you put it like that, it sounds so simple,' said Polly.

Tarnie looked tired when he popped his head round the bakery door that evening, but genuinely surprised.

'Wow,' he said.

Polly smiled. She was exhausted too – she'd barely slept – but she couldn't believe how much progress she'd managed to make tidying up the bakery. She'd even cleaned the ovens, cold and greasy from long-term neglect, which were now all ready to burst back into life.

'I haven't seen it looking like this . . .' his voice went a bit distant, 'in years.'

'How is she?' said Polly.

Tarnie shrugged. 'Belligerent. They want to do a full psych observation and she told them where to stick it.'

'Ha,' said Polly. 'Good for her. I like that she's an equal opportunities insulter. Did she eat my brioche?'

'She did,' said Tarnie. 'She told me it was awful, but she ate the whole thing.'

'Well THAT's a good sign,' said Polly.

Tarnie looked around again.

'It's a shame she's so pig-headed and stubborn,' he said. 'I mean, you need a job, right?'

'I DO,' said Polly fervently.

'It seems obvious to me,' said Tarnie. 'You do the baking, she stays front of house, you work together.'

Polly straightened up.

'Er,' she said.

'What?' said Tarnie, looking confused.

'Um, she hates me?'

'So what? It's just a job. Jayden hates me.'

'Jayden worships you,' Polly said. 'And ten hours a day

149

in this tiny space with her? It would be a disaster, trust me.'

'So what are you going to do, sign on?'

'Can't I be a fisherman?'

He smiled. His teeth looked very white in his sun-browned face.

'You've got to be born to it.'

'Well that's racist.'

'No, I mean it. If you aren't born doing it, it's just too awful.'

Polly glanced at the ovens.

'Maybe I could work here for a bit . . . just until she gets back.'

Tarnie shrugged again. 'Do you think you're up to it?'

'I don't know,' said Polly with total honesty. 'Do you?'

Tarnie smiled. 'You know,' he said, 'I think you could do anything if you tried.'

She smiled back at him. 'Except fishing,' she said.

'Well, yeah, except fishing.'

Polly slept late the next day, and was woken by a loud roaring sound followed by a persistent honking.

'Who's that?' she said, pushing open her window. It was a glorious day, fluffy clouds bouncing across the horizon like children on their way to the beach.

It was Huckle, on his ridiculous motorbike. He had pushed his goggles up on to his helmet.

'Hey!' he said. 'How you doing?'

'Fine,' said Polly, taking a deep breath of sea air. 'What are you doing?'

He looked confused. 'It's today, remember?'

Polly shook her head. It was hardly like her diary had been stuffed with social engagements.

'Er, no?'

'Neil.'

'What about Neil?'

'We're taking him to the sanctuary. We arranged it on Saturday?'

Polly had completely forgotten. In fact, she realised in dismay, she'd pretended to herself it wasn't happening at all.

Polly's first inclination was to say no. No no no. Now that Neil could fly, he liked to follow her around more than ever before. He was at war with the kettle and danced around it as it boiled; even though she told him to keep away, he tended to prance up towards it as it whistled, and occasionally peck the side aggressively. On one occasion he had succeeded in clicking it off, which he obviously saw as a major triumph.

'Move, you,' said Polly, clicking it on now, to Neil's bossy consternation. She couldn't believe she'd put this to the back of her mind, even with everything else that was going on. But she couldn't keep a puffin as a pet. It was wrong. It was cruel. Everyone had said so.

Still, it seemed to have come so soon. She stroked his feathers and absent-mindedly fed him a little of the leftover brioche. Neil snuggled in to her finger as if he knew.

'Oh for goodness' sake,' she said crossly. 'Okay, let's get this over with.'

'You look like you lost a quarter and found a nickel,' said Huckle when she finally emerged, after a very quick shower and shrugging into her favourite faded jeans and old Converses.

Polly just looked sad.

'Come on,' said Huckle. 'You know, where I grew up, you couldn't get too attached to the animals.'

'What was that, a farm?' said Polly, crossly.

'Er, yeah. A farm,' said Huckle.

There was a short silence. Polly looked at the sidecar.

'Am I seriously meant to be getting in this thing?'

'No,' said Huckle. 'Just follow me. Neil can fly and carry you in his claws.'

He handed her a retro black helmet with a little bib on the top of it like the front of a cap, and a large round pair of goggles.

'Has a German warplane crash-landed in a nearby field?' asked Polly.

'Thank you, Huckle,' said Huckle. 'For giving up your own time and effort to try and help somebody else.'

Taking a deep breath, Polly jammed the helmet down over her curls and levered herself into the sidecar. It was surprisingly comfortable; a leather cushion ran all the way along the inside and her legs were stretched straight out, so that it was like a luxury sleeping bag. Once she had settled Neil, who had his head out of his box, looking around him, Huckle revved the throttle, put his foot down – he was wearing large black boots – and the machine took off.

It was just as noisy from the inside; it startled the birds from the trees. She also hadn't expected it to create such a stir. Every street they went along people pointed, children laughed, and old men smiled to see them. Polly felt it was a little like being famous.

The causeway was open, its bricks shining in the morning sun, and then they were across, and Huckle opened her up on the quiet country lanes. They sped round bends, past great fields of meadowsweet; herds of uninterested cows, standing round their water troughs chatting; and some beautiful palomino ponies, galloping through a hilltop field. Above them as they began to cross the peninsula, the sharp caws of the seagulls gave way to sparrowhawks circling flawlessly in the air, and spring thrushes chirruping in the hedgerows. Rabbits flashed across the road in little bobs of soft fur and the wind whipped across the bike, although in her cosy sidecar, with its helpfully provided blanket, Polly wasn't cold at all.

If it hadn't been for the task ahead – she kept her hands tightly clasped round Neil's box – she would have loved the ride. From time to time Huckle would turn to her, as if to check she was enjoying it, but it was far too noisy to do anything other than nod, at her sudden glimpse of a sunlit cove and bouncing water appearing through the hills, or an old grey Cornish stone farmhouse that could look both austere and cosy, with its slate roof amid the rolling green. Being so close to the road meant she felt part of the country she was travelling through, and although they saw few cars, cyclists and walkers all seemed please to see them, some even waving. She was exhilarated by the time she saw the turn-off, a brown National Trust sign with 'Puffin Sanctuary,' written on it. Her heart sank. Don't think about it, she told herself. Think about other things. She glanced at Huckle's long thighs, supremely confident in charge of the bike. Okay, maybe not *that*.

The countryside up here to the north was far rockier and wilder; the wind more chilling. This side of Cornwall gave on to the Irish Sea, with its cold storms and wild cresting waves. A perfect environment for a cold-water bird, she told herself. Think how much fun he was going to have with his one point four million new best friends.

She had thought, before she left, about doing something to Neil to mark him somehow, in case she ever wanted to visit him again. She supposed she could ask them when they got there, but they might think she was stupid. And she could hope he'd remember her, but that really WAS stupid. He was a bird, she was a girl. It was never supposed to work out. She smiled ruefully at the thought and swayed into the turns and twists of the little road – the bike was actually quite a smooth ride, once you got used to how close to the tarmac you were.

Huckle had rung ahead, and there was a nice young girl with a sturdy netball-playing figure and a no-nonsense Kiwi accent expecting them.

'Let's take a look at the little fella, then,' she said, lifting Neil with practised ease out of his box. Neil glanced back at Polly in a panic.

'It's okay,' she said. 'It's okay.'

'So, broken wing?' The girl was handling him gently and

154

attentively, checking him all over. 'You've done a really nice job, yeah?'

'Er ... okay.' Polly realised to her horror that she was having some trouble controlling her voice.

'Course you've packed a bit of beef on,' said the girl sternly to Neil. 'You'll need to speed up a bit, little fella, get in there and get your share of fish.'

Neil eeped and tried to inch closer to Polly, but the net-ball girl had him in a firm grip.

'Can I ... I mean, is there any way I can tag him?' said Polly. 'Just in case ...'

'In case you wanna come back and say hello?' The girl scratched her head. 'Well, I can't ... I mean, they do tag, but only for checking on migration. I'm not sure I'd have a tag that wouldn't be misleading, know what I mean?'

'That's okay,' said Polly. 'It was just an idea.'

'Look,' said the girl. 'You're doing the kindest thing for him, you know that, right?'

Polly nodded, her lip trembling.

'He's not a pet. He's designed to flock and mate and pair and raise his young, just like everybody else. And he deserves that chance, don't you think?'

'Yes,' said Polly, steadying herself. 'Yes, I do.'

'Good on yer. Right, come on down and we'll release him.'

Over the crest of the hill there was a path (signposted with little puffins) down to a huge rocky outcrop jutting out into the sea. Polly gave a gasp. There were so many birds there it would have been impossible to count them. They were everywhere; large, small, orange-beaked and black-beaked. They were cawing, diving into the water, hopping around or just standing squarely on the rock, gazing inscrutably out to sea. They were like a huge black and white carpet; it was an extraordinary sight.

'He'll be well cared for.'

Polly picked up the box. Neil obviously sensed something was up; he was hopping up and down in a frenzy, his head turning at all the other birds in the air.

'It's like he knows,' Polly said.

'He does know,' said Huckle, and he gently put his arm around her. With his other hand he brought something out of his pocket.

'Here,' he said. 'I wonder if we could maybe use this?'

It was a little tag that he used to seal off his wax honey containers; made of plastic, it fastened tightly, but it was light. On it was written quite clearly 'Huckle Honey'.

'I wasn't sure ...' he went on.

The breezy Kiwi girl looked at it.

'Oh yeah,' she said. 'That should do it. And it won't get mixed up with any of the studies. Brilliant.'

Polly looked up at him.

'Thank you.'

'Not a problem,' said Huckle. He took the tag and put it gently round Neil's left leg. Neil immediately started pecking at it crossly.

'Ssh,' said Polly. 'Don't do that. Otherwise ...'

She picked up the little bird and rubbed his feathers behind his ears, just what he absolutely loved, for the last time. Then she rubbed noses with his beak.

'You,' she said, 'were the first friend I ever met here. Thank you for that.'

She looked into his black eyes.

'Now, off you go,' she said. 'Off you go, fly free. Make friends, build nests.'

She set him down on a rock. He was utterly engrossed by the chattering and fluttering of the thousands of other birds all around him. Then he took a little step forward, then back again, looking at her inquisitively.

'No,' she said, her voice cracking again, just a little. 'It's okay. Go on.'

Neil pattered forward a little further. She caressed his head one last time, then stood up.

Carefully, tentatively – he was noticeably fatter than the other pufflings – he jumped off the rock and hopped to the next one. Immediately, the other puffins there gathered round to have a look at him. There was some chatter and fluttering.

'Don't bully him,' Polly called out fiercely. Neil turned back briefly. Polly got out her phone to take one last photograph, but by the time she'd got the camera lined up, she realised to her great sadness that she could no longer recognise him amongst the cluster of hundreds of other birds.

'Oh Huckle,' she said. 'Which one is he? I can't see him.'

'Ssh,' said Huckle. 'Look.'

A group of the birds had risen into the air, converging on where a young man in a colourful polo shirt was distributing fish. Sure enough, in the middle of the group, struggling a little, but definitely holding his own, was a slightly portly puffin with a little tag on his left leg. Polly watched till he soared over the cliffside, caught up amongst all the other birds, and eventually disappeared from sight.

Huckle gave her a squeeze and they turned to head back along the path. Polly was too upset to speak.

'I know it's stupid,' she squeaked finally. 'He's only a bird.'

'Neil was not only a bird,' said Huckle fiercely. 'He was the finest puffin I ever met.'

This brought Polly perilously close to a half-laughing, half-crying breakdown, so she kept her mouth closed.

'There's a café here if you're hungry,' said the cheery Kiwi girl, but when they stuck their heads in, not only did it smell of cold chips and unhappy bank holidays, but it was covered with pictures of puffins, cuddly puffin toys and puffin memorabilia. It looked entirely unappealing, but time was getting on.

'Are you hungry?' Polly asked Huckle.

'I'd rather eat puffin,' said Huckle. 'Sorry, was that insensitive?'

'YES,' said Polly.

She turned back to the girl.

'Thanks for everything you've done,' she said.

'No worries.'

'Here, this is my mobile number and this is my email address ...'

The girl looked at the piece of paper uncomprehendingly.

'If he doesn't thrive or ... if anything happens to him ...' Polly's voice choked up.

'Er, yeah, all right.' said the girl, unconvinced.

'Come on,' said Huckle. 'Let's go.'

The girl gave him a look. 'Nice to meet you, yeah?' she

said in a tone that even Polly in her sad state recognised as flirtatious.

Huckle gave her his broad American farm boy smile and guided Polly back to the motorbike.

Polly decided to wait to have a cry until she was safely in the sidecar and nobody could see or hear her, apart from some visiting children, who couldn't believe that anyone who got to ride in a sidecar could possibly be so sad they would cry.

She knew she was being ridiculous and overdramatic, and she couldn't imagine what Huckle must think of her, but even so. Neil was only a little baby bird, but he had made her feel less alone at the loneliest point in her life. She was allowed to miss him. She wondered if this was what having children was like. Then she remembered her mother telling her that God made teenagers horrible so that you were happy when they left home, which explained a lot.

Eventually she got over her crying jag and realised, looking out through her goggles, that she didn't have a clue where she was. They weren't retracing the obvious route home; instead, they seemed to be driving down the north coast, the sea bobbing in and out of view every time they traversed a hill. She looked enquiringly at Huckle, but he was checking the road signs with a confused look on his face and didn't notice. Then her foot touched Neil's empty cardboard box and she had to concentrate hard on not crying again.

With a screeching howl from the brakes and a manoeuvre that nearly jolted Polly out of her seat, the bike made a sudden right turn down a sandy track.

'Sorry,' mouthed Huckle beneath the noise of the engine. Polly could see why he'd nearly missed the turning; it wasn't signposted at all. She wondered where it led.

The bike bumped down the unpaved track. She'd expected it to lead to a farm, but instead it ducked down alongside a flat field and then up over some sand dunes, where a number of jeeps were parked up. Huckle pulled up alongside them, and stopped the bike. The sudden silence after the noise of the engine felt almost overwhelming.

Polly climbed out of the sidecar and stretched.

'Where are we?' She looked around. Huckle glanced at her, amused.

'Have you stopped crying?' he said.

'Er, yeah,' said Polly. 'I think so.'

'It's okay to cry, you know.'

'I do know,' said Polly, rubbing at her face to get rid of mascara traces.

They stood at the top of the dunes and looked down. Polly gasped. They were at the very top of a long golden sandy beach. It was immense; it seemed to stretch on for ever. Huge blue waves pounded it, a rolling surf that went on for miles.

The beach was almost completely deserted except for one wooden shack and the bobbing heads and wetsuited bodies of about half a dozen surfers out in the water. Polly could only get a measure of the scale of the waves by how tiny the figures looked dancing on top of them.

'What IS this place?' she said. Even this early in the season the surfing beaches were all absolutely mobbed, surfers pushing and shoving each other out of the way, often having fights. But here . . .

'It belongs to Reuben Finkle,' said Huckle. 'He's like some Silicon Valley whizz-kid, yeah? Made an absolute mint selling top-secret defence gizmos. Retired at twenty-eight to surf all day.'

'Impressive,' said Polly. 'Oh my God – what, this is his beach?'

'This is his beach. His house is up there. It's completely secret. But he lets a few friends use it from time to time.'

'No way.'

'I knew him back at Wharton ... Anyway ...'

Polly looked around. It was exquisite. The sun had come out and was making the fine sand glow. It felt like the first really warm day of the year.

'Come on,' said Huckle. 'Are you hungry or still too sad?'

'I am sad,' said Polly. 'But also a little bit hungry.'

Huckle took off his boots and socks and left them by the bike, and Polly did likewise with her Converses, then they both rolled up their jeans and slid down a dune. Polly fell on her bum and Huckle laughed at her and she stuck her tongue out at him, feeling almost normal.

The wet sand when they got down to the water's edge was delicious; the water itself was still bracing, but lovely to splash through, so Polly did.

'It's amazing some people have so much,' she said. Reuben Finkle's house had come into view, an amazing modern glass circle that looked like something Tony Stark might live in.

'Yeah,' said Huckle carefully. 'But isn't it wonderful that he preserves something as beautiful as this? And he does a lot for ocean conservation.'

'He sounds like a great guy.'

'He's a yutz,' said Huckle. 'But he does a lot for ocean conservation.'

After waving to some of Huckle's buddies on the surf, they arrived at the little wooden shack Polly had seen from the dunes. It was painted white and, she saw as she got there, was actually a little café; there were tables and chairs sprinkled roughly about, a full bar and an open-plan enviably equipped kitchen.

'Wow,' said Polly. 'Impressive. Why don't people just come down and vandalise this place? The local kids must know. The road's like right there.'

'They do know,' said Huckle. 'They dream that one day he'll let them come here too. Plus there are lots of rumours about CCTV and guards with machine guns.'

Polly glanced at him. 'Seriously?'

'Oh, they're just rumours,' said Huckle. 'Probably.'

They sat down at one of the tables. It was comfortably warm, not too windy, the sun a gentle healing presence on Polly's neck. She sighed with relief.

'It's beautiful.'

A short, wide man with an army haircut and a boyish, petulant face full of freckles came out from the kitchen wearing a white apron over his shorts.

'HUCK! MY MAN!'

Huck raised his hand and did some kind of complicated high-five manoeuvre, which failed at the last moment. The cook punched him quite hard on the shoulder.

'He has a chef?' said Polly before she could help herself.

'Who has a chef?' said the short man.

'Sorry,' said Polly. 'I was just asking about the man who owns all this. Hi. I'm Polly.'

'And I'm the man who owns all this,' said the man, sticking out his hand. 'And I like to cook. But I also have a chef. Actually I have three chefs. Yeah. Cool. Reuben Finkle. Good to make your acquaintance. You a friend of Huckle's, huh? Huh? Yeah? Am I right? A special friend? A special sexy friend?'

He winked widely at Huckle and made a small movement with his hips. Polly could see what Huckle meant about Reuben being a yutz, even if she didn't know the meaning of the word.

'Polly here is going through a bit of a tough time,' said Huckle in his slow, deliberate way. 'So I thought I'd bring her down to the best food in Cornwall, cheer her up.'

'That's the way, that's the way. Do you want a martini?' Reuben looked at her and snapped his fingers. 'No. No, I know what you need. You need a margarita. Am I right or am I right? Margaritas make all the bad stuff go away. Until you wake up in the garbage. HA.' He let out a slightly surprising barking laugh.

'Um . . .'

Polly was having a very confusing day. Huckle gave a slight nod in her direction.

'Er, that would be lovely,' she said.

'Light beer, my man? Light beer for the light-haired farm boy in the corner?'

'Sure,' said Huckle. 'Hit me.'

Reuben came back with their drinks and sat down. He was actually quite relaxing to be with, because he talked non-stop about how much surfing he'd done, how many ladies he'd had down partying with him (Polly had thought partying meant having a nice party, but it seemed to mean drinking until you were technically unconscious), what an amazing summer they were all going to have and how much money he'd turned down for his estate from a Russian oligarch who'd threatened to have him sent to Siberia, but it was all right because Reuben was kung fu trained and had apparently frightened him out of it, and did she like *Star Wars*?

Polly replied that she did like *Star Wars*, or at least she liked Harrison Ford in *Star Wars*, whereupon Reuben got a slightly cross look and said that the new films were vastly underrated and people had to re-evaluate them, which he then proceeded to do at some length.

Not having to talk meant Polly could basically tune out and just enjoy the sound of the surf and the blueness of the sky and, she found, the comforting casual presence of Huckle, his large frame draped over the battered wooden chair, his long feet with neat short nails buried in the sand. His eyes were the same colour as the sea. She knew it was the (excellent) margarita, but she suddenly felt an urge to put her own feet in his lap. She banished the thought immediately. She was getting a very strong vibe from Huckle, and that vibe was: I will be absolutely very nice as long as you don't ask me a single thing about my personal life or get too close.

And that was fine. It wasn't like her own life was free of complications. She thought back to the girl at the puffin park.

164

It seemed highly unlikely that Huck was a man short of offers. And that being the case, he was almost certainly choosing to be alone for a reason.

At one point, without interrupting his flow of consciousness, and whilst asking Huckle what colour he should paint his new helicopter, Reuben jumped up and started cooking. The smell and sizzle of wild garlic and onions in a pan made Polly realise how hungry she was, and the margarita had gone straight to her head. She could see Reuben eyeing up a wine fridge. He thought for a moment, then selected a very cold Chablis.

To clear her head and to stop herself watching Huckle, whose heavy-lidded blue eyes appeared to be fluttering a little – it was hard with someone so laid-back to work out whether he was actually asleep or not – she got up and followed Reuben into the kitchen.

'You cook?' she said.

'I love to cook,' he said. 'I'm brilliant at it. If I hadn't been a computer genius I'd have had like nine Michelin stars. That's two more than the most anyone has ever had.'

She smiled. 'What are you cooking today?'

'I cook whatever we catch,' he said. 'We have a couple of fresh langoustines I got this morning. It's coming to the end of the season but they're still pretty good, water's still cold.'

'She cooks,' said Huckle sleepily from out the front.

Reuben eyed her beadily. 'Oh yeah?' he said. 'Probably not better than me.'

'No, I'm sure I don't,' said Polly. 'And I'm not really a cook. I'm more of a baker.'

She flushed as she realised this was the first time she'd said the words out loud. It must be a combination of the alcohol and Reuben's exceptional self-confidence.

'But I love your kitchen.'

He smiled at her with satisfaction.

'Yeah. It's top of the line. Cost a quarter of a million sterling. Flew it in from Germany.'

Polly nodded politely.

'Want to make us something to go with lunch?'

'Um,' said Polly. 'I'm not sure now. I'd probably break something in your very expensive kitchen.'

'Don't be dumb,' said Reuben. 'I'd just like totally buy a new one.'

Suddenly Polly spied something out the back.

'Oh my God, is that a brick oven?'

'Sure is,' said Reuben. 'It's been on an hour, too; it's good to go. You can't have an outdoor kitchen without a brick oven. What would you do for pizza? I'd rather die than eat bad pizza. I make great pizza.'

'I see,' said Polly, smiling. She was warming to Reuben. 'Well, if you like, I could dish us up some socca.'

He opened the iron front of the oven. The heat pulsed out, scorching. Then he straightened up.

'Some what?' His brow was furrowed. Polly guessed that there was little Reuben disliked more than hearing things he did not already know.

She smiled. 'Well, have you got any chickpea flour?'

'Of course,' said Reuben sullenly. He picked up a walkie-talkie that was clipped to his belt.

'Chickpea flour. Stat.'

'It's kind of a pancake,' explained Polly. 'But it's good, you'll like it.'

Reuben eyed her up.

'Okay,' he said. 'Fish with pancakes on the side. That'll do us.'

The flour was brought by a housemaid, who smiled politely but didn't say anything as Polly thanked her. Polly wondered if she didn't speak English.

'So,' said Reuben, watching her as she laid out the ingredients. 'You boning Huckle, then?'

Polly nearly dropped the eggs.

'Why?' she said. 'Would *you* like to?'

Reuben burst into his barking laugh again.

'Hey, Huck,' he yelled. 'You got a firecracker here.'

Polly mixed the dough expertly, adding more chickpeas and water and throwing it until it was as thin as she could make it. Then she carefully oiled the oven hot plate and poured on the mixture, expertly flipping the dough after a couple of minutes. The underside had satisfying black popped blisters on it. After a minute on the other side, she pulled it out with the long stick left by the oven for this purpose, popped it on a plate with plenty of salt and pepper, quartered it and gave it to Reuben to try. He was so greedy he barely blew on it and burnt his mouth.

'Ow. Goddammit,' he said. 'Stupid goddam super-hot oven.'

'It's a great oven,' said Polly. 'I'm jealous.'

After a second he tried a second bite. Then he polished off the lot.

'Oh man,' he said with his mouth full. 'That's amazing.'

'I know,' said Polly. 'They're good, aren't they?'

She made another one for Huckle, which Reuben insisted on eating, then finally got one to him. Then the surfers came in and were so appreciative she got through three batches before Reuben even remembered to put the fish on.

The surfers were big, friendly guys, mostly Brits. The last person to emerge from the water, though – unpeeling her wetsuit to reveal a gorgeous red spotted bikini, and pushing back long blonde curly hair – turned out to be one of the most beautiful girls Polly had ever seen. She looked like a bikini model from an American sportswear magazine. Her golden skin was lightly tanned and completely free of make-up; she had feline green eyes and a wide, full mouth. Even Huckle opened his eyes in appreciation as she walked up the beach, a beautifully embroidered kaftan thrown over her long, lithe body. Polly wondered what it would be like to be able to do that – did she even notice that eyes followed her wherever she went? Was she just completely used to it? Would she wake up at fifty and wonder when the world had changed?

The girl casually grabbed a bottled beer from the fridge, took a long draught as though she was in a commercial and then pressed herself up against Reuben like a cat. She was nearly a head taller than him.

'Hey, babes,' she said. Reuben grunted at her. 'That smells amazing,' she said. 'You should have come out this morning, it's nuts out there. Fabulous.'

'Yeah, whatever,' said Reuben sulkily. He didn't offer her a piece of the socca.

The goddess turned her attention briefly to Polly, who had the uncomfortable sensation of being scanned by a machine and instantly categorised as non-threatening. She felt like offering her hand to be stamped.

'Hi,' said the girl, with a wide smile that showed her perfect white teeth. 'I'm Jaz.'

'Er, hi, Jaz,' said Polly. 'Polly.'

Jaz looked at Polly, who was making more socca, and frowned.

'He's letting you use his kitchen?'

'Jaz, wanna sit down?' said Reuben. 'We're kind of busy here.'

Jaz gave a ravishing pout but retreated back to the other surfers, who surrounded her like a queen.

'Cor, your girlfriend is GORGEOUS,' blurted out Polly without thinking. Unusually for Reuben, he didn't reply.

Lunch was fried langoustines in garlic and lemon on a bed of fresh peppery rocket salad. They all tucked in heartily, the Chablis a perfect accompaniment to the meal along with the hot sun and the daft banter between the surfers as they talked about hanging tens and sex wax and other surfing terms Polly didn't understand.

She was, she realised, enjoying herself.

After the meal, and coffee, and a large box of American candy that Reuben passed around, the boys headed out into the water again.

'Can you surf?' said Huckle.

'Yes,' said Polly. 'I have the perfect surfer's physique, hadn't you noticed?'

Huckle shrugged. 'Seems strange to grow up in Cornwall and not surf.'

'Well I grew up in Devon.'

169

The maid was back, Polly noticed, unobtrusively cleaning up around them. Imagine someone doing that for you and not even noticing.

'Thank you,' she said. The girl glanced up quickly, then returned to her work.

'The thing is,' said Reuben. 'You gotta ... you gotta surf, man.'

'It looks hard,' said Polly.

'No, I don't mean SURF,' he snorted. 'Obviously it's like totally a metaphor.'

'I didn't realise that,' said Polly.

'You gotta follow your bliss. You heard that term?'

'Is it American by any chance?' From the opposite side of the table she could feel Huckle smirking at her response.

'Like all the best things, baby,' said Reuben, winking. 'Yeah! You gotta follow your bliss. Only way in life. You gotta do what you love. When you figure out what you love to do, do it as hard as you can and everything will be awesome and you can surf. And that will make you happy. What makes *you* happy?'

Polly shrugged. 'I suppose ... Well, baking bread. Baking things. But I don't know if I could do it all the time, as a job. Wouldn't that take the fun out of it?'

'What, getting paid to do it?' said Reuben, aghast. 'God, no. That makes it even more fun, don't you see?'

Polly looked around.

'Maybe,' she said.

'It's all right if your bliss is hacking into computer systems that saves the American government from Chinese copyright thefts and makes you billions,' said Huckle. 'That's helpful. My bliss makes me about two bucks a jar.'

170

Reuben shrugged. 'Doesn't matter. You're happier here than you were trapped in Savannah, right?'

It was as if someone had suddenly opened a fridge door. The entire atmosphere plummeted through the floor. Huckle froze and tilted his head towards the sea. Reuben seemed completely oblivious.

There was a very long pause. Finally Jaz shook her long hair and jumped into the conversation.

'Yes, I followed my bliss and look where I ended up.'

Reuben gave her a sharp look.

Polly figured it was probably time to be on their way. Huckle jumped up immediately at the suggestion.

During the trip home, they couldn't speak over the noise, but Polly had a lot to think about. Huckle was recovering from something; that much was obvious. And Reuben was a tricky character, completely oblivious to what people thought of him or what he was saying. On the other hand, what he had said about following what she wanted to do ... Could she?

'Thanks,' she said when Huckle dropped her off. 'Your friend is interesting.'

Huckle lifted his goggles.

'He liked you,' he said. 'That doesn't happen often.'

'He wasn't very nice to his girlfriend.'

Huckle smiled. 'Oh, she's not his girlfriend. He's surrounded by women all the time. They have their eyes on the prize for sure.'

'Oh!' said Polly. 'That's kind of ... Wow. I never thought.

Really? The money? But she's so stunning, she could have anyone ...'

'Don't knock it,' said Huckle. 'It's a tough old world out there. People have to do whatever they can to get by.'

'Well, yes, I know that,' said Polly.

'Not everyone has a gift like yours.'

It took her a moment to catch on to the compliment.

'Really?' she said, flushing.

Huckle shrugged. 'Duh,' he said. Then he looked a bit embarrassed for a second and reached into the back of the bike.

'Um,' he said. 'I bought this for you when you were drying your tears at the park.' He handed her a little plush toy puffin.

'Oh,' said Polly. She felt very wobbly and emotional as she took it. Huckle hadn't drunk any wine at lunch, but she had. 'Oh. Thanks.'

'Really? I wasn't sure if it would make things better or worse.'

'As long as I don't call him Neil 2 and keep him in a box,' said Polly. 'No. Thank you. Thank you.'

Huckle looked relieved and embarrassed at the same time.

'I had a lovely time today,' Polly said. 'I'm sure Reuben didn't mean to be rude.'

'On the contrary,' said Huckle. 'It's one of his hobbies. But I'm used to it.'

He kissed her, fleetingly, on the cheek. The motorbike fired up with its usual throaty roar, and she watched, clutching the cuddly puffin, all the way up the cobbled street until he disappeared from sight.

Chapter Twelve

Polly wouldn't have admitted to anyone how much she missed Neil that night. It was so stupid; he was only a bird, he wasn't a guard dog or anything. But every creak woke her; every clank of the masts outside; every seagull's cry. She did not sleep well and wearily decided at five o'clock that enough was enough, and she might as well call it a night. She took to kneading some sesame bread, thinking as she did so that she might send some over to Reuben as a thank you. In fact, she'd make breadsticks too, they'd keep longer.

At seven she heard the fleet coming back in and happy shouts that indicated that the catch had gone well. She took a coffee down for Tarnie, and the fresh breadsticks, which didn't need to rise like the bread.

'Hey there,' said Tarnie, smiling. He looked tired but happy. 'We had a good run.'

'Brilliant!' said Polly, hoping he would take a few days off and get some rest.

'Where's Neil?'

'Ah,' said Polly, and explained.

'Well I am sorry to hear that,' said Tarnie. 'I didn't ever notice him being a particularly miserable or unhappy puffin.'

'I know,' said Polly sadly. 'But everyone else said it's for the best. Anyway.'

'Anyway yourself,' said Tarnie. 'I've got news for you. They've agreed to discharge Gillian if she gets some help in the shop and lets a community nurse pop round. I've found you a job!'

'You're not serious?' said Polly. 'She's agreed to have me?'

'Of course,' said Tarnie, unwilling to divulge how much coercion had actually been required.

Polly thought of Reuben telling her to follow her bliss. Then she thought of how much money she had left in the world, the number of jobs she'd applied for (38) and the number of interviews she'd had (0).

'Brilliant!' she said, deciding to ignore her doubts and go with her gut. It was a job! She could do it! She'd worry later about working for someone who didn't like her. If Gillian Manse fired her, at least she'd have broken her duck. 'When do I start?'

'Er, tomorrow,' said Tarnie. 'She gets discharged today and she can show you the ropes tomorrow.'

Polly didn't really want Gillian showing her the ropes, so she popped over to the bakery in the afternoon to see if she could figure out for herself how to fire up the ovens. They were still clean and sparkling and she looked around the room, nervous and excited at the same time. All of these ovens! She was going to be in charge of all of them! She ran her hands over the wooden surfaces of the units; peered into the vast mixers that kneaded the dough. Maybe there would be no more central buying-in, she hoped. That was what was making the bakery fail. She'd already spent more time than she would have liked with one failed business. She wasn't going to let it happen again.

While she was inspecting the ovens, there was a knock on the back door. A strong-looking man in his fifties with the ruddy cheeks of someone who spent their life outdoors was standing there.

'Is it true?' he asked in such a strong local accent Polly could barely understand him. 'Is it true, me lover?'

'Um,' said Polly. 'That depends.'

'That they're going to start baking again? That they're bringing the baking back?'

Polly smiled. 'I think we're going to have a shot.'

The man put out his hand for her to shake.

'I'm Ted Kernesse,' he said. 'I used to deliver flour here, back in the day. She was a sensational baker, Gillian Manse.'

'Really?' said Polly. 'It wasn't very good when I got here.'

'Nah, she switched to the bought-in, didn't she? Lost interest after … that business,' he said, taking off his hat. 'Anyway. Will you be wanting the flour back?'

'I suppose we will, yes. How soon can you get started?'

'It'll be outside your door in the morning,' said Ted. 'Where's your yeast going to grow?'

'I don't know,' said Polly, suddenly nervous. She'd only ever used dried yeast.

'Well, just stick it in a pot in the fridge, let it get on wi' itself.'

'I'll do that,' said Polly. 'Gosh.' She looked around anxiously. 'It's a lot to learn.'

'I think it's grand you're doing this,' said Ted. 'It'll be really good for Mount Polbearne. And Gillian.'

Polly's heart plummeted. She really was very nervous about working with the woman. Maybe she had bitten off more than she could chew.

'Ah, you'll be fine,' said Ted as if reading her mind. 'Her bark's worse than her bite. Although her bite is pretty bad to begin with.'

Polly smiled at him hopefully.

'That's the spirit.'

Just as Ted had promised, there was a huge sack of flour outside the back door at 5.30 the next morning, along with six pints of milk and a plastic Tupperware container with a note on top: 'A little present'. Ooh, thought Polly, popping it open. But instead was a plastic container reeking heavily of sourdough mould.

'Oh God,' she said, pushing the pungent mix away from her.

'Well I don't know how you're going to get on if you can't even manage THAT,' said a crotchety voice.

The enormous figure of Gillian Manse pulled the back door wide open and watched as Polly lugged the enormous sack indoors. It weighed a ton. Polly had slightly expected a thank you or a hello or at least a bit of embarrassment – she'd saved the woman's life, after all – but apparently it was not to be.

'It's a present from Ted,' said Polly. 'Er ... hello.'

'Hello,' said Gillian. They faced each other.

'How are you feeling?' asked Polly.

'I'm feeling fine,' said Gillian. 'As I've been telling those dratted doctors. It's ridiculous. Don't you ever dare do that again.'

'I will not,' said Polly fervently.

'Well, come in if you're coming,' Gillian said ungraciously, stepping aside.

'Have you got any coffee?' said Polly. 'I could really do with one.'

'Why don't you actually start work before you have a break?'

Polly bit her lip. Remember you don't have a job, she told herself. This is what it takes.

Polly did her best to keep her head down that first day, but it wasn't easy. Everyone who came in was delighted to see her, particularly those who'd been in on the secret bread run. Gillian, however, watched her like a hawk the entire time, breathing down her neck, barking orders, never failing to point out a mistake, however tiny, which unsettled Polly so much she started to make more of them.

Everyone respectfully asked after Gillian's health, but she shut them down rudely, and Polly found herself trying to smile ingratiatingly to make up for her rudeness. The fact that they all then went on at great length about how wonderful the day's bread was didn't help matters either. This was going to be just as tricky as Polly had feared.

At about 3.30, when everything was gone and they were beginning to think about closing up, there was a loud banging on the back door. Polly looked at Gillian nervously.

'Do you know who that is?'

'No,' said Gillian. 'Answer it.'

Polly opened the door tentatively, to find a big burly deliveryman with a huge truck open at the back. The truck was completely blocking the narrow street.

'All right,' he said crossly. 'I've been waiting for the damn sea to clear half the day. Where's your chimney, then?'

'What?' said Polly. 'Um ... ' She was a little discombobulated.

'You're the bakery, right?'

'Er huh.'

'Got a delivery here. A brick oven. Needs a chimney.' He scratched his chin.

'No,' said Gillian. 'No, that's not for us. Take it away, please.'

The man shrugged. 'Can't do that. It says on the form.'

Gillian folded her arms. 'Well it can unsay it.'

'Hang on,' said Polly. 'Er, can I see the form?'

'Don't know what good that'll do,' said Gillian. 'He's not having my chimney.'

Polly ran her finger down the sheet. It did seem in order – the Mount Polbearne Bakery. Then she saw it. A little note at the bottom. *Follow your bliss*, it said. And the signature – big, flashy – *Reuben Finkle*.

'NO WAY,' she breathed, completely overwhelmed. 'He bought me an oven!'

'Who bought you an oven?' said Gillian crossly.

'Er, this bloke ... friend of a friend,' said Polly.

'We don't need an oven. There's nothing wrong with our ovens.'

'Yes, but with this,' said Polly, her eyes shining, 'we could make ciabatta. Flatbreads. Bruschetta. Just all the most amazing things . . .'

'Can we get a refund on it?' asked Gillian angrily. 'Can I have the cash? I don't want all that foreign muck.'

'No!' said Polly. 'No, can't we—'

'No refunds, love,' said the driver, starting to look pissed off.

In one sense, Polly thought, Gillian was right: the fireplace wasn't really big enough, although if they moved a few things about . . . No. She could tell by the look on Gillian's face that this wasn't going to happen. But, it suddenly occurred to her, there was another space . . .

'We could put it in the Beach Street bakery,' she said. 'Below me. There's room there, isn't there?'

Gillian's brow furrowed. She didn't want the oven, but on the other hand she wasn't going to turn down anything that was free. Polly looked at the floor. She didn't want to catch Gillian's eye and annoy her so much she'd say no on purpose.

After a long pause, during which the driver glanced at his watch, Gillian said, 'Aye, all right then. Just keep it out of my way. And it better not cost me a penny.'

'It won't.'

Polly sat in the cab of the truck with the driver and his mate as they drove the short distance to her building. Gillian had handed over a key to downstairs, not realising that she could already get in.

The dust was as thick as ever. Polly hadn't had enough cash even to fix the glass Neil had broken the night he'd flown in. The men looked around in consternation.

'Seriously?' said the driver. 'I mean, this is a pricey bit of kit.'

Polly looked at it, smiling. Even though obviously the shop wasn't hers, it felt like the oven was.

'I know,' she said. 'This is just the start. You stick it in, I'll make some tea. Oh crap, I forgot to get milk again.'

Chapter Thirteen

Polly had hoped that as time went on, she and Gillian would learn to shake off their rough edges, get along a little better. Nobody had to like the people they worked with, not necessarily.

But if anything, she found things getting harder. Gillian seemed determined to fight her on every single suggestion, so she made none. She brushed past Polly rudely in the shop, and would let her bake only the most basic white bread – although now her bread was getting so good, so light and tasty, just through sheer practice. The shop was busier, cleaner than it had been in a long time. But this just seemed to make Gillian more resentful than ever. Polly became quieter and quieter, but even this was annoying, it seemed.

Coupled with the early mornings, and using every spare minute to begin quietly cleaning up the downstairs bakery so she could start playing with her new oven (she'd sent a very grateful thank you card to Reuben. She didn't know his full address, but was reasonably confident it would find him),

Polly felt tired and demoralised. And the money was . . . well. She hoped she wouldn't suddenly develop holes in her shoes, otherwise she was going to have to fix them with gaffer tape.

She was trudging her way home one grey Saturday when her phone went off.

'RIGHT,' said Kerensa. 'I'm on my way. I think you must have finished with the wound-licking by now.'

'What?' said Polly, unwilling to admit that she felt she might have exchanged one set of work problems for another.

'I'm on my way. For a night out. The bright lights of Mount Polbearne!'

'Ah,' said Polly. 'There aren't really any of those.'

'There must be somewhere everybody goes.'

There was the large pub on the harbour with the dark wooden door. It was incredibly old and still had its original courtyard where tavern visitors would have stabled their horses. Now the courtyard was full of tables and chairs, and as the evenings became warmer, they had started to fill up on Friday and Saturday nights. Polly had wanted to venture in for a pint, but felt nervous. The fishermen must go some-times, but she didn't really want to ask; they had their own lives. She hadn't seen Huckle in weeks. She really really, she realised, wanted some company that wasn't going to tut at her for spilling flour on the work surfaces.

'Well, it's probably not what you're used to . . .'

'I don't give a fuck, darling, I just need to get out of this hellhole.'

'Internet dating gone wrong again?'

'They're all scuzz, Pol. All of them. All the half-decent men have been snapped up.'

'Ha,' said Polly, only just realising. 'I'll tell you what there are a lot of in Polbearne.'

'Mixologists?' said Kerensa hopefully.

'No,' said Polly. 'But it is absolutely stuffed to the gills with blokes.'

'I'm getting in the car.'

Kerensa turned up that evening wearing a ludicrously in-appropriate pink minidress with her hair dyed bright red. She looked a little alarming. Polly was so pleased to see her she nearly cried.

'SO!' said Kerensa. 'The famous new life!'

She looked around.

'Like what you've done with the place,' she said.

'Thanks,' said Polly. She hadn't managed to do much, but the scrubbed floors and the pale stripped-back table, together with one or two of the nice art prints she once used to wander round galleries choosing at her leisure and paying for on her credit card – ha! – hanging on the plain walls, plus of course her wonderful window and extraordinary view, had made the place far more cosy than it had been before.

'I can't believe we haven't seen you,' said Kerensa. 'Is it just too much fun here?'

'Oh Kerensa,' said Polly, opening up the lovely bottle of fizzy stuff her friend had kindly brought, and keeping her own very cheap bottle of rosé at the back of the fridge. 'I have been horribly ...'

It was very hard to say the words.

'I've been lonely,' she said simply, staring out of the window.

183

Kerensa looked at her, and filled two mismatched glasses.

'Me too,' she said. 'And before you say it, yes, I have a fabulous job, blah blah blah, and loads of friends ... but I miss my bestie. And I really want someone to come home to, but they're all superdicks. And not in a good way.'

The sun was going down over the bay. It was exquisite; great tendrils of bright pink stretching out and lighting up the clouds. Kerensa strode over to look at it.

'This is quite cool, you know.'

'I do know,' said Polly.

'And you're working?'

'Yes. That sucks. But ...'

'I thought it sounded perfect for you.'

'You haven't met my boss.'

'Ooh,' said Kerensa. 'Boss from hell?'

'No,' said Polly. 'Boss from wherever it is hell sends people who are too annoying to work for.'

They chinked glasses.

'To not being lonely,' said Kerensa quietly. 'Oh CRAP, that is the most depressing toast we've ever made. How about, to constantly being fabulous?'

'Much better,' said Polly, incredibly cheered to see her best friend.

They went to the pub in the end, Kerensa forcing Polly into a brightly coloured top – 'Otherwise I'll look like the town good-time girl.'

'Well, one, you are that, and two, what did you think this place would be like?'

'St Ives,' said Kerensa gloomily. 'I thought I was going to pick up Prince Harry.'

Polly laughed. 'Oh Kerensa, it is so very good to see you. Come on.'

The evening was mild, and the old courtyard of the pub was cheerfully lit up with lanterns on the tables and little candles in glass jars everywhere. A waitress went round taking orders, and before long Kerensa and Polly were stuck back into dissecting their lives, gossiping and sharing their news as if they'd never been apart.

'Have you heard from Chris?' Polly asked on her third glass, when she'd finally plucked up the courage.

Kerensa shrugged. 'Now and then. He's over the worst.'

'Is he still living at his mum's?' asked Polly.

'Yup.'

'You know, he hasn't contacted me. Not even once, to say how are you doing or something.'

'I know,' said Kerensa. 'I called him on it.'

'You did? When did you see him?'

'At Shanoosha and Michael's fortieth – which you didn't come to, by the way.'

Polly shrugged. She didn't like to admit that the presents would have been expensive; that it would have been horrible to stand there amongst all their successful professional middle-class friends with their mortgages and Volkswagens and pregnancy bumps and talk about being a minimum-wage assistant in a bakery. She couldn't have borne their sympathy and pity.

'No,' she said. 'But Chris was there?'

Kerensa winced. 'I think he got a bit overexcited at the free cocktail bar.'

'They had a *cocktail bar*?'

'Pure swank,' said Kerensa. 'Anyway. He was a little ...'

'How's he looking?'

'Tired,' said Kerensa.

'Oh God,' said Polly. 'What did he say?'

'He asked how you were doing. And when I told him you'd moved and had a new flat and a job and everything, he was ...'

Polly's heart sank. She knew the answer.

'Was he jealous?'

Kerensa nodded. 'He thinks it's all right for you, apparently. Thinks it's easy for you to get on with your life because you didn't really care about the business in the end, he was the creative talent, blah blah.'

Polly's eyes stung with tears at the unfairness of it all.

'He ruined my life, Kerensa. It's WRECKED. Look at it! Just because I'm not sulking at my mum's house ...'

'I know that,' said Kerensa. 'I told him. I told him he was wallowing.'

'What did he do?'

'Got pissed and tried to pull the cocktail waitress.'

Polly grimaced in sympathy. 'Oh God, poor Chris.'

'Poor Chris nothing,' said Kerensa fiercely. 'He has to man up and get through this. He's treated you appallingly.'

'He did his best,' said Polly.

'He did nothing of the sort. He got all huffy every time there was a tiny little setback. You can't run a business like that.'

'No,' said Polly, thoughtfully. 'But really, how dare he? Assuming I'm having a fantastic time and doing brilliantly. For crying out loud. It's awful. My life is dreadful. It's a total failure and a disaster and I hate it here and basically ALL OF IT.'

There was a sudden unexpected hush in the crowd. Polly realised that someone was standing behind her. She turned round. It was Tarnie. He looked very embarrassed.

'Er, sorry,' he said. 'I was coming over to say hi, but you sound busy ...'

'Oh God,' said Polly, crestfallen. 'Oh GOD, I didn't mean you. You're the only good thing to happen to me here. Hey, Kerensa, this is Tarnie.'

'Hell-oo,' said Kerensa, drawing out the last syllable. Polly gave her a look. Then she glanced back at Tarnie. She supposed he did look quite smart in his civvies: he had on a plain shirt, very soft worn jeans and Converses.

'Hey, what's up?' came a soft American voice, and Huckle and Reuben hove into view from the other side of the bar, both of them holding pint glasses.

'I hate this bar. Why are we in this bar? This is a terrible bar. This is bad beer. They should serve good beer. I'm going to buy this bar,' Reuben was saying. He didn't say hello.

'Polly was just talking about how much she hates her life,' said Tarnie gravely.

'I didn't ... Shut up,' said Polly, flushing bright red.

Kerensa turned round. She looked like a child in a sweet-shop.

'Hello to you too,' she said.

'Do *you* hate your life?' asked Tarnie.

'Not any more,' said Kerensa.

In the end, they all sat down together: six or seven fishermen, the American boys, plus a few of the surfers who'd joined them. Jaz was not amongst them today, but there was Felicia, a ludicrously beautiful Eurasian girl with black hair that stretched all the way down her back. She was trying to get Reuben's attention and failing, and ended up having to squeeze on to the bench next to Jayden. Jayden's facial expression was comical. He was frozen to the spot as if he didn't dare move, gazing at the goddess next to him.

'Can you stop staring at me?' she said softly.

'Um, are you going to have me arrested?' asked Jayden, his mouth completely dry.

'No,' said Felicia, tossing her hair.

'In that case, maybe not. I'll try. But probably not. Oh God,' said Jayden.

Felicia turned away from him. Polly wondered if this happened to her all the time. It probably did.

'Tell her your funny joke you told me,' she whispered to Jayden.

'I can't,' he said, eyes wide. 'I can't see straight.'

'Women like men who make them laugh.'

Jayden coughed. 'Um, Felicia?'

Felicia graced him with a flicker of her feline eyes. 'Yuh?'

'What do you call a crocodile wearing a vest?'

'I don't know.'

'An investigator.'

'A what?'

The colour drained from Jayden's face.

'Oh SHIT, I got that wrong. I mean, what do you call an ALLIGATOR . . . Oh, never mind.'

Felicia turned her back again and Jayden sat on his hands and stared fiercely at the table, his ears pink. Polly smiled and turned back to Kerensa. She preferred Jaz so far, but they were all pretty impressive.

'This place is more glamorous than I thought,' said Kerensa. 'Who's the annoying one?'

'Do you mean me?' said Reuben, who clearly had bionic hearing. 'Are you talking about me? I'm not annoying. Huckle, tell them I'm not annoying, I'm cool.'

'Of course you're not annoying,' said Felicia languorously. 'Darling, that's just rubbish.'

Kerensa rolled her eyes. 'Oh God, is he really, really rich?' she said loudly.

'Yes,' said Reuben.

'Thought so,' said Kerensa, shooting Felicia a triumphant look. Felicia turned away, which landed her back facing Jayden, who went bright red again and started scratching his neck. Polly got up to go over to Reuben.

'Thank you for my beautiful oven,' she said. 'Did you like the breadsticks?'

'If I had made them they would have been better,' he said. 'But they weren't bad. They needed more pepper.'

'I'll try and remember that,' said Polly, smiling at him. 'It was a really kind thing to do.'

'It was nothing,' said Reuben. 'I've forgotten all about it. It was like two cents to me.'

'Well, thank you for the two cents,' she said.

'Who's your friend?' Reuben asked casually. 'She's very rude. I like that in a woman.'

'That's Kerensa. Do you want to meet her properly?'

'No.'

'Kerensa!' said Polly, beckoning her over. 'This is Reuben, who gave me the lovely oven.'

'I've got a helicopter,' said Reuben.

'I hate helicopters,' said Kerensa. 'They're rubbish.'

Tarnie brought over another bottle of wine for the table, and cider for Jayden and a couple of the other fishermen. He pulled up a chair next to Polly.

'So how are things?' he said awkwardly. He normally found Polly easy to talk to, but this was a big group of people; it was a bit tricky.

'Honestly,' said Polly, 'I am so grateful to you for finding me a job.'

'But . . .'

'But,' nodded Polly. 'Oh man, Tarnie, she's killing me. She won't let me bake any proper bread, only cream horns and stupid doughnuts and pasties and pale white stuff. Which she's now talking about ordering in anyway because I'm too slow, apparently. She doesn't want to change or get better or anything.'

Tarnie nodded.

'Doughnuts were Jim's favourites,' he said finally.

'Oh Lord,' said Polly. 'I do know; I know that she's grieving and everything. I am doing my best to be helpful and useful and all of that, but it . . . it feels like I'm being continually punished for something.'

She took another sip of her drink and smiled ruefully. 'This will sound nuts, but I kind of had this fantasy of myself . . . making things better. Like, she would have someone to share the workload and could unburden herself, and maybe I could find the inner kind person inside sort of thing. Stupid.'

'I think that's a nice fantasy to have,' said Tarnie kindly. 'But I'm not sure . . . I'm not sure she hasn't been so bitter for so long that everything's kind of . . . just sealed over.'

'I do feel sorry for her,' said Polly stubbornly. 'But she is really, really mean to me, every single day.'

Huckle came over and pulled up a chair. He didn't see the look Tarnie gave him, but Polly noticed it.

'Hey,' he said, in his expansive laid-back drawl. 'How you all doing?'

'I'm just having a moan about my job,' said Polly. 'The job I've only had for two weeks. I'm not a very impressive specimen.'

Huckle frowned. 'Did you put Reuben's oven in?'

'It wouldn't fit in that bakery,' said Polly, 'so I had to put it in the other one, the one under my flat. But Mrs Manse won't have a thing to do with it, thinks it's foreign. She just wants pasties and big white buns.'

Huckle frowned again. 'The summer season is coming, right?'

'Er huh.'

'And she owns the property you're in, right?'

'Yeah.'

'Well, I don't see how it would be much more expensive if you divided up the labour. You work on the harbour and make bread with Reuben's oven, and she stays in the shop on her own and just does cakes and pasties. You don't need to fall out about what she wants to do, and she doesn't have to try and sell bread that she doesn't want to, so she saves all that time and effort, and you're not in competition with each other because you're basically the same company.'

All three were silent for a moment.

'You know, that could almost work,' said Polly. 'The only problem is, if *I* mention it to her she'll just say no

191

immediately. She always says no then thinks up reasons later.'

She tried so hard not to look at Tarnie it made the corner of his mouth twitch.

'You want me to propose changing everything AGAIN?' he said, taking a slurp of his pint.

'Don't you see?' said Polly. 'I know she doesn't want me in the shop.'

'Mmm,' said Tarnie.

'But she knows the workload is too much for her.'

'Mmmm.'

'And she's got the space to do it.'

'What about all the people who go into the wrong bakery for what they want?'

'We're two streets away,' said Polly. 'I think they'll manage. But she wouldn't have to handle as much stock if I did the bread.'

Tarnie hated to admit it, but it wasn't a bad idea.

'And,' said Huckle, 'if you're as good as we think you are, people will come to you just for your bread anyway. And also my honey.'

'You want me to sell your honey?'

'In return for the brilliant idea I just gave you?' said Huckle. 'No, you're right, it would be completely unreasonable of me to ask you to sell my honey.'

'No, of COURSE we'd sell your honey,' said Polly, excited. 'That's a great idea.'

Tarnie looked at his hands. He was, he realised, jealous of them planning something without him.

'OOH,' said Polly. 'I am quite excited about this. Except

of course she'll say no and then I'll have to go back to working for her and it will be even worse because I'll have dreamed of the taste of freedom.'

The drinks kept going down, and there didn't seem to be any closing time. By midnight, Polly was a little tipsy, her head full of plans and schemes for the downstairs space. Kerensa had ended up arguing with Reuben all night, about politics, feminism, gun control, freedom of the internet and literally anything else two people could possibly have a difference of opinion about. Eventually Jayden stood up. He was quite stewed.

'And now!' he shouted at Andy, who ran the bar and the chippy single-handed and in tandem, which made it a lucrative spot. There was a chorus of 'Oh no!' from the other fishermen.

Andy bowed, and went over to the CD player.

'If this doesn't impress the ladies, nothing will,' said Jayden.

'Er oh,' said Polly, but Kerensa was already sitting up eagerly. Felicia was rolling her eyes.

'Nothing *you* do will impress the ladies!' shouted Kendall, and Jayden flicked him the Vs.

'Archie! Tarnie! Kendall!'

The men grumbled and shuffled, but to Polly's astonishment they got up nonetheless. The other punters in the pub had gathered round, obviously well aware of what was about to happen.

Andy pressed a button on the CD player and a long, lamenting horn sound started up. Then it launched into a minor-key jig, which sounded exciting and melancholy all at the same time. It was wild music, and Polly felt her heart lurch with it, its strangeness and beauty. Then, to her utter astonishment, the men began to dance; with some embarrassment at first, then less and less as they got into it, bending and tilting, their heels banging hard on the rough wooden planks of the pub floor. It was a proper sailor's hornpipe; Polly had never seen one before, and as the music got faster and faster, the men twirled in time, looking ancient and young all at once, and she clapped her hands in delight as Tarnie flashed her a huge smile of white teeth, and they dipped in and out of each other, all twirling, until the music came to a hectically fast climax and the entire room erupted in whoops and cheers of applause.

Polly rushed up to Tarnie, closely watched by Huckle. Tarnie was pink in the face but couldn't stop smiling.

'That was amazing,' she said.

'Ach,' he said, shyly. 'My grandad taught me. It's just . . . it's just a local thing.'

'It's VERY SEXY,' said Kerensa loudly behind Polly. 'It's a shame you can't be sexy like that, Reuben.'

'I am totally sexy,' Polly heard Reuben say, but Andy was calling last orders now, and it was time for closing up.

'What a terrible little shit,' said Kerensa as a chauffeur-driven Bentley arrived at the bottom of the cobbled street. Felicia piled in after Reuben, who had barely spoken a word to her all evening.

'Oh, I'm sorry you didn't have a nice evening,' said Polly, still on a massive high after the boys' dancing. She linked

194

arms with her friend as they went to get some chips for the way home. Polly had never seen Kerensa eat chips. She wasn't even sure she'd know how.

'Oh GOD, these smell like heaven,' said Kerensa, breathing in deeply.

'You can eat them too,' said Polly. 'You know, if you like.'

Doused in salt and vinegar, in the still warm night air, washed down with a couple of cans of Fanta, they were absolutely delicious. The two girls ate sitting on the harbour wall, kicking their legs. The boys had gone their separate ways, waving and hollering. Jayden was taking a boat back to the mainland; Polly wondered briefly about whether he should be drinking and sailing, but he pointed out with a straight face that men had been doing that on Mount Polbearne for eight hundred years and they probably weren't going to stop tonight, then he gave another little deft click of his heels, and all she could do was giggle and wave good night.

'I had a great time,' said Kerensa.

Polly looked at her carefully. Could it be? Was Kerensa actually . . . *eating a chip*?

'What?'

'I thought you said you hated that guy. I heard you both shouting about George W. Bush.'

'Yes, I did hate that guy. But I quite enjoyed arguing with him, do you know what I mean?'

'No,' said Polly. 'I don't like arguing with anyone, ever.'

'Oh,' said Kerensa. 'Well, when you meet someone who's such a rude jerk, you don't have to hold back, you can just let it go.'

'Hmm,' said Polly. 'You should work in the bakery.'

Kerensa looked at her. 'And what about you, Little Miss Popular?'

Polly flushed and concentrated on her chips.

'I don't know what you're talking about.'

'Those two totally divine men is what I'm talking about. How on earth did you manage that?'

'I haven't managed anything,' said Polly. 'There's not a lot of women in this town, is mostly what that is. And neither of them fancy me anyway. Well, Huckle certainly doesn't.'

'He was certainly paying you a lot of attention.'

'I don't think so,' said Polly. 'He has a' – she lifted up her fingers into quote marks – '"tragic past". As soon as anyone mentions his private life, he clams up like a trap. Seriously, I do think he's cute, but I'm not an idiot; he's patently not up for it.'

'And what about the other one?'

'Tarnie?' said Polly. 'You're joking, aren't you? He's got a beard.'

'He's got a BEARD? That is the STUPIDEST reason I have ever heard for not dating someone. He's got a BEARD? Brad Pitt has got a BEARD. Johnny Depp has got a BEARD. George Clooney has got a BEARD. Ben Affleck has got a BEARD. Do you need me to go on? I will pull Mark Ruffalo into this if I have to.'

Polly looked uncomfortable. 'He's been really kind to me.'

'Yes,' said Kerensa, making a crude gesture. 'He's trying to get into your oilskins.'

'Only because there's not a lot of women around,' said

Polly. She looked at Kerensa sideways. 'You seriously think he's hot?'

'Let me see,' said Kerensa. 'Tall, fit, muscular, piercing blue eyes, strong jaw ... Polly, have you gone blind?'

Polly found herself staring at her chips again.

'Oh, I'm sure it's just because I'm new in town.'

'So what?' said Kerensa. 'Why he fancies you doesn't have to matter, does it?'

'No one ever fancies me,' said Polly.

'That's normally because they see me first,' said Kerensa sagely. There was a pause and they both burst out laughing.

'Shut up, you daft mare,' said Polly.

'Seriously, though,' said Kerensa. 'Oh boo hoo, woe is me, my life is a disaster. And here you are in this place which is' – she waved her arms around slightly drunkenly, indicating the horizon – 'absolutely gorgeous, in a cute little quirky flat—'

'Dump,' said Polly.

'No, flat,' said Kerensa. 'You've made it your home. With a job of your own and a whole group of new friends – plus one jerk – and a whole new life. I mean, seriously' – they chinked Fanta cans – 'that really is amazing, Polly.'

'When you put it like that, it sounds better than it is.'

'It is what it is,' said Kerensa. 'Chris is at his mum's getting pissed and making passes at waitresses.'

Polly looked around. Although there wasn't another person in sight and the chippy had closed, the sea was never quiet; she could hear the gentle splash at the harbourside and the clattering of the masts.

'Well,' she said. 'Well. I suppose. It's all right ...'

'Where's my smiley friend?'

Polly bit her lip.

'Come on! Where's that smile? I used to see it all the time.'

Polly grinned at her. 'Shut up!'

'HA!' Kerensa laughed. 'I knew you were coming back to us.' She put a finger to Polly's forehead. 'Now all you need is a LEETLE bit of Botox to get rid of these worry lines ...'

Chapter Fourteen

Polly slept in the next morning, which was something of a novelty. When she woke, Kerensa was gone, heading back to town and shopping and all the busyness. Polly had assumed she would feel jealous, hadn't been a hundred per cent sure before Kerensa's visit that she wouldn't just grab her friend's arm and beg her to take her back to Plymouth with her.

But instead, as she padded over to the stove to put the coffee machine on, she realised how glad she was not to be heading back to the world of noisy radios and commutes and traffic jams and drive-throughs and packed shopping centres. It was as if Kerensa had given her the gift of seeing Mount Polbearne through a prism which made it a lovely place; somewhere people would like to be.

She checked her phone. There was a message on it from Reuben. *I'm in love with your girlfriend*, it said. *Please tell her to call me straight away. I'll send the jet.*

Polly laughed out loud and was briefly disappointed that Kerensa wasn't still there so she could see her face. She headed over to the window with her coffee, just in time to see Tarnie turn up, waving when he caught sight of her.

'What are you doing today?' he yelled.

'I'm scrubbing a horrible black filthy room just in case I get to run it as a bakery,' she said, making a face.

'No you're not,' said Tarnie. 'It's Sunday, and it's the most beautiful day ever. So. Come fishing with me.'

'You're taking me to work?'

'Nope. This is just for fun.'

'You fish all week then you fish for fun?'

'Do we have to debate this shouting out of high windows?'

Polly smiled. 'Okay. Do we need a picnic?'

'No,' said Tarnie. 'Well, you know, anything you have lying about.'

Polly thought about the wholemeal bloomer she'd left to rise the previous evening out of sheer habit.

'I need to get the boat ready,' said Tarnie.

'Good,' said Polly. 'I'll be there in forty minutes.'

By the time she'd washed and changed, the bread was ready. It was warm and stunningly fragrant. She packed a jar of honey and a knife, a roundel of local cheese she'd bought from someone at the side of the road, some early Pink Lady apples, a large bottle of water and, on a whim, the macaroons and posh white wine Kerensa had brought her as a gift, 'because you can't get this stuff in Hicksville, right?' about which she had in fact been exactly right.

It was a perfect day, sunny and warm, with a little cooling breeze that sent tiny rags of cloud scuttling across the sky. The water was a light inviting blue. Polly dithered for a few minutes and eventually, feeling nervous and a little daring, tossed her swimming costume into her rucksack before she ran downstairs. Halfway down, she paused, wondering what was missing, and then realised that of course it was Neil.

She had expected Tarnie to be on his fishing boat, but that wasn't what he had meant at all, as it turned out; he was standing next to a little white rowing boat with a small engine at the back.

'Welcome to my yacht,' he said, smiling.

'Well I think she's very pretty,' said Polly, accepting his hand as she stepped off the wharf.

'Have you got a hat?' he asked.

'Oh no,' said Polly. 'I didn't think.'

'It gets pretty bright out there,' he said, tossing her a hat with lots of little pockets up the side.

Polly jammed it over her strawberry-blonde hair. 'Does it suit me?'

Tarnie smiled. 'You look about five.'

'I'm taking that as a no,' she said, taking it off again. 'What are these pockets for? Worms?'

'You have a real obsession with carrying animals about your person,' said Tarnie. 'Anyway, no. Hooks and flies mostly, but leave that to me.'

'Are you insinuating I can't fish?'

'Can you fish?'

'No, but you shouldn't assume.'

Polly put on her lifejacket. Tarnie smiled.

'What? Do the cool kids not do that?'

'Sorry,' said Tarnie. 'It's my fault. I assumed you could swim.'

'Of course I can SWIM.'

'Well then, I don't think you have to wear that – unless you want to. I'll be gentle, I promise.'

He set his hand on the tiller, and Polly took off the very bulky lifejacket and sat down on the little wooden bench at the front. Tarnie had been right: the boat jerked just once to start, then cut very smoothly through the white-tipped waves. This early in the morning there was nobody else out on the water, just a few fishermen standing forlornly at the end of the jetty, holding out for a catch. The sun shone down warmly and Polly was surprised at how much she enjoyed the sensation of the little boat zipping speedily along. The engine was noisy, so they didn't talk; she just watched as the great mount shape of Polbearne faded behind them in the morning mist, its clustered buildings and cobbled streets sweet and soft-looking in the haze. It was odd, she realised, but she almost thought of it as home.

Ahead was the open sea, suddenly thrilling in its endless expanse.

'It's gorgeous out here,' Polly said, settling back and enjoying the wind and sun on her face; as she grew warmer, she put her hand down and let it trail through the waves. It felt delicious.

After forty minutes, she saw a little something jutting out of the water. As they approached it, she realised it was the tiniest little island, a minuscule outcrop of land in the middle of nowhere.

'What's that?'

'I don't think it even has a name,' said Tarnie. 'Bird Island, maybe.'

As they drew closer, Polly saw that it had a rickety wooden jetty.

'Somebody lives here?'

'No, you couldn't live here. But in the past someone came and stayed from time to time; a hermit, I think. Some rich local second son who'd never quite got on in the world. He used to be ferried out here with his supplies, stay for a few months, then head back for the winter.'

'What on earth did he do?' said Polly.

'I think he just stared out to sea,' said Tarnie, tying up the boat and giving her a hand out. 'I really don't know. Maybe in the days before television people were just more easily pleased.'

Sure enough, up from the jetty, and a narrow yellow beach, were the abandoned remains of a rough-hewn stone house.

'Wow,' said Polly.

'I know,' said Tarnie, looking over at the graffiti. 'In the summer, kids steal their parents' boats and come and do stuff here. You should probably admire it from a safe distance.'

There were also the remains of several campfires.

'Can we build a fire?' said Polly.

'Strictly illegal,' said Tarnie. 'But yes.'

They walked around. There were large ash trees bent over on one side where the wind blew in from the sea, and little flickering flashes as rabbits scampered past. It was a lonely place – the mainland was merely a fine line in the distance – but beautiful too.

'What did he do for water?' asked Polly suddenly.

'Oh, he had a rain butt. No shortage of that stuff, not really.'

'No,' agreed Polly.

'And the fleet would pop in from time to time – we come past here every day, and there's the Looe sailors of course.'

Polly nodded.

'Okay,' said Tarnie. 'Ready to fish?'

Polly had been nervous about taking somebody's eye out with a hook, but Tarnie showed her how to cast back properly, and they sat on the jetty waiting for something to tug. Tarnie said that because there was vegetation, there was lots for the fish to eat, and they were lucky they were the first people here that day. 'Make your cross face at anyone else who comes,' he added.

'You make YOUR cross face,' said Polly.

Tarnie smiled, his eyes looking very blue.

'Actually,' he said, 'when people see that someone else has already got here, they tend to pass on. It's a little small for a nice quiet day out for everyone. So. We've bagsied it.'

'Our own private island,' said Polly wonderingly. Tarnie grinned at her again.

Polly was first. She felt the sudden tug on her line and wondered what it was; then she stood up and nearly fell in.

'Woohoo!' she yelled. 'I've got one! I've got one!'

Tarnie smiled. 'That's it! On you go, start reeling it in! Pull it!'

'Oh my goodness!' said Polly, excited, as the large silvery shape started to become visible, frantically jerking and splashing under the surface. 'Oh God, oh no, I'm killing a fish.'

Tarnie looked at her.

'Polly, it's a bit late for that.'

'I know, I know ...'

She winced and was on the brink of dropping the rod.

'Do you want me to take it?'

She nodded quickly, slightly cross with herself for being so squeamish. Tarnie came up behind her, and very casually gently removed the rod from her hands, then, as she stood aside, started to reel it in.

The sun glinted off the water and the silvery scales as the fish twisted and turned right to the top of the filament. It was a herring, a big one too.

'I'm so sorry, Mr Fish,' muttered Polly.

'This is a bad time to go vegetarian on me,' said Tarnie, as he expertly picked the fish off the hook. 'Okay,' he added. 'You may want to look away for this bit.'

He reached into his fishing bag and took out a long silver knife, then quickly and smoothly began to gut the fish. Polly peered through her fingers. Tarnie smiled at her.

'You're a squeamish lass,' he said.

'I know,' said Polly. 'I know it's pathetic. I normally only buy them sealed in plastic from the supermarket.'

'Well then you've never tasted a real fish,' said Tarnie simply. 'Now you go and get some sticks.'

'Seriously?'

'Seriously.'

It was rather lovely wandering through the little wood, an emerald canopy shading her from the sun. She went as deep in as she could, picking up sticks on the way. Birds cooed overhead, but there was nothing else to be heard. It was completely beautiful and very still. Polly felt like she understood why so many people in Cornwall still believed in pixies; it was such a magical place. She took a deep breath of

205

the fresh salty air and smiled with something that felt alarmingly close to happiness.

By the time she got back, Tarnie had caught several more fish, and she gave him the sticks and he set about building a neat little fire.

'But this is illegal,' she said.

'Yes, if you're a drunk teenager who might set the entire island on fire,' said Tarnie. 'Let's try our best not to do that, shall we?'

Soon he had it crackling, and he took out some tin foil, butter, lemon and parsley, and wrapped the fish up and rested them on stones near the blaze.

Polly removed the bottle of wine that Tarnie had had the foresight to leave in the sea to keep it nice and cool, and tore apart the fresh bread, which was still warm inside. They buttered it and ate it with the fish, which had a sensational smoky taste from the fire. Their fingers got greasy because Polly had forgotten to pack napkins, and they both managed to burn themselves from time to time, then they had to throw the bones back into the water, when maybe that wasn't the most ladylike Polly had ever felt.

It was the best meal she'd ever eaten in her life.

The cool wine and the hot sun were making Polly feel sleepy. She rolled over and grabbed one of the apples from the picnic bag. As she bit into it, she caught Tarnie looking at her. Something in the atmosphere shifted.

'Apple?' she said.

He blinked for a moment. 'Er, no thanks.' He looked away. Then he looked at her again. 'Um,' he said.

Polly realised immediately that Kerensa must have been

right. After all, she thought, looking around her: this spot, this lunch, this day. This wasn't just about friendship, otherwise he'd probably have brought his mates along. This was something else.

They sat in silence for a moment, then Tarnie got up and walked across the sand towards the sea.

'I'm hot,' he announced. Without warning, he pulled off his shirt – he was lean, slighter than Polly had expected; all sinew and tight muscle, with a couple of fine scars tracing up his side – and, leaving on his long shorts, he dived straight into the surf.

Polly watched him for a long time. He was clearly a strong swimmer and didn't surface until she was almost starting to worry about him. Then she saw his dark head appear, like a seal, and he waved.

'What's it like?' she called.

'Refreshing,' he shouted back.

'That always means bloody freezing,' she said.

'Burk burk burk burk.'

'Don't make chicken noises at me!' said Polly. She did feel hot, and a bit sticky. 'You're not meant to swim after a meal anyway. Or did they disprove that?'

'Burk burk burk.'

Before she realised what she was doing, she ducked back into the wood and slipped on the cherry-print vintage swimsuit she'd bought online back in the days when buying nice things was simply the kind of thing one did for fun. She wished she had a mirror. On second thoughts, she was glad she didn't. She would only start picking faults and worrying, and she hadn't exposed her skin all winter, so of course she was going to be pale. For those reasons too she decided that the best thing to do was just take a run into the sea, charging towards it before she had the chance to consider it and change her mind.

It was not refreshing. It was not even cold. It was absolutely bloody arctic.

'EEK!' screeched Polly, feeling her insides constrict as she splashed about in agony. 'What IS this?'

Tarnie burst out laughing. It was strange to see him so relaxed; he was bobbing up and down on his back quite happily.

'You get used to it,' he said. 'A bit of cold water never hurt anyone.'

'Yes it does! All the time!' yelled back Polly, the shock still deep in her lungs. She dived under again. The water was miraculously clear out here, practically Mediterranean. She felt a fish nudge her leg and managed not to squeal.

Finally she felt herself getting used to the water. She surfaced next to Tarnie. The sun felt delicious as she lay on her back and waggled her hands to stay afloat.

'Well this is lovely,' she said, smiling.

Tarnie looked at her. His eyes were suddenly very blue, his teeth very white. And it seemed like the easiest thing in the world to bob a little closer to him, to close her eyes to the sun and the bright blue sky; to let him pull her in and kiss her.

It had been the contrasts: the warmth of the sun and the coldness of the water; the roughness of his beard and the softness of her skin; the freshness of the open air and the closeness of being with someone again after so long, someone new, and exciting, and different.

All the way back in the boat, Polly lay replete, slightly giggly, a little sleepy, feeling quite unlike herself. She was in the front, facing him. Occasionally they would share a smile, a glance. Otherwise she trailed her hand once again in the water, just enjoyed the lovely sense of being in her own body, in her own time; not worrying about the future or dreaming about the past, or distracting herself with daily chores, but simply, truly being and feeling. The sun was starting to sink and a few of the clouds were tinged with pink. She was happy, she realised. She was happy.

The boys were already loading up the sloop when they puttered gently back into Polbearne harbour. There was enough good-natured waving and cheering for Polly to realise they were both going to be the object of some ribbing. Tarnie had gone pink too, not just from the sun.

'Ach,' he said, grinning at her by way of apology.

'I'm guessing you can't come back?' she said, boldly.

'I have to work,' he said. He gently put out his rough, calloused hand and stroked her face. She nestled into it.

'Soon, though,' he said, his intense blue eyes meeting hers.

'Soon,' she whispered.

'HELLO,' said Jayden, helping her off the boat. 'DID YOU HAVE A GOOD DAY?'

'All right, Jay, settle down,' said Tarnie gruffly.

They looked at each other.

'Um, thank you for a lovely day,' said Polly.

Tarnie stared at the ground.

'Er, it was my pleasure,' he said. Then in front of all the boys, he leant in and kissed her gently on the cheek. Blushing, Polly retreated with her wicker basket.

'You did what?' said Kerensa. 'On an ISLAND? Oh GOD, I am so jealous.'

'Why don't you go out with one of the millions of people who ask you out all the time?'

'Because I have standards,' said Kerensa. 'Oh God, I didn't mean that the way it came out.'

'You SO did,' said Polly. She was sitting with her feet up on her window ledge, sipping a beer, watching the sun going down and feeling ridiculously contented. 'But that's okay, because today I don't mind.'

'Because you have the sex hormones making you crazy.'

'I don't feel crazy,' said Polly. 'I feel good.'

'That's their secret,' said Kerensa. 'That's what they do.'

Polly rolled her eyes. 'I thought you were the one telling me to get back on the horse.'

'That's true.'

Polly remembered something.

'Oh, that little American bloke is in love with you.'

'HA,' said Kerensa. 'Well tell him from me he's disgusting.'

'You know he's incredibly rich.'

'Oh well, let me whore myself out to someone I don't like for money,' said Kerensa. 'Thanks for the wonderful advice.'

Polly took another sip of beer.

'Well,' she said. 'It was lovely. Gorgeous.'

'Yeah, all right,' said Kerensa. 'Listen, could you call Chris sometime?'

'Why?' said Polly, suddenly jerked out of her reverie.

'Nothing. It's just ... he's awfully down. I think he feels that you're doing well and he's doing so very badly. He's a bit bitter.'

'How can *I* help?'

'I don't know,' confessed Kerensa simply. 'Perhaps you need to convince him to face up to things and move on.'

Polly sighed. 'Yes,' she said. 'Yes, I'll call him.'

'Women are always better at getting on with their lives,' said Kerensa. 'Did you know that? Men are terrible. That's why they're always getting married by mistake.'

'Hmm,' said Polly. 'Or maybe you should tell him to call me.'

'Try not to sound too happy and sexed up.'

'I'm ...' Polly smiled. 'Well, maybe a teeny tiny little bit.'

'Good,' said Kerensa. 'About bloody time.'

Chapter Fifteen

Polly was still smiling the next morning, and her smile only grew wider as she explained her new idea to Mrs Manse – her in one bakery, Gillian in the other, but Polly handling all the heavy lifting – and found her to be quite amenable.

'For as long as you're here,' she sniffed, which counted as encouragement coming from Mrs Manse.

'Well if this works out, I might stay,' pointed out Polly, but Mrs Manse gave her a dark look and hoisted her bosom ominously. Polly could tell, though, that the idea of being in her own shop without Polly getting in the way was making her happier, even though she was reluctantly coming round to the idea of Polly doing all the baking, or at least realising it was beyond her own capabilities.

So Polly uncomplainingly worked a sixteen-hour day helping Mrs Manse rearrange things back to how she wanted them, and moved the flour over to the other building.

It was dilapidated, of course, but workable now that it had stopped raining all the time. If she could get it running and make a little money, she could have it patched up for the winter. She was slightly shocked to find herself planning so far ahead, but she couldn't help it. She felt the excitement bubbling up inside her. Her own bakery! Well, not exactly, but ... She must phone Huckle and thank him for the idea. And maybe Tarnie would come in later and ... She blushed at the memory and told herself sternly to get to work.

She remembered as she turned on the big plug for the electricity to start up how nervous she'd been the first time she'd gone down there, for poor little Neil. The oven fired up first time with the wood placed in there – Reuben had bought absolutely top-of-the-range, and it gave out an astonishing heat. She could use the traditional ovens to bake the standard loaves, and there was plenty of opportunity to do more with the big industrial mixers, but she figured starting simple was the best way. Mrs Manse was going to pay her on commission and take her loaves, but would also stick to her original pasties and sandwiches to begin with, and they would see how they went from there. It was a very informal arrangement. Polly sensed that Mrs Manse would have done almost anything to get her out of there. Only by clinging on to the idea that it wasn't personal – Gillian didn't really like anybody – could she avoid getting her feelings hurt.

She put her first six loaves of focaccia into the wood-burning oven and immediately burnt her fingers on the long serving stick. She also burnt the bread. It took three shots of fresh dough for her to finally bake a loaf properly – it went far faster than she was expecting – with the right amount of olive oil and the right balance of salt and rosemary.

When she finally managed it, however, the difference in quality was unbelievable. It tasted like nothing else she'd ever made before: crispy and sharp on the outside; soft and yielding inside. The scent was heavenly: the warm fragrance of baking bread with a slightly burnt, crispy smell cutting through it. It was all Polly could do not to stuff the entire thing in her mouth.

Next she tried a pissaladière, with some slow-cooked onions. It was even better; the onions caramelised in the smoky heat of the oven, becoming soft and sweet and contrasting with the sharpness of the anchovies and olives that she'd sprinkled on top. Next, her cheese loaf was infused with a toasty, melted mellowness.

This oven, Polly thought, looking at it sideways, was making her a far better baker than she could ever have been without it. She texted another thank you to Reuben and invited him over any time. Then, tentatively, she picked up the ancient 'Closed' sign on the door and pushed it round to 'Open'.

Nobody could resist strolling in to see what was going on – either that, or the smell simply physically dragged them in. Within fifteen minutes Polly had attracted what passed in Mount Polbearne for a crowd. She put out little tasters on the top of the counter with toothpicks sticking out of them so people could sample them.

'SAMPLE,' she said to Jayden, who couldn't speak, his mouth was so full. 'That means you take one to see if you like it.'

'I DO like it,' said Jayden, murkily. 'I like it a lot. That's why I'm eating more.'

'No, now you buy some.'

'Oh,' said Jayden. 'I thought it was too good to be true.'

'You're in a shop.'

'Oh, yes,' he mumbled. 'Can I have some of those?' He pointed to some cheese breadsticks she'd made up. 'How much are they?'

'Ooh, good point,' said Polly. 'I should probably have thought that one through. Um, a pound?'

Jayden counted out three coins carefully.

'I would like three.'

'Are you sure? They're quite big.'

Jayden looked at her.

'I went to Exeter once and ate four Big Macs,' he said. 'I was sick, but I did it.'

'Congratulations,' said Polly.

'Best day of my life,' said Jayden.

He looked crafty for a minute.

'So, um, have you spoken to Tarnie?'

Polly gave him a look.

'I would hate to ban you from this shop,' she said sternly.

'Wow, you're turning into Mrs Manse,' said Jayden.

Polly shook out one of the paper bags she'd carted down from the other bakery.

'Off you go,' she said, wrapping up his breadsticks.

'I'll tell him you said hi,' said Jayden cheekily.

'I'll tell him to kick your butt,' said Polly, then realised she'd said that far too close to the elegantly dressed woman who'd just stepped into the shop.

215

'Oh, sorry.'

'That's all right,' said the woman. Judging by her accent, and her clothes, she wasn't local.

'You new around here?' asked Polly, feeling a tiny secret thrill at the idea of there being someone in Polbearne even newer than herself.

'Yes, well . . .' The woman glanced around. 'We were looking for a holiday home – you know? Somewhere to buy to get away from it all? We want somewhere really quiet, but the problem is, the really quiet places don't have a lot going on, no restaurants and so on.'

She was pretty, Polly supposed; very thin, with highlighted hair and fuchsia lipstick.

'Well yes,' said Polly. 'That's *why* they're quiet. No restaurants or things to do.'

'So you see my problem,' said the woman. 'We want unspoiled, but with amazing traditional fare and local produce and so on.'

'That is a problem,' said Polly, thinking she'd probably be better off in one of the bigger resorts. 'Have you thought about Rock?'

The woman shuddered. 'Oh yes, ghastly. Full of awful second-homers sitting outside restaurants braying.'

'And that totally isn't what you want to do?'

To her credit, the woman smiled.

'Ugh, I know. But we want to be first! It's not easy at all!'

'Well I can't help you with that,' said Polly. 'But I can provide you with bread.' She indicated the loaves nestling in new baskets she'd bought from the pound shop but which actually looked pleasantly rustic.

The woman studied them for a moment. Then her face suddenly brightened.

'Is that . . . is that a *sun-dried tomato*?'

Polly picked up the tomato loaf.

'Certainly is.'

The woman's eyes widened even more.

'And is that a . . . *wood-burning oven*?'

'Yup.'

Polly gave her a little of the bread to try. She ate a morsel, then squeaked loudly.

'Henry! Hen!' she called in loud, carrying tones to the huge Range Rover that was taking up most of the road outside. 'I think we've found it! We've done it! The Hambleton-Smythes will never even have HEARD of this place! It'll be our undiscovered gem!'

A beefy man with the collar of his pink rugby shirt turned up got out of the car. He was a lot older than his wife.

'Thank Christ,' he said to Polly. 'She needs bragging rights or nothing ever gets done. Seems a pretty enough place.'

'I'll bring my decorator down to choose us a house,' said the woman.

'I'm not sure there's anything for sale,' said Polly. She'd seen Lance the plump estate agent in the pub on Saturday night and he'd been pretty glum about the whole business.

The couple started laughing.

'Oh, they always sell to me in the end,' said the man.

'Yes, they do, darling,' said the woman.

'Everyone has their price. Now, I'll take one of everything you've got. Not for you, though, honey pie. Don't want you puffing up, do we?'

217

'No, Hen,' simpered the woman. 'I'm just your ickle baby pie.'

Polly watched them after they'd gone, the man delving eagerly into the large paper bag. She felt obscurely guilty that she'd let something in that didn't quite belong in Polbearne – she felt fairly sure that if they'd gone to Mrs Manse's shop, the big man wouldn't have left his Range Rover parked right over the street like that. On the other hand, all the locals had come in that morning, from Muriel in the corner shop, to Patrick the vet, who'd kindly enquired after Neil and bought a white sliced, to the steady procession of fishermen, partly to eat, she knew, and partly to have a gander at the woman who'd pulled Tarnie. She felt something tugging at her; part of her wished she hadn't come back with him in the boat in full view of everyone, although there wasn't much she could have done about that. She wondered when he was going to phone her.

He was *going* to phone her, surely? Of course he was. This wasn't some gruesome date set up in a loud nightclub where they'd shouted at each other all night, or an awkward dinner in a mid-range restaurant where they'd tried to find common ground on sport or music or politics. This was something organic, wasn't it. Had arisen naturally out of the time they'd spent together? Surely. That was it. So she didn't have to worry about him phoning, because of course she'd see him – he worked right outside her window – and when she did, it would be easy and sweet and not at all awkward, even with a bunch of friendly fishing folk sniggering in the background.

She thought back, slightly embarrassed, to the day before. She had got carried away, of course she had. Under normal circumstances she wouldn't have . . . but what with the beautiful day, and having fun for once . . . She resolved not to feel guilty about it.

It had been strange, too, her first time in so very long. The feel of his body, different from Chris's, which had grown soft and slack in the years they'd been together; too much take-away food, too many nights hunched over the computer or the drawing board, too much beer at the weekend. Tarnie had felt sharp and angular. Not better, or worse, she thought: just different. But that was to be expected after being out of the game for so long. You weren't going to click with anyone first time; you needed practice to get used to one another, she was sure of it.

She rubbed her neck, then made up another batch of the little cheese sticks; they were proving hugely popular. The honey loaf sat in the corner – possibly a little bit ambitious for the clientele so far, but that was okay, she could give it time. And sure enough, by two o'clock she'd sold every single thing in the shop. People turned up later, and went away disappointed.

She glanced at her watch, then counted the takings. Mrs Manse would be pleased, surely – if anything pleased her. And now that summer and the tourists were upon them, it struck her that it might be possible to finish work at two every day. She tried to keep down a rising excitement. If she could do this every day – and it was a big 'if', depending a lot on her difficult boss – it would be a job, a real, proper job.

And so different. She made bread, she sold it. She thought back to when she and Chris had worked together: the endless schmoozing for possible contracts; all those exhausting nights out, discussing future work in endless meetings, trying to get to a yes, trying to plan ahead, trying to deal with constant changes and a million different ways of doing things.

Whereas here, if people wanted a bun, they bought a bun. If they wanted some bread, they bought some. If they didn't, they didn't. There was something earthy, something very real in the transaction that she'd simply never known before. If she didn't make the bread, she wouldn't make any money and she wouldn't get paid. If she did, and it was good, she'd have people coming back – even buying a house to be closer to where she did it.

Suddenly, here in the little Beach Street bakery, it all felt possible. It really did.

She turned the sign on the door to 'Closed' and started clearing up. She would have to become a bit more tidy and efficient while she worked. Or maybe she could get someone in to help part time with the cleaning. That could work too. She was trying to keep down the fizzing excitement when her phone rang.

Her old mobile had been paid for by the business; handing it over to Mr Bassi had been one of the most humiliating moments of her life. She'd got a new, cheap one, but she hardly bothered to use it or give the number out; when she was ready to see her friends again, she promised herself, she would. She definitely would.

The number was unknown. It must be Tarnie, she thought. She smiled, suddenly much more nervous than she'd felt before. What were they going to do? Would they go on a date? It was suddenly ridiculous to imagine Tarnie sitting nicely in a restaurant or a cinema; Polly had never even really seen him inside. He wasn't an indoors creature at all; he belonged in the open air, with the salt spray in his hair.

'Hello?' she said cheekily into the phone, much more confidently than she felt. 'How are YOU doing?'

'Not so good,' came a voice, dourly.

'Chris?'

'Well, yes, who did you think it would be?' He sounded low, defensive.

'Um, no, of course. Hello! How are you doing?'

Polly's new, hard-won happiness suddenly dropped away and she felt her leg twisting round on its ankle with awkwardness. After everything they'd been through, everything she'd tried . . . She remembered what Kerensa had said about everyone being worried about him.

'Hey. Are you okay?' she said.

'Well I hear you are,' Chris said heavily.

Polly looked round the little bakery. Its windows were still cracked. But it had character.

'Um, you know, it's been a struggle,' she said quickly. 'What are you up to?'

'What do you think I'm up to? I'm living at my mum's trying to get my life back together.'

'Is she well?' asked Polly. Chris's mum had always liked her, but her face had taken on a drawn, hunted look as things had started to go wrong.

She felt Chris scowl down the telephone.

'She says she's getting fed up with me. Like you did.'

'Chris,' said Polly, trying her best not to get riled, 'I didn't get fed up with you. Things went wrong, remember?'

There was a long pause.

'Yeah, of course I remember,' he said. He sounded bitter.

Polly bit her lip.

'So, I thought I'd maybe come and see you, yeah?' he continued defensively, as if he expected her to say no.

She thought about the little flat, and everything that was going on, and how she was waiting to hear from Tarnie. This wasn't ideal timing. But of course she had to see him; of course she did.

'Well?' he said, when she didn't reply immediately. 'What's up, moved on?'

Polly knew it was Chris's insecurities coming out in the harsh words.

'Um, well, no, you know . . . Of course you should come. Please. Do.'

'Kerensa says you're out in the sticks on some crazy island.'

'Does she?'

'I could do with a bit of piece and quiet. My mum's doing my head in.'

Polly felt frustrated. She couldn't help it. She was finally moving on, getting past it; she had barely thought about Chris, if she was absolutely honest with herself, had buried the sting and the hurt and got on with other things. But that wasn't fair on Chris.

'Yes, of course,' she said. 'Come whenever you like.'

Chapter Sixteen

The speed with which the Little Beach Street Bakery (so called to differentiate it from Mrs Manse's establishment, even though that was only larger by about three square feet) took off surprised everyone, not least Polly.

She experimented every day with different flavours, and soon learned what worked well. Chorizo was a massive hit, even if she had to order it from the mainland and nobody knew what it was; corn fritters likewise. Anything that looked even vaguely like pizza would sell out before ten o'clock in the morning.

Polly was thinking that she was going to need an assistant pretty soon, as the tourists started to flock across the causeway, but the long hours on her feet were offset by the joy she felt at two o'clock when all the stock was sold and she could clean up. On a couple of occasions, trying to avoid everyone in the village knowing their business, she hopped upstairs to be with Tarnie, who was also free in the afternoons, and they grabbed some time together, the sun streaming through the windows, the air full of the smell of salt. But they didn't seem to be a couple as such, she noticed: they didn't go out for dinner – where would they go? They sometimes joined the others in the pub, but they couldn't quite handle the ribbing and would seat themselves apart.

Nevertheless, Polly felt good. She felt the gradual stirring of her body back to life as the days grew warmer and warmer and the summer became beautifully, properly hot and the little town came to life. She would wake every morning with the sun's first pink rays, to knead and grow the bread, to try new things, to savour the smells, to put on the coffee, to greet her new friends, and catch up on village gossip. Everyone quickly got into the habit of stopping by, especially when she bought paper cups for the good coffee machine and started selling that too. Patrick would drop in to complain about mangy cats; Muriel would appear declaring that her feet were killing her; Andy from the pub would amble over just before lunchtime to pick up rolls for his barbecues, and Huckle would drop off his honey.

The tourists would flood in, looking surprised to find such a lovely place, and Polly would happily listen to the jingle of the till. When she carried the takings over to the other shop, Mrs Manse would grunt at her, but Polly soon learned that if she made the older woman a cup of tea, she had absolutely no objection to listening to the gossip second hand, making occasional tutting noises. Polly wouldn't in a million years have called it a friendship, but it was definitely well en route to a thaw.

And every night she would fall into bed with the sunset, exhausted from hard work, getting browner and feeling better and stronger every day, her old life receding like the waves on the little sandy beach just round from the old lighthouse, where she and Muriel occasionally escaped for a much-needed sit-down and natter.

And now Chris was coming, bringing that old life to Polbearne.

Polly looked carefully at the sofa – her treasured sofa – and pulled it out and made it up into a bed, feeling apprehensive.

He'd called to say when he was getting here and she realised, without even needing to glance at her tidal chart any more, that the causeway would be under water then. She told him this and he said, well, it was too late, he had set off now, and she'd sighed and said all right, she'd figure something out.

Down on the harbour Tarnie was nowhere to be found, but Jayden was unfurling nets, in the most unenthusiastic way possible, and jumped up when she offered him some extra buns to take her over the causeway and pick up Chris.

It was a fine afternoon, just starting to turn to pink on the distant horizon, when they set off across the water, which had washed steadily over the cobbles of the causeway until every stone disappeared and they were an island once more. The seabirds were calling and the mainland seemed very far away, and Polly sat in the back of the boat – she clambered aboard with ease nowadays; she was as comfortable with getting on to a boat as she would be getting in a car – and grinned as Jayden gunned the little engine.

'You are the Formula 1 of tiny little boats,' she said, and he smiled appreciatively.

'You're the second run I've done today,' he said. 'I'm starting up the taxi service again.'

In the summer, the fishing crews ran the tender as an unofficial taxi cab to ferry stranded daytrippers back to their mainland campsites and hotels after they'd been tempted to stay too long at the Mount Inn. The set price was as much as they could get away with, with the only stipulation being that all cash thus fleeced was then put behind the bar and the rounds shared.

'You're basically pirates,' Polly had said when she had learned of it, and they had all grinned and nodded in agreement.

'Been busy?' said Polly. There weren't many incomers yet, and the locals knew the tide times like the back of their hands.

'Aye,' said Jayden. 'I took Tarnie back to see his—'

Polly wasn't really concentrating. In fact, there was every chance that if Jayden hadn't cut himself off very obviously and blushed like a demon, he'd have got away with it.

He could have said 'new boat' or 'allotment' or literally anything that came into his head, but Jayden's head could be a large, cloudy expanse sometimes, and instead he stood there, bright pink, his hand rubbing at the back of his neck and his mouth agape like a fish.

Polly didn't notice at first. Then she idly traced the conversation backwards and sat up, swallowing hard.

'His what, Jayden?' she said, trying to make her voice sound calm and unconcerned. Inside, her heart had started to race.

'Er, his nothing,' said Jayden, hopeful that she might leave him alone.

'No, not nothing, Jayden,' said Polly in a prim voice. She looked at him straight on, but he could barely meet her gaze.

There was a long silence. Polly wasn't going to break it.

'Um,' said Jayden eventually as they drew closer to the mainland. Polly could already see Chris's mum's little white Polo in the car park.

'Yes?'

'Um . . . his wife.' He muttered the last words in a rush, his eyes fixed on the bottom of the boat.

'His . . .' Polly had to make absolutely sure. 'Jayden, did you just say "his wife"?'

Jayden nodded his head guiltily.

'Tarnie's married?'

'Aye.'

'And you knew this?'

More staring at the floor.

'Aye.'

Polly felt the blood rush to her head and realised her hands were shaking. Well, she supposed this explained why they hadn't progressed much beyond the occasional drink. Something else occurred to her.

'And . . . can I assume that everyone in town knows this?'

Jayden shrugged.

Polly swore, loudly, and threw a pebble that was lying in the boat into the water.

'Oh for crying out loud. Why didn't you tell me?'

'Not my business,' mumbled Jayden.

Polly thought furiously. She hadn't asked . . . well, it had never occurred to her that she needed to, and he didn't wear a ring – mind you, that would be dangerous in his job anyway.

She always used to double-check with those flashy chancers she and Kerensa came across in bars in Plymouth in their younger days: the naval officers on shore leave looking for a bit of fun; the businessmen in town. But of course recently it had never mattered to her; she and Chris had been together for so long. It was always Kerensa doing all the heavy lifting; Polly gave off an 'I'm taken' vibe, and it had worked just fine ... And now she'd made the most amateur, rookie mistake of all. She felt unbelievably stupid.

'Oh bloody hell,' she said. 'BLOODY hell. I can't believe nobody told me. Why didn't Mrs Manse tell me?' She answered her own question. 'Because she doesn't like me. Why didn't Huckle tell me?'

'That weird American?' said Jayden. 'Why would he know?'

'What's she like?' said Polly. 'Oh God, tell me they don't have children.'

Jayden shook his head.

'She doesn't like the fishing,' he said. 'She lets him work the season, keeps house back in Looe. He comes and goes.'

'FRIG,' said Polly. 'He must have thought I was easy pickings.'

Jayden looked heartbroken.

'I don't,' he said. 'I think you're nice.'

'Thank you, Jayden,' said Polly.

They were coming in to the jetty and Polly hadn't discovered half of what she needed to know.

'So does he do this every summer?' she demanded. 'Find a newbie and go for it? Am I just this year's model? Oh God, that island. He probably goes there all the time.'

Anyone less like a practised seducer than Tarnie she would have found hard to imagine. But then again, maybe that was his special skill. Making himself seem all rough and unsure, whilst knowing what he was doing the entire time.

Jayden shook his head firmly.

'Neh,' he said. 'He's scared stiff of Selina. I've never seen him do this before, honest.'

Polly glared at him.

'It's true,' he said.

As the boat approached, Chris got out of the car, the breeze slapping spray against his forehead.

'This your boyfriend?' said Jayden.

'Not quite,' said Polly. 'Good God, you're all sex maniacs.'

She hauled herself up on to the jetty, furious but knowing she had to put it behind her for now, block it out of her head. It briefly occurred to her that if she had been tempted to feel a little bit smug when meeting Chris, that had now been well and truly kicked to the kerb.

Chapter Seventeen

Polly studied her ex, trying to ignore the ferment inside her. He looked different. Only three months apart, but it seemed longer. He didn't look quite as pale and pasty as he had when the business was going under. His hair needed cutting, but it rather suited him a little longer. He had regained all the weight he had lost, and added a bit more, and the bags under his eyes appeared to be there for good. He was wearing an old checked shirt and jeans that looked slightly too small for him.

'Hey,' he said warily.

Chris for his part was struck by the change in Polly. She seemed distracted; rangier. Her skin had taken on a flattering light tan from being outside; her strawberry-blonde hair was casually pulled up in a ponytail, as if she didn't care who saw her. Fronds tumbled round her face; the effect was pretty. She too was in old jeans, and a red T-shirt with powdery stuff on it; he assumed it must be flour. She looked younger than she had done; less strained. He felt a guilty stab, suddenly; he had had a lot to do with that.

'Hey,' she said. They looked at each other awkwardly, not sure what the right form of greeting was after so long apart. Then she said, 'Come here, you' and opened her arms, and he gave her a tentative hug. Polly noticed immediately the familiar smell of him; to Chris, Polly smelled different – there was a scent of baking, a hint of salt water.

'Wow,' he said finally. 'You look really good.'

It suddenly struck Polly that she hadn't made an effort for him coming. In the early days she would have made a big deal about getting done up for him; chosen what to wear carefully and put on lots of make-up. Now she only had a smear of lipstick on. She realised why – partly because it hadn't occurred to her, and partly because of course she had thought she was dating somebody else – and felt immediately foolish. She tried to banish Tarnie to the back of her mind. She couldn't think about that just now.

'Er, well,' she said. 'Thanks. So do you.'

There was an uneasy pause, then Jayden coughed and reminded them that when the tide went out again he had to take a really awkward route round the headland, and Polly scampered down into the boat. Chris followed with his overnight bag, rather more clumsily.

'So you've got your sea legs, then,' he said, and Polly just smiled, whilst inside she wanted to die.

Jayden, obviously mindful of the trouble he'd caused already, was completely silent on the way back, with the result that it felt not unlike being rowed across the Styx by the ferryman. As they rounded the point into the bay, Polly looked at Chris, gratified by the expression on his face as the

231

first rays of sunset hit the little town and made the slate and stone glow golden. The windows glinted, the cobbles shone, and the masts of the boats chimed.

'Wow,' he said. 'Is this it? It's really pretty.'

Polly smiled proudly. 'I know.'

'But you're in the middle of bloody nowhere.'

Behind her, Polly could feel Jayden scowling.

'That depends on where you're standing,' she said. 'A lot of people like it this way.'

'What's it like in the winter?'

Polly thought back to the hammering storms and wild loneliness of earlier in the spring.

'Cosy,' she said quickly.

Chris looked unconvinced and took out his phone, seeming surprised when he couldn't get a signal.

Jayden dropped them off without another word, just a slightly apologetic glance in Polly's direction, which she didn't reciprocate. One thing at a time. She didn't know what she was going to do when she saw Tarnie, but it wasn't going to be pretty.

'I thought we might go for a drink,' she said, wishing suddenly that there wasn't just the one pub in the entire town. But Tarnie was over on the mainland anyway and she hadn't heard from Huckle in weeks.

'Perfect,' said Chris. 'Do they do fish and chips? I'd love some proper fish and chips.'

'They certainly do!' said Polly, glad that, so far at least, he didn't seem to have come to Mount Polbearne just to give her a hard time.

They put Chris's bag upstairs in the flat above the bakery.

It had become a lot more cosy and pleasant since she'd started fixing up downstairs; the ovens kept it toasty warm, and it no longer felt damp and dank as it had done. She'd also – Tarnie had driven her – gone to the storage place one Wednesday afternoon and fetched her pictures, books and rugs, all the things Chris had never wanted in his minimalist paradise. There was now a warm red rug on the floor, and rows of books on rough brick and plank shelves, and some abstract landscapes that Chris had said looked like a child had done them, but Polly had liked them for exactly that reason. Cushions were scattered on the impeccable grey sofa. The effect was cluttered, but inviting and cosy.

'Wow,' said Chris, his face constricting. 'Ha. This is a bit of a change from the Plymouth flat.'

Polly gave him a sideways glance.

'I mean, it's lovely.'

'Tea?' she said, fetching out her mismatched crockery and the leftover buns from lunchtime.

Chris nodded, and she laid the table by the big window, where the sunset was now making an enormous pink and purple display, as if showing off just for them.

'So,' she said gently as she put her cup down.

Chris stared into his own cup, then out of the window.

'You're running that bakery downstairs?' he asked in disbelief.

'Yes,' she said. 'I know it doesn't look like much, and I'm running it for someone else, but you know ...'

'How can you even bake for that many?'

233

Polly shrugged. 'It's just practice. You know … all those weekends …'

She didn't have to finish the sentence. All the weekends he hadn't come home from work, or insisted that they couldn't go out as he was too stressed, or was recovering from a dreadful hangover after attempting to drown his sorrows, a technique that rarely worked well, or for long.

'This is just upscaling.'

Chris shook his head. She could see from his face that he was startlingly, terribly jealous.

'Um, you know, it's not that great,' she said. 'I mean, it is freezing and I have to get up at stupid o'clock and the locals can be REALLY AWFUL and …'

She was babbling, she knew, but she didn't know what else to do.

'Yeah, well, things are going really well for me,' said Chris quickly. 'I've been working with some websites … I mean, mostly for exposure, but it really gets my name out there, you know?'

Polly did know. People getting free creative work, saying it was in return for publicity – who wouldn't dream of not paying their plumber? Or for a loaf of bread, for that matter.

'That's great,' she said. 'And how's your mum?'

Chris frowned. 'Um … she's all right. She thinks I should go and live on my own again. But everywhere to rent is a total shithole. I mean, you got lucky.'

Polly bristled a bit at this.

'It's really hard out there.' His face was contorted, and he was whining like a disappointed child.

'I know,' said Polly, and as gently as she was able said, 'Have you thought about maybe another line of work?'

'What, like making cakes?' Chris scoffed. 'No, you see it's kind of different for me. I'm a professional.'

Polly decided it was best they leave before she hit him with the teapot.

In the pub, with their fish and chips and a bottle of white wine in front of them – fortunately apart from Patrick the vet there was no one else in there she knew – she cleared her throat.

'So,' she said awkwardly, filling their glasses. 'Um. The flat.'

'Yes,' said Chris. 'Right.' His face went a little pink and he cleared his throat, as if announcing something. 'I've been thinking about this. Now that you're earning, I thought you could take the mortgage on fresh. And I'll move back in and look for a job. Then when I'm on my feet again, you can move back to Plymouth and get a proper job, and Bob's your uncle, we'll just go on like before and we'll save the flat.'

Polly took a long swig of her wine. Here was Chris, finally saying the words she'd been dying for him to say for six months – no, longer than that. The last two years. She found herself blinking rapidly.

'But I have a job here,' she found herself saying.

She forgot how convinced she'd been – she'd told Kerensa enough times – that Mount Polbearne was a temporary measure until she got back on her feet; that they were having a trial separation until the good ship Polly and Chris righted itself again.

Plus her wages were hardly going to stretch to rent *and* a mortgage.

'Yeah, but, you know …' Chris gestured around. 'This one-horse town. It isn't you, Pol. It isn't us, you know?'

Polly thought of their joint fantasy: two hip young professionals, living in a fashionable apartment, getting ahead in business, going to smart meetings, trendy bars. That girl … she barely remembered that girl now.

She took a deep breath, turned round and stared out to sea. The lighthouse swept its great beam around, illuminating the cobbled streets, the harbour wall, the seagulls fighting like teenage boys drunk on cider, the little white road signs. She could only just see the jutting, crumbling facade of the bakery on the harbour, gulls soaring overhead.

She steadied herself, looked at Chris, whose face was anxious. She realised that he was worried about her answer. And she realised that she hadn't known – not properly known, deep down – till that precise second exactly what her decision was going to have to be. She had always said the move to Polbearne was going to be temporary. But regardless of the ups and downs, it had come to mean to her much, much more.

'I think,' she said, swallowing hard. 'I think maybe it is me.'

There was a long silence. They both stared at their glasses.

'What do you mean?' said Chris, finally.

Polly felt a painful lump in her throat and suddenly had to fight back tears.

'I mean, I don't think … I don't think I want to go back to how it was.'

Chris frowned. 'You don't want to run a business any more. That's okay, we can't do that anyway, not for two years. But we can still keep the flat with you covering the—'

'No.'

Polly realised how seldom she had said no to Chris. In fact, most of her time with him had been spent trying to make him happy. No wonder, she thought ruefully, she had ended up being seduced by the first bloke who'd come along. That thought made her feel sick and she squashed it back down.

'You're not serious?'

The lighthouse beam swept over them one more time. In the harbour the fishing boat lights came on, and Polly felt a tug deep down as they started chugging their way out to their long night's work ahead. Muriel and her husband passed by on an evening stroll. Sitting on the harbour wall were a couple of early holidaymakers; a boy and a girl with their arms around each other, the boy stealing kisses into the girl's long hair. Overhead, a few stars were starting to pop out in the clear night sky.

Polly shrugged. 'I think ... I think ... I mean, at least for the time being, but—'

'You work in management!'

'But the Little Beach Street Bakery ... I'm doing something I love,' said Polly. 'And I love this place. I can't explain; it's magical.'

Chris made a sour face. 'You're burying yourself to hide from the truth.'

'Maybe I am,' said Polly. 'Maybe I am. That the business failed.' She made her voice as gentle as she could for the next words. 'And we failed, Chris. We tried our best, but we failed.'

He looked up at her, the bags under his eyes heavy and sad.

'Yeah, well, you know, bloody recession, fricking Tories ... We'll get back on.'

'No,' said Polly. She put her hand on his. 'I wasn't good for you. I pestered you and fussed you and you didn't like it. You need someone you can look up to, not someone who runs around after you.'

Chris looked tearful suddenly.

'I just want things to be back how they were.'

Polly remembered suddenly the time when they had just met. He was so handsome, so young and clever, with his port-folio full of art and design, wonderful lettering, ideas. The two of them had looked good together; they were dynamic, out to conquer the world. They were so sure of themselves. They could never again be the people they were back then.

'I know,' she said, feeling heartbroken, and very, very tired. 'I know.'

Chris took the sofa, Polly the bed, but neither of them had any chance of sleep. They both lay awake, staring at the sea in Chris's case, the ceiling in Polly's, as everything went round and round her head. Had she made a terrible mistake by not agreeing to move back to town? Was this her last chance to live a 'normal' life as everyone expected: get engaged to Chris, find a nice little job in an office some-where, maybe one day have a baby? She wasn't getting any younger; if she didn't do it now, would she turn into Mrs Manse? She had to resist the occasional temptation to get up and go and hold Chris and tell him yes, it would be fine, they'd be okay, they could do it, let's just start over. Because she knew, deep down, that it would not be fine.

At four in the morning, Chris gave up and, as quietly as he could, slipped out of the apartment to find something else to do. Polly heard him go, and was about to get up and go after him when she realised, finally, that she was falling asleep, trapped in that sinking paralysis of limbs, and could not go after all.

Polly slept till eleven on Sunday morning and woke up with a start. She couldn't remember the last time she'd had so much sleep; she felt completely fresh, warm, almost brand new. She went to see if Chris had come back in, but there wasn't a trace of him to be found anywhere; it was as if he'd never been there. He was always so tidy. No note, nothing.

She thought back over the previous night with a sense of rising panic before telling herself that no, she had done the right thing. She had made the right choice. She switched on her beloved coffee machine, and felt lighter. As if the worry of what to do about Chris had been an invisible burden she'd been carrying around and was now lifted. Yes, it hurt – and yes, her future was now an open book, anybody's guess. But she had done the right thing, she knew that much. To go back now would be a second failure, and she wasn't sure she would come through that again.

She peered out of the window and suddenly saw a crowd

of villagers staring at her. She gasped and jumped back, checking that her dressing gown wasn't gaping open. What was everyone doing there?

She scrubbed her face and dressed quickly and ran downstairs, suddenly worried. Had someone broken in? Or had one of the local teens done some graffiti? Why was everyone looking at the bakery?

When she got outside, in jeans and a striped T-shirt and bare feet – the day was promising to be scorching – she stopped short and put her hand over her mouth.

Although he was gone – and she felt instantly bad for thinking he had stormed off – Chris had left her something. Restless, unable to sleep, he had gone down to explore the shop in the early dawn light – Polly no longer locked the connecting door between the bakery and the apartment – and stumbled across some old tins of grey and white paint that were stored in the back. With his artistic eye and exquisite taste, he had painted the peeling, cracked exterior a new, soft pale grey – the same colour as her sofa – and in his lovely flowing script had written above the window:

The Little Beach Street Bakery

Proprietor, Ms P. Waterford

Established 2014

Chapter Eighteen

Summer had turned on its full beam, and every day saw families marching across the causeway with buckets and spades and shrimping nets, the children squealiing if the waves made it over the cobbles, everyone hurrying as the tide came in again, the inevitable few who left it too late having to scurry, or hail one of the fishing boys.

Word had got out. The smart couple, Henry and Samantha, had bought a house at the top of the village; a large, rambling Victorian place with a huge garden, a massive greenhouse and hollyhocks climbing the walls. They were constantly bringing visitors over, on the pretext of introducing them to some of the 'best bread in Cornwall' but in reality to show off and swank about how they were the first second-homers to discover the place. They made a big show of how well they knew Polly, using her name constantly and suggesting new flavours for her to try, which she often would.

If the queues kept up, she was going to need an assistant – she was selling out earlier and earlier each day. Mrs Manse, as it turned out, much to Polly's relief, turned out to be both absolutely eagle-eyed about the paperwork – which meant Polly didn't have to do any cashing-up or accounts – and very hands-off as a boss. Polly secretly suspected that the Little Beach Street Bakery was making a lot more money than the other place. At the very least, she had noticed that Mrs Manse had bought a new fridge for cold drinks and a freezer for ice cream, and had cut her bread and sandwiches way, way back. The pasties, of course, remained.

Polly had managed to avoid Tarnie completely, which in a village of fewer than a thousand people was something of an achievement. Sometimes, when the wind was blowing in the right direction, she would hear his gruff tones early in the morning and would groan, because that meant it was time for her to get down to the ovens. She worked and she worked and she worked; her arms grew toned from kneading and lifting, and she fell into bed at night too exhausted to do much else than pass out, which was useful.

Although Tarnie didn't come into the shop, the other fishermen did, and chatted to her and always bought, she noticed, a little bit more than they needed. She figured Tarnie was behaving pretty shabbily given that he owed her a massive apology, but she wasn't going to dwell on it. She threw herself into her baking. She cultivated the sourdough Ted Kernesse had given her – a disgusting yeasty fungus that lived in the fridge and divided itself like a living thing (it was, she reminded herself, a living thing) – and started making a darker, stronger bread called a campagne. It was a hard sell to begin with – people wanted their trusty sliced white – but she persevered with the free samples, knowing herself what an incredibly addictive flavour it had, and sure enough it became one of her best sellers. To placate the traditionalists, she also experimented with a Jamaican brioche that was so sweet it was practically cake. Spread with jam at four in the afternoon, it might be the only thing to trump the local cream tea.

She was clearing up one Saturday afternoon when she heard a familiar noise rattling down the cobblestones.

She hadn't seen much of Huckle at all – she'd guessed it was the busy season for bees or something – but they'd nearly sold out of the four boxes of honey he'd given her to sell on and she needed to pay him. She smiled and went downstairs.

When he saw her, Huckle's face fell.

'What?' she said.

'Oh hon, what's the matter with you?'

Polly searched her head.

'Um, stuff,' she settled on, it being safest. She realised she'd neglected to put on any make-up, and couldn't remember the last time she'd washed her hair. Burying yourself in your work was okay, she realised, up to a point, and perhaps this was the point.

'Where's pretty Polly?' he asked with a half-smile playing around his lips.

'I think you should take me as you find me,' said Polly crossly.

'I know,' said Huckle sadly. 'I'm not meant for the modern age.'

'Where you come from, does everyone look like Dolly Parton?'

'I'm sure there's a happy medium somewhere,' said Huckle cheerily. 'But you'd like Dolly.'

'I would, but she wouldn't approve of my wardrobe.'

'She wouldn't,' said Huckle. 'I shall just politely avert my eyes.'

'HUCKLE!' said Polly, half exasperated, but half flattered that he'd noticed what she looked like; not many people did these days. 'Anyway, hang on, I have some money for you.'

'That is a sweet, sweet sentence I haven't heard for some time,' said Huckle. 'And I have something for you too. But we have to go back to mine, and you'll have to sleep in the spare room; the tide's up tonight.'

'What is it?' said Polly, mystified. 'I don't like it when I can't get home when I want to.'

'Come on, I've been waiting for this! Anyway, what else are you doing?'

'That's not the point.'

She looked around.

'This better be good.'

'It is good. You'll see,' promised Huckle. 'Cancel all your glamorous plans and come with me. And bring the money!'

Huckle had to pick up one or two things in town, which gave Polly an opportunity to quickly wash her hair. She didn't bother too much with the blow-drying, though, not if she was getting in that sidecar again. She opened up her built-in wardrobe, thinking as she did so that she should probably get the rest of her stuff out of storage, or else get rid of it. In a lot of ways, though, it was nice living with so little. She had got used to doing without her ghds or more than one handbag, and she hadn't missed all that stuff a bit.

She rifled through her little-used space – she mostly wore jeans and a T-shirt for working – and was suddenly surprised by how much was actually in there and what she'd once deemed essential. She let her fingers run across smart evening tops, dark work suits and crisp white shirts – had she really ever done so much ironing? The clothes looked uncomfortable, lots of buttons and scratchy material. She could barely remember the Polly who had dressed like this, who had looked like this. She supposed Kerensa could. She and Kerensa used to go and get their nails done together, sometimes even a facial. She laughed to herself at the idea of having her nails done now. She glanced at them; they were squared off and stubby, easier to keep clean when they were in dough all the time.

A waft of her favourite perfume – Chanel's Eau Première – filtered through the air, and Polly had the sudden, weird memory of clearing out her grandmother's cupboards after she'd died. It had been impossible to believe that Granny was dead with the smell of her favourite scent still so prevalent. It was silly, of course; Polly herself hadn't died. But it was a little like looking at the wardrobe of someone from long ago.

She shook her head at her daft ideas as she combed out her hair – it had grown, way down past her shoulders. Normally she just pulled it back into a ponytail, but tonight as it dried naturally it curled, and she let it lie there. Once upon a time she would have ironed those curls out mercilessly, but now she didn't seem to mind them half as much.

At the end of the row of untouched clothes was an old summer dress Polly had forgotten about in the long winter months, and had barely worn before then. It was a faded vintage flower print, on soft cotton, with a full skirt and a pretty boat neck. It wasn't like her at all; she'd bought it on a whim, thinking that when she and Chris weren't working so hard, they'd maybe go and catch a festival, hang out somewhere. Of course, they had never stopped working.

Polly threw the dress on over her head, surprised that it hung loose on her – clearly all that heaving flour about was coming in at least slightly handy – and went and looked at herself in the mirror the only way she could get a full-length view – standing precariously on the side of the bath. Her toenails needed painting, she reflected, but apart from that ... She put on a quick swathe of BB cream, leaving her nose with its little sunshiny freckles (normally she would have submerged them completely), opened her eyes up with a little sooty mascara and added a coral lipstick. She tucked her strawberry-blonde hair, lightened by the sun, behind her ears and gave herself an experimental smile.

'Excuse me, ma'am, but I'm here for Miss Polly Waterford?'

'Huckle, stop it. It's me,' said Polly, whacking him with the box of Jamaican bread she'd brought along.

'Yeah, she normally looks like kind of a drudge, so you, Cinders, cannot possibly be her.'

Polly found herself blushing and looked around before

she climbed into the sidecar. Sure enough, some of the fishermen were gathering in advance of that night's fishing expedition. She was going to get the most terrible reputation. Well, there wasn't much she could do about that. She felt like sticking her tongue out at them all.

'Okay, Cinders,' said Huckle when she had put on her helmet and goggles. 'Chocks away!'

It was the most beautiful evening. Insects hummed and danced in the meadows, the headlights catching them as the bike swung round corners. The sky was violet, huge, the stars popping out. Dusk released the heavy scent of hedgerows and wild poppies, rambling wild roses and the comforting scent of freshly tilled soil, waiting for the new seeds. Polly breathed in deeply. The fragrance was intoxicating. She looked up at Huckle, concentrating on the road, his powerful thighs driving the machine forward. He caught her watching him and smiled, and she instantly indicated that he should concentrate again on the road, smiling to herself and settling back to enjoy the bird calls and the perfumes and the vastness of the sky.

They turned up the rutted track. Huckle had obviously been pretty certain she would come; all round the beautiful little garden outside the cottage were dotted candles in glass holders. In the trees were fairy lights.

'Fairy lights?' said Polly.

'I know, they were here when I got here,' said Huckle. 'I

figured I'd keep using them until we have a major electrical fire.'

But Polly couldn't stay sarcastic for long. The little cottage looked absolutely beautiful. The night was still warm, but Huckle moved ahead, poked a little brazier with a Zippo lighter and it flared into life.

Polly looked at him with narrowed eyes.

'This is all very . . . seductive-looking,' she said.

'I know,' said Huckle, taking her seriously. 'I'm really sorry about that. I only realised just now. I didn't mean it to be; it's just Reuben's out of town. Do you want to go home?'

'I didn't say that,' said Polly. 'Seriously, I'm your second choice after Reuben?'

'No,' said Huckle. 'I was just making it nice for him, otherwise he gets sniffy. I apologise.'

Polly smiled. The night was warm, but she moved closer to the fire anyway; there it was even better.

'Go on then. Show me your great amazing thing. And if this is a motorbike with *two* sidecars, I'm going to be spectacularly unimpressed.'

'Nooo,' said Huckle, disappearing into the house. He reappeared with two flagons and a large corked jug.

'I am already interested,' said Polly.

Huckle placed the jug on the table between them and uncorked the top. Polly leaned forward to smell it, then sat back quickly.

'WHOA,' she said.

'I know,' said Huckle.

'That is . . . what is it?'

'It's mead,' said Huckle proudly. 'Brewed it myself out in

the back. People aren't getting through my honey fast enough. It's peeing off my bees. Now congratulate me on my mastery of English idiom.'

'I dislike a peed-off bee,' said Polly, peering into her flagon as Huckle poured them both generous measures.

'Is this right?' she said. 'Are you meant to drink it in beer containers? Isn't it more like wine?'

Huckle gave her a look. 'Have you never seen any Viking films? You drink it by the pint whilst going AHA!'

'AHA!' they said, clinking flagons.

Polly took a mouthful. It was strong, yes, but it tasted delicious too: warm, sweet, full of honey but with a darker flavour.

'Wow,' she said. She looked at Huckle. 'You know, this is pretty good.'

'Thank you,' said Huckle, beaming. 'It took a lot of … plastic canisters.'

'I think you could sell this too.'

'I like the way you're thinking,' said Huckle.

They chinked again, then Polly remembered to give him the money from the honey sales, which he also liked, and they chatted easily in the darkening air.

Later, they got up and rummaged around for some local cheese to have with the bread Polly had brought, as well as a huge bowl of strawberries Huckle had picked from a nearby farmer's field in return for a couple of jars of honey ('I've gone almost totally to barter,' he said). As soon as Polly stood up, she realised that she was squiffed. That stuff was lethal.

'I think,' she said with some difficulty, 'that someone has stolen my legs.'

'That happens every time I make this,' said Huckle, slurring his already slurred words. 'I must try and brew something that leaves you with your own legs. Or someone else's.'

'I'd like Elle Macpherson's,' agreed Polly, and found herself completely hilarious.

'Oohh!' she said suddenly. 'Look!'

At first she had thought they were sparks from the brazier, now keeping them cosy as the night grew chillier, but as she stared at them they started to take shape, and she saw they were in fact tiny glowing insects.

'June bugs,' said Huckle, then glanced at her. 'Fireflies. I didn't know you got them too till I moved here. Lots where I come from.'

'Neither did I!' said Polly. She stood up, fascinated if a little wobbly. 'They're beautiful.' She watched as the insects traced intricate patterns on the air, leaving behind just a faint impression of their iridescent trajectory. 'Oh wow. I'd like to keep one in a jar, if it wasn't really really cruel.'

'Well, just enjoy them as they are,' said Huckle expansively, waving his arms around. 'Live in the moment. Don't take a photo, don't try and grab it and freeze it for ever. Let's just enjoy the fireflies.'

'And perhaps,' hiccuped Polly, 'another glass of this most delicious mead.'

Later, as the fire burned low and they grew quieter and the fireflies had flown away, Polly found herself getting pleasantly cosy and drowsy, wrapped in a blanket Huckle had brought out for her that smelled of woodsmoke.

'Why did you come here?' she asked lazily. 'I mean, you know ALL about me ... I'm assuming you know all about me?' she said.

'Er, yeah,' said Huckle apologetically. 'Things get around. Sorry. Bad guy. Bad bad guy. Bad guy.'

'You know I had absolutely no idea ...'

'Oh yeah. Bad guy.'

'I would never, ever do that, you know? How could you do that to someone? Then go home to their bed at night?'

'Did you really like him?' asked Huckle gently.

Polly heaved a great sigh and tilted her head all the way back till she was staring at the stars.

'Well, I wasn't in love with him or anything like that. But it had just been so long, you know? And things had been so tough. So I thought, well, hey, this will be a bit of fun. I'm such an idiot. I was with my ex for most of my adult life one way or another, and I ... I don't know the rules. I really don't. They may have totally changed, I have no idea. I'm like one of those rubes who comes to the city for the first time and loses all their money to someone playing three-card monte on a street corner.'

Huckle laughed. 'Yeah,' he said. 'You are the first and only person ever to make a mistake with that kind of stuff.'

Polly smiled wryly. 'Yes, but in front of the entire town and everyone I'd only just met.'

'Whose sympathies, if it helps, lie entirely with you. Jayden is incensed about it. I think he has a Mrs Robinson crush on you.'

'Oi!' said Polly, putting her head down. 'Just "crush" would have been fine, okay?'

251

'Okay,' said Huckle. 'And Tarnie is miserable.'

'Good,' said Polly. 'Oh Lord, that sounds horrible. I just … It was just really embarrassing, that's all. REALLY embarrassing. I feel like … some daft girlie.'

'I don't think you're like that,' said Huckle.

'Oh no?' said Polly, hopefully.

'No. I think you're a daft grown woman.'

Polly hurled a cushion at him and he caught it and laughed.

'Go on then,' she said. 'You know all my grubby little secrets now.'

'All of them?'

She gave him a look.

'Your turn. Men don't just choose to up sticks and move somewhere with no reason. So tell me.'

'Or what? You'll do something bad to a firefly?'

'No. I'll … I'll be very cross with you.'

'I am shaking in fear.'

'And I will tell everyone you pee in your mead.'

'You would not do that.'

'Try me.'

Huckle squinted at her oddly for a minute. Then he looked into the fire and let out a big sigh, stretching out his long legs in front of him.

'Oh what the hell,' he said. 'Maybe it would make it easier to tell someone.'

Polly smiled encouragingly at him.

'If it helps, I'm completely pissed,' she said. 'I'm not going to remember any of it in the morning.'

Huckle laughed. 'Ha, yeah, well there is that. But you can't breathe a word of it to anyone.'

Polly leaned over laboriously and held out her littlest finger.

'Pinkie promise,' she said.

Huckle put out his big warm pinkie and they joined them solemnly. 'Pinkie promise.'

He refilled their glasses.

'Well,' he said. 'Once upon a time . . . I was a management exec in Savannah, which is in Georgia, the state where I grew up. And I liked it. It was full on, no holidays, crazy hours, but I was young and I was good at it and I loved my job, so that was all fine, you know?'

Polly nodded. 'I remember,' she said, then she went quiet so he could talk.

'And I met a girl who worked there – a woman, I should say. Candice. She was . . . is beautiful, really sharp, really switched on.'

So far this was sounding familiar to Polly. She sipped thoughtfully.

'And, well, I fell for her. Hook, line and sinker.'

So that's the kind of woman he likes, Polly found herself thinking, a bit ruefully.

'And she felt the same way, totally, and we made all these plans about how we'd work hard and build up our cash, then maybe get married one day, downsize – I was already so into the honey – and all that.'

Polly nodded. 'Sounds like a great idea.'

'That's what I thought.'

There was a long pause.

'And?'

'Oh. And. Apparently that lifestyle is harder to give up than

I realised. Every year it was "next year, next year", and she'd get promoted again, then I'd get promoted again, then she'd want a cool new Lexus, then a cool penthouse apartment, then we both started travelling a lot for work, then we never saw each other, then it was all expensive restaurants and bars ...'

'This is sounding very familiar,' said Polly.

'And it was fun, you know. Doing that yuppie thing. All the cool spots, lots of people around.'

Polly nodded. It *was* fun.

'So?'

Huckle shrugged. He looked oddly embarrassed.

'Well, after all that, and after all we'd said ... she met someone who made more money than me. And so it turned out that downsizing to the country wasn't exactly what she was after at all.'

'Oh no,' said Polly.

'It's all right,' said Huckle. 'It was my fault, I was completely nuts about her. I must have stifled her really. I was so sure I knew which way our lives would go. I had it all planned out.'

He smiled, a little painfully. Polly thought how she had had it all worked out in her mind too, with Chris.

'So why ... how did you end up here?' she said.

'Hah. I kind of stormed off in a fit of pique ... said I'd do it anyway. Bought the first ticket I could find.'

'You came here by MISTAKE?'

He shrugged. 'My dad was English, I have a passport. I knew Reuben was around here somewhere.' He rubbed his eyes. 'But, yes. Kind of. A bit.'

'But you like it?'

Huckle shrugged. 'Yes, some of it.'

His face looked pained.

'I am a little lonely. God, I can't believe I just said that out loud.'

'It's okay,' said Polly, reaching out and stroking his leg. He looked at her hand, as if he had no idea what it was doing there, and she snatched it away immediately, mortified.

'And I miss the penthouse . . . Savannah's a great town.'

'Sounds it,' said Polly. 'Surely you can swallow your pride now and go back?'

He smiled. 'I guess so. I just . . . it's hard, you know.'

'I do know,' said Polly, looking at him for a long moment. She felt stupid when he got up out of his seat.

'Now don't forget to take some painkillers before you go to sleep tonight; this stuff can really settle on your head,' he said. His voice had changed, as if he was pulling himself out of his memories.

'Thanks,' said Polly, immediately forgetting this advice.

'So yes. Doing something else . . . it definitely makes me . . . it makes me feel better,' said Huckle. 'Definitely better.'

'Good,' said Polly. She poked the dying embers of the fire, then looked at him. Whatever moment had been between them had faded away. But she was glad she knew now, at least; that it was no longer a mystery between them.

'Well,' she said, trying to perk up the mood. 'That's not as bad as I'd thought it would be. I really did think you'd shot a man in Reno just to watch him die.'

Huckle half smiled, but no more than that. He was staring into the fire now, as if he'd completely forgotten she was there. Polly wondered about Candice, what she was like – she'd bet

255

she always had her nails done – and how Huckle's lovely dream of a family in the country had turned so sour. She sighed.

'Well, I'd better turn in,' she said.

Huckle had made her up a lovely little single bed, crisp white sheets tucked in with a heavy embroidered patchwork quilt over the top. It was cosy and fragrant in the little thatched cottage, and she could feel sleep creeping up on her very quickly. Just before she gave in to it completely, she sneaked a last peek out of the tiny mullioned window. Huckle was still exactly where she had left him, staring mournfully into the flames, the empty flagon of mead discarded by his feet.

Chapter Nineteen

At first Polly couldn't figure out where she was. There was a heavy scent of honeysuckle coming through the little window, and a buzzing sound in the air. There was a second wonderful scent too, of coffee brewing, then joined by bacon frying. She sat up happily, then realised, looking at the thoughtfully placed Advil and pint of water beside her bed, that she had forgotten to take her medicine. She did so now. The sun was bright through the curtains.

'Oww,' she said, pushing open the little arched wooden door. Huckle was up already, wearing loose farmer's boy dungarees with no T-shirt. The effect should have been ridiculous but was actually rather lovely; he had a little chest hair, not too much, and it was soft and golden. Polly realised she kind of wanted to stroke it, and promptly put her hands behind her back.

'Morning.'

Huckle smiled his lazy smile at her.

'Hey.'

He seemed in much better spirits than the night before, back to his normal laid-back self.

'How are you?' she said. 'Apart from the dungarees.'

He looked at her for a long moment, then said, 'You know, actually I feel okay. I feel fine. I'm glad I told someone.'

Polly shook her head. 'Maybe you had a lucky escape. Maybe you just weren't right for each other.'

Huckle nodded. 'Yeah. Yeah. Clearly. That's what I try to think ... well, on good days. Yeah. How are *you* feeling?'

'Bad,' said Polly. 'I forgot the Advil and the water and stuff last night.'

'Here,' said Huckle. He poured her a large glass of apple juice. 'Drink this.'

'I thought you Yanks drank orange juice.'

'Your orange juice is unspeakable,' he said. 'It's got bits in it. Your apple juice, on the other hand, just about passes muster.'

Polly gulped the lot down thankfully.

'That's better,' she said. The door to the cottage was wide open and the sun was pouring in. It was a radiantly beautiful day.

'Coffee?'

'Yes!'

'Bacon?'

'Yes!'

'Pancakes?'

'WOW! I think I'm in love with you!' said Polly. It was meant to be humorous but came out suddenly all wrong. 'I mean with pancakes,' she amended hastily. 'You wear dungarees. I'm in love with pancakes.'

'Actually, they're overalls.'

When the pancakes arrived, they were crisp on the out-side, soft and yielding on the inside, served with crackling bacon and a thick swoosh of maple syrup.

'Okay, this is the best breakfast I've ever had,' said Polly through a mouthful. 'Seriously, if you ever think you're get-ting skint, open a B and B. I'd move in.'

Huckle smiled. 'Well I don't think I'm quite there yet. But glad you like 'em.'

After they'd finished, Polly would probably quite happily have crawled back to bed, but Huckle asked if she'd like to come and see the bees, and she agreed that she would, with some trepidation. Huckle had a spare suit and put her in it, then took her down to the hives.

It was fascinating. Huckle set up the smoke machine to calm the bees down when he got in amongst them; he scooped up some of the honeycomb, but not so much that they would get overexcited. He pointed out the great fat queen, unmistakable and so exceptional that Polly goggled at her, feeling fear and fascination in equal measure.

He showed her how to card off the honey from the combs, and let it plop in golden rounds into the jars, with the sticky scent and the buzzing and the wild flowers blooming all around them, and she enjoyed herself hugely.

Just before lunch, though, she knew she had to get back.

She kissed him lightly on the cheek and he drew her in for a hug.

'Thanks,' he said. 'I needed a friend. Can you keep it to yourself?'

'Yes,' said Polly. 'Can you keep it to yourself that I accidentally slept with a married guy even though absolutely everybody within a hundred-mile radius knows already?'

They shook on it.

Even with Huckle's revelations, it still counted as the nicest evening she'd had in a long time, and she had a spring in her step as she walked. Huckle had offered to take her on the bike, but she'd turned him down; she could do with clearing her head, and it was a lovely day.

She had finally made a friend, a proper friend, not some bad fisherman who wanted to lure her to his naughty island. As she thought that, a smile crossed her lips. Just a little one. Really, as Huckle had shown her, it wasn't the worst thing in the world, was it? To let herself be slightly misled by someone. She should chalk it up to trial and error. At least she'd broken her duck. And if everyone in the village thought she was a terrible slag, well, they should try going out in Plymouth on a Saturday night.

It had been a daft thing to do, but it wasn't worth beating herself up about for ever. Life went on.

As she walked – she'd decided to take the coastal route rather than the country roads, which meant striking out across open moorland – she felt the wind building up. Gently at first, but more and more insistently as she went on. Great black and grey clouds, heavy and portentous-looking – the first for weeks – appeared as if out of nowhere, blotting out first a portion, then half, then the whole of the sky. Polly started to move faster as the rain arrived, and then to run, but eventually she stopped and gave in to the inevitable: she was going to get drenched, and there was nothing she could do to stop it. She held her hands up and let the rain course down her body. It was warm, but quite refreshing, a bit like standing in a shower. Hangover completely gone, she was suddenly aware of feeling incredibly free, more alive than she had felt in a long time.

'ARRR!' she shouted loudly, open to the elements, all alone on top of a hill. A part of her was aware that she was being a bit crazy. Another part felt like giving voice to it. It was kind of mad, but nobody could see her up here, and it felt so good too, to get out all the frustrations of the last few months – oh Lord, years.

'RAAAA!' she roared at the sky. 'AARRRGH!' She spun in circles under the huge heavy drops.

'Feeling better?' observed a quiet voice.

It was Huckle, standing right behind her with a huge black umbrella.

'JESUS!' said Polly, jumping out of her skin. 'Where the HELL did you spring from?'

'Er, sorry,' said Huckle. 'I just saw the rain coming on and thought you might need some shelter. I didn't know you were re-enacting *Wuthering Heights* up here.'

Polly was furiously embarrassed.

'Go away,' she said. 'You're like a creepy stalker.'

'Oh come on. I thought it was cute,' he said.

'SHUT UP,' said Polly warningly. Her face felt suffused with red.

'Well, would you like the umbrella?'

Water was getting in her eyes, running down her cheeks, soaking her to the skin. Huckle, slowly at first, then more determinedly, passed the umbrella across. Of course, as he did so, the rain got to him too, and in no time at all, he was nearly as drenched as she was. The huge black brolly hovered uselessly between them, Polly refusing to take it, Huckle refusing to stop offering it to her. Suddenly a great gust of wind snatched it, lifting it high above them over the moor, where it danced and tossed on the air.

Huckle and Polly glanced at each other wordlessly, then both of them dived off after it. Polly's wet hair slapped against her forehead and her shoes squelched as she charged along, feeling as tossed and thrown about by the weather as the umbrella itself, in the heart of the storm. Huckle, his long legs striding fast and far beyond her, his arms wide open to the water and the gusting air, had his head thrown back and was laughing at the craziness of it all. They leapt and threw themselves at the brolly, which always managed to tear itself away from them again, until finally they cornered it when its spokes got caught in a tree. Huckle lifted Polly up without difficulty. Polly grabbed the umbrella and waved it about triumphantly as Huckle gently placed her back on the ground with her treasure. She turned to him, watching the raindrops roll off his long eyelashes, which were surprisingly dark for such a fair-haired man, his blue eyes crinkling, his hair slicked back against his leonine head. She stood for a second in his arms, and suddenly thought it would be the easiest thing in the world to reach up and . . .

No. No, she couldn't. She'd just been through this entire exact thing. Had she or had she not just been yelling about her liberation?

'Actually,' she found herself saying, realising how much colder it was getting all of a sudden, and that her teeth were beginning to chatter. 'Actually you know I think I *will* take that brolly after all.'

Huckle bent down in a courtly way.

'Ma'am, may I walk you home?'

'No,' said Polly, 'You'll miss the tide back.' And she turned and marched happily back towards Polbearne.

Huckle stood and watched her go. Then he swept back his mass of hair out of his eyes, and strode back the other way, towards the cottage.

Chapter Twenty

Polly had never known a nicer bath. She lit the stove, to make the little apartment all toasty and heat up the boiler; then, while that worked itself up, she made up the dough for the morning, with the most immense cup of tea she could muster. She used up all the hot water in the tank by filling the bath to the brim, throwing in the very last of the posh smellies she'd got for her birthday the previous year – she remembered that birthday: they had all gone out to some fancy new restaurant that charged a fortune for tiny cubes of vegetables, and she'd been so nervous about their credit card, even though her friends, led by Kerensa, had insisted on paying for her share – until the entire flat was warm, steamy and scented.

Even though it was only early afternoon, it felt like night-time in the middle of winter; there were no daytrippers today. Polly couldn't believe the speed with which the weather had asserted itself, blowing in across the sea in a tearing rage. Thunder rumbled ominously and lightning rent the roiling sky, occasionally coinciding with the lighthouse beam, which had been switched on early that day. Polly soaked for a long time, reading her book, until she was warm again from the inside out, then put on her oldest, softest cotton pyjamas and woollen socks, and propped herself up at the window to look out at the storm.

Suddenly, to her horror, she saw Tarnie's Land Rover appearing and the boys getting out. They looked miserable, defeated, their shoulders slumped. They couldn't possibly be going out in this, she thought. They couldn't be.

Without thinking, she pulled on her old mackintosh and ran downstairs and out into the worsening wind.

'You can't!' she howled, crying out to make herself heard above the storm. 'You can't be going out in this.'

Tarnie looked at her, and she remembered she was furious with him. His piercing blue eyes were sorrowful.

'Aye, Polly, hello,' he muttered, casting his eyes to the ground.

'Also,' said Polly.

'Aye, reckon,' he mumbled. 'I'm sorry, you know.'

'It was so cruel,' she said, suddenly forgetting the weather, but still shouting. She'd managed to avoid him so successfully, but here she was right in front of him. 'So cruel, you know. You took advantage of me.'

'I know,' said Tarnie, blushing furiously red and shaking his head. 'I shouldn't have. I'm so sorry.'

'My whole life had come crashing down and you made it worse. Why?'

Tarnie looked up then, and his eyes were very blue and clear against the crashing grey sea.

'Because I thought you were so lovely,' he said gently.

The wind went out of Polly's sails completely.

'Well ... That's STILL BAD.'

'I know,' said Tarnie. 'I'm sorry. It was an awful thing. Me and the missus had been going through some hard times and I was ... I was very lonely.' That word again.

'Well you shouldn't have taken it out on me,' Polly said severely.

'No.'

Tarnie scratched the back of his neck. The other fishermen were looking on. It was hard to keep things quiet in a village.

'Can we be friends?' he ventured finally. 'Please? Like I should have kept it?'

Polly waited a second.

'Well, all right,' she said.

Tarnie put his hand out awkwardly and Polly took it.

'Kiss!' shouted Jayden, but Kendall instantly stuck his hand in front of his mate's mouth.

'Well now,' said Polly. 'I don't have anything for you to eat today.'

'Reckon that's all right,' said Tarnie.

Another peal of thunder shook the purple sky.

'You guys are amazing,' said Polly admiringly.

'I hate this job,' said Jayden.

'Must you go out in this?' said Polly, looking up, horrified. 'It's awful out there.'

'Seen worse,' said Tarnie. 'Damn it all.'

Polly looked at him. 'It was very naughty to send Jayden to buy your bread.'

'I know,' said Tarnie. 'But come on. I have to live without you; I don't think I could bear to live without your sand-wiches too.'

'Are you going to be good from now on?' she said.

Tarnie nodded furiously. Then he took a book out of his back pocket: her *Alice in Wonderland*.

'Thanks,' he said. 'I really did enjoy it.'

'Good,' said Polly, slipping it inside her mac. Big globules of rain were falling on them. 'I still can't believe you're going out in this.'

'It's just weather,' said Archie, loading up. 'Just the wind and the rain.'

'Well, be careful out there.'

'She's a stout little ship, she'll outrun it,' said Tarnie.

'Aye, and so's your wife,' shouted Kendall, and the boys guffawed. Tarnie ignored them, and cursed roundly, and Polly backed away.

She watched them clamber into their yellow oilskins, clip-ping their nets and checking the winch. Suddenly their huge yellow sou'westers made a lot of sense. Inside the tiny galley, someone had already set tea to brew.

'Godspeed,' she said, under her breath, then she turned and left, back up to where her bathwater was still waiting (she'd kept it to wash some clothes in) which was thankfully still hot.

Polly couldn't concentrate on anything that evening, think-ing of the little fleet bobbing out on the ocean, the boats so tiny under such a furious sky. Maybe the fish were easier to

267

catch when the waters were swirling and bouncing like this; maybe they couldn't sleep either. She tried to phone Kerensa and then her mum for comfort and a chat, but she couldn't get any reception at all – the storm must be interfering with the masts – and she finally gave up.

She'd expected to be awakened at the usual early hour – she rarely needed to set her alarm – by the boats coming back and the fishmongers' vans rattling up the cobbles. That night, however, her sleep had been disturbed, by crashing thunder and heavy seas. At one point she'd woken up completely knotted in her blankets, unable to breathe, convinced she was on the point of drowning; she could feel the ocean pulling her down, the boat collapsing above her, everything disintegrating into heavier shades of blue and black, the panic and the twisting. She was drenched in sweat, her heart thudding in her chest, her eyes wide open. The storm was still raging around the house, and she jumped suddenly as something hit the window. To her horror, she realised it was a wave, thrown with incredible force right over the harbour wall, across the street and up to the first floor of the building, as if a huge being had simply picked up a handful of water and hurled it at her full force. The noise was tremendous.

When she'd finally calmed down, she fell back into a calmer sleep, filled with the heavy scent of bees and a quiet buzzing. And when she awoke, it was indeed to her phone buzzing with messages from the intermittent signal, and the great clouds clearing away, the storm blowing itself out. She jumped up in panic, realising immediately that she had slept in, that it was late.

She grabbed her phone: 7.30. Damn, damn, DAMN. The

first loaves should have been in two hours ago; she had to open up in half an hour. There wasn't even time to make coffee; she had to move, and fast. She pulled on a top and jeans, and galloped downstairs, where she turned the ovens up as high as they could go, heated the wood-burner up (she kept it smouldering all night, otherwise it would take too long to heat in the morning) and hammered out her loaves on their racks without her usual care or finesse. There would not be much choice today.

She finally had them all in and was starting on the rolls when she glanced out of the front window and noticed that there were a lot of people out there. At first she thought they were waiting for her to open up, but they were facing away from the bakery, all of them peering out to sea. Nobody was speaking, nor really moving, except to occasionally mutter something into their telephones, or stare at them as if they had some kind of an answer.

'ALL HANDS!' she heard.

She turned the 'Closed' sign to 'Open', pinging the door as she pulled back the lock and opening it on to vicious grey skies and heavy clouds. No wonder she had slept in; the sun had not come up at all.

'What is it?' she asked Patrick, who was standing there with his three dogs, out for their morning constitutional. But when she followed his gaze, she realised. There was nothing in the harbour. No boats at all, apart from the dinghies belonging to the weekend potterers and the old lags.

'The fleet,' she said in shock, and Patrick nodded as she put her hand out to steady herself. 'Oh my God, where's the fleet?'

'We're waiting to find out, Pol,' said one of her older

269

regulars. 'They say they've got one or two up Looe way, managed to beach themselves in the night.'

He looked at the sky, still grey, the wind still pulling at the trees, the rain still plopping down.

'I reckon they can head back now.'

Polly's heart was in her mouth.

'Oh God, but Tarnie said he'd get ahead of the storm. He said.'

Patrick touched her arm reassuringly.

'I'm sure he did. I'm sure he's washed up, having a big English breakfast somewhere.'

'Phone him,' said Polly sharply, but Pat shook his head.

'The phone masts are down,' he said. 'Last night was a doozy. No one can get through to anyone.'

Polly's hand went to her mouth. She turned towards the end of the harbour wall closest to the causeway.

'ALL HANDS!' she heard a man's voice shout once again in the distance. Several figures were charging along, pulling on yellow oilskins, heading for the white RNLI shelter. Then they were bringing the bright orange boat on its runners straight down into the freezing water with a splash and jumping on board.

'Why didn't they go out before?' Polly asked crossly. 'Why are they only going out now?'

Patrick turned to her seriously.

'They've been out three times,' he said. 'This is the fourth search today. When they run out of fuel or can't go any further, they come back.'

'Oh God,' said Polly. 'Oh God. I'm sorry. And they haven't found them?'

'Not yet,' said Patrick, grimly.

'One of the village teenagers came tearing up shouting, 'There's a wreck! There's a wreck over on Darkpoint Bay! A big 'un, too!'

Patrick stiffened. 'Oh no. That'll bring folks out in force.'

'One of the fishing boats?' said Polly in horror.

'Neh, a great big cargo ship! Full of stuff an' all!'

Several of the young men who had up until now been looking tired from their stint on the lifeboat suddenly appeared a lot more awake.

'The police will be down,' warned Patrick. 'You loot it and you know where you'll end up.'

Following the others blindly, Polly walked across the causeway and over the top of the headland. At first, she couldn't work out the scale of what she was witnessing. It was as if a skyscraper had fallen sideways on to the land. Part beached, but part submerged too, it was the largest thing she had ever seen. It must have been more than two hundred metres end to end, and looked hideously unnatural lying there: a gigantic supertanker loaded with crates, which were now floating about on the surf.

'Fuck,' said Patrick sharply. 'Oh God, please let there not be oil.'

'What about the crew?' said Polly anxiously. She narrowed her eyes and could just about make out six or seven tiny, frantically waving figures sitting on the front end of the prow.

'We'll get the doc out,' said Patrick. 'But meanwhile ...'

Polly looked at him. 'Can I help? I don't think I can just hang about.'

'Of course,' said Patrick. 'Oh Christ. If there's oil ...'

Polly could barely take it in as they scrambled down the cliffside with the other villagers. Muriel was there from the shop.

'Oh my, those poor men,' she said. She looked around. 'They used to do this on purpose, you know,' she told Polly.

'What do you mean?'

'Wreckers, you know? They used to show a light to lure ships ashore. Then kill the sailors and take the swag off the boats. Was a huge living round here.'

'You are kidding?' said Polly. 'No wonder everyone looks so nervous.'

The real problem, they saw as they reached the beach, would be getting the men off. The closer they came, the more immense the structure appeared. Sure enough, a helicopter from the nearby air-sea rescue base could soon be heard flip-flipping its way over the coastline. The lifeboat was bobbing round the bottom of the ship: it must have looked like the side of a vast cliff from down there.

'I wonder if it's going to land,' Patrick said, looking up at the sky. But as the helicopter hovered there, they saw a sling rope descend with a man attached to it.

'Wow,' said Polly. The men on top of the sunken ship were waving their arms excitedly. She could make out one lying there, obviously injured.

'You know,' said Patrick. 'What everyone could really do with is some tea and probably something to eat. Do you think you might be able to . . .'

'Open the shop?' said Polly before he had even finished the thought. 'I probably should, shouldn't I? There's going to be loads of people down here.'

272

'Especially if there's oil.'

'Oh God.'

The men on top of the sunken ship were loading their injured comrade into the sling with the man from the helicopter. People were filming it on their phones. Polly wanted to watch, but she saw the sense in what Patrick was saying – people were going to need a lot of tea, the media was going to be here and she had bread in the oven. She turned round to leave.

The other thing about having to hare back to the shop, even if she was missing all the excitement, was that she was instantly so busy she didn't have much time to think about Tarnie and the boys, out there somewhere. Where? The sea was calmer now; they could make it back if they tried. Were they drifting? But why hadn't they been picked up by now? Everyone was out looking for them; she'd heard it on the radio. The man on the radio was also saying it was an unprecedented storm, far worse than forecast. There were calls for the meteorological services to explain themselves, and fears for insurance companies.

Polly filled an old urn that she found in the back of the shop, and Muriel brought four boxes of dusty, unsold, commemorative Mount Polbearne teapots, a ton of plastic cups and some milk from the minimart. They carried down the table from upstairs and set it up in front of the bakery, offering free tea and bread to anyone who needed it. The boys who were doing shifts on the RNLI boat came back chilled and shivering and despondent; helicopters were covering the area, but the fishing zones were widespread. Television crowds had already sprung up, even though the causeway was barely passable. They were taking the long way round by boat, or forcing SUVs through the water, however dangerous this was. The storm had been widespread, but Polbearne and its men had taken the brunt of the devastation; they had been ground zero.

Finally, at 11 a.m., there was some good news: *Free Bird*, one of the ships in the fleet, had let off its emergency beacon and the rescuers had somewhere to head for. The boat had been blown more than thirty kilometres from its normal fishing grounds; its electronic equipment had been knocked out, its mast was broken and all the nets were gone. No one on board had seen *Trochilus* or the other two boats.

Free Bird was towed back to shore, and crowds lined the harbour to cheer it in. Crying wives held up children, who were unsure what was going on but were taking happy advantage of the free buns and cuddles. Polly looked up from handing out food – she had put some more loaves in, and a large batch of buns; she would have to square it with Mrs Manse later, but she didn't know what else to do – and checked her phone for the millionth time for a signal. Oh God. It might technically be summer, but the water was so cold out there in the depths, certainly cold enough to kill a man. With a start, she remembered her dream the night before: being pulled down, far into the depths, the light fading and turning to black. She found her hands shaking; it couldn't have been a vision, surely. She didn't believe in those sorts of things.

The day went on endlessly. At two, rescuers found the

survival capsule – a kind of tent boat – of the *Lark*, with all five men on board, bobbing towards Devon. The *Lark* itself had sunk without a trace; they had only just made it out in time. They were driven back to Polbearne by the Devonshire police, quiet, pale and shaking as they were met by their families. Likewise the *Wiverton*, whose emergency beacon had got stuck and hadn't worked. An eagle-eyed helicopter pilot spotted the bobbing neon-yellow shape in the water and managed to winch the men to safety.

'HEY!'

Polly looked up, bleary-eyed. She had baked and handed out food all day, waiting, waiting for news. She blinked. This was the last person she had expected to see.

'What are *you* doing here?'

Kerensa made an innocent face. 'You're joking, aren't you? They've filled the place with unbelievably hot helicopter pilots.'

She came closer to Polly.

'Are you okay?'

Polly shrugged. 'One of the boats isn't back yet.'

'Is it the one with the sexy beardy?'

Polly swallowed and nodded. Several people from the village came up to pat her shoulder and thank her for her contribution.

'Move over,' said Kerensa, and she started buttering rolls. 'I can't believe you aren't charging for this. It's no way to run a business. Actually you should charge treble to all the rubberneckers.'

Polly gave her a look.

'Okay, okay, just saying.'

A substantial figure approached slowly, holding a large tray. Polly squinted in the watery sunlight.

'Who's that?' asked Kerensa. 'Oh, is it the old boot?'

'Ssh,' said Polly as Mrs Manse came into earshot. She looked at what Polly was doing and sniffed. Polly bit her lip, worried that she was going to get a telling-off. This wasn't her business, after all; she didn't get to make these kinds of decisions. Mrs Manse surveyed the makeshift stall, surrounded by people – it had become something of a focal point – and harrumphed crossly. Then she banged down the large tray. It held the entire day's selection of cream horns and fancies.

'I'll need that box back in the morning,' was all she said before turning round and marching back up the road.

'Well, well,' said Kerensa, as Polly started handing out cakes to hungry crew and passing children.

As evening fell and the RNLI boat came back for the sixth time, empty-handed, Polly felt her fears beginning to grow again. During the day, as the other boats had been recovered without much worse than some bruised ribs and a couple of broken wrists, cuts and bruises here and there and a bit of exposure, her hopes had steadily risen until it had felt as if any second now Tarnie and his boys would turn up in a police car, full of stories about their adventure.

But it was getting late. The rescued fishermen who'd managed to prise themselves away from home were all in the pub, and the rest of the villagers and the media had gathered round to hear their stories – which would inevitably get more and more thrilling as the evening went on, and the boys became braver in their cups.

Every tea bag, every drop of milk, every last bun was gone when Polly shut up shop and packed everything away.

'Come on,' said Kerensa. 'Let's take a walk. I want to see the salvage boat anyway.'

'The tanker?'

'Uh huh.'

'You want to see a boat lying on its side?'

'Now you put it like that – yes.'

Polly didn't want to go to the pub, didn't want to hear about everyone else's close brush with death, endure people asking her if she'd heard anything, assuming she would have because of course they all knew about her and Tarnie … No, she couldn't do that.

'Okay,' she said.

The sky was now soft and golden-hued. The sea was quietening down. It was almost impossible to believe the force and power of what had ripped through just a few short hours before. Polly had never given the weather much of a thought when she had lived in Plymouth. It was wet or dry, that was all. But here she lived so close to the thin line between the land and the sea. The sea dictated everything: whether they could cross the causeway, whether the men could work, even whether she could leave the building. It was part of the warp and weft of everyone there. As she and Kerensa tramped across the dunes in silence, she understood finally what it actually meant to have the sea running through your veins.

The other side of the headland was still buzzing with

people too; Polly hadn't seen such crowds in months. Police were setting up a cordon – she wondered why, until Kerensa pointed out that it would be to stop looting.

'But if it's all gone overboard anyway, why can't people just have some?' said Polly.

'Because they'd fight and steal and because the next time a boat appeared on the horizon they'd wreck it?' suggested the pragmatic Kerensa.

'No they wouldn't,' said Polly, but some of the teens down on the beach looked a bit tasty, almost daring the police to let them have a go. On the upside, there didn't appear to be any oil.

'What are those?' she asked, pointing to where some things were bobbing up and down in the water, tiny against the looming, ominous outline of the vast ship.

'I don't know,' said Kerensa. 'Let's go and have a look.'

They scrambled down to the beach, where a policeman told them to get back. Just as they were about to do so, there was a sudden loud noise and a ridiculously flashy long-nosed boat charged into view. It was made of pale brown wood and looked like something from the 1950s, but it moved like a bullet. In the back were luxurious leather seats and a low bow. It turned in front of them in a flashy arc, sending up a massive spray of water into the air.

'Yeah, Officer?' came a loud, grating familiar voice. 'We're here to pick up these chicks.'

'Chicks?' said Polly.

Kerensa had already run forward to have a look. In the beautiful boat were Reuben, driving, and Huckle.

The policeman waved the girls on.

'Don't climb on the wreck,' he shouted. Orange patrol boats and white police boats were circling it anyway, protecting it from scavengers.

'I'll buy it,' said Reuben crossly, reversing close into shore so the girls could splash aboard. Huckle stretched out a hand to help them in.

'Nice,' said Kerensa, looking round approvingly at the walnut-lined interior.

'It's my Riva,' said Reuben. 'It cost eight hundred thousand dollars; it's just one of my little boats.'

'Actually, I hate it,' said Kerensa, turning away from him disdainfully.

'Hey,' Huckle said gently to Polly. The way she looked was worrying him: there was nothing there behind her eyes, no ready smile or warm glance. 'How are you?'

'Have you been looking for them?' asked Polly urgently.

'No,' said Reuben. 'We thought today would be a good day to take a pleasure fucking cruise.'

'Ignore Reuben,' said Huckle, putting his hand on her arm. 'Of course we have.'

Polly shook her head. 'I couldn't get you on the phone. Where are they? Why can nobody find them?'

'They're probably at the bottom of the ocean, like, being eaten by sharks?' said Reuben. He put the boat in gear.

'Shut up, rude friend,' said Kerensa.

Reuben looked at her.

'You're very attractive to me,' he stated loudly and with no conceivable sense of embarrassment whatsoever. 'What expensive gifts do you like?'

Kerensa ignored him and sat as far away in the boat from

him as possible. They moved slowly ahead. At first Polly couldn't quite make out what was holding them up. Then she saw that they were pushing through something. It was very peculiar, but the water was absolutely full of . . .

'Are those . . .' she said, suddenly roused to action.

Huckle looked at her and gave a half-smile. 'I know. Everything else must have sunk. But . . .'

Spread out for miles, under a pinkening sky, were thousands upon thousands – uncountably many – of little yellow rubber ducks. Some had moustaches, some had pink hats, some were dressed as golfers, or demons, or were wearing policemen's helmets, but they were all little yellow ducks.

'They must have been in one of the crates,' said Huckle. 'And burst free.'

'The ducks ESCAPED?'

'Kind of.'

'Look at them!' said Kerensa. 'Roaming free!'

'Not so cool for Toyota,' said Huckle. 'According to the internet, they had a huge shipment of cars on this boat. I don't think they'll be driving out of here.'

They all looked down, wondering morbidly what was beneath the boat.

'I'm going to open a diving school here,' said Reuben suddenly. 'It'll be the best diving school in the world. People can dive down and pretend to drive underwater cars.'

'That's a shit idea,' said Kerensa.

'Hush,' said Huckle. Polly didn't say anything at all.

They pushed through the field of yellow ducks, bobbing up and down on the water, and as they cleared the headland, Polly gasped.

It looked like a regatta. Right across the horizon, as far as the eye could see, there was nothing but boats. Tiny rowing boats, great racing sloops, fat pleasure cruisers, bright orange rescue boats, little black tenders. Every one of them patrolling the water, looking for a sign, looking for a clue, looking for the lost fishermen.

'Oh my God,' said Polly.

The Riva joined them, cruising past the little island – Polly could barely look at it – and onwards up to the main channel, where they would have to watch for ferries. They waved at other boats as they passed, but mainly kept their eyes on the water for any trace – a lifejacket, a piece of cloth, a floating radio transmitter, a piece of mast – of something that would give them a clue as to the whereabouts of the missing boat.

Afterwards, Polly would remember this trip as if it lasted for days, even though it was only a few hours. She trailed her hand in the water – it was still warm despite the sun starting to go down – desperately scanning the horizon and staring beneath the waves, as if she could see something there if she gazed hard enough. Reuben would open up the throttle and shoot them to another space and they would look again, then go on . . .

Polly couldn't believe that Tarnie – so tough and hard, yet vulnerable underneath – could possibly be gone. He was the best captain in the fleet; all the others said so. He was so strong. He wouldn't have let anything happen. And Jayden, so mouthy and so young, who hated fishing; and little Kendall. But they'd been raised to it; salt water ran through their veins. They had to come back, she thought fiercely; they had to.

She scrubbed at her eyes, then trained them on the horizon again, squinting so hard into the sun she could barely see.

'Darling. Wrinkles,' said Kerensa, rubbing her back. She could see how distraught Polly was; obviously concerned for the young men she'd met, and horrified by the disaster.

Polly looked at her uncomprehendingly.

'Don't squint,' Kerensa told her.

She called up front.

'Us girls are going to look for the boat away from the sun. You boys do the sun side. You look good with crow's feet.'

'I look good in anything,' said Reuben, who was sporting a horribly bright pair of pricey Oakley sunglasses.

'Is that what your girlfriends tell you?' said Kerensa.

'Yeah,' said Reuben. 'And they're all models, so they should know.'

'That's right,' said Kerensa. 'When they're coked out of their heads at parties wearing two plastic bags for shoes and a swan on their heads.'

Reuben pouted. 'You obviously don't get invited to those parties.'

Kerensa gave Polly a look, but she was miles away and didn't seem to hear what anyone was saying. Huckle watched her with concern. He wanted to put his arm around her shoulders: she was looking cold, and the sea was picking up again. The sun was setting and a chill had settled. But he didn't want to send mixed messages, didn't want to startle her. Instead he very gently touched her hair.

'Hey,' he said.

She looked up at him, her eyes brimming with unshed tears.

'We have to find them,' she said.

'We're doing everything we can,' pointed out Huckle.

Reuben had a fully packed hamper with chilled champagne and fresh lobster and smoked salmon sandwiches, but nobody felt like eating. Instead they continued to cruise until it was nearly pitch black, a heavy navy darkness hanging in the air. The sea was growing rougher again, and a man with a loudspeaker hailed them from a helicopter, shouting at them to go home, that the RNLI would continue the search.

'We can't leave them out here for another night,' said Polly, her teeth chattering.

'We have to,' said Huckle. 'Otherwise the RNLI will be looking for us too.'

He took off his jacket and put it round her shoulders. She didn't notice. He looked at Kerensa.

'I'm worried about her,' he said.

'I'll take her home,' said Kerensa, cuddling Polly close.

Huckle would rather have taken her home himself; he didn't want Kerensa getting her drunk on wine and making her feel worse, but he didn't say anything. They had one of Reuben's cars parked up on the mainland and would bring the boat again tomorrow.

The harbour was still busy and everybody anxious when they got back: police, press, and people washing down their boats, everyone asking each other if they had any more news. Kerensa hustled Polly upstairs and into a hot bath and made her some cheese on toast, which Polly left untouched. Then Kerensa, knackered, suggested bed – it was after ten – but Polly refused. She let Kerensa have her bed, and sat by the window in the sitting room, googling the news endlessly; trawling Twitter for updates on her little phone. She watched as the crowd finally dispersed for the night, and the lights winked out along the harbourside. She felt desperately tired, but when she closed her eyes all she could see was Tarnie's chiselled, serious face, his bright blue eyes, the cheery youth of his crew; she heard his voice telling her of the peace he only ever felt out at sea, under the stars.

'Please,' she found herself saying. 'Please.'

She must have dozed in her chair, because the next time she opened her eyes, the stars had moved in the sky and the earth felt muffled. She stood up and looked out of the window. There was the familiar figure, standing silhouetted on the harbour wall.

As if in a dream, Polly moved to the door, pulling a blanket off the sofa, unable to help herself.

Outside, the moon made everything brighter than it had seemed inside; it was quite easy to see. The waves were high again, pounding the harbour wall, but nothing like as bad as they had been the night before. It was cold, though; she wrapped her checked blanket around her head and shoulders and tried not to think about how cold it would be out at sea.

She moved closer to the figure. Mrs Manse, as usual, was standing as still as a statue. Polly swallowed, but did not speak, simply standing beside her.

After five minutes of scanning the horizon, of waiting for the lighthouse beam to swing round, Polly felt her teeth begin to chatter.

'This is how it is,' came the voice from beside her. Mrs Manse didn't sound her usual snappy, angry self. She sounded resigned, sad, serious. 'This is how it is. We stand and we wait. We women. This is what we do.'

Polly looked at her.

'Does it help?'

Mrs Manse shrugged. 'It doesn't bring them back.'

Polly nodded. 'But you think it might?'

Mrs Manse was silent for a long time. The lighthouse beam swung round again. Finally she spoke.

'I don't know what else to do,' she said.

Polly bit her lip.

'I always thought,' said Mrs Manse quietly, 'that if I don't come one night, that will be the night he comes home ... with the very last of his strength, only just enough to climb the harbour wall ... and if I'm not here to help him, he won't make it.'

Polly understood that completely.

Mrs Manse turned suddenly, her large body stoic and unmoving in the wind.

'Please,' she said, in more urgent tones. 'Please go home. Don't get like me.'

'But I need to wait for them,' said Polly.

Mrs Manse shook her head. 'Not like this,' she said, with desperation in her voice. 'Please. Not like this. Don't do this to yourself.'

Polly pulled the blanket more tightly round her.

'I can't think of anything else.'

'But wishing doesn't do it,' said Mrs Manse crossly. 'Don't you see? Wishing doesn't do it.' She looked Polly straight in the face. 'Please,' she said, imploring her now. 'Please go home.'

Polly gazed out one last time, scanning the horizon. Her head felt fuzzy, full of cotton wool.

'Please,' said Mrs Manse. 'Don't. Don't be like me.'

Polly looked at the old woman, who, shaking now, was so desperate to escape from the trap of her life, but so unable to. It was like Polly was suddenly waking up. What was she doing? This wouldn't help Tarnie, or anybody else.

'Can you ... Do you want to come home with me?' she said. 'Have some tea?'

'I can't,' said Mrs Manse, shaking her head. 'But you can. Please. Go. While you still can.'

'I can't leave you out here.'

'You have to,' said Mrs Manse. 'It's all right. I know what I'm doing.' She bravely attempted a half-smile, her eyes still on the dark horizon.

Without thinking about it, Polly put her arms around the woman and gave her a tight squeeze, then she pressed her lips to Gillian Manse's lined cheek.

Chapter Twenty-One

Back in the flat, Polly settled in her chair again, warming up with the blanket over her. Oh Lord, where were they? A part of her thought they couldn't possibly survive another night out there, another night like this. She tried to imagine them dead; all their energies and worries dispelled into nothing. The idea of them blanked out was odd, shocking. She had been here less than four months, and already they were part of her life.

At about five she must have dozed off again, because when she woke up, it was to a huge noise, and light was streaming in.

There was a bang. Then another bang. Polly jumped. What the hell? What was happening now? Her first thought was that the big boat was breaking up in the water, being pulled apart by the waves. But the noise was closer to home. Then she thought it was the fishermen, hungry and home, crashing at the door. Or, a darker side of her suggested, returned drowned, banging on the window . . .

Her eyes popped open in a huge adrenalin rush of panic and fear.

It took her a few moments to focus as dawn light flooded the room. The bang came again. She looked at the window, and gasped.

Outside, a small black bird with a large orange beak was frantically trying to get her attention.

She ran to open the window. It couldn't be. It just couldn't be. But there it was: on his leg – grubby and covered in who knows what from what had evidently been a long journey – was a plastic seal, with the words 'Huckle's Honey'.

'NEIL!' she screamed, as the window went up and the little puffin hurled himself into her arms. 'NEIL!'

The bird flapped his wings happily and made an eeping noise. Polly covered him in kisses. He smelled a little oily and fishy and the best thing ever as she shed tears on to his feathery head. He put up with the affection for quite a while, rubbing the side of his head frantically against her finger, but his eyes were darting around the room.

'Are you hungry?' said Polly, realising. 'Of course you are. You've flown a REALLY long way. Come on.'

Her untouched supper was at the top of the bin, so she fished it out and put it on a plate. Neil eeped happily and dived into the food. Once he'd eaten his fill and drunk water from a saucer, he flew happily round the sitting room, as if rechecking his territory, returning every now and then to peck at the crumbs.

'I am so pleased to see you,' Polly said, unable to stop her happy grin as he returned to perch cheerfully on her shoulder, like a pirate's parrot. 'You've got too thin.'

She tickled his tummy.

'Not enough white carbohydrates. Too much seaweed and fish. Better for your brain, but you still came back, huh?'

Kerensa appeared, yawning, at the doorway.

'Are you talking to a bird?' she said. 'Or am I still asleep?'

'Not just any bird,' said Polly. 'Look! It's *my* bird! He flew right across the county to come back to me! He made it all the way! Neil, you're amazing.' She smothered him in kisses.

'Er, okay,' said Kerensa, recoiling slightly. She glanced around the room. 'Any news?'

Polly grabbed her phone.

'No messages,' she said. 'The system's back up. But there's no ...'

All her joy at seeing Neil again suddenly evaporated. Her whole body slumped. 'Oh GOD, Kerensa. Oh God.'

'I'll put the kettle on,' said Kerensa hurriedly. 'A cup of tea. And something to eat.'

Polly slumped back into her chair, Neil hopping all over her making concerned noises. As Kerensa went to put on the kettle, however, they heard a noise. A strange noise coming from outside.

'What's that?'

It was the tolling of a bell from the old ruined church. It was the only piece of the steeple still standing. Not pealing, as Polly heard on Sundays, when people came from all around to the ancient place of worship that some said pre-dated Christianity altogether. It was not wedding bells, or happy, joyful Easter bells. This was a low, repeated tolling, a dong dong dong. It sounded dolorous and sad.

'What *is* that?' repeated Kerensa, forgetting the tea. They both pulled on their clothes – Polly couldn't remember seeing Kerensa with bed-head before – and ran downstairs, Neil in Polly's arms.

Everyone else in the village was also down on the harbour, milling around, rubbing their eyes, some in pyjamas, some hastily pulling on mismatched jumpers. It was just after 6 a.m.

At first, there was nothing to see. Then, slowly, a tiny dark shape appeared on the horizon. It picked up speed gradually, then came into focus.

'Bloody hell,' said Polly.

A murmuring started up amongst the crowd.

The boat arced back and forth over the waves, which were just starting to glisten in the sunlight.

'It's almost like they're … showing off,' said Kerensa. 'Hmmm.'

And sure enough, as the boat came closer, they could see that it was the Riva.

'But they came in last night,' said Polly.

'They dropped you off last night,' said someone who'd obviously been there. 'Then they went out again.'

'In the dark?'

As if in answer, the Riva turned, and the girls caught sight of a huge spotlight attached to the front.

The boat was getting closer and closer, setting up plumes of surf. Finally, the bell still tolling its deep, ponderous note, it whizzed to a flashy halt in front of the harbour wall. Reuben waved merrily from the driver's seat as Polly, and everyone else, frantically checked the number of people in the back.

Not counting Huckle's yellow head, there were four passengers.

Four.

But the fishing boat that had chugged out of Polbearne two nights ago had left with five people on board.

Chapter Twenty-Two

Everyone at the harbour wall immediately surged forward in silence. The entire village was there. Two ambulances were lined up waiting. Huckle was off the boat first, looking tired but pleased, and put down his arm to help the other men up on to the jetty.

First was Archie, the softly spoken bosun. His face was pale grey and drawn, his eyes dancing around the harbour as if he didn't recognise where he was. The paramedics ran forward with silver blankets. As he limped his way very slowly up the pier, everybody started to clap. Somone surged forward with a cup of tea to press into his hand, and somebody else gave him a tot of whisky.

Next was Kendall, looking even younger under his big yellow hat. His mother came charging down the cobbled road in her slippers, screaming and yelling, and his four brothers – all of whom had been on board the other fishing boats that had already safely returned – let out great cheers and yells. Polly couldn't see over people's heads, and even with Neil pecking at them, she couldn't get through the throng to see what was happening. Her heart was pounding harshly through her chest, her breath coming in gasps as she struggled to see.

John was next, and there was a collective gasp as his two young children ran to him, screaming, 'Daddy! Daddy!' He was wobbly on his feet as he knelt down and let them fly into his arms. Polly glanced over the heads of the crowd and spied Mrs Manse, standing back. Her face was as impassive as ever.

Finally, strapped to a stretcher that two ambulancemen had taken on to the jetty, came Jayden, looking very pale and drained, one leg at a strange angle under its blanket. He was barely conscious.

And then the boat was empty.

Without thinking, Polly charged through the crowd towards the jetty to see for herself, to check – and was caught, suddenly, strongly, in the huge bear-like arms of Huckle, who held her tight in his strong embrace.

'What?' she said, briefly struggling, but Huckle was so big and strong, there wasn't much she could do. He twisted her close to him and whispered, 'Hush now' in her ear. 'Hush.'

Still wriggling, Polly turned her head, and suddenly she understood. Because standing at the empty boat, keening, her entire body doubled over in a paroxysm of grief, was a petite red-headed woman, and Polly knew instantly who she was.

'Oh my God,' said Polly. 'Oh my God.'

'We're not done,' said Huckle fiercely, exhaustion clear in every line on his face. Indeed, the lifeboat was already firing up down the slip. But Polly, her eyes clouded by tears, was looking over at the returned fishermen, in a huddle with their families, friends, reporters. Their faces, after the first excitement at being home, were grim. Polly found she couldn't stay where she was and indicated to Huckle. They limped over together.

Kendall was talking. His young face had aged ten years. Someone was supporting Tarnie's . . . Polly couldn't think of her as his widow; she could barely think at all. Her insides had turned to ice water; it was the worst, the most terrifying news she could ever have conceived of.

Kendall was incoherent with grief, even as the television cameras rolled in his face.

'He wouldn't . . . he couldn't . . . He had to get Jayden on, he wouldn't let him . . . It was all . . .' He dissolved into weeping. Polly had to put it together herself, later, from the newspapers, as she and Kerensa sat silently in the flat, staring out at the empty harbour, the milling journalists, the confused tourists.

When the *Trochilus* had reached the centre of the storm – it was far worse than the reports had predicted; worse, in fact, than the region had seen for thirty years, a catastrophic differential of high and low pressure colliding at speed – their mast had broken and they had realised their situation was hopeless. Polly imagined them being tossed about like driftwood on waves higher than a three-storey building, lifting them up and hurling them violently down again. She couldn't bear it.

They had launched the life vessel at the very last moment – Polly remembered Tarnie telling her it was always best to stay on a ship if you possibly could – but the mast had snapped off and landed on Jayden's leg, smashing it horribly. They had tried desperately to keep the lifeboat and the ship together, and Tarnie would not leave Jayden's side until he'd freed him. With huge effort, he had managed to get Jayden into the lifeboat – Polly could see it all vividly, knew Tarnie would never have given up on Jayden, knew that he was doing for Jayden what he was never able to do for his friend Jim Manse – but by that time the fishing boat was nearly under. Even as the men had desperately tried to grab Tarnie's arm, even as they had thrown out ropes and hands and inflatables, the suction of the boat had pulled him down. The lifeboat too had been sucked beneath the waves, but when it had resurfaced – the pyramid-shaped yellow survival vessel eventually doing its job and righting itself – there was nothing else in the tumult of the tossing seas but the occasional piece of flotsam. The storm and the current had carried them further and further away as they had sat in a dazed silence, trying to keep Jayden conscious, struggling to deal with the loss of their captain, their livelihood, their entire world.

The last lifeboat had returned after another twenty-four-hour stint. It was needed elsewhere and decisions had to be made.

Boiling the kettle for the hundredth time, staring out of the window, listlessly kneading bread, Polly could not bear to think what it had done to Selina when she'd heard that news.

And people came. Everyone needed to talk about it, again and again and again. The worst thing was that without a body there could be no funeral, no laying to rest. But people

295

needed to talk about what had happened, needed to grieve, and they congregated around Polly's shop.

Everyone in the town had their own story, their own version of events. Someone had had a premonition in a dream; someone else had had a visit from a ghost. Nobody seemed to know exactly what was going on with Jayden, the boy who hated fishing. He was in hospital in Plymouth, and would recover, and the hospital had told the people from all over the country who were sending gifts and cards to understand that there were so many of them they might be shared amongst other patients.

Something, it was clear, needed to be planned, but as an incomer – and worse, one who had a connection to the deceased she desperately didn't want spread any further – Polly didn't think it was down to her to do it.

'But we should do something,' she said.

They didn't have a vicar on the island, but a local woman had offered to do a service in her church in Looe. Kerensa argued that they should hold it in the ancient church high up on Mount Polbearne itself, even though it had been deconsecrated long ago.

Selina had gone back to her mother's on the mainland, and whilst they couldn't begin to share her pain, nonetheless the local community had to acknowledge it – hers, and the pain of the men left behind, who felt guilty, as well as having been terrified to within an inch of their lives.

On the Monday morning of the second week after the accident, the phone rang. Polly was elbow-deep in flour and asked Kerensa – who had come to Polbearne again to be with her friend – to answer it.

'Hello, Pol,' said Reuben, sounding sleepy. 'Wassup?'

'It's not Polly,' said Kerensa. 'It's Kerensa.'

There was a hurried shaking noise at the other end of the phone. When Reuben spoke again, he sounded a lot more awake and had dropped his voice by about an octave.

'Well hull-oo,' he said, as manfully as he could muster. Kerensa rolled her eyes. 'What can I do for you?' he said.

'Well,' said Kerensa. 'We were thinking of having a commemoration of the boat and Tarnie. We're probably going to have it in Polly's shitty little apartment. You can come if you like.'

'Oi!' shouted Polly crossly. Neil hopped up and down in the sink, where he was amusing himself. In amongst everything else, Polly had managed to find time to call the sanctuary.

'Er, hi. I think I have one of your birds that's escaped?' she'd said.

It was the same cheery Kiwi girl as before.

'Oh! You know, we haven't missed it. We've got, like—'

'A million and a half, I know. But this one is wearing a special honey tag.'

'I remember you! Are you the one who loved your puffin?'

'I think every puffin deserves to be loved,' said Polly.

'Yeah. But don't you live on the south coast?'

'I do,' said Polly proudly. 'He made it all the way home.'

She waited for the girl to be incredibly impressed and say something about how Neil was the most amazing puffin she'd ever heard of.

'Well,' said the girl. 'You can bring him back if you like.'

Polly looked at Neil. The bird regarded her with his beady black eyes. He eeped quietly.

'You know,' she said. 'I think we're all right.'

Kerensa and Reuben were still talking on the phone now. Reuben seemed to be incensed that they didn't expect him to host.

'I got a dance floor! I got lighting! I got access to DJs and a fully stocked champagne cellar,' he was saying. Polly could hear him from the other side of the room.

'It's not a party,' said Kerensa. 'It's a wake, numbnuts.'

'I think everyone should have this when they die,' said Reuben. 'It's what I want.'

'He's got a point,' said Polly.

'Anyway, what are you guys going to do, make some toast?' Reuben continued.

'I like toast,' said Kerensa.

'Fine,' said Reuben. 'When I'm flying in the sushi chef, I'll fly in a toast chef too.'

Kerensa and Polly looked at each other. Polly nodded her head. 'We should do it. The town needs it.'

'OKAY,' said Kerensa, as if she were doing Reuben the most massive favour, and ended the call.

'You know, you should be nicer to him,' said Polly. 'He took that boat out and found the rest of those men. He was really being quite heroic.'

'Well, one, he was showing off as usual,' said Kerensa.

'You're harsh,' said Polly.

'And two, it was Huckle who made him do it.'

'You don't know that.'

'I do. Reuben told me. Well, I suggested it and he couldn't deny it.'

'I can't believe you really dislike this guy but you've still managed to persuade him to host the entire thing.'

Kerensa rolled her eyes.

'There is a reason *I'm* still in business.'

'Low blow.'

Kerensa stuck out her tongue.

'Come on,' said Polly. 'We've still got a lot of work to do.'

Chapter Twenty-Three

Kerensa, true to her word, managed to arrange for the vicar to perform a service of remembrance in the old church. It would take place on Saturday, followed by a blow-out at Reuben's place. Polly hoped the weather would be fine. They told everyone in the village.

The media, thank God, had mostly gone home. But they had left an unexpected legacy behind. When people had seen the news reports on the 'tragic tidal village', they hadn't thought about the fishing so much as the beautiful upwards sweep of the town towards the picturesque ruined castle; its quaint cobbles; its lovely little artisan bakery; its sun-dappled waters. Within a day, they were descending en masse as daytrippers – not just ghouls, but genuine holidaymakers too. Kerensa went back to Plymouth, and Polly missed her helping around the place; she was run off her feet. Anything she baked was snapped up at the speed of light. She was so busy she could sometimes forget everything that had happened. Then she would glance out of the window, looking for the chattering masts, the banter, the jokes, the shouting of the fishermen, the familiar tall figure with the piercing blue eyes, and he would not be there, and it was like being hit in the stomach with a cannonball all over again.

On Wednesday, she was closing up the blinds when she saw a thin, bent figure approaching the harbour wall. The daytrippers were all on the beach; it was a ravishing day, and a quiet postprandial heat had overtaken the town. There was nobody else around. Polly made a cup of tea and took it outside, sitting down on the wall next to her.

'Hello,' she said. 'I brought you some tea, but I'll leave if you want to be alone.'

Selina looked up at her, blinking in confusion.

'Hello, sorry, I don't . . .'

'I'm Polly Waterford,' she said. 'I was a friend of Tarnie's . . . Well, I mean, I knew all the fishermen. I work just over there.'

'Oh yes, the bread shop.' Selina smiled sadly. 'He talked about the bakery all the time. He loved your bread.'

'Look, I don't want to intrude . . .'

'No,' said Selina. 'It's fine. I just had to get out from my mum's. All those cocked heads and "Are you OKAY?" all the time. You know, in that really soft voice so that people can show how caring they are. FUCK, I am tired of it.'

Polly nodded.

'So then I have to say "Yes, I'm okay" to make THEM feel better. Seriously. For the rest of my life.'

She twisted the wedding ring on her left hand.

'How could you possibly be okay?' said Polly, genuinely

301

confused. 'What a stupid question, like they think you might be a monster.'

'YES,' said Selina. She went quiet again. They both stared out to sea.

'Except I *am* a monster,' she said. 'Because I am SO fucking FURIOUS with him. I TOLD him. I TOLD him not to go to sea. I begged him not to be a bloody fisherman. Everyone knows it's dangerous, and there's no bloody money in it. And he was away all the time, here – I mean, who can live here, it's half a bloody island, for heaven's sake. Seriously, we nearly broke up about it all the time, we fought and fought and fought about his damn job, and then what does he do?'

Her eyes were filled with tears.

'He only goes and proves me bloody right, the bloody bastard. BASTARD. I am SO cross with him.'

She wiped her face furiously. 'Oh God, again with the tears,' she said. 'Sorry. Sorry for venting. Do *you* think I'm a monster?'

'I think that makes perfect sense,' said Polly, feeling awful. She liked this woman. Silly Tarnie.

'I miss him,' said Selina. 'Oh God, I miss fighting with him.' She snuffled. 'And I wish everyone would stop talking about him like he was some kind of saint.'

'I know,' said Polly fervently.

'He could be a right dickhead. But he was MY dickhead.'

Polly put an arm around her shoulder.

'Do you think they'll let me put that on the memorial stone?' Selina was half hiccuping, half laughing.

'Well, the amount of money people have sent in to pay for it, you can probably have anything you like,' said Polly, and

they both half laughed and half cried at that, and eventually
Polly said sod it, hang on, and went up to the flat and grabbed
a bottle of wine from the fridge, and they sat on the sea wall
and drank it from plastic cups, and Polly let Selina tell annoying Tarnie stories all afternoon until people started filling up
the town again and recognising Selina, and she scowled and
said it was like being the worst kind of celebrity ever, super-
widow, and left. They both hugged when she went.

That week was the busiest ever in the shop. Mount Polbearne
was famous now, and everyone wanted a piece of it. Henry and
Samantha, the incoming couple, who were in the middle of vast
overhauling building works, came in brimful with excitement.

'Well, we are QUITE the talk of Chelsea!' said Samantha.
'I don't think house prices are going to be static for long! All
the DRAMA!' she trilled.

Polly winced, then looked outside. The Range Rover was
parked across the cobbles, blocking the road again. She wondered gloomily if they'd have to get a traffic warden.

'I don't suppose you'd fancy also opening an artisan
butcher's?' asked Henry hopefully. Today his cords were
pink. They matched his blowsy cheeks. 'That kind of thing
really helps.'

'What? God, no,' said Polly. She watched one of the
fishermen pass the window with his arms full of yellow ducks.

'I see someone's got an enterprising spirit,' said Henry.
'Hmm. I wonder if *he'd* fancy opening a butcher's.'

Polly looked at them.

'So, are all your friends moving here?' she asked politely.

'Deffo! Binky and Max and Biff and Jules and Mills and Pinky and Froufrou are already calling their agents, aren't they?' said Henry to Samantha.

'Oh good,' said Polly, putting their specially ordered gluten-free loaf (for which she charged enough to pay her fuel bill for a month) into a paper bag. 'Oh good.'

Saturday dawned glorious and perfect. There were a couple of puffy white clouds breezing across the sky, but otherwise it was a technicolour blue. It reminded Polly of the day Tarnie had taken her out on his little boat, and it took her three times longer than usual to get ready, because every time she thought about that day, she cried all her make-up off and had to do it again. She spoke to herself fiercely. She was not going to make an idiot of herself. She wasn't. Tarnie had been a friend, that was all, whom she had known for a few months. She didn't deserve to selfishly grab a slice of the grief – the real grief, the huge, never-ending, life-shattering heartbreak. That belonged to his family, his old friends, Selina. She had no right to intrude. She had to lock it inside, be strong, not embarrass herself.

Thankfully Kerensa turned up bright and early to catch the tide. She looked insane but also fabulous, in a short – slightly too short – black lace dress, dramatic make-up and a fascinator with netting.

'Oh my God,' said Polly, rubbing under her eyes for the thousandth time. 'You look like the black widow.'

'Good,' said Kerensa, turning on the coffee machine. 'What do you think? Too much?'

'You only met him once,' said Polly.

'I know,' said Kerensa. 'But I thought that if anyone was suspiciously searching the church for likely bits on the side, they'd skip over you and assume it was me.'

Polly gasped. 'That's brilliant.'

'I know.'

'Thanks,' said Polly, dissolving again.

'It's all right,' said Kerensa kindly, patting her on the shoulder. 'You wouldn't have looked as good as me even if you were trying.'

But Polly knew what she was really saying, and simply bawled in her arms until there was nothing left in her.

'Better?' said Kerensa.

Polly nodded.

'Then go have a shower.'

'I've had three. It's only cold water left.'

'Even better, it'll tighten up the pores.'

Polly did what she was told, then Kerensa, looking on sternly and bringing out the waterproof mascara, sorted her out in a plain black short-sleeved dress made up of a silk skirt and T-shirt top.

'Fine,' she said. 'Just sit quietly at the back and try not to draw attention to yourself. Have you met his family before?'

Polly shook her head. 'Only Selina.'

'Good, they won't recognise you. You'll be fine, do you hear me?'

Huckle and Reuben met them at the church, both looking unusually sober in dark suits and ties. Reuben didn't pass up the opportunity to tell them that his tie and shoes were sharkskin, 'the most expensive skin you can buy', which Kerensa quickly told him made him a biological terrorist.

The church, once the focal point of the community, stood at the very top of the village, a walk up the stepped pavements. Originally built in the Middle Ages, when the town was still connected to the land, it had fallen into disuse as the causeway closed over, and had been deconsecrated at the end of the nineteenth century. It was more like a ruin now than a church, with its old stone walls and paved floors; there was no roof, just birds' nests high in the crumbling stonework. It was a nice spot to picnic outside, even amongst the ancient gravestones, and the view out to sea on three sides was absolutely magnificent: boats dotted here and there, the sky a massive flag waving over their heads.

Seats had been brought up from the tiny village hall for older people to sit on, but the church was so crowded that most people were standing along the walls or sitting on the floor, or on rocky outcrops where the flagstones had been broken or taken away. There was a murmur of low voices, men standing awkwardly in their best suits, slightly red-faced in the heat. At the front, sitting with their heads bowed, were two people who Polly realised instantly were Tarnie's parents. She knew that after his father had retired, his mother had insisted they move to the mainland, in search of a little more excitement. She also hadn't been happy that Tarnie had been a fisherman; she'd had higher hopes for her only son. She had the same bright blue eyes as her boy, Polly could see, presently so misted and unfocused she looked blind.

The man did not raise his head, but she could see Tarnie

in the slope of his shoulders, in the rangy build, in the shadow of his jaw, and she took a sharp intake of breath. She could not bear to think what must be going through his head, this fisherman. A woman shepherding several small children and looking harassed and worn down had to be Tarnie's sister.

Next to them was Selina, in a pretty black dress that showed off her thin collarbones. Polly smiled an apologetic smile at her, and Selina gave her a look of such open pain it made Polly's heart constrict. She was being supported by her mother and various other relatives, and looked too frail to even stand up.

Mrs Manse was sitting, ignoring everyone, straight-backed and uncomfortable-looking, in one of the chairs. In black, she resembled Queen Victoria. Polly tried to wave and received a disapproving look in return.

The entire town was there, even, Polly was surprised to note, the newcomers, Samantha and Henry, who looked awkward and out of place. She gave a little wave towards them too. Then they all stood, anxiously, waiting for something to happen.

Finally, the female vicar from the mainland appeared, coming in through the ruined walls like everyone else. She made her way to the front and cleared her throat, and everyone immediately sat up attentively.

'Good morning,' she said. 'And thank you all for coming on such a beautiful day. I know the circumstances are unusual, but I feel that even if we cannot bury our brother Cornelius William Tarnforth, we can celebrate him.'

At the sound of his name, his mother gave a stifled wail.

'Not all deaths are tragedies,' continued the vicar. 'But this one was.'

She went on to talk about how well known Tarnie had been in the community, how loved by his family, how missed he would be; then various people got up and said a few words, told stories Polly hadn't heard: about his habit of dropping fish in on people who didn't have much money to spare, about the lifeboat-manning shifts he took on in his spare time, some ridiculous story about pushing over a cow that Archie told through gulping sobs and that wasn't very coherent.

The vicar read from the Bible.

'And it came to pass, that, as the people pressed upon him to hear the word of God, he stood by the lake of Gennesaret,

And saw two ships standing by the lake: but the fishermen were gone out of them, and were washing their nets.

And he entered into one of the ships, which was Simon's, and prayed him that he would thrust out a little from the land. And he sat down, and taught the people out of the ship.

Now when he had left speaking, he said unto Simon, Launch out into the deep, and let down your nets for a draught.

And Simon answering said unto him, Master, we have toiled all the night, and have taken nothing: nevertheless at thy word I will let down the net.

And when they had this done, they inclosed a great multitude of fishes: and their net did brake.

And they beckoned unto their partners, which were in the other ship, that they should come and help them. And they came, and filled both the ships, so that they began to sink.

When Simon Peter saw it, he fell down at Jesus' knees, saying, Depart from me; for I am a sinful man, O Lord.

For he was astonished, and all that were with him, at the draught of the fishes which they had taken:

And so was also James, and John, the sons of Zebedee, which were partners with Simon. And Jesus said unto Simon, Fear not; from henceforth thou shalt be a fisher of men.

And when they had brought their ships to land, they forsook all, and followed him.'

Then, at a prearranged signal, the men Polly recognised as fishermen shambled to the front of the congregation and started to sing.

> *Eternal Father, strong to save,*
> *Whose arm hath bound the restless wave,*
> *Who bid'st the mighty ocean deep*
> *Its own appointed limits keep:*

The voices swelled louder and louder now, joined by most of the others there.

> *Oh hear us when we cry to thee*
> *For those in peril on the sea.*

Polly glanced over and saw Tarnie's father trying, and failing, to mouth the words. That was when she lost it completely. Trying very, very hard to be quiet, she buried her head in the inner lining of Huckle's jacket and sobbed and sobbed. The lining was never the same afterwards.

Oh Christ, whose voice the waters heard,
And hushed their raging at thy word
Who walkedst on the foaming deep,
And calm amidst its rage didst sleep:
Oh hear us when we cry to thee
For those in peril on the sea.

Reuben, or rather the wildly expensive party planner he'd got in from London – he was sparing absolutely no expense – had sent coaches over to pick people up and take them to the wake.

It was a beautiful day as they boarded the vehicles, the men already loosening their ties and taking off their jackets. Not a cloud in the sky, just bright blue as far as the eye could see, the sun hot and delicious on the increasingly brown shoulders of the holidaymakers, beachcombers and scavengers. Most of the goods from the wrecked tanker had either sunk or been removed from the ship, and fortunately the oil had been successfully contained, thanks to the quick thinking of one of the young engineers on board, who'd managed to close the bulkhead doors as the ship was going down. Polly had been amazed to learn that this behemoth had been crewed by fewer than a dozen men. Archie had explained to her that their great fear in the lifeboat had been that a huge cargo ship would simply not notice them; that a boy would be asleep at the radar, or simply assume they were a large fish, nothing worth bothering about.

The coach they were on was quiet, nobody quite sure what to expect. Polly sat next to Kerensa and in front of Patrick and his wife.

'You're not bringing the bird?' Kerensa had asked back at the flat after the service.

'Um,' Polly had replied. Secretly she wanted Neil there for comfort. Also, Tarnie had liked him a lot. They had compromised on not for the service, but yes for the wake. Kerensa had changed into a sun dress but Polly decided not to; it felt disrespectful.

'No,' said Kerensa. 'It's disrespectful not to go and have an amazing time. He would have liked that.'

'I think he'd have liked to still have been here,' said Polly.

'Yes, having a good time at a fantastic party thrown by an idiot,' said Kerensa, looking in the mirror while putting on more lipstick.

Polly hugged her.

'Thank you for all your support,' she said.

'What support?' said Kerensa. 'I thought you were a total moron coming out here. I thought you'd be back in ten days, crying, with your grey sofa. In fact . . .'

'What?' said Polly.

Kerensa fiddled with her phone, then showed it to Polly.

'What is that?' she said, looking at the picture of a nice house.

'It's a house,' said Kerensa. 'In the . . .' She cleared her throat before she could bear to say the word. 'In the *suburbs*.'

'What about it?'

'I was thinking about buying it, you idiot. For when you came back. So you'd stop being so bloody stubborn and come and live with me. I've missed you, you doof.'

Polly flung her arms around her again.

'I love you,' she said.

'I know,' said Kerensa, hugging her back. 'But even with everything that's happened, I still think you're happier here.'

Polly started to well up again. 'Oh God . . .'

'It's true, though, isn't it?' said Kerensa. 'It's like you're really living, for the first time in years.'

They clutched each other in front of the mirror, and for a second they were teenagers again, sneaking out of Polly's tiny bedroom clutching bottles of alcoholic ginger beer.

'Let's go get 'em,' said Kerensa. 'Don't let me get super-pissed, I don't want that weird American midget pawing at me.'

'And don't let *me* get super-pissed and accidentally say something awful to Selina,' said Polly.

Kerensa gave her a look. 'What about pawing tall, hunky blond Americans?'

Polly rolled her eyes. 'I cannot imagine him getting super-pissed enough to even think about me.'

Kerensa smiled. 'Anyway, are you bringing that bird or not?'

Neil eeped at them.

'Of course I am. He's already wearing his bow tie,' said Polly.

Now it was Kerensa's turn to roll her eyes.

The coaches – there were three of them – wound round the warm golden hills and headed towards evening. Singing could be clearly heard emerging from at least one of them, which indicated that several of the men had come out of the service and headed straight to the pub. Patrick was fascinated by Neil's story, even if he was in agreement with Kerensa that he probably oughtn't to be wearing a bow tie.

'It's smart,' said Polly. 'He can wear it to greet his host, then I'll take it off so he can play.'

Patrick smiled. 'Excellent. I think everyone is going to need cheering up.'

The secret turn-off to Reuben's beach was less secret tonight; it was lit up with lanterns, beaming in the narrow little road. Two large men wearing headpieces stood at the entrance with high-beam torches and unfriendly expressions. They glanced over the coach and had a word with the driver, then waved them in.

The long lane down to the beach was entirely lit up with braziers either side, giving the early evening a cheery, exciting glow. Already Polly could hear the sound of distant drumming. She looked nervously at Kerensa, who was already wearing her 'desperately unimpressed' look.

'Come on,' Polly said. 'This is going to be something special. I think you're right; for Tarnie's sake we just have to go with it. You don't have to talk to him.'

'That's true,' said Kerensa. 'Cor. I reckon he's spent a FORTUNE on this.'

Someone with luminous paddles directed the coaches in and parked them up, and everyone descended nervously in ones and twos.

313

'This way, this way!' shouted a bossy woman in a high-vis jacket, indicating the pathway brightly lit by candles across the dunes. They followed it, some of the women stumbling already in their heels. Polly took her sandals off. The sand was still warm beneath her toes from the heat of the day. It felt delicious.

Over the last dune, where the beach became visible, everybody stopped and stared.

'Oh my,' said Kerensa.

The entire beach was strung, somehow, with bright white lanterns. The little café had had a huge covered bar attached to the side of it. There were lines of black-and-white-clad waiting staff standing with large trays of drinks, and already the beach was full of the most glamorous, beautiful-looking people – obviously friends of Reuben – in chic outfits, chatting animatedly and starting to dance. There was a huge DJ stage set up, but at this point a band was playing some sensuous reggae. The most amazing barbecue smells hung heavy in the air; the atmosphere was stupendous.

'Bloody hell,' said one of the Polbearne lot, a little intimidated. This was a far cry from their normal world of the pub and the sea.

'Well, this is what I call a send-off,' said someone else, but they still didn't move.

Finally, the waiters stepped forward to serve them all with champagne. Reuben picked up two flutes himself and brought them over to Polly and Kerensa. The two stunningly lovely girls he'd been talking to looked instantly pouty.

'Hi. Welcome to my brilliant wake for Tarnie. It's very kind of me to do it,' he said, presenting them with their glasses.

'Do you buy yourself attention like this often?' said Kerensa.

'Stop being rude,' ordered Polly. She gave Reuben a hug and a kiss. 'You were a hero, a true hero, and this will be the best send-off ever. His family will never forget it.'

'I know,' said Reuben.

There were boys still out on the surf, where the tide was high, but when they finished they would come in, strip off, have a beer. The barbecue turned out to be a pit in which whole pigs, rubbed with spices, were being roasted and expertly crisped into rolls. On the other side was a massive bonfire, crackling up to the sky, to keep them warm later in the evening. There were pictures of Tarnie up in the covered bar. Polly paused in front of one of them, a candid shot of him mending a net. It had been taken at exactly the same angle as how she used to see him from the flat; it was like she was looking out of her window.

The entire beach was lit up, but the most astonishing backdrop of all was the sky, bestowing a bright pink and purple sunset as if ordered in especially. Polly wouldn't put much past Reuben.

Waiters circulated with sushi and other hors d'oeuvres, but as soon as the band had a break and the DJ started up with 'Get Lucky', Polly and Kerensa realised what they wanted to do.

Dancing was their escape, a way to deal with all their pent-up emotion. They danced as the sun went down, watching the boys mess about in the water; watching Muriel from the minimart drink too much too fast in excitement at being out before collapsing in a chair with a kindly-brought cup of tea;

watching Archie and his wife standing shyly to the side, slightly overcome and very close to one another; watching John's children charging about shrieking and laughing, chasing each other with water pistols that seemed to have been conjured from nowhere.

They talked and laughed and made a million new friends, and danced with boys or with each other or on their own. Polly felt her shoulders free up, her cheeks ache with laughter in the midst of such sadness, her feet bare, her black dress floating out around her. It felt as if everyone there – those who had cheated death, who had cheated the calamity in their community – was intent on celebrating life and happiness and the sheer beauty around them, and it made Polly dance and twirl even faster.

Huckle sipped his beer slowly, watching her. The party was full of beautiful young things – Reuben's usual rent-a-mob of trust-fund hanger-ons, models and semi-professionals – but he wasn't interested in any of them, even though he could tell from the looks and the flirtatious chat and dancing from some of the girls that they would like to turn the evening into something more. Huckle was six foot two, blond and blue-eyed; finding girls had never been a problem for him. Finding a girl who wouldn't break his heart, on the other hand ...

He thought back to Polly, pounding up the jetty the day Tarnie had not come home, and took another slow swig of his beer.

Polly couldn't have said how late it was, but the stars had changed position. The party wasn't slowing down, though; if anything, it was getting more hectic, the bar serving faster, the food still circling, more and more people dancing, including a hugely successful boy band who'd been playing St Ives and had dropped in on their way back to London.

Suddenly the DJ turned off his set and Reuben stood up to take the mike. There was mass cheering, and some of the girls jostled their way to the front to make sure he could see them there being supportive.

'So, yeah, I know, greatest party of all time, right?' he said nonchalantly.

'Seriously, he's like Kanye West without the humble, modest side,' sniffed Kerensa, who'd sidled up. Her skin was shining from the dancing and her make-up had run a little, but it made her look rather endearing, Polly thought, younger and less carefully put together.

'But we're here to honour our brother Tarnie – and all our brothers who did come home.'

'Thanks, Reuben!' shouted one of the girls. Reuben smirked.

Kerensa tutted. 'Seriously.'

'He did do an amazing thing,' said Polly.

'It'll be even more amazing when people stop going on about it.'

'So, anyway . . .'

A fisherman from one of the other boats stood up.

'Oh Lord,' said Kerensa, who, Polly suddenly realised, was drunker than she'd thought. 'He's going to sing "My Way" or something.'

The fisherman walked up to the mike, looking out nervously at the crowd of people. Everyone cheered. The rest of the fishermen went and stood beside him. Jayden was there in his wheelchair, looking thin and anxious, but also incredibly pleased to be there.

'Um,' said the man. 'I just want to say thanks. To Reuben. But to each and every boat that went out looking for us.'

A huge cheer went up.

'To the tireless emergency services.'

A clutch of very drunk ambulance drivers waved merrily.

'To everyone who . . .' His voice cracked a little and he raised his glass. 'To everyone who never gave up on us.'

'To everyone who never gave up,' chorused the partygoers.

Jayden was now pushed forward, and coughed anxiously. Apart from the distant waves, there was total silence.

'And to say goodbye to our boy, these are a few words,' he said, fumbling with a piece of paper, 'from Robert Burns. He's a poet.'

He put his hand up in the direction of the sea.

> *An honest man here lies at rest*
> *As e'er God with his image blest;*
> *The friend of man, the friend of truth,*
> *The friend of age, and guide of youth;*
> *Few hearts like his, with virtue warm'd,*
> *Few heads with knowledge so informed;*
> *If there's another world, he lives in bliss;*
> *If there is none, he made the best of this.*

Next one of the fishermen struck a chord on his guitar, and the rest of them came forward. Polly didn't recognise the song, but everyone else obviously did, as they all joined in.

I wish I was a fisherman,
Tumbling on the seas
Far away from dry land
And its bitter memories
Casting out my sweet line
With abandonment and love
No ceiling bearing down on me
'Cept the starry sky above
With light in my head
You in my arms
Woohoo!

She felt Kerensa take her hand as the fishermen, strong and low, sang a further two verses, with everyone joining in lustily on the last lines. Just as they finished, a tiny piercing light shot across the horizon.

'Look,' said Polly, astonished that it was so late and the party had gone on for so long. 'It's dawn.'

As the last notes of the guitar died away, the fishermen followed someone who appeared to be organising everything, who waved them all off the stage down towards the water's edge, where there were sixteen Chinese lanterns – the number of men back home from the sea – and one larger one. Two men helped Jayden out of his wheelchair as the orange lanterns were lit, and the fishermen lifted them and let them sail high, high into the breaking dawn, lighting up the last stars in the sky.

'Thank you to the sea,' said Reuben, speaking simply for once. 'For delivering our souls home. And look after our brother.'

Everyone stood watching the floating beacons of light soar

higher and higher over the waves. There was reverent silence for a second, then they all burst into a storm of cheering and applause.

'And now: PARTY HARD!' said Reuben. 'That's an order!'

The DJ whipped immediately into a huge banging summer hit about wishing someone a good morning, and how they had to watch the sun come up, and everybody started dancing again, and hugging each other, and talking about how amazing it all was, especially when the DJ followed it up with 'Praise You'.

The young fishermen were suddenly celebrities as far as the London crowd were concerned. Polly passed Jayden in his wheelchair. She hadn't even had a chance to talk to him; she knew he had a nurse keeping a very strict eye on him – he shouldn't have been out of hospital at all, but Reuben had pleaded with them to make a special case. He was sitting next to a ravishing girl with dark hair and huge brown eyes who was nodding sympathetically as he described his terrible plight and how brave he'd been in the face of death. She kept putting out her hand and stroking his arm sorrowfully. Polly caught his eye and he gave her a huge wink. She smiled to herself.

Over in the café, a crack team of chefs were serving up coffee and delicious-smelling bacon rolls along with Buck's Fizz. Polly helped herself to breakfast and sat on a rock next to Huckle, who was watching the fishermen, surrounded by friends and family, bursting with happiness.

'Hey,' he said, pleased to see her. Very pleased. 'Enjoying the party?'

'It's amazing,' said Polly. She realised suddenly that she

was starving; she hadn't had much time to eat in the last week or so. 'Everyone's having such a good time.'

Huckle smiled that low, lazy smile.

'Are you?' she asked.

'Oh sure,' he said. 'I always have a good time.'

In fact, he didn't sound happy at all. Polly looked at him. The first rays of the sun were just starting to spread. One touched his hair, turning it golden. She thought about everything she'd learned about him. And how sure she was that it was he who had made Reuben take the boat out again. Reuben of course hadn't mentioned that.

'Do you?' she said.

'Well, put it this way,' he said, looking out to sea. 'If there's a more beautiful place to be sad, I don't know it.'

She put down her Buck's Fizz suddenly and turned towards him. His deep blue eyes gazed at her, unreadable as ever.

Dammit, thought Polly suddenly. I have nothing to lose. She had already staked everything on coming here; on changing her life, on baking the bread. Every risk she had taken had paid off far more than if she'd stayed in Plymouth, living a safe life in a little flat with a little job and a little mortgage. Every leap into the unknown ... well. Her thoughts flitted briefly over Tarnie. Well, almost every leap.

She shook her head. She was overthinking everything.

'I ...' she said. She realised suddenly that her hands were shaking. Well, she had been up all night, she supposed. Lots of booze, not enough food. Down on the sand, the ambulance boys and girls were all tearing off their clothes and running screaming into the water. Five seconds later, it seemed like everybody was at it. There was a mass of people swimming and splashing. She smiled at the exuberance of it all. Their spot under the palm trees suddenly felt a lot quieter and more secluded, even if it was getting lighter every second.

'I should ...' She half smiled.

'You seem to be talking even slower than I do,' said Huckle, but she could see a sudden tremble in his mouth, or was she imagining it? She steeled herself.

'I should have liked ... I should have liked to try and make you happy,' she said. It came out in a rush, tailing off to a whisper, but she knew, as she looked up at him under lowered eyelids, that he understood. He took a deep, slow breath. Suddenly what had started on a whim was going to be terribly important for her to hear.

'Polly,' he said. The soft, treacly way he spoke her name made her feel as if she was setting herself up for disappointment. That he would apologise and explain – as he had done already – that he wasn't in the market, that Candice had left him too raw, that they'd been through this.

She felt the touch of his huge, rough hand underneath her chin, lifting it up so she was looking directly at him. The music and the sounds of the revelling swimmers seemed to fade away. She was conscious of nothing but his piercing blue eyes, his handsome face. He seemed to be searching for something; looking at her like nobody else had looked at her before: hungry, curious, but also something else. Like he had finally found what he was searching for.

Just for a second – a delicious second – the entire world froze, and Polly realised suddenly that he was going to kiss her. For that long moment, she knew that this kiss would be everything she had ever dreamed of, everything she had ever wanted, and that after this, whatever happened, she might not want to kiss anyone else ever again.

The force of him took her by surprise; she had, she realised, expected his kiss to be gentle, tentative, as laid-back as the rest of him, but instead he kissed her fiercely, hungrily, like he was the drowning man, and she his only hope of rescue.

Chapter Twenty-Four

Polly didn't know how long the kiss lasted. She didn't know where she was or what she was doing, only that her whole body jumped as if she'd been given an electric shock as soon as their lips met; that instantly, without even thinking about it, she was responding to him, her whole being concentrated on their mouths and their hands and her desperate, sudden urge to press herself to him, to be close to him, to be under his shirt and against his skin, burying her face in his chest and breathing in the heady sweet scent of him. She felt greedy, abandoned, completely oblivious to the other people there.

Then she heard someone call her name.

'Wow, Polly, go.'

It was one of the fishermen, the one who played the guitar; she wasn't sure of his name. He was drunk and shouting and suddenly she realised what she was doing, and when, and in what circumstances. It was wrong. She pulled back, horrified.

'What?' said Huckle, half drunk on lust. His hair was tumbling across his forehead, his eyes were glazed.

She stared at him. He looked gorgeous. But still . . .

'I . . . I can't,' she said. 'Not . . . No.'

Huckle's eyes flashed.

'I see,' he said. He should have guessed: she still had a thing for Tarnie.

Polly wanted to explain to him that the circumstances were wrong – and not just wrong, but publicly wrong, in front of everyone. But his face had already shut up like a stone.

'I mean . . . I just mean, not here.'

'No,' said Huckle. 'Of course not, ma'am.'

He glanced at his watch.

'It's getting pretty late. Or pretty early. One or the other. I think I'd better be heading back . . .'

Polly nodded miserably. She didn't want him to go, but it didn't seem appropriate . . . not at all.

'Me too,' she said.

Across the beach, people were sprawled round the bonfire; chatting, sleeping, making out.

'Um . . . can I . . . see you later?'

'It's a small part of the world,' said Huckle, his eyes fixed on the glittering sea.

'I'm sorry,' said Polly.

Huckle shrugged. She looked at him, desperate for his gentle smile once more, or his open laugh, but of course it did not come. He had turned into a statue. She looked at him once more, then turned round and headed off back down the beach.

'Shit,' said Huckle to himself as she walked away. 'Shit shit shit.'

Chapter Twenty-Five

Polly stumbled back across the beach, a huge lump in her throat. She couldn't make out anyone's face; everything was a blur. Somebody else shouted her name, but she couldn't or didn't want to see who it was. She headed back to the dance floor to find her shoes and maybe her bag, but she couldn't seem to see Kerensa anywhere. She wasn't in the water, or in any of the beautiful white wooden cabanas Reuben had set up everywhere for groups of people to talk quietly in.

She found her eventually, behind the café area – basically where the bins were. She spotted the fuchsia dress before she took in what else was going on.

'Kerensa!' she shouted. 'Come on, let's go.'

When she peered a bit closer, she realised that Kerensa was trapped in a massive teenage clinch. With one of the surf instructor types, Polly thought; must be. Then she blinked again and realised that—

'Oh for crying out loud,' she said, feeling that her own dramas never quite took precedence over Kerensa's.

Kerensa came up for air. Her face was puce and her dress was completely open at the front. She looked overheated and roundly overexcited.

'Oh, hi,' said Reuben.

'What are you two doing? You hate each other!'

'I'm really good at kissing,' said Reuben. 'And all that stuff.'

Polly looked at Kerensa in consternation.

'Er, he is,' confirmed Kerensa apologetically. Her lipstick was all kissed off. She looked completely wanton.

Polly rolled her eyes.

'Seriously?'

They both looked at her.

'Er . . .' she rubbed her neck. 'I was just going to go.'

'Okay,' said Kerensa. She didn't move.

'I was going to go home . . . with you.'

Kerensa frowned. Reuben put a proprietorial hand on her thigh.

'I'm not going home yet,' explained Kerensa. 'I'm going to have sex with Reuben.'

'Oh God, you two are both as bad as each other.' Polly was trying really hard not to cry.

'Can Huckle not take you home?'

She immediately choked up.

'It doesn't matter,' she managed eventually. 'I can catch the coach.'

'Good,' said Reuben, turning to Kerensa. 'Come with me to my giant bedroom. I have, like, the most enormous . . .'

'OKAY, see you later,' said Polly.

'. . . bed,' said Reuben.

Polly tramped back over to where she'd left Neil eating sandwich leftovers. He was sitting in a rock pool looking guilty.

'Neil,' she said in dismay, looking at the mess next to him. 'Were you sick?'

Neil eeped and hopped into her arms.

'Oh Christ, I can't even look after my own bloody puffin. Don't eat until you're sick, my love.'

'Eep,' said Neil.

Cradling him, she followed the groups of people making their weary way towards the waiting buses. She found a double seat near the back, made sure Neil was comfortable in his rucksack, emptied the sand out of her shoes and almost immediately, before she had time to think, fell fast asleep.

The next day, Sunday, was miserable. Polly slept till eleven, then woke and remembered Huckle. What had she been thinking? Why couldn't she have waited, gone somewhere Tarnie's mum and dad weren't, for example? And couldn't he understand why? She pictured the stony look on his face, and remembered again how closed he had been when she had met him, how it had taken a while to get to the sweet boy underneath. She sighed. She would ring him. No, she would ring Kerensa and ask her what to do.

Not surprisingly, she couldn't get through to Kerensa. She tried not to be jealous of her glamorous friend, and of course she hadn't the slightest interest in Reuben, but the idea that Kerensa was spending all day in a luxurious bed doing exactly what she'd very much wanted to do herself was a little hard to stomach.

She went to call Huckle, then frowned and hesitated. She didn't want to look as if she were throwing herself at him. Instead she threw herself into work, drinking lots of orange juice and making up her yeast and sourdough mixes for the coming week. The little village was thronged. Some holiday-makers came up and knocked on the window, but she shook her head sharply. She really did need some help in the shop, she thought; she would turn into Mrs Manse if she didn't keep an eye on it. She cursed herself for being so self-pitying and concentrated on making up decorative bread plaits to hang over the door; she'd meant to do it for ages, and now she had the time and the energy, she thought crossly, but no one who cared what she was up to. She baked with all her heart until she had tired herself out, and slept again early, cross at the merry sounds of the holidaymakers just outside her window.

She was woken at ten that night by her phone buzzing. It was a text from Huckle. She immediately jumped up, wide awake and delighted. Had he realised he'd made a big mistake? With a faintly wobbling hand, she picked up the phone.

She checked the text carefully, drawing in breath.

Sorry to bother you, but can you show the beekeeper the way?

Oh well, she thought. A bit formal, but they were back on friendly terms. Surely they could take it from there? She thought again of the softness of his lips, the roughness of his skin, his sweet taste.

Why, where are you off to? she texted back.

The answer, when it came, made her want to throw the phone across the room.

Just dropping in to Savannah for a time.

She stared at the screen, half laughing, half crying in disbelief. This wasn't a planned trip, was it? Surely he'd have mentioned it. And arranged things with the sodding beekeeper.

No, this must be a last-minute thing. It was, she recognised with utter fury, exactly what he had done the last time he'd been in a relationship that hadn't worked out. He'd fled the country. No way. She couldn't believe it. She stared at the phone, shaking, then threw up her hands. Oh, for heaven's sake.

Huckle had been more affected by the rescue than he had let on. He had come all the way round the world looking for something safe, and the precariousness of life on that little rock had shaken him to the core.

Added to this was what had happened between him and Polly. It had taken him so long to open up after his relationship with Candice, so long to get over it and heal. And the second he did so, and met someone that he thought was safe, and kind, and gentle, she too had been thinking about somebody else.

He was, he thought, safer at home. His experiment had failed. He didn't want to wait about, to see all the same old faces every day. He needed to get away. With barely a thought, he packed an overnight bag and caught the first train to London.

Tell him to come to bakery, Polly texted back, eventually.

Huckle stared at his phone. Well, there it was. Proof that

330

whatever he'd thought there was between them was nothing at all, nothing real. She barely seemed to remember ... Or maybe she just didn't care. He stared in disbelief around the airport lounge, full of sleepy-looking businessmen. Was this his life, then? Just women who liked other guys more? Maybe men like that fat guy over there with the ten-thousand-dollar watch on, drinking vodka in the middle of the afternoon. Or that businessman shouting into his phone.

Thanks. You're a pal, he texted back, slightly bitterly.

Polly stared at Huckle's text for a long time. It looked to her very carefully worded to imply nothing more; she was nothing more than a pal, someone useful in a spot of organisational difficulties. He was letting her down gently. She sat on her bed and wept some bitter tears. Neil drank them, to let her know he cared.

The next morning, she opened up as usual. People were busy and ready for something to eat; the season was in full flow now and the combination of the town's fame and the beautiful weather meant it was looking like a vintage year for tourism. Polly figured she should probably think about putting some little wrought-iron tables and chairs across the road by the harbour, so people could sit out and drink their coffee and eat something. That would make a lot of sense; she wondered if it would be allowed. And how she could manage it.

As if in answer to this, two figures appeared at the doorway. It was Mrs Manse and a limping, but patently healing, Jayden.

'This boy needs a job,' Gillian stated shortly.

'I don't want to go fishing any more,' he said, smiling.

'Did you know girls LOVE to ask about my leg?' His face was a cheerful pink.

'Do they?' said Polly. It was hard not to smile seeing him up and about again. 'How's it healing?'

'Do you want to see it?'

'Is it gross?'

'Of course not,' said Mrs Manse. 'I'm not getting a boy in to work with an open wound.'

'I'm glad to hear it,' said Polly.

Jayden showed her his leg. There was a huge chunk out of his calf and a white-lined skin graft under the bandage.

'That is disgusting,' said Polly.

'You should have seen it before,' boasted Jayden. 'I looked like a butcher's shop. You could see the bone and everything. I made a health assistant faint.'

'Er, well done. Sorry, you want me to do what?' said Polly, confused.

Mrs Manse sniffed. 'It seems like you might need some help round here.'

Polly blinked and caught on.

'Oh.' She looked at Jayden severely. 'Can you work, young man?'

'They kept me on the boats for long enough,' said Jayden, which Polly reckoned was fair enough. 'I can gut two hundred fish an hour. I reckon I can probably help out with a bit of bread.'

He looked defiant and a little nervous. Polly felt her heart go out to him.

'Do you really want this job, Jayden?'

Suddenly his face showed the child he must have been. There was a suggestion of tears in his eyes.

332

'There's nothing else here,' he said. 'I don't want to move. Please, please, please don't make me go out to sea again. I can't.'

He spoke the last sentence in a monotone, staring at the floor, and Polly could only guess what it had cost him to say it.

She looked at Mrs Manse, who nodded once, abruptly.

'Okay,' said Polly. 'Yes. I do need help. I need more stock. And you can sweep. Can you sweep?'

'I've been sweeping up fish guts for years.'

'Can you get up early in the morning?'

'I never got to bed in my last job.'

Polly smiled. 'As long as I can keep you from wolfing all the stock, I think this might work out all right.'

She stuck out her hand. 'No cheek though, okay? Well, you can be a bit cheeky to the customers, but Mrs Manse is your boss and I'm your second boss, okay?'

Jayden looked at her hand in wonder, then pumped it up and down, beaming.

'Yes! Totally! Yes! You won't regret this!' His face was completely transformed. 'Can I start now? Let me sweep something.'

'I will let you do that,' said Polly, smiling back. 'And I'll teach you how to knead. And of course, Mrs Manse, anything he can do for you, any fetching and carrying, when he's fully healed ...'

'I'm fine,' said Mrs Manse shortly. In fact, the other bakery was open for far fewer hours these days, and Polly had seen confused-looking shoppers gazing at its bare cabinets more than once. The Little Beach Street Bakery was bringing in enough to allow Gillian to work less, and Polly could only think this was a good thing. It didn't exactly help her decide when she could ask for a raise, but she was just too relieved that it was working out to complain at this point. Plus, Mount Polbearne's other shops only stretched to fish and chips and buckets and spades. She wouldn't have much to spend her money on anyway.

'Well, in you come then.'

She led Jayden through the shop. She had asked Chris to print up some aprons in the same font as he'd done above the window, and she was also stocking some cards that advertised him as a sign writer, with a picture of the Little Beach Street Bakery on the front. Quite a few had been picked up by holidaymakers and daytrippers. Painting physical things rather than doing design online ... that might just be the way forward for Chris, she thought. Well, she hoped.

She gave Jayden a tour of the baking area.

'Wow,' he said, watching her stoke the big wooden oven, check a rising batch that smelled heavenly, sniff the sourdough, splash in a little milk to a fresh batch. 'There's quite a lot involved in this.'

Polly gave him a look.

'What did you think, that I just went to the back of the shop with a fishing rod and caught some bread?'

Jayden looked awkward.

'Is that like a joke? Like one of your funny jokes and things? You may have to tell me if it's one of those, so I can laugh.'

'You don't have to laugh,' said Polly. 'How does your leg feel? When will you be up to lifting things?'

'I can lift things now,' said Jayden. 'Mostly I'm keeping the bandage on to impress girls.'

'Oh good,' said Polly. 'Okay, in the morning ...' It suddenly struck her how lovely it was to be able to hand this work over. 'In the morning I need you to bring in the new bags of flour from outside. Then dust and sweep every surface. And clean out the ovens – just the crumbs, though; leave the patina. That's the slightly greasy stuff. It's good for bread.'

'Really?'

Polly looked at him.

'Do you love my bread?'

'I do,' said Jayden.

'Then I'll get you on kneading ... Oh my God, that means I can take a break. Then you can take a break! Jayden, this is going to be brilliant.'

Jayden grinned. 'And I get to stay inside all day?'

'All day,' promised Polly.

'And I don't need to start till five thirty?'

'Nope.'

Jayden smiled with pure happiness.

Things weren't helped that first morning by a) Jayden not knowing where anything was or what the different types of bread were called or where the bags were or how to work the till, or b) every single local person who came in, which was most of them these days, having to stop for twenty minutes to have a full and detailed chat with Jayden about the accident, his new job, his poor mother's nerves and his future prospects. Eventually Polly set him up in a corner to do chatting and handled all the serving herself. He could make himself useful in other ways.

Sure enough, she had him mopping when she finally noticed an awkward-looking man hovering near the doorway.

'Can I help you?' she asked.

The man, who had a rather spotty neck and slightly greasy dark hair and was wearing a suit and tie, coughed politely.

'Er,' he said. 'I'm ... I'm here about the bees?'

For a second Polly didn't realise what he was talking about. Then she remembered.

'Oh yes,' she said. 'Hu—'

She realised, suddenly, crossly, that just saying his name made her feel bad.

'I heard you were coming,' she said shortly. 'Actually, let me just wash my hands – Jayden, you wash your hands too,' she commanded quickly. 'Just do it every fifteen minutes, in fact.'

'Roger,' said Jayden, who was humming a little song as he mopped the kitchen. At this rate the Little Beach Street Bakery was going to be gleaming.

'We close up at two,' she said to the man. 'Can you wait till then?'

The man nodded awkwardly, his Adam's apple bouncing up and down. Then he went out and sat on the harbour wall, staring out to sea. Jayden and Polly could see him from the shop. It was rather peculiar.

'He doesn't look like a beekeeper,' said Jayden.

'What does a beekeeper look like?' asked Polly, cross that she'd been thinking the same thing.

'I don't know,' said Jayden. 'Not like that. Can I have a sandwich?'

'You can,' said Polly. 'Every day you can have a sandwich and one loaf for your mum, but no more, okay? You're a growing boy, you'll eat the profits.'

Jayden nodded and tore into a cheese croissant.

'I will never get tired of these,' he said with satisfaction.

Polly smiled. 'I'll show you how to make them, if you like.'

His eyes widened.

'No way!'

'But eat plenty of fruit and vegetables too,' she heard herself saying.

At 1.45 Polly could stand it no longer. She left Jayden on his own to sell any remaining stock and tidy up. He could take the till over to Mrs Manse and she'd cash it up. She didn't think Jayden would ever steal anything, but even if he had a mind for a bit of mischief, the mere mention of the words 'Mrs Manse' seemed to have a terrifying effect.

She went back out to the man.

'I'm Polly Waterford,' she said, putting out her hand.

'Er, Dave,' he said. 'Dave Marsden.'

His local accent was thick and his hand was a bit sweaty. He seemed very nervous.

'Hello, Dave Marsden,' said Polly. 'Okay, it's a bit of a walk out to Hu— the cottage, but it's the only way, unless you have another mode of transport?'

Dave shrugged. 'Naw. The bus dropped me off.'

'Okay, fine. Let's go, then.'

She passed him a bottle of water – she'd brought two,

speculating, correctly, that he wouldn't have his own – and they set off across the causeway, along the country lanes and towards Huckle's turn-off. Dave, in his suit, started sweating almost immediately. It was a hot day.

'So,' said Polly, after they'd walked for thirty minutes in silence. 'How did you get into working with bees?'

There was another silence. Polly took a sideways glance at Dave. He had gone absolutely beet red, right to the very tips of his ears.

'Um,' he said.

'What?'

They had turned off the lane and were walking along the shaded track towards the little cottage in the woods.

'Er,' he said. 'I don't really . . .' He coughed. 'I haven't spent much time with . . .'

Polly gave him a shrewd look.

'You've been hired to look after some bees. You know that, right?'

Dave suddenly looked very much like he might start to cry.

'Aye,' he mumbled, staring at his shoes, which were getting covered in mud and early-fallen leaves.

'I mean . . .' said Polly. They were nearly at the cottage now. 'I mean, do you actually know how to look after bees?'

'I . . . um, I looked up some stuff on t'internet.'

'You what?' said Polly.

Dave swallowed hard. He was sweatier than ever.

'I'm sorry,' he said, looking about five years old. 'I'm sorry. I really, really need this job. The temp agency just keep not having anything, then they asked if there was anyone with bee experience and ... I don't know what I was thinking. I was ...'

He rubbed his eyes.

'My girlfriend's pregnant,' he said quietly. 'I were just ...'

Polly shook her head.

'Good God,' she said. 'What if they'd needed someone down at the tiger farm?'

Dave looked at her in surprise that she wasn't cross with him.

'Are you going to phone the agency?' he mumbled. 'Because they'll drop me for ever.'

'Do you know ANYTHING about bees?' asked Polly. She pushed open the gate.

'I told you ... I did read some stuff on the internet,' said Dave. 'But I've forgotten it all now.'

'You have?' said Polly. She thought back to the night she and Huckle had spent here, so comfortable with one another. So happy. He had showed her then, she supposed. Everything she needed to know, really.

The garden, a little wilder perhaps than the last time she had been there, had, with the heavy rain from the storms, then the bright sunshine, overbloomed into full mid-July blowsiness; it was almost too much. Great big pink fuchsias and roses, their petals trailing, grew wild around tree trunks; every square of grass was littered with daisies and meadowsweet, so it was less of a lawn, more of a meadow. There was even some bougain-villaea, shocking in its bright pinks and purples, and the collection of apple and cherry trees were heavy with fruit,

339

windfall already collecting round their roots. Polly couldn't resist trying a cherry, but they were small and sour. Perfect for jam, she thought. Sour cherry jam on a good country roll.

Down by the stream, the hives buzzed excitedly. Lots of the bees were nosing in and out of the flowers, their vibration humming in the air.

Dave was no longer red. He'd gone white.

'Christ,' he said. 'Them's big buggers, ain't they?'

Polly turned to face him.

'You are kidding me?' she said. 'You're not frightened of bees?'

'Are those even bees?' he said, gradually backing away. 'They look more like hornets. I mean, some people die from bee stings, don't they?'

Polly stared him out.

'We're going to put the suits on,' she said firmly. 'Come on, they're in the shed.'

The shed was open, as she'd known it would be. You would have to be a particularly unusual and committed burglar to make it all the way to Huckle's house.

Dave looked at the suits hanging up and rubbed the back of his neck again.

'What?' said Polly, rather cross now.

'Nothing,' said Dave. 'It's just, I get really claustrophobic. I mean, I've got a note from my doctor and everything. I don't ... I mean, I don't really think I could get in one of those suits.'

'So when you looked up beekeeping,' said Polly, 'I mean, did you actually look it up, or did you look up "World of Warcraft, bee edition"?'

Dave looked more embarrassed than ever.

'I really wish I hadn't told them I could do this,' he said.

'Not as much as I do,' said Polly. She glanced at her watch. It would be early in the morning where Huckle was. And she didn't really want to speak to him, not after . . . well. He could certainly have called her if he had something to say. And he had not.

The cottage was giving her a terrible, indefinable ache. How much she would have loved, she admitted to herself, letting her mind stray where it shouldn't; how much she would have loved them to leave Reuben's beach, to come back here, with the heady scent of flowers, and the complete and utter privacy, and squirrel themselves away, doing nothing but make love until . . .

'So, er,' said Dave. His spotty neck seemed worse than ever; he kept picking at it. 'I mean, do you want to phone the temp agency?'

Polly sighed.

'When's the baby due?' she asked.

'September,' said Dave. His face perked up a bit. 'It's a little girl. Our first. We want to call her September. My mum reckons it's silly, but we like it. Because she's going to be born in September, you see?'

Polly rolled her eyes.

'Yes. I do see.'

She sighed again.

'Okay, so I'm NOT going to phone the agency. But you can tell them they're just to pay you for today, okay?, and that we don't need anything else. Then get yourself to a building site; they're recruiting in town, doing loads of renovations.'

This was true. House sales were picking up all over the area, and scaffolding was sprouting like mushrooms as people demanded roof conversions and open-backed indoor/outdoor kitchens.

'Er huh,' said Dave. 'Only I'm a bit afraid of—'

'Heights?' said Polly.

Dave nodded. Polly smiled.

'Okay, okay. Do you think you can find your way back to town?'

Dave looked doubtful.

'Along the track, follow the signposts,' said Polly patiently. 'And good luck with the baby, okay?'

'Thanks,' said Dave wholeheartedly. 'I mean it. Thanks so much.'

'Off you go,' said Polly severely. She watched him march away, looking around him curiously, then wiping his forehead with his suit sleeve and pulling off his tie. She shook her head, then suited up as Huckle had shown her. It hurt so much to remember them laughing together, and him trying to tickle her through the suit. Hadn't there been something between them even then? Or had she imagined it all? Obviously, yes. She sighed. It was a physical pain.

She went down to the hives, glad that she hadn't brought Neil, who would not have liked it at all, and tried to remember everything Huckle had shown her. She smoked down the hives to make the bees quiet, then cleaned out the dust, added some sugar syrup in case they were hungry and scooped up some of the lovely thick combs, ready for pulling out. It didn't take long, and it was quiet and restful in the garden with the little bubbling stream babbling away to itself, and the occasional drifting dandelion puff. And even though she knew it was unutterably pathetic, demeaning, and everything she was trying so hard to get away from in her life, she felt closer to Huckle doing it. Even though it didn't matter now, even though he'd gone – and might never come back – a tiny bit of her could pretend. He could be in the house now, having a nap. The motorbike was still there too ...

She opened her eyes, cross with herself. This was stupid and wouldn't get her anywhere. But at least she was keeping the bees alive.

Chapter Twenty-Six

The weeks passed, with no word from Huckle, but Polly simply carried on.

She was impressed by how well Jayden was doing. He was brighter than he'd seemed, and so happy and relieved not to be on the boats any more he bounced into work, his leg barely troubling him, heaving flour about with ease, taking care of all the cleaning, chatting nicely to the local customers and curtly with the incomers (he hadn't travelled very widely).

Polly had upped her baking as a result, meaning the shop didn't empty till three or later, which was fine because now they could both take breaks. And something else had happened too: a new restaurant – a proper restaurant, with white linen napkins and real glasses, not just bottles of Fanta – had opened up in one of the tumbledown buildings along the front. They got their fresh fish from the boats that had been hired or bought afresh with insurance money by the fishermen who were once again plying their trade along the harbourside – and their bread from Polly!

It had been very exciting. Samantha had come into the shop one morning, introducing the son of a friend of hers from London, announcing him as *the* most talented young chef, who was going to put Mount Polbearne firmly on the map – Polly had not commented on this – and urging him to try Polly's speciality breads. To Polly's huge gratification, he had pronounced them excellent, and put in a daily order that she baked along with the rest. Samantha, very kindly, had negotiated a fee on her behalf that was substantially more than Polly had been expecting, though when she saw the prices on the menu – the restaurant was called 'Mount's' – she didn't feel guilty. Living the quiet life she'd adopted here, and working incredibly hard, she was actually starting to make some money. Mrs Manse had agreed that she should have a share of the profits, and there was absolutely no doubt they were on the rise, for both of them. Polly was able to take all her restaurant earnings and put them away for safe keeping. It wasn't much, but it was a real start.

She finally managed to grab lunch with Kerensa, who'd been mysteriously out of reach, only contactable occasionally on the telephone. She appeared to be in sex prison or something; whenever they spoke, she always sounded a bit breathless and half naked. They turned up at Mount's, looking around it curiously. It had been an old bucket and spade shop that had gone bust without anyone bothering to remove the old fixtures and fittings, or pick up the post. Now it had been completely transformed; it had flagstone floors and cool white walls, white tables with little lemon trees on, and a glass frontage with a perfect view of the harbour. There was a new terrace too, where people could sit outside, but Polly and Kerensa stayed indoors, as it had been colonised by a group of very noisy people talking about Chelsea.

Kerensa looked awesome, Polly had to admit. She was suntanned, and had put on a little bit of weight, just enough to make her pleasantly rounded rather than over-worked-out; her eyes had a dreamy, sleepy expression and her skin was flawless. Polly saw what it was. She looked happy.

'Look at you,' Polly said. 'You've vanished off the face of the earth. Because you've got a boyfriend! Reuben is your boyfriend!'

'God no,' said Kerensa. 'No. He's my ... er, shag toy?'

'Bleargh,' said Polly. 'That's disgusting.'

Kerensa's phone beeped with an incoming text. She glanced at it, gave an infuriatingly smug smile and put it face down.

Polly rolled her eyes.

'Mash note?'

Kerensa took a sip of her sparkling water and changed the subject. 'Goodness, this place is coming up in the world.'

Their waiter was a gorgeous boy in his early twenties; Polly had no idea how he'd ended up here. He took their order solicitously, and Kerensa insisted they have a glass of Sauvignon Blanc too, whilst Polly mentally wrote off going back to work that afternoon.

'So,' she said, treading carefully. 'What about your job?'

Kerensa looked down at her plate.

'Um,' she said.

'WHAT?'

'Er, well, Rubes called the office and threatened to buy the company and sack everyone in it if they didn't let me have a leave of absence,' mumbled Kerensa, at least having the grace to sound embarrassed.

'Kerensa! Are you a kept woman? What happened to "the house I live in, I bought it"?'

'I did buy it,' protested Kerensa. 'It was either that or he threatened to hire me as a consultant. I am going straight back. Just as soon as I've got this very annoying man out of my system.'

There was a long pause. The phone beeped again, and Kerensa smiled and texted something back.

'You're right,' said Polly. 'This is totally a casual fling that you can take or leave.'

'No, no, hang on, I'll stop.'

Polly rolled her eyes. 'I think you're in love with him.'

'He's a doof,' said Kerensa, but fondly. 'You know, there is something very sexy about somebody who tells you they're going to be fantastic and then is.'

'Well now,' said Polly, pleased. 'I've always liked him.'

'Have you heard from Huckle?'

Polly took a large gulp of the delicious freezing cold wine that had just shown up. Kerensa had told her in advance that she was paying for lunch so shut up, and they had both ordered the oysters and the whitebait, which was a lot fancier than what Polly normally liked, but she found to her surprise that she was enjoying it.

'Because it was weird, wasn't it, him shooting off like that? When's he back?'

Polly hadn't told a living soul about the kiss she and Huckle had shared at the party. She was too ashamed, especially after Tarnie.

'I don't know, she said.

She was heading down to the cottage every couple of days to collect the honey and keep an eye on things. She hadn't told Huckle it wasn't the temp agency doing it; he'd have felt guilty and hired someone else. Anyway, on these glorious long summer days it was actually very enjoyable to be outside: the drowsy humming, the heavy scents, and everywhere the astonishing flowers. Plus the honey was a good seller in the shop.

Kerensa put down her glass.

'Nothing happened between you two, did it?'

Polly nodded slowly.

'HURRAY! Great! I knew it! He's a total hunk!'

'Yes, and he's gone back to the States,' said Polly, trying to be brave.

'For a bit,' said Kerensa. 'Probably getting his affairs in order so he can fly back and do you senseless.'

Polly shook her head sadly.

'No,' she said. 'It didn't . . . it didn't go well. It was just . . . it was so weird it happening at Tarnie's wake and everything and I got a bit spooked . . . and he pulled back, did that funny closed-up thing again. I think . . . I think I totally freaked him out and now it's all gone wrong.'

'Oh don't be ridiculous,' said Kerensa crossly. 'Call him and tell him you made a terrible mistake and he has to stop being a nobber and come home.'

Polly shook her head. 'He hasn't called, emailed, nothing at all. He left the country. I think I have to see that as a very clear message.'

'Yes, a very clear message that you're both total idiots,' said Kerensa.

348

Polly bit her lip.

'No,' she said. 'He told me before that he wasn't ready for a relationship. He'd just come out of something really serious. Anyway, if a boy likes you, he'll come and get you. Like Reuben did.'

'What are you, in the 1950s?' said Kerensa crossly. 'That's nonsense. Call him.'

'It was just a kiss.'

'Sometimes that's worse. Oh, I don't mean that. Oh Pol. You have had some rotten luck.'

They both fell silent.

'I'm such an idiot,' said Polly. 'I really thought he was ...'

'There's no doubt he likes you,' said Kerensa. 'He's always looking for you. He doesn't talk to anyone else, just sits in his chair giving it the big Owen Wilson. Then you turn up and it's like his eyes suddenly open; he's suddenly there.'

'Really?' said Polly, then, quickly, 'Oh. It doesn't matter. It doesn't matter now. He probably won't come back.'

Kerensa paused. Polly wondered if she would try a comforting lie, but in the end she didn't.

'He might not,' she said. 'But you'll be all right, yeah?'

'Of course!' said Polly stoically, taking a large slurp of her wine. 'I've got Neil.'

'Exactly!' said Kerensa.

And they chatted about other things, and decided in for a penny, and ordered a bottle of the delicious white wine and had a hilarious afternoon after all.

Chapter Twenty-Seven

Huckle found it both comforting and a bit weird how people hardly commented on his being back. It was like he'd just been on holiday. Which he had, he supposed.

His mother was pleased, of course, but she was so used to him being away in the 'big city', which was what she called Savannah, doing things that she didn't really understand, that going to a totally foreign country wasn't much different to her. His buddies were glad to see him, and made lots of cracks about warm beer and cricket, and whether he'd developed a weird accent. He spoke to a firm of consultants he knew, who took him on immediately, and found himself working regularly in offices around town. The hours were long, but the work wasn't difficult – it was quite nice to engage his brain again, at least for now – and the money was amazing. As his quiet way of saying fuck it, he rented an apartment just like his old one, as far away as possible from the quaint town houses of the old city, which reminded him too much of England: a glass box, way up in the sky in a new high-rise. He had hardly anything in it; it was not at all cosy, had no rugs or eiderdowns or thatched roofs. And it was cool.

He had to put Mount Polbearne out of his life now, remember it as a dream. There was a harbour in Savannah, full of big beautiful boats: pleasure cruisers and the gambling riverboats that still patrolled the slow, silty mouth of the great Savannah river and the swampland beyond. But there were little boats too, and Huckle walked past them of an evening, when the temperature dropped a little and it was possible to go outside without feeling you were in a steam oven. The harbour front at Savannah was pretty, lined with shops and bars and the smell of churros and barbecue, and teeming with happy plump tourists wearing matching T-shirts. But Huckle went to listen to the chattering masts. Sometimes he would close his eyes.

At the back of his mind he knew he had to sort out the little apiary when his lease ran out, go and tidy his stuff away in England.

It would be best, he surmised, not to see anyone when he went over. Maybe Reuben, briefly, though Reuben couldn't be trusted for a millisecond not to charge over to Polly and blab about everything. But he couldn't ... He told himself he didn't want to lead Polly on, he told himself it had been just a passing summer friendship at a time when they both really needed a friend. That was all.

But of course, he realised, if they really were friends, they'd be chatting right now. Every day, in fact. He'd have liked to chat with her, tell her more about his life and how he was doing and what Savannah was like: he would love to show it to her.

But she was in love with a dead man. He'd been hurt before; it wasn't going to happen again. And look how busy she was, how the bakery was thriving; she wouldn't have the faintest interest in him. Best put it behind him, stay where he belonged. And anyway, he'd forgotten how much he liked it here: the easiness of getting everything, the choice in the supermarkets, his cool apartment, the noisy bars. It wasn't that bad, he told himself.

Even so, he still walked down to the harbour most evenings, just to listen to the masts.

It was always going to happen, sooner or later. Savannah wasn't that big a town, and sure enough, one beautiful pink-tinged Sunday evening, when Huckle was considering going to a movie then browsing the bodega, he ran into Alison, Candice's elder, skinny sister.

'Huckle!' she said, clearly only pretending to be surprised. 'I didn't know you were back in town ... Well, I'd heard something.'

'Sure,' said Huckle. 'Hi.'

'So how was England? Lots of rain? Beer warm? Did you play cricket?'

'Er, yeah,' said Huckle, feeling uncomfortable.

'Well, great to see you, gotta run.'

'Er, how's Candice?' said Huckle, quickly.

'Well, she's just great!' said Alison. Huckle waited for the stab in the heart, but surprisingly, it didn't come. Instead, to his amazement, he felt mildly interested; quite pleased, in fact.

'Cool,' he said with a huge smile. 'Well, tell them I said hi.'

'I'll do that,' she said, heading off into the sunshine.

He knew that, Candice being Candice, she'd be straight on to him, and sure enough, he was barely back in his apartment before his email pinged, asking him to meet up for coffee. She didn't mess about.

They carefully avoided their old haunts and met the next day outside the office where he was working. She looked, as ever, good: worked-out and muscular, very blonde, her heels tapping on the sidewalk. Mentally Huckle contrasted her with Polly – long strawberry-blonde hair floating around her shoulders, the soft freckles on her nose – then blinked the image away.

'Hey,' he said. 'You look great.'

'Yeah,' said Candice. 'I'm on this new meal plan. You look good too.'

'Yup, me too,' said Huckle. 'I just eat bread all the time.'

She arched an eyebrow.

'That stuff is pure poison.'

'Soy latte?'

She smiled. 'Always.'

They sat by the window.

'So how was England? Does it rain all the time? Did you play cricket?'

'Oh no,' said Huckle. 'It rains a bit. Sometimes. But not like here, where it's like a monsoon. It kind of spits on you a bit and gets real windy, then it's gone. But at the moment the weather is beautiful. It's not hot and sticky like here, it's maybe high seventies?'

The thermometer next to the water tower in Savannah had been showing 94° that morning.

'So you wear a T-shirt, but maybe take a jumper for when the sun goes down. And the town, right, it's got all these tiny little stone houses that look like they're climbing on top of each other. Some of the sidewalks have stairs in them otherwise they're too steep to get up. And there's only a few roads and they all lead to the harbour, and in the morning if you get up early you can see the fishing boats come in with the night's catch, and you can buy some right there and then and they slit the fish for you and take out the guts and it's the freshest fish you can possibly imagine. And right on the harbourside there's a little higgledy-piggledy shop . . .'

He paused for a moment, then went on. Candice looked at him curiously.

'It's a bakery, the most amazing bakery I've ever been to. Every morning from first thing you can smell the wonderful scents rising up from the baking bread, and when she opens her doors, you can buy the bread warm straight out of the oven, and tear bits off and sit on the harbour wall, and after half an hour most of the town will come by for a bit of chit-chat and to buy their own bread, and that's how Polbearne wakes up of a morning.'

His face was completely lost in reminiscence.

'Sometimes, if you're really well behaved, the girl who runs the bakery will bring you a cup of decent coffee too. But you mustn't bother her, she's very busy.'

Candice raised her eyebrows.

354

'Sounds like you know this baking woman quite well.' Candice herself never cooked; she got her meals delivered from a nutrition company. 'Sounds like she's a good friend,' she went on, looking at him. She hoped he had found someone else; it would make her life a lot easier not having to feel guilty.

Huckle sighed.

'Oh, I didn't want to complicate things,' he mumbled. And he told her about the fishing boat disaster.

'Jeez,' said Candice. 'That's awful. But was she serious about this Tarnie guy?'

'I don't know,' admitted Huckle.

''Cause it sounds to me like you like her a lot.'

Huckle shrugged.

'And she might have liked you too. In fact I think you might have been a total pair of idiots.'

'Thanks for that,' said Huckle, taking a long sip of his coffee. 'How's . . .'

Candice went a little pink, and smiled.

'Er, you know . . . now that I've heard all about Little Miss Bakery, I am a lot less bothered about telling you this, but Ron and I are getting married.'

'Congratulations!' said Huckle, and again to his amazement, he found that he genuinely meant it. Ron and Candice were well suited he did three triathlons a year.

'Thanks,' said Candice. She looked at him.

'You were so daft to run away like that,' she said. 'Well, that's what I thought at the time. But now . . . I'm not sure it didn't suit you. You look well, Huckle.'

He smiled. 'Oh, anywhere suits me.'

355

Candice arched an eyebrow.

'Hmm,' she said as they stood up to go. 'Stay in touch. If you're staying.' She gave him a quick kiss on the cheek.

'Sure,' said Huckle, watching as she clip-clopped her way down the sidewalk.

Chapter Twenty-Eight

They were all gathered in Polbearne's new posh restaurant, summoned for a meeting by Samantha and Henry, who, despite being incomers, had somehow contrived – as well as providing the local builders with a huge amount of work, and persuading several of their posh friends to buy tumbledown cottages, which pleased everybody – to take over the running of the town. They had called a meeting about 'the Greatest Danger of our Time', according to the posters they'd put everywhere, and nearly everyone had turned up obediently, partly interested, partly because there wasn't much else to do now the summer rush was slowing down, and partly because they suspected, correctly, that Samantha and Henry might provide free wine.

Patrick was there from the vet's; Muriel, of course; Mrs Manse, sitting alone imperiously; Archie and Kendall from the boats, and Jayden. Polly was sitting at the side, with Neil, stifling a yawn.

'What's going on?' she asked Patrick. She knew that the

unspoiled, unmodern ambience of the village was what appealed to him about Polbearne. He felt they had something there, an unbroken link to the past – several of the older residents still spoke a little Cornish they'd heard at the feet of their own grandparents. The idea of change terrified him.

Just then, Samantha stood up and pinged her glass.

'Now, I'm sure you've all heard the news,' she said, which she knew wasn't the case because she'd only got it herself from a planner she'd made a huge effort to cultivate on the mainland so he'd let her build a roof garden.

People shook their heads, and Samantha explained.

The new summer rush had never slowed, not even for a second, but it wasn't that that was changing things; it was the wreck. The police had sealed off the beach, and special ships had come along and siphoned all the diesel off the ship – about forty thousand gallons – but there was still a lot of merchandise on the bottom of the ocean and the ship needed to be taken away for scrap. Every day, ducks were washing up; taken by the tides, they had been found as far away as Exmouth, and Land's End.

But back in Mount Polbearne, the problem was local. Lorries and diggers and diving vessels and personnel needed to get into the town to work, and they needed to get back at night-time, regardless of the tides. The new residents wanted building work done to their houses, which also meant trucks and lorries and diggers. And they wanted to drive their cars. Daytrippers too didn't want to risk getting stranded or take an overpriced ferry boat back to the mainland. The talk had been around for years, but it had started to gain more and more momentum, particularly when a car broke down one summer

Sunday on the causeway just as the tide came in, and the family inside, including very young children, had had to make a heart-stopping dash for it as the water lapped around their knees. Something had to be done, was the general consensus, and the local council, delighted with the regeneration of the area, had applied to the central development fund for a bridge to connect them to the mainland.

There was a gasp around the room, then an immediate burst of noise.

Some people thought it was a great idea. It would open up the town to more people. It would mean you could go and do a supermarket shop and not worry about getting back in time. It meant no more being stranded in the wintertime when the storms made the causeway impassable for days. It meant the fishermen could get their fish to market faster, and that people could live on the Mount and commute. Jayden was very excited, pointing out that he wanted to go to a nightclub in Plymouth and flash his new-found 'indoor job' status. The fishermen grumbled a bit about the imminent loss of their water taxi income, but most understood that there was no halting progress, that it had always been just a matter of time. Patrick, of course, was valiantly opposed.

'Well can't they all go and live in those places, then? The pizza-ordering places? And we can keep this as a place where you can't order a pizza.'

Polly suddenly felt like she'd love a pizza, but didn't feel she could mention it. Maybe she'd make some in the shop. Maybe, she thought suddenly, she could *be* the pizza concession – she had the oven, she'd just need to work slightly different hours. It would be tricky, but not impossible, and given the amount of hungry men currently working in the town, probably extremely popular.

'Hmm,' she said, in two minds.

'Abso-bloody-lutely not no bridge!' thundered Henry in his pink cords. 'We'd get all sorts in here.'

All the Polbearnites, including Polly, rolled their eyes, and helped themselves to another glass of the wine Henry was paying for.

It was a lot to think about, and the main topic of conversation of everyone who came into the shop, along with the fact that a famous pop star had tried to buy the lighthouse.

'The LIGHTHOUSE is for sale?' said Polly in amazement. She still had broken nights, despite spending a lot of money on blackout curtains. How could you live in that?

'Well no, it's fine when you're inside it,' said Muriel. 'It's the only place in Mount Polbearne you *can't* see the damn light.'

'Hmm,' said Polly. 'Is the pop star going to buy it, then?'

'No,' said Muriel. 'They wouldn't let him put in a fireman's pole and a helter-skelter.'

'Why does planning say you can't have a helter-skelter but you can have a bloody great eyesore bridge?' said Patrick, who was picking up a bloomer. He had given two interviews to national papers (who were very in favour of maintaining Polbearne's traditional ways, regardless of whether any of the locals wanted to go to a supermarket or not) and was feeling commensurately proud of himself.

'Good point,' said Polly.

She wandered over to the lighthouse after another night of being kept awake. It was as dilapidated as the rest of Mount Polbearne – or half of it, at least, given how much gentrification was going on, a gentrification which, it was occasionally pointed out to her, she had helped start. Nobody had lived in the lighthouse for a long time, since the beam had become remote control; the black and white stripes were peeling, and the little granite cottage next to it was small and functional. It was completely impractical as a project. But she couldn't quite get it out of her head.

Every two days, rain or shine, she went to Huckle's cottage to look after the bees. It had turned into her constitutional, her own form of exercise, until it was just out of habit, more than anything else, or some kind of weird talisman. She cleaned out beds, removed dead bees and checked on the queen; sterilised and filled the honey pots and carried them back in her rucksack, Neil sitting on some newspaper on the top. The honey continued to sell well in the shop, and she put the money aside carefully for Huckle when he came back. But she'd heard nothing; of course he wasn't coming back. For all she knew, his ex had greeted him off the plane with open arms, apologising for breaking his heart, begging him to go back to her.

Polly came back to the harbour one afternoon after a honey trip and to her great surprise ran into Dave the temp.

'Hello!' she said. It was late August. Not quite so light in the morning when she got up to start the day's baking, but still warm, and the soft summer air had a touch of cooler breeze about it. 'How's your girlfriend?'

'Good!' he said. He was looking more cheerful, although his spots were still there. 'She had the baby early.'

'Oh no,' said Polly. 'Is she all right? Did you call her Augusta?'

'No,' said Dave. 'We wanted to call her September, remember?'

'Yes,' said Polly. 'But I thought maybe because she was born in August ...' Her voice trailed off. Dave still looked utterly uncomprehending. 'Well,' she said. 'That's wonderful.'

He smiled again. 'She's amazing.'

'So what are you doing back here?' asked Polly. 'Tell me you're not working on the new bridge. You'll never manage it.'

He shook his head. 'No. I heard there's a place going on a fishing boat.'

It was true. Despite high unemployment in the area, it was still difficult to persuade men to go into fishing, which was seen as dangerous, uncomfortable and poorly paid. Jayden's place on Archie's new boat hadn't been filled.

Polly looked at him sternly.

'Dave,' she said, not wanting to waste Archie's time. 'Are you sure you're not frightened of fish?'

Dave shrugged.

'Dunno,' he said. 'I only really eat fish fingers. I'm frightened of sharks, though.'

'There's only little sharks out there,' said Polly.

'Little sharks are the most poisonous,' he said. 'Or no, hang on, is that spiders?'

'I don't know,' said Polly.

Archie came over.

'Come on then,' he said to Dave. 'You know this chap?' he asked Polly.

'Um, a bit,' said Polly, unwilling to dump Dave in it.

'Reckon he's up to it?'

'Be nice to him,' said Polly. 'He's just had a baby.'

Archie's face broke into a smile. 'Oh congratulations,' he said. Polly smiled to herself about what an old softie he was.

'Have you got kids?' asked Dave.

Archie smiled. 'Three. Well, three plus . . .'

Polly turned to him.

'No way!'

'Yes way. And not just us.'

'What do you mean?'

'Well, Bob at the chemist's got another on the way. And Dave at the pub. And Muriel.'

Polly shook her head.

'MURIEL? How far along?'

'Yup, you got it.'

Polly thought about it.

'Seriously? The wake?'

Archie shrugged.

'It's going to be the first baby boom in Mount Polbearne for about two hundred years. We're going to need a school.'

'No way,' said Polly. 'That's amazing. And I'm guessing all the boys will be called Tarnie.'

'Well they won't be called Cornelius,' grunted Archie. He turned his attention to Dave again. 'Are you afraid of hard work?'

'Not sure,' said Dave.

'Can you handle a knife?'

Dave looked dubious.

'Oh well,' said Archie. 'It'll give me some practice with babysitting. Come on then, soft lad.'

Dave followed him, rigid with terror. Polly watched, smiling, as he wobbled and slipped on the jetty. Archie had to practically lift him on board. Polly shook her head. Well. They would see.

The tide was out, and on the cobbled causeway Patrick was taking lots of photographs. It was odd, thought Polly, as she returned to her flat and sat at her window, opening a beer; the idea that the village might change from the way it had been for hundreds and hundreds of years. And that she had arrived to see the very end of it. The thought made her sad.

Her phone rang.

'If this is someone calling me to tell me that they're pregnant, congratulations,' said Polly. 'I do christening cakes.'

'Not quite,' said Kerensa's overexcited voice. 'But the next best thing . . .'

Chapter Twenty-Nine

They had immediately convened a summit for the next day. Reuben had offered to helicopter Kerensa over, but she had declined.

'Well you're an idiot!' said Polly. 'I'd love to go in a helicopter. I think the rest of our lives should be spent just riding round and round in Reuben's helicopter.'

They hugged in the pub courtyard.

'We're getting married!' shrieked Kerensa. Every time they'd spoken recently, Polly reflected, she'd sounded like she was going to explode. Reuben must be rubbing off on her. 'We're getting married! WAAAH!'

Polly marched up to the bar and ordered champagne. Dave looked very doubtful, but managed to dust something down from the back of the fridge.

'Since when is my bankrupt mate ordering champagne?' frowned Kerensa.

'AHA!' said Polly, smiling. 'You're not the only one with news.'

The post had come that morning – the postie always brought it into the bakery. Jayden had never had a letter in his life and was always fascinated by what arrived, even though it tended to be flour invoices and a lot of bank paperwork. Today there was a large cardboard envelope with Do Not Bend printed on it, addressed to Polly, handwritten. She recognised the lovely hand-writing, dusted the flour off her hands and opened it, puzzled.

Carefully she extracted the contents, and gasped. It was a painting: a beautiful, architecturally precise rendering of the Little Beach Street Bakery, with the masts and sails in the foreground, the bread in the window, a tiny watercolour sug-gestion of her inside. It was ravishing.

'Chris!' Polly said in delight.

'That sulky guy?' said Jayden, squinting at the painting. 'That's REALLY good,' he added with feeling. 'I wish I could do that.'

'Isn't it?' said Polly, her heart swelling. 'He hasn't painted like that in such a long time. Oh, how lovely of him.'

There was a note attached. Polly read it, and her hand flew to her mouth.

'Oh my God!' she yelped. 'Oh my God! We've sold the flat! We've sold it! And we did all right ... we've paid off our debts! Oh my God, we're going to be discharged! WHOOP!'

And she turned up the radio and danced around the counter with Jayden, who hopped willingly. Neil squawked and jumped up and down so he didn't miss out on the fun.

'I don't know what that means,' Jayden said. 'But it sounds good.'

'It is GREAT!' said Polly. 'Oh my God. I'm free! I'm free! I have money! I'm free! I can . . .'

She sobered up.

'Wow, I could move.'

Jayden looked at her.

'Why would you move?'

'You've changed your tune,' teased Polly. 'Of course I'm not going to move away from Polbearne. I mean out of the flat. Oh my God. But I could buy out Mrs Manse. Or I could put a roof on the flat. I could . . .'

She glanced down at the paper once more. 'Okay, I couldn't do that much. But STILL!'

And that was the reason for the happy raiding of the petty cash tin to buy some champagne. Polly also, unselfishly, gave the picture to the nice young men at the restaurant, who sold it almost immediately for a fortune and straight away got him to do more, which also sold. She finally kept the tenth one for herself, before she priced herself out of the market.

'So,' said Polly, settling down at their table in the courtyard, unable to keep the grin off her face. Kerensa had hugged her and told her how wonderful it was and how you wouldn't believe she was the same person after what a terrible rotten old misery-guts she'd been six months ago, to which Polly had rolled her eyes and said seriously, she wasn't *that* bad, and Kerensa had said, okay, no totally, you were brilliant, and so happy, and then they both fell about laughing.

'So what about that guy you hated?' said Polly.

'That was before I had sex with him,' said Kerensa. 'Man.'

'All right, all right, no more,' said Polly. 'Not to someone who is never going to have sex again and has settled for being a successful businesswoman. Congratulations!'

'I know!' said Kerensa. 'This is going to be awesome. We're going to have the most immense wedding ever.'

'Ha,' said Polly. 'You're starting to sound like him.'

'We're very similar in a lot of ways,' said Kerensa. 'Except he's really annoying and I'm not.'

Polly smiled.

'And you have to be my maid of honour,' said Kerensa, swigging her champagne.

'I am FAR too old for that.'

'Nonsense. You have to. I have to have about a billion bridesmaids anyway; we're getting married in America.'

'No way!'

'Yes way. Reuben's family have some massive estate up in Cape Cod on the ocean, which is apparently quite nice.' She tried to say this in a way that indicated it wasn't at all a big deal, but the two of them couldn't keep it up and fell about laughing at that too.

As if magnetically drawn by the champagne cork popping, posh Samantha popped her head into the pub courtyard and came towards them, stopping several metres away as the sunlight washed across Kerensa's absurd, bird's egg engagement ring and blinded everyone within range.

'OH MY GOODNESS,' she said. 'NEWS!'

'It is news,' said Polly. 'Do you want some fizz, or are you pregnant too?'

Samantha joined them immediately and peppered Kerensa with questions about the size of the Cape Cod estate, the number of guests, the catering options. Then she went quiet, put her immaculate hands on her tiny lap – her own engagement ring was huge, but nothing on Kerensa's, which technically qualified as a weapon – and sighed.

'You know, I don't think any of our friends have ever been to a wedding like that.'

Polly and Kerensa exchanged looks.

'Of course you can come,' said Kerensa kindly.

Samantha let out a tiny shriek of joy.

'Now of course you know Reuben is insisting on a *Star Wars* theme . . .'

The girls left the pub later, quite tiddly, and wandered over to the dock, where the boys were making a commotion. Polly looked over. Dave was holding up a gigantic fish, his face red with pleasure.

'You didn't catch that?' she said. Dave was beaming. The fish was the size of his chest.

'First big cod I've seen round these parts for a few years,' said Archie. 'Those quotas must be working.'

'And *Dave* caught it,' said Polly, trying to keep the disbelief out of her voice.

'You're kidding, aren't you? This boy's a natural-born fisherman. Scared of nothing, he is.'

Dave was beaming. Jayden came out from the bakery to take a photograph.

'I love fishing,' Dave told him. 'I don't know how you could have given it up.'

Jayden rubbed his fingers down his white apron. His

tummy was already showing the signs of his career change, promising to emerge into a very impressive belly in the years to come. Being Jayden, of course, he had no malice in him.

'That's really cool,' he said. 'Are you going to sell it to Andy's chippy?'

He lined them all up so he could take a group photo.

'We should put this in his window,' he said. 'So that everyone who goes there thinks that all their cod comes from that fish.'

'And he can put his prices up even more,' muttered someone. Andy had not been slow to take advantage of all the new trade, particularly at high tide. But his fish and chips remained as hot and crackling and salty as ever, the fleshy fish generous and silken, with plenty of scraps in the bag, so no one minded too much really.

Kerensa and Polly made their now traditional drop-in to get some chips and Fanta, then sat and kicked their legs on the harbour wall.

'Aren't you on a wedding diet?' teased Polly.

'Sod that,' said Kerensa. 'Anyway, God only knows what I'm going to be wearing.'

Chapter Thirty

Things were changing, thought Polly as she moved through the town, taking the cash box to Mrs Manse. She had to excuse herself to get out of people's way, there were cars nudging their way down roads that were far too narrow to take them, and people were looking oddly at Neil perched on her shoulder, which made her feel like a weird cat lady and was extremely annoying. Although the bakery was doing so well, she still wasn't sure about so many new people in her home, and the bridge would make it even worse. The no-bridge campaign was still running strong, but could they really halt progress?

She hadn't been over to the old bakery in a little while; Jayden tended to deal with all that. As long as Mrs Manse was barking at him, everything seemed all right with the world. So she was a little shocked as she approached to see Gillian cowering behind the counter as a man Polly had never seen before gesticulated at her.

Without thinking, Polly marched right in. The man was

wearing red trousers and had a loud, abrasive London accent. His face was as red as his trousers, and he was shouting so loudly, spittle was coming out. Neither of them saw her enter.

'You can't charge for this shit!' he was yelling. 'You can't eat this! I'm going to get trading standards on you! If a supermarket did this, they'd get shut down. You can't rip off decent people like this for awful bloody sandwiches! It's a cheek! This mayo is on the turn.'

Polly felt suddenly completely torn between her love for good, decent, honest food – which she really did believe in – and defending what now felt, beyond all measure, like her home town, her people.

She coughed loudly. The man turned round, still furious. He was big.

'Excuse me,' she said, and as she did so she felt her accent get more Cornish, more local than the generic southern English it normally was. 'This is our town, right? And if you don't like our sandwiches, you are more than welcome to pee off right back where you came from.'

'But they're bloody stale.'

'That's how we like them,' said Polly, folding her arms defiantly. 'Now I would suggest it would be a good idea for you to leave. In fact, tell everyone else you know not to come by either, because if they're all horrible thugs who bully old ladies, I think we're better off without you, don't you? Now do you want to keep abusing an eighty-year-old, because I have Officer Charlie on my speed dial.'

She held up her phone menacingly.

'This place sucks,' shouted the man angrily. 'I hope you all go to hell.'

'So do I,' said Polly. 'If it would keep the scum out.'

The man crashed the rickety old wooden door so hard the entire shop shook. Polly looked at Mrs Manse; she was white.

'What's wrong with you?' Polly said, trying to make a joke of it. 'Normally you could run nine guys like that out of town before breakfast.'

Mrs Manse leant on the counter top. The man had thrown the sandwich across it, and there were smears of old salad cream everywhere. Her hands were shaking. Polly still tried to make light of it.

'Don't you think I'm turning local? Do you think I'd pass muster?'

Mrs Manse didn't say anything, just stared at the counter. Polly put the cash box down and went round to her.

'Look,' she said. 'Sit down a minute, okay? He's just one stupid man. Don't let it get to you. He's patently a total idiot.'

Mrs Manse shook her head.

'They're everywhere,' she said, sitting down heavily on a stool. 'They're here now. That's how it is. And they're going to build this bridge and then it will truly be a disaster.'

Polly tilted her head.

'Well, we have a lot more visitors. That's good, isn't it? We've never taken more money. We're going to do well, give you a comfortable retirement.'

'I'm nearly eighty,' said Mrs Manse. 'I don't want to do this any more.'

Polly looked round the dusty, neglected shop.

'Well,' she said. 'I have ... not very much, but I have a little bit of money that I might be able to—'

Mrs Manse shook her head. 'I don't want your money,' she said. 'You keep paying me rent, you can keep the rest. I have plenty put by. I'm going to go and live with my sister in Truro. They've got bingo.'

'Well, that sounds ... that sounds good,' said Polly, trying to be encouraging. 'Are you sure you want to leave Mount Polbearne, though? You've lived here all your life.'

'And it's brought me ...'

Mrs Manse trailed off. Polly suddenly felt that Gillian should have been playing bingo with her sister a long time ago. What the old woman said next took her completely by surprise.

'I need to thank you, you know,' she said.

Polly looked at her.

'Excuse me?'

Mrs Manse nodded.

'Before you came ... I couldn't leave. I couldn't go. You know. The town would have died without a bakery. Yes, I hated the work; it was my husband's idea for me really. But I did it for him and I did it for the town, because it was my town and no other bugger would.'

Her face looked distant.

'And I lost Alf and Jimmy, and well, that was ...'

There was a long silence.

'But then you came with your fancy ideas and your daft words for a basic bloomer and your stupid plans to make things different ... and, well, it worked. Some of it,' she added. Polly smiled to herself.

'And now they don't need me. There's more and more of 'em, and they don't need me. They'd rather go somewhere young that lets seabirds walk in the flour.'

She harrumphed this last bit. Polly patted her on the shoulder.

Mrs Manse's eyes lifted and looked out.

'I knew,' she said. 'I knew when that boy Tarnie never came home. Those other boys came home, but my boy never did.'

'I know,' said Polly respectfully.

'I know now, I do, you know. I know . . .'

Her voice trailed off; she looked a little confused.

'I know he isn't . . . I know they won't . . .'

Her old hand clasped Polly's suddenly, with surprising strength.

'I hope they're together, Jim and Cornelius. Wherever they are.'

Then she burst into tears.

Polly moved fast, turning the shop sign over to 'Closed' – it wasn't like the Little Beach Street Bakery, where there'd be a huge queue down the harbour by now; nobody was passing at all. She locked the door and immediately went into the back of the shop and switched on the kettle.

'Nice cup of tea,' she said. 'Nice cup of tea.'

'They don't come back,' said Mrs Manse.

And although Polly knew she meant her husband and her son and Tarnie, she couldn't help thinking of someone else, someone whose hair glinted in the sun, who was so far away . . . As the kettle boiled, and she kept a worried eye on Mrs Manse, she wondered, wasn't she doing kind of the same thing? Keeping everything nice for Huckle, just as Mrs Manse couldn't bear the idea of not being there to greet her menfolk when they came home? Just in case? There wasn't any more chance of Huck coming back, not really. Not at all. It had taken Gillian Manse a very long time to face the truth. When would Polly face it?

She made Mrs Manse drink the tea, then took her upstairs to her little flat and, without much difficulty – the old lady was still mumbling – persuaded her to get into bed. She called Archie and asked him to track down Mrs Manse's sister in Truro, then she sat in the stifling flat, waiting for the doctor, who had to wait for the tide.

As she waited, she noticed that the photo, the old photo she'd seen in the drawer, had been taken out and put on top of the cabinet that housed the television, freshly dusted and polished. Gillian had been speaking the truth, Polly realised; she had accepted what had happened to her boys, and knew that they wouldn't be coming home again.

The doctor arrived looking harassed.

'The sooner they get that bridge sorted, the better,' she said. 'This is ridiculous, it's medieval. How do you guys live like this?'

Polly looked at her.

'We like it,' she said, defensive again.

The doctor checked Mrs Manse over and declared her physically fit, if clinically obese. She sniffed loudly. 'Though you might just call that normal these days. All that white bread.'

Polly decided she didn't like the young doctor.

'She's a little confused, though. I would say it's almost certainly just a dizzy spell to do with her age, and I would

376

suggest that whatever she does now, she doesn't stay on her feet for too long.'

'I think she wants to go and play bingo,' said Polly.

'Perfect,' said the doctor. 'Is she still working?'

'Runs this place single-handedly.'

The doctor shook her head.

'That won't do. That won't do at all.'

'It's all right,' said Mrs Manse sleepily. 'This ... this girl is going to run it for me now. Aren't you, Polly?'

Polly realised that this was the first time Mrs Manse had ever used her name. She normally just referred to her as 'you'; as in 'you've ruined this village'.

She squeezed Mrs Manse's wrinkled old hand.

'Of course I am,' she said. 'I promise.'

Chapter Thirty-One

The seasons had rolled around and new shops had opened in Polbearne: a bespoke fishmonger that paid the men well for their catch, next to the beautiful seafood restaurant; and a children's clothes and knickery-knackery shop that Polly was astonished to see could actually make a living.

Both bakeries too were thriving; they had hired another member of staff and Jayden oversaw the running of everything with ease, handling the main baking and the grunt work and leaving Polly to experiment with new tastes and flavours and techniques, which she enjoyed. She had also got a lovely mention in a Sunday newspaper, which pleased her. She had been on one or two dates, once with a surfer friend of Reuben's, who turned out to be very chatty on the subject of surfing and almost entirely uninterested in anything else, and also with an architect who was working on one of the conversions, but nothing had quite clicked, even as she told herself that what she and Huckle had had was a friendship gone slightly awry, and that was all. Anyway, she was far too busy to worry about that, what with Christmas with her mum, her brother and his children, Reuben and Kerensa and Kerensa's parents. It all got a bit embarrassing when Reuben and Kerensa kept snogging over the Christmas crackers, but there was a big service up in the old church building, everyone freezing but giving thanks for a year that could have been so much worse, and the whole thing was brilliant fun.

But as spring and the wedding approached, she found herself getting a bit nervous again. She settled on a cool 'Hey, how are you?' approach, but then of course if Huckle turned up with his ex – if he turned up with anyone – she knew she would be gutted.

Most people didn't even know about her and Huckle; didn't even ask. Kerensa asked did she want him disinvited, and Polly pointed out that he was Reuben's best man. Kerensa said screw that, Reuben did anything she told him to, and Polly could only smile and say don't be ridiculous, it was a tiny kiss ages ago. Who could possibly still be bothered by something like that?

Come the early spring, pop pop pop, the babies all arrived: one Tarnie, one William, Tarnie's middle name, two Cornelias and a Marina. (One of the Cornelias belonged to Samantha, who had been pregnant after all, just so slender she didn't recognise the fact.) People started regularly talking about Polbearne needing a school, which inevitably led to some of them saying 'and a bridge'. The village was still very split. It would be touch and go come the quarterly planning meeting.

Reuben and Kerensa were hoping their wedding ceremony

would 'blow everyone's socks off'. From Mount Polbearne only Polly was flying out, as maid of honour, which made her really nervous. Samantha couldn't because she was pregnant. Archie had been invited but couldn't be persuaded to leave his new baby, the apple of his eye. Jayden was needed to mind the shop.

Polly practised being calm and collected, telling herself that Huckle would probably barely remember her: just some girl he hung out with for a bit, on that holiday he took. She wondered how utterly impossible this was going to be when she had to turn up dressed as Princess Leia, complete with doughnut ears.

'Why don't YOU have the doughnut ears?' she had hissed furiously on one of the many occasions she and Kerensa had had cause to fall out about it.

'Because I'm going to be the *young* princess,' said Kerensa. 'Reuben thinks the later, prequel episodes are terribly under-rated.'

'That's because he's wrong about everything,' grumbled Polly, trying to plait her hair up again.

'Wear the wig,' counselled Kerensa.

'No chance,' said Polly. 'I look like an actual mad person.'

'But if you have red doughnuts you'll also look mad.'

'Strawberry blonde,' said Polly. 'And this was your fiancé's stupid idea. Seriously, is everyone coming like this or is it just going to be me?'

'Everyone,' said Kerensa. 'All five hundred. Reuben is taking it extremely seriously.'

'FIVE HUNDRED?'

'But it's okay,' said Kerensa. 'You don't know any of them.'

'Great, that helps. Who's Reuben going to be anyway? Luke?'

'No! Darth Vader. It's going to be hilarious.'

'You're not serious.'

'Totally! It's going to be fab.'

'You're getting married to Darth Vader.'

'It's sexy.'

'It's asthmatic. And evil.'

'Well I think it's going to be really special.'

Five hundred of Reuben and Kerensa's friends and relations were booked in to hotels close to the seafront mansion, but Polly was only interested in seeing one. She couldn't sleep a wink on the long flight over, couldn't eat. When she got there, too late for the rehearsal, about which Kerensa was furious – 'You won't walk at the right speed' – she wished more than anything else that the hotel would let her into the kitchen to make up some dough to calm her nerves. Instead she lay tossing and turning in the vast luxury suite, trying not to worry about how tired and jet-lagged she'd look in the morning. Finally, at about four a.m., she drifted off, waking, very late, to the most beautiful American morning. The sun shone; the Atlantic looked far bluer and wider, it seemed, than it did from the other side. Polly ordered breakfast in bed, looked at the white costume hanging on the back of the door and groaned loudly.

She couldn't force anything down but a cup of coffee. She was terrified of seeing him again, particularly when Kerensa, banging furiously on her door, hauled her away to an elaborate hair and make-up session. When she saw her hair twisted into their ludicrous headphone shapes, she wanted to burst into tears. Kerensa on the other hand looked rather good: pale make-up and an extraordinary kimono-style dress, incredibly huge and elaborate, with her hair perched on top of her head and what was clearly about four other people's hair pinned on for good measure.

'Wow,' said Polly.

'I know,' said Kerensa. 'Amazing, huh?'

The wedding was outdoors, on a completely perfect lawn. There was a bower leading down to the water's edge and chairs laid out with large bows tied to their backs. The bows were black and had pictures of the Millennium Falcon on them.

'Who are all these people?' asked Polly wonderingly.

'Oh, everyone loves Reuben,' said Kerensa complacently, and Polly gave her a hug.

'I love you,' she said.

'Watch the kimono.' Kerensa grinned. 'You too. I have invited all his sexy rich friends. There must be SOMEONE at this wedding who won't move to another continent if you kiss them.'

'They'll move *before* I kiss them, the second they see this bloody headphone hair . . . Oh my God, are those Ewoks? They must be boiling.'

The familiar *Star Wars* music, played by the Boston Symphony Orchestra, struck up as they finally reached the French windows leading out to the lawn. Their path was scattered with black and white rose petals. Polly squeezed Kerensa's hand.

'EEK!' Polly said.

'YAY!!' said Kerensa back.

Kerensa's dad, of whom Polly had always been fond, was trying to look as dignified as possible whilst dressed as Obi-Wan Kenobi. Father and daughter embraced, then Kerensa, steady as a rock in her huge costume, indicated for her flower girl, Cadence, Reuben's extraordinarily fat but very pleasant sister, who was dressed as a red handmaiden of some sort, with horns, to throw blood-red rose petals in front of their feet.

Polly stepped out clutching a bunch of white flowers and feeling so nervous she thought she was going to throw up. At first she gazed at the ground where she was walking, but as people started to clap (they obviously did this at American weddings), she raised her head.

And there he was.

Reuben had to be standing on a box, or wearing high heels or something, because assuming it really was him in the black Darth Vader mask, he appeared miles taller than usual. And next to him, managing somehow to look calm and as stupidly handsome as ever, dressed as Han Solo in a rather fetching leather jerkin, was Huckle.

Polly bit her lip and carried on walking. Gasps were greeting the arrival of the bride behind her. This was good; Polly felt there weren't as many eyes on her now. She'd been instructed to go down the aisle then stand to the left of the rabbi, on the bride's side. Huckle of course was on the other side. But he came towards her immediately, holding out his hand. She swallowed hard.

'Hello,' he said quietly.

'Hello,' she replied, and as if he'd never been away, he

planted the softest kiss on her cheek and led her over to his side, despite Reuben harrumphing crossly.

'I like your hair.'

'Shut up,' she said, her heart thumping.

'No, I mean it.'

'You're wearing a jerkin. How could I possibly take what you have to say seriously?'

They arranged their faces into expressions of suitable solemnity as Kerensa, looking truly like a queen, took her place next to Reuben, hissing at Polly to go round her other side. Polly pretended not to hear her. She also noticed that Reuben was wearing platform boots.

Inside, her whole body was like fireworks, exploding with joy. She couldn't keep the smile from her lips or the glow from her face as Huckle gently took her hand. All the difficulties, the separation, the long, cold winter months, the lonely nights, the long days, the fact that seeing him again was temporary; all those things dissolved just being near him.

'Where's Neil?' he whispered.

'Did you know they don't give out passports for seabirds? It's a disgrace.'

'Well if you stay here long enough, he'll probably find us.' Polly smiled.

'If everyone has quite settled down,' said the rabbi, rather tersely and giving them a sharp look, 'we can begin.'

'My queen,' recited Reuben in a low monotone, reading from a card. 'May the Force be with us as we travel through the galaxy of life. I pledge never to turn to the dark side ...'

'Bit late for that,' whispered Huckle, and Polly smacked him.

384

'. . . but to stand for ever in the illumination of our love. I vow to fight the evil empire and you may take your place at my side as we rule the galaxy.'

'I will,' said Kerensa.

She took out her own card. Polly bit her lip very, very hard.

'My Jedi, my love. I take your hand and accept your pledge. May the Force be strong in us. Remain a Jedi and I will stand by you.'

'I will,' said Reuben, the heavy breathing from his mouth-piece making it come out as a rasp.

Polly felt herself getting vaguely hysterical. It didn't help that after they'd crushed the chuppah, and it was announced that Reuben could kiss his bride, he couldn't get his helmet off. Mostly people were clapping and didn't notice straight away that there was a titanic struggle going on. Kerensa tried to help, but couldn't raise her arms in her enormous dress. The rabbi had to step in and try and unfasten him, with Reuben expostulating furiously the entire time.

Polly felt an insistent hand on hers.

'Come with me.'

'We can't leave yet.'

'We'll be back before he's got that thing off.'

Huckle drew Polly out through the side of the flower-entwined bower – nobody even passingly looked at them – and down a little slope to the beach, where nobody could see them.

And down there, he took her hands.

'I am so sorry your boyfriend died,' he began, carefully.

Polly looked at him.

'I ... I was fond of Tarnie,' she said. 'But he wasn't ... It was awful that he died, but we'd ... you know, we weren't together.'

'You acted like it was wrong.'

'Oh Huckle!' said Polly. 'THEN! It felt wrong THEN! At his FUNERAL! Not FOR EVER, you big doof!'

She saw the slow, lazy grin crack across his face, and found she couldn't help it; there was no holding back now. She hurled herself into his arms and kissed him, fiercely, the two of them rolling down the dune towards the surf.

'I thought it was for the best,' he said, when they came up for air. 'But if I'm honest ... if I'm honest with myself, I couldn't believe how much I missed you, how much I thought about you. Every day, every minute, every second. I've been waiting for this.'

'I've been dreading it,' said Polly.

'Why?' asked Huckle.

'In case you were back with your ex ... in case you had someone else.'

Huckle shook his head. 'God, no.'

'But to leave and not to contact me ...'

'I thought you were grieving for Tarnie and I would only get in your way.'

And as they kissed, the entire wedding party – C-3PO, R2-D2, plenty of Ewoks, a very unhappy Jabba the Hutt and a Jar Jar Binks who'd almost got turned away at the door – appeared over the top of the dune, coming down to get their photographs taken. Polly instantly felt guilty for behaving badly at her best friend's wedding, until Kerensa, right in the centre of the group, moving very slowly as befitted her queenly status and uncomfortable garments, came towards her with her bouquet of blood-red roses outstretched.

'I'm not going to throw these,' she said. 'I can't lift my arms anyway. I think they are just for you.'

The rest of the wedding was a riot of excess: oysters and fresh Maine lobster, a new cocktail, rows of immaculate waiters, and a famous eighties band who were truly terrible in every way, though the people in costumes rivalled it. There was a choreographed dance by the bride and groom that nobody who saw it ever forgot; four hours of speeches during which six people fell asleep, and a cabaret performance by a famous stand-up comedian and a dancing dog.

It was all completely wasted on Polly and Huckle, who liberated a bottle or two of the Krug and stayed down by the water's edge, completely wrapped up in one another. Huckle remembered that he should go and make his best man's speech, but when he got to the vast marquee and saw people fanning themselves and passing out all over the place, he simply sidled over, hugged his friend (whose plastic carapace was uncomfortable to the touch and felt increasingly sticky, though Reuben refused to remove it) and whispered in his ear:

'Do you want the full version or the short version?'

'MAKE THIS HELL END,' breathed Reuben through his regulator, whereupon Huckle held up his glass and declared:

'To my friend Reuben, the best, the most heroic yutz I ever met in my life, and his wife, who is of course far too

387

good for him,' and the entire room exploded into clapping and cheering, from relief more than anything else.

'Now, Reuben's early life was somewhat challenging,' said a short elderly man dressed as Luke Skywalker and looking not very happy about it, as he got to his feet brandishing a sheaf of notes as thick as a telephone directory. The room collectively groaned. Huckle was glad that Reuben's face wasn't visible, as he grabbed a plateful of wedding cake (there had been nine of them) and another bottle of fizz, and ducked back outside.

He stood for a second, just looking. The sun was setting behind them, and the sky was filled with pink and yellow, a soft, clear light that lit up Polly's hair, which had come loose from its ridiculous buns and was falling in soft waves over her shoulders. She was standing perfectly still, gazing out to sea with a pensive, faraway look on her face, his ridiculous jerkin resting lightly on the shoulders of her white dress. He wasn't used to Polly being still; she was always doing something, five things at once sometimes: laughing, eating, baking, clearing up, taking money . . . She was normally a ball of energy. To see her so soft and still like this . . . His heart simply leapt in his chest.

'Hey,' he said, very quietly. She turned her head and smiled at him, as the huge waves crashed on the surf.

The hotel they were both staying in was oddly bare; fashionable, Polly supposed. It had wooden floors and clapboard walls and pale colours everywhere. They'd got there hours before the rest of the party, as a massive disco band had arrived at the mansion and was forcing everyone to dance.

'It was starting to look less like fun and more like a marathon of endurance,' observed Huckle gently.

'Oh, you know Reuben,' said Polly. 'No top he can't go over.'

Huckle smiled. 'Quite.'

'Oh, I brought you this.'

She pulled out a pot of his honey.

'Ha!' he said, looking at it, marvelling. He had put that side of his life away so completely, it barely felt like his at all.

He looked back at Polly.

'Well, I am hungry,' he said simply.

Polly, emboldened by the champagne, and the long wait, and the desire to finally seize the moment – to seize something for herself – pulled off the top of the white costume she was wearing in one movement. Underneath, she had nothing on.

'God,' breathed Huckle. 'Look at you.'

Polly's skin, usually so fair, had taken on a golden hue, freckles popping up in the sunshine, and her strawberry-blonde hair had lighter streaks in it.

'You're so beautiful,' he said, as the dying rays of the sun caught her hair through the dormer windows. 'So beautiful.'

Polly knew she wasn't, not really. But here, in this room, in this light, with this man, she felt like she was. And that was enough. She drew closer to him – at last! at last! her nerves were screaming – but even though she was trembling, she was also patient. She was going to take her time; enjoy every second. His huge broad chest, once she got his shirt off, was brown, with light golden hair across it. She wanted to bury herself in it. He picked her up and sat her on his lap as if she weighed nothing at all, and before he kissed her again, he buried his face in her hair.

389

'Oh God,' he groaned. 'I want you so much.'

Polly looked up at him and smiled.

'That,' she said, 'is useful.'

Huckle laughed his slow, lazy laugh. Then he picked up the honey, dipped his fingers into it and, with long, languid strokes, rubbed it into her small breasts. Polly giggled.

'That is going to be so sticky,' she said.

'I'll get it all off,' promised Huckle.

Then the time for laughing was over, and everything became suddenly more serious, more intense, as they lost themselves utterly, body and soul, in one another, until neither could tell where one began and the other ended.

'Were those . . . fireworks?' said Huckle, finally.

'Yes,' said Polly, her eyes full of stars. Then she focused again on the room.

'Oh God, they actually are fireworks, aren't they?'

'Either that or we're under advanced military attack.'

Outside the window, sure enough, was the single most enormous fireworks display Polly had ever seen. The sky was filled with furious explosions and enormous noises. A great red glittering heart was flickering and puttering over the sea. Polly and Huckle looked at each other and burst out laughing.

'It's almost,' said Huckle, 'like someone's trying to tell us something.'

They dressed swiftly and ran down to the beach again, away from where everyone else was being served picnic hampers as the fireworks entered their thirtieth exhausting minute, and lay back in the dunes in each other's arms, watching the show.

Chapter Thirty-Two

Nobody made it up in time for breakfast the next day, but Polly managed to catch up with Kerensa before she left on her round-the-world safari honeymoon the next evening. There was a huge brunch, but Polly was too excited to eat. She grabbed Kerensa by the door, meaning to apologise, but Kerensa got in there first.

'God,' she said. 'I am SO sorry. I never got to see any of my friends at all, spent the entire time shaking hands with big old white men and posing for photographs. Look! Ow! My face hurts! This must be what it's like being famous. It totally blows.'

'But did you have a good time?' said Polly.

Kerensa nodded madly. 'I loved every second,' she said.

'Where's Reuben?'

Kerensa looked slightly awkward.

'Er. He's just ... I mean, the helmet was a bit hot ... It's just a precaution.'

'What?'

'He's a bit dehydrated. They put him on a drip.'

'He's in HOSPITAL?'

'He parties hard,' said Kerensa defensively.

'He does!' said Polly. 'Oh my. Well, I will see him ... very soon.'

'And where are you going?' said Kerensa. They went into the dining room of the hotel, which had been laid out with every foodstuff Polly could imagine: bagels, smoked salmon, eggs, croissants, fresh fruit of every kind, a juice squeezer, pancakes and waffles, champagne of course everywhere, hash browns and sausages.

'Goodness,' said Polly. The Plymouthites were sitting at a table in the corner, and they all cheered Kerensa as she walked in. And then did a double-take at Polly.

'We thought you'd gone!'

'We thought you didn't talk to us any more!'

Polly realised it was the first time she'd seen many of them since she'd taken herself out of town. She had felt so ashamed, so embarrassed, she hadn't let any of them near her. Looking round at the kind, interested faces, their obvious pleasure at seeing her again, she found it hard to believe now that she had been too proud to ask for help, so certain that nobody else would understand what she was going through. They scooshed up to make room for her and launched into loads of questions about what she'd been doing since she left Plymouth. When she told them, they were gratifyingly impressed, and Kerensa smiled secretly to herself.

Huckle had slept late, had slept better than he had in months, in fact, and came down and spotted her laughing and joking with her friends, who had already made plans to come down to Mount Polbearne over the summer. He smiled nervously and she looked shyly back at him, the events of the night before etched clearly on her memory.

'Hey,' she said, getting up. One of her friends let out a quiet 'woop' and she hushed them quickly.

'This is my friend Huckle,' she said, with as much dignity as she could muster, but the smile spilling from her face betrayed her utterly.

'You,' said Rich, one of her old friends who worked in marketing. He pointed a finger at her. He was still quite drunk from the night before, and the Buck's Fizzes were now helping him along too. 'You are NEVER coming back to Plymouth.'

'Come with me,' said Huckle, when they surfaced later. 'Come have a look at Savannah.'

Polly swallowed. She supposed Jayden could mind the shop for a little, but he couldn't bake like her. Quality would slip faster than you could say bath bun. But Huckle wheedled, and before she knew it, he had booked her a seat on the plane, and she called home and it was decided.

But she didn't have long.

'Wow,' said Polly, looking round the minimalist apartment with its floor-to-ceiling glass. Outside, the lights of Savannah seemed far below. 'I can't believe you live here.'

'Now that we've christened the bed, I'm never leaving,'

said Huckle, lying back, his arms behind his head, a picture of total contentment.

Polly gazed at his body, which she had dreamed of so often. To see it laid out for her was almost too much.

'Mmm,' she said, and he smiled back at her.

'So,' he said. 'What do you want to do tomorrow? I can send you to the mall.'

'Why, what are *you* doing?' she asked, surprised.

Huckle bit his lip.

'Well, I have to go to work. So I thought you might like to, you know. Shop for a few things.'

'What things?' said Polly, suddenly worried. 'I never shop.'

Huckle shrugged. He had thought, he realised on some level, that as soon as he got her back here, she would stay, would be so happy just to be here, that it would all be perfect.

'Okay,' he said. 'DO NOT SHOP! I order it. Stroll around. Have a look at Savannah. It's gorgeous here.'

He stood up behind her and embraced her as they stared out of the window together.

'We don't have to live here for ever, you know,' he said. 'Go look at the old section; they have these most gorgeous houses there, on garden squares. We could live in one of those.'

Polly turned round, hurt.

'But I have a house.'

'You rent an apartment that lets rain in,' Huckle pointed out.

'At the moment,' said Polly. 'But I was thinking of . . .'

She hadn't really been thinking of it seriously, but suddenly it came out.

'I was thinking of buying the lighthouse, actually.'

Huckle actually laughed.

'You're not serious?'

'I might be.'

'That old falling-down lighthouse? It'll be worse than the flat.'

'Not with a bit of care and attention.'

'And all that light!'

'Actually, when you're IN the lighthouse, you don't see the light,' pointed out Polly. 'It's the only place safe from it.'

Huckle shook his head.

'I love your crazy ideas.'

'It's not . . .'

They both fell silent, sensing disagreement.

'Are you going to have a fireman's pole?' said Huckle eventually.

'Maybe,' said Polly, trying not to sound defensive. 'Anyway.'

'Anyway.'

Huckle sat down on the bed, and they looked at each other.

'Sorry,' said Huckle slowly. 'But I thought . . . I thought you'd come and live with me. Here.'

Polly blinked several times.

'But I came to the wedding.'

'Yes, I know, but, you know. To me too. No?'

'No,' said Polly, half lying. 'I mean, I wanted to see you, but . . . it wasn't till I actually did see you . . .'

Huckle nodded. 'Yes! And hurray!' he said. 'I mean, COOL, look at us! Look at us, we're amazing. Aren't we?'

395

Polly nodded.

'And you're here . . .'

His voice tailed off. He had to admit, he had thought about it. Wouldn't it be lovely for Polly not to have to get up at five every day, slave her guts out, get covered in flour, behaving like an indentured servant to Mrs Manse, whom she hated, living in that shack of an apartment? Wouldn't it be lovely for her to be here, in a lovely home with him, taking a rest, having some time off? He assumed that that would be exactly what she wanted, what she would like . . . He had plenty of money, he could pay for everything . . .

He tried to explain this to Polly, realising as he did so that what had seemed perfectly logical and reasonable in his head wasn't coming out well at all now that he started to say it. Her face was looking more and more concerned.

'But it's mine now,' she tried to explain. 'The bakery. Mrs Manse has retired to her sister's. She's left everything in my hands. It's my responsibility.'

'But you can bake here,' said Huckle, gently kissing up the side of her neck. 'Hmm?'

Polly pulled away from him.

'Have you got this all planned out?' she said, her heart beating at a million miles an hour.

Huckle shrugged and looked at the ceiling, then at her.

'I have nothing planned out,' he said. 'But oh, I want you so much.'

They were the words, Polly realised to her horror, that she had longed to hear; had been desperate to hear for a long time. She wanted to be with Huckle, she dreamed of him, she thought of him all the time. All her joy in the bakery she had wanted to share with him, every funny story, every high surf day. Just to be near him now, to breathe in his scent, to be in what she had always felt as the glow of his company, that had lit her up whenever he was around . . . He was offering her the world, she realised.

She gazed at him, felt his soft, strong hands caressing her shoulders.

'But I can't leave,' she said. 'I can't leave Polbearne. I've worked so hard to make something mine.'

'And you deserve a rest,' said Huckle. 'Just stay a while.'

She gazed into his intense blue eyes.

'Couldn't *you* move?' she asked imploringly.

Huckle swallowed. 'But Polbearne,' he said. 'It was . . . it was a time out for me. It wasn't my real life. My work, my job . . . I can't make little pots of honey for the rest of my life.'

'Some people do,' said Polly, quietly.

'It was amazing, but seriously. I can't live somewhere I can't get to see you unless the tidal conditions agree with me.' He laughed. 'You have to admit it's a bit crazy, that place.'

Polly leapt back as if stung.

'It's my home now,' she said. 'Anyway, they're talking about building a bridge.'

'A bridge!' said Huckle. 'Now that's a BRILLIANT idea.'

But he quickly saw from Polly's face that it was not.

Polly only had one day left on her ticket. Huckle showed her round Savannah, hoping that she would fall in love with it, and she was polite, and certainly appreciated its beautiful buildings, but it was dreadfully hot still, and hard to stay out for long. There was not much left to say; instead they made love, and they cried, then they'd sleep, then wake up and cry before starting all over again.

'Let me tear up your ticket,' Huck begged. 'Just walk away. You've done it once, you can do it again.'

'But I can't,' said Polly miserably. 'I owe it to Mrs Manse, and Jayden, and I've worked too hard to build this up. It's the first thing I've ever done for myself. You can surely see that.'

He nodded, heartbroken.

'But you can do it again. Can't you? Now you've done it once?'

'I don't think so,' said Polly. 'I can't even work in America. I couldn't possibly do that here.'

'Well don't do anything,' pleaded Huckle. 'Don't do anything. Just come and live in my bed.'

She laughed at that.

'I don't know how long that would work. You couldn't come back to Cornwall? You're great at skipping countries every five minutes.'

Huckle looked so sad.

'But my home ... my family, my job, everything ... I don't know if I could do it again. I'm a grown man. I have to behave like one.'

She nodded. She understood.

What they'd had had been a dream, just an idle fantasy. They weren't teenagers. They were grown-ups, with responsibilities.

'I can't believe I was your holiday romance,' said Polly, not even bothering to wipe the tears that were still dripping from her eyes.

'You weren't . . . you aren't,' said Huckle. 'We'll find a way. We have to.'

They clung to each other when the cab turned up to take her to the airport.

'You probably shouldn't go,' pointed out the cabbie helpfully.

'Don't,' Huckle said to Polly, his face distraught. 'Please,' he said. 'Please, this isn't the end. This can't be the end. Not again.'

She just looked at him.

'Don't you think it'll make it worse?' she said. 'If we . . . if we pretend? If we keep pretending?'

Huckle shook his head furiously.

'Nothing can be worse than this,' he said. 'Nothing.'

They stood, the cabbie sighing and looking at his watch, the traffic honking furiously as it circumnavigated them.

'I don't want you to go,' said Huckle.

'I don't want to go,' said Polly.

'Go, don't go,' said the cabbie. 'The meter's running.'

It took every ounce of strength Huckle had not to chase the cab straight down 8th Avenue and grab her back into his arms. At any second he expected her to jump out of the door and come running to him. But she didn't.

Stunned, numb, too exhausted even to cry, Polly sat with her back against the torn and gritty old leather of the green and white cab, and stared into space.

Chapter Thirty-Three

There was always work, of course. And Polly had plenty of other things to occupy her. She had already decided that she was going to put the tiny bit of money left over from the Plymouth apartment towards a deposit on ... Well, no, it was ridiculous. She would never get it. Samantha and Henry's friends had already mentioned what a hoot it would be to live in a lighthouse, and Polly felt resentful, as she walked past it occasionally with Neil, looking up at its little windows, its faded stripes, that it would be bought as a holiday toy for someone to show off about, when she knew – she was really sure – that she would love living there.

She wondered what Huckle would think, then shrugged it off. He had called every day; sent emails. That morning he had sent a poem, and she had wondered whether she shouldn't stop talking to him, because it hurt too much.

I make seven circles, my love,
For your good breaking

I make the grey circle of bread
And the circle of ale
And I drive the butter round in a golden ring
And I dance when you fiddle
And I turn my face with the turning sun till your
   feet come in from the field.
My lamp throws a circle of light,
Then you lie for an hour in the hot unbroken circle
   of my arms.

She had stared at it for twenty minutes, then kneaded the dough so hard she thought she would dislocate her shoulders.

Now she sat on the harbour wall, watching the sun turn golden in the sky and waving the lads off on their way to work. Dave looked suntanned and happy, bantering with the rest of them. Jayden made them sandwiches every day at a reduced rate, and he brought them down to the boats and stopped for a chat. She'd wondered if he missed fishing at all, but he had laughed so heartily at the thought of it, she never asked him again. In fact, he looked the part more and more every day; he was a born baker.

She went home and looked at Kerensa's ludicrous honeymoon pictures on Facebook, then made herself a simple supper and only looked at the poem another eight or nine times. After she'd eaten, she forced herself down to the pub for another of Samantha's interminable meetings about how to stop the bridge. They seemed interminable, Samantha boldly pointed out, because there wasn't a bridge yet, so they were obviously working. Samantha brought her baby along; Muriel had hers too, and Polly thought of the changes she'd seen in the last year as they got ready for the summer season again.

Samantha was talking, but Polly was miles away.

'What do you think?' she snapped in Polly's face.

'Er, yeah, fine,' muttered Polly, trying to pretend she knew what was going on.

'So it's decided!' said Samantha, to general groans. 'Polly had the casting vote!'

'What have I just agreed to?' said Polly worriedly to Jayden, who was looking cross right beside her as they went to the bar.

'The sit-in,' said Jayden. 'Well, stand-in. Samantha's getting the press down and we all have to stand holding hands along the causeway to stop them building the bridge.'

'But we'll drown!' said Polly. 'This is a ridiculous idea. It'll totally prove their point that we need a bridge!'

'I know,' said Jayden dolefully.

'And the water is freezing! It's only spring.'

'I know. And I want to go to a nightclub.'

'Just go to a nightclub,' said Polly, slightly exasperated. 'Book a bed and breakfast or something.'

Jayden frowned.

'Wow,' he said. 'I could! Now I have all this money!'

'What money?' said Polly, narrowing her eyes. He was on minimum wage.

'All the money I'm making now,' said Jayden happily.

'You're not telling me it's more than you made as a fisherman?'

'LOADS more,' said Jayden. 'Wow, a B and B. Imagine. They make you breakfast and everything.'

'Yes,' said Polly. 'Yes, they do.'

The human chain was scheduled for Easter weekend, the first big holiday of the season, and three days before the local council was scheduled to vote. The town was going to turn out on the causeway as soon as the first tide had gone down, and stay till the second, with banners and songs. The second tide would come up about five o'clock, by which time, they hoped, their point would have been made.

Kerensa and Reuben were jetting in from the current leg of their honeymoon (Porto Cervo in Sardinia – Kerensa said all the rich women were completely awful and Reuben kept trying to buy her really ugly handbags, and they had decided to settle for just lots of sex instead) to join them for a bit of solidarity (and, Polly suspected, a chance for Reuben to zip around in his Riva).

The mornings were getting lighter, and Polly was up, for once, with the bright pink dawn that morning, baking extra lots of buns for the post-human-chain barbecue they had planned on the little shingle beach. She had overheard Lance the estate agent complaining in the pub about not being able to shift the lighthouse unless they got the damn bridge, and was feeling tentatively hopeful about it.

And it was a lovely morning, she thought, whistling cheerfully as the wonderful scent she never tired of rose from the ovens and she looked forward to seeing her friends. She'd persuaded a gang of Plymouthites to come down for the day; Chris might even join them. Apparently, his new girlfriend was a radical artist with big nose studs who made pictures with blood in them. Polly rather liked the sound of her. Neil hopped over and she ruffled his feathers affectionately and gave him a quick kiss on the beak.

'It's going to be a nice day, Neil,' she said gently, looking out of the bakery window towards the east, where bright golden rays were just beginning to bounce off the top of the water, then straight ahead, where she could hear the fishing boats chugging back in. Not much changed in Polbearne, and she wanted to keep it that way. Not for the first time, she wondered if she was turning into Mrs Manse.

Chapter Thirty-Four

Huckle knew it was time; had known for ages, in fact. He had got no response to his poem, which he had thought might spark something – he'd believed it, wanted to believe it so much he'd almost gone to the airport, for God's sake. But no. He had to sort that area of his life out now, move on. Everything was going swimmingly in Savannah, work was busier than ever, he could go out every night if he wanted to, though he rarely did. It needed to be done; he'd been putting it off too long. He shut his office door and pressed 9 for a long-distance outside line.

First the house. He called the rental place, who were so overjoyed that they would have a prime property to rent in the up-and-coming region of Polbearne, the new hotspot, profiled in all the Sunday supplements, that they didn't even charge him an early vacancy fee. They had a list of downsizers a mile long, apparently, who had fallen in love with the quirky area and thought keeping bees would be a perfect next step.

He asked his PA to bring him a cup of coffee, then phoned the temp agency to cancel the beekeeping contract – the new tenants were moving in in a week, so one more visit should do it.

The woman on the other end of the phone was confused.

'Sorry, Mr Skerry, but you cancelled your temp service.'

'Er, no?' said Huck.

'Yes, it's quite clear here. Mr Marsden came back saying you no longer required a temp. He's now left the agency, I'm afraid, or I could ask him. We haven't been sending anyone, not in months.'

Huckle thanked her, and wondered. Polly had brought him all that honey when she came, and it had been fresh. Not just fresh, wonderful; he'd made a mental note to congratulate the temp, and then, in the turmoil of what had happened with Polly, had completely forgotten all about it.

It dawned on him slowly. What an idiot he'd been. What on earth . . .

Suddenly, in his mind's eye, he saw her like she was standing right in front of him. Saw her walking through the avenue of trees – such beautiful trees, he remembered – rain or shine, summer and winter, every day, simply going there to tend his bees, on top of everything else she had to do. His eyes blinked away tears. All those months when he'd thought she was in love with the memory of a ghost; all those months, in the mud and the wet, she had tramped across the causeway and up to his house, and tended his goddam bees.

He looked round at his office – the novelty of being busy once more was fast wearing off. He thought of the snarled freeways and the humid, sticky evenings, the tie that felt far too tight around his neck, his buddies sending him group messages about going to watch a baseball game, the files teetering high on his desk, his promise to take his mother to church on Sunday, the invitation to Candice and Ron's wedding, which looked as if it would be just as over the top as Reuben's. His entire life piled up around him, holding him in, and all he could think about was those goddam bees. Well, not quite all.

Without realising it, he had pulled off his tie.

'Oh man,' he said to himself, running his hands through his hair. 'Man. Susan!'

His PA was holding his black coffee hopefully. She was madly in love with him.

'Er. I have to . . .'

He couldn't think of what to say. The last time he had left he had gone quietly, taken time out under his own rules. This time it didn't seem to have anything to do with him; his legs were moving of their own accord. He absolutely couldn't believe he was doing it again. But he was.

'Yeah, I have some . . . some things to take care of.'

'Anything I can help you with?'

Huckle shook his head.

'Er, no. Not . . . No. Er. Can you book me a cab to the airport?'

He didn't call anyone, didn't speak, didn't stop to think. He barely slept on the plane, but the long train ride from London to Looe knocked him out completely and the guard had to gently shake him, having noticed his destination on the reservation on his seat. Huckle was extremely grateful.

The cabbie chattered non-stop all the way to Polbearne about how incredibly successful the place was becoming, how they might get a new bridge and that would change everything. Spring was coming in, and many of the little winding roads were papered with pink and white blossom. Between the rolling hills, the sea still sparked. Huckle gave a sigh. He had forgotten just how beautiful it was.

The taxi driver got so far up the lane and no further; Huckle turned and thanked him, and got out with his leather overnight bag. Feeling leadenly tired after his incredibly long journey, he almost limped up the familiar avenue, the thick carpet of petals beneath his feet.

At the little cottage gate he stood for a second and put his bag down. Then he slipped off his shoes and socks so he could sink his bare feet into the cool, soft grass. He could hear once again the reassuring babbling of the little brook and the low, gentle hum of the bees.

'Hiya there, guys,' he murmured, overwhelmed with tiredness and, oddly, the most extraordinary relief.

He noticed, to almost no surprise, that his bee coveralls had been scrubbed clean and hung up tidily. The hives themselves were humming along in immaculate condition. The wax had been scraped away, the honey perfectly jarred. He looked at the trees with the fairy lights and remembered the night they'd spent drinking mead. He smiled. All his mead dreams turned to dust for a well-paid job back in an air-conditioned office. No. No no no.

Quick as a flash, Huckle pulled off his smart travelling suit, ran in and out of the shower, bouncing with excitement and sudden adrenalin, and pulled on jeans and an old T-shirt.

He charged out of the house, not even locking it, eating toothpaste for speed. Thank God the motorbike started first time, because he was beyond thought now. He wasn't thinking, he wasn't planning, he wasn't doing anything rational at all. It felt wonderful.

He sped along the little lanes, narrowly missing a huge lorry carrying vast amounts of scree, and pulling up with a roar at the end of the road leading to the causeway. The tide was coming in; there was a stern sign warning people not to use the causeway within two hours of high tide. He was well within the window, but he didn't care. He barely noticed that there were loads of vans and cars parked there, some with television insignia on the side, and a small crowd of people standing around; all he wanted to do was get on the causeway before it closed.

Then he saw it. Right along the causeway. A massive line of people; the whole of Polbearne, holding hands, all the way from the mainland to the Mount.

'What's going on?' he asked Muriel, who was standing on the end, a cute baby in a sling on her back.

'HUCKLE!' she screamed. 'Oh my God, you're back! Polly's right at the other end!'

'What are you doing?'

'We're protesting. We don't want a bridge!'

'No bridge, no bridge!' chanted the crowd, filmed by the television crews.

Huckle broke into a huge grin and took Muriel's arm.

'Quite right too,' he said. 'NO BRIDGE, NO BRIDGE!'

But he could see that the water was already lapping up the side of the causeway. He took a worried look at the baby.

'How long are you going to keep doing this?' he asked.

'I know, we're nearly done,' she said, and just as she spoke, a bullhorn went off.

'CLEAR THE CAUSEWAY! CLEAR THE CAUSEWAY! MOUNT POLBEARNE FOR EVER!' called a voice Huckle recognised as Samantha's.

There was a surge of people coming off his end, and he had to struggle his way through.

'Nope, we're done now,' said Jayden, looking officious in a reflective jacket. 'Come on, sir ... Oh, it's YOU.'

'Yes,' said Huckle.

'Well, we all have to be off the causeway by five. Come on, it's the law.'

'I just want to see Polly.'

'She's on the other side – you can see her in the morning.'

The water had started washing across the causeway now, and everyone was hurrying off with damp feet.

'I'll just go quickly.'

'You won't make it,' said Jayden. 'And I'm on this side, I can't take the boat out.'

'I'll be fine.'

'It's freezing,' said Jayden. 'You won't. Don't be an idiot.'

Huckle grinned. 'My being an idiot days are over,' he said. 'Apart from today.'

And he broke past Jayden's arms and started pushing his way against the tide of people. He shouted her name – 'Polly! Polly!' – but he couldn't see her.

Polly was one of the last people to come off on the Mount Polbearne side: there had been a rush, and she had hung back to let the others go, especially the little ones. Polbearnites were superstitious about being on the causeway when the water came in, and rightly so, she knew.

Anyway, she was only wearing flip-flops; she didn't really mind the cold water stealing across the tops of her toes. It was going to be the most spectacular sunset. She glanced up at the buildings, which looked as though they were on fire, listening to the chatter and laughter of people going past her, happy with their day – the turnout had been amazing, the causeway full. Patrick had been interviewed for a newspaper again, so everyone was happy.

She didn't hear it for a long time, but something caught her, something on the wind, and even though the water was now uncomfortably high, she stopped, turned, looked around at the distant figure. Someone was still out there. Her heart stopped. Then she recognised him.

Everyone else had gone; the causeway was closed. But he was here. He was here, that was all, and Polly started to run.

He was running towards her just as quickly, with the same determined look on his face as she had, staring straight at her. The water was splashing round her ankles now, the sun a great glowing ball in the pink-streaked sky as they collided in the middle of the causeway. Without a moment's hesitation or a single word being spoken, Huckle lifted her up as if she was made of thistledown and spun her in his arms and kissed her full on the mouth, and she returned it hungrily, as if there had been no separation between them, as if it were

411

the same kiss they had started at the wake: the same power, the same force. Huckle felt like a man dying of thirst in the desert who'd been given a glass of water. Polly didn't think at all.

It was only when the water was lapping up to his thighs that Huckle reluctantly drew away.

'I think we may have to get out of here,' he said, gently putting her down. Polly laughed at the splash of the cold water.

People were shouting at them from both sides as they waded, helpless with laughter, back to the Mount Polbearne side, hand in hand. The waves came in with incredible speed, the freezing water up to their chests as they were hauled out by friendly hands. Archie gave them a scolding, but they looked at each other and giggled again. It was just so astonishing to Polly that Huckle was here, in front of her again, grinning his big farm boy grin. She wanted to run her fingers through his thick cornstalk hair.

'Can I make some kind of totally terrible joke about wet clothes and getting out of them?' he asked.

'You,' said Polly, 'can do whatever you like.'

She took him up to the big room she loved so much, that had haunted his dreams, with the sea view, the view of clear, pure blue, darkening now. The boats were all out. Good. Polly shut Neil in the bathroom and came back, a little nervous all over again.

'Are you hungry?' she asked.

'Not sure,' said Huckle. 'Yes.'

And she fetched the fresh bread, and the new honey.

Later, happy, sated, Polly snuggled under the blanket with Huckle, breathing in the wonderful warm scent of him, stroking the light golden curls that covered his chest – he was so extraordinarily beautiful to her – and fell into a deep sleep.

Coda

'Seriously?'

'Seriously!'

The funny thing was, in the end, it was the picture of the two of them embracing, the sun setting behind them, up to their waists in water, that had done it.

FOR THE LOVE OF MOUNT POLBEARNE, the caption had said, whereupon the council had voted against the new bridge five to three, and that was that. And Lance had sighed heavily, and slashed the price of the old lighthouse.

They were standing at the top of it, a room that had windows on all sides, and gave the dizzying sensation that you were right out at sea, or flying like a bird above it. It had the same wobbly wooden flooring that Polly was leaving behind in the flat (there were plans to possibly turn that into a little café), and the paint was peeling on the walls. Neil was flying around it happily.

'Where will we even get the circular furniture?' said Huckle, but Polly could see he was just as taken with it as she was. It was damaged, messy and scruffy – but then, as Polly had pointed out, so were they, and that seemed to be working out just fine. And Huckle could not have denied her a thing.

'But I want a fireman's pole,' he said.

'Anything,' said Polly. 'I can dance round it if you like.'

'I would like.'

He smiled at her. 'Won't you miss the light?'

She looked at him, then looked out again at the beautiful, dancing golden sea.

'You're my light,' she said quietly, and he pulled her to him, burying his face in her mass of hair.

And Polly looked over his shoulder through the huge ceiling-to-floor windows and saw the little fishing fleet heading out for their evening's work. As usual, a flock of seagulls followed behind them, chattering angrily, as the clouds blazed with gold. She could see something – a fish, or possibly a seal – jumping and splashing at *The Tarn*'s bow. They often did this, like they were playing. But tonight, somehow, it felt different; it felt like the spirit of someone watching over the boat; the spirit of Tarnie, perhaps, still with them somehow. Even though she knew it was daft, she still couldn't shake it, as she stood there in the lighthouse, safe in the ring of her loved one's arms.

'Godspeed,' she murmured to the boats, and those who sailed on them, remembering once again Tarnie's song:

> *I wish I was a fisherman*
> *Tumbling on the seas*
> *Far away from dry land*

415

And its bitter memories
Casting out my sweet line
With abandonment and love
No ceiling bearing down on me
'Cept the starry sky above
With light in my head
You in my arms
Woohoo!

Acknowledgements

Thanks, first off and always, to Ali Gunn, OF COURSE, and absolutely to the stark-staring amazing team at Little, Brown, particularly my wonderful editor Rebecca Saunders; someone else's wonderful editor Manpreet Grewal, whom nonetheless I pester fairly regularly; the sensational Emma Williams and the equally wonderful Jo Wickham and their teams; David Shelley and Ursula Mackenzie, a formidable duo; Charlie King, Camilla Ferrier, Sarah McFadden, Patisserie Zambetti, Alice, the board and my lovely friends and family, here, there and everywhere.

The more eagle-eyed amongst you might think, AHA! That grumpy lady's name, Gillian Manse, is very much like that of esteemed novelist Jill Mansell – a bitter vendetta? And I will say nothing can be further from the truth: Jill is quite lovely in every way, and she bid to have her name included in the book in last year's Comic Relief auction.

On that subject, there is a lot concerning itself with the sea in this book. There are two amazing organisations which help sailors in dreadful conditions: one is the RNLI, of course, www.rnli.org, who I'm sure you've heard of; the other is the Fisherman's Mission, www.fishermensmission.org.uk, who do a simply astonishing job helping people in this treacherous line of work. Donations have been made to both of these organisations from the proceeds of this book.

And lastly, the song which is quoted throughout, 'Fisherman's Blues', is by The Waterboys and I love it dearly, and if you'd like to hear it whilst you're reading, it's here: www.tinyurl.com/fishermansblues but I would also recommend their entire back catalogue.

As ever, all the recipes in this book have been tested by me – in the case of the easy bread, about once a week.

And do, please, get in touch: it's www.facebook.com/thatwriterjennycolgan or @jennycolgan on Twitter.

Very warmest wishes,
Jenny xx

Life is sweet with

Jenny
COLGAN

EASIEST WHITE BREAD

Now here is an absolute starter for bread. It could not be simpler, is just the thing for a lazy Sunday when you're just kind of flolloping about. It will allow you to flollop about whilst also giving you a real sense of accomplishment. If you have ever thought, 'hmm, that is just not for me, that weird bread stuff', then I really really hope you give this a go.

It is the easiest bread you can ever make. You can't really go wrong and the second you taste it you will immediately realise why people like baking.

700 g bread flour
1 sachet dried yeast
400 ml warm water
1 level tbspn of salt
1 level tbspn of sugar

Sift the flour, then warm it slightly in the microwave (I do 600w for one minute). Add the yeast, salt and sugar, then the water. Mix.

Knead on a floury surface for a few minutes until it's a nice smooth ball.

Leave for two hours whilst you read the papers or go for a stroll.

Knead again for a few minutes.

Leave again for an hour whilst you take a nice relaxing bath.

Heat the oven to 230 degrees and grease a bread tin.

Leave in the oven for 30 minutes, or until it makes a hollow noise when tapped on the bottom.

Leave to cool as long as you can stand it, then devour.

CHEESE STRAWS

Another easy-peasy, but delicious, savoury recipe.

Pre-heat the oven to 200 degrees. Butter and line a baking tray.

Combine 120g of soft butter with 450g of cheese (I KNOW it's a lot. These are for sharing and parties and things. I like extra mature cheddar but any hard cheese will do – the Dutch ones are fine. Nothing soft or blue).

Add:
250 g of flour
1 tspn of salt
chilli flakes to your taste
plenty of pepper
1 tspn of baking powder

Roll into plasticine snakes, just like at primary school. Size and dimension is up to you but if they're too thick they will taste a bit stodgy.

Bake for 15 minutes or until crunchy.

SWEETCORN FRITTERS

These are my husband's absolute favourites so he gets woken up with them on his birthday. Actually, I should make them more often now I think about it; they're lovely and tasty and easy.

Beat 1 egg.

Add a tablespoon of water, 1 cup of flour, 1 small tin of sweetcorn (or half a standard size, or double everything else and use the whole tin) and 1 tspn of baking powder.

Season to taste (in our case, we use lots of salt and pepper).

Form into cakes and fry on a medium heat. Take off and drain on kitchen roll. Yum!

CINNAMON ROLLS

These are ACE, delicious, and will make the ones you buy in *cough* high-street coffee emporia seem rubbish.

1 cup milk
¼ cup butter
1 packet yeast
¼ cup sugar
1 beaten egg
3½ cups flour
½ tspn salt

For the inside:
1 cup brown sugar
1 tspn cinnamon
½ cup soft butter

For the top:
Icing sugar
Water

Grease and line a large baking pan.

Heat the milk, butter and sugar gently together in a saucepan, then allow to cool.

Combine with the yeast, egg, two cups of the flour and the salt. Then beat the rest of the flour in slowly.

Knead for five minutes, then leave for one hour to rise.

Mix together all of the inside ingredients.

Roll out the dough and cover with the inside mix. Then (this is the fun bit) roll up the dough and cut into slices, like a Swiss roll.

Leave these for another hour to rise (on their sides), then bake for 25 minutes at 180 degrees. Leave to cool (just for a bit; no need to deprive yourself any longer), then ice.

FOCACCIA

I once had a focaccia-off with a chef friend. He beat me hands down, OF COURSE, but we were lucky enough to be using an outdoor oven, which gave them both such a lovely flavour. Anyway, whack your own oven up; 220 degrees will give it a good taste (but watch out for burning).

500g flour
1½ tspn salt
325 ml hand-warm water
1 sachet yeast
2 tbspn olive oil
Cheese/rosemary/anything you fancy for the top

Mix the flour and salt.

Mix the yeast with the hand-warm water. Add this and the oil to the flour/salt mix.

Knead for ten minutes. Leave for one hour, warm and covered.

Stretch out the dough into a long shape, about 20cm by 30cm, then leave for another forty minutes.

Press your fingers into the risen dough to make little indents and cook for twenty minutes at 220 degrees.

Remove from the oven and add the cheese, herbs and some more drips of olive oil. Then give it another five minutes in the oven.

BAGELS

Bagels can be a little fiddly but they're hard to find where I live and sometimes NEEDS MUST.

  4 cups bread flour
  1 tbspn sugar
  1½ tspn salt
  1 tbspn vegetable oil
  1 packet instant yeast
  1¼ cups hand-warm water

Mix the ingredients together to form a stiff dough.

Knead for ten minutes.

Cut into eight pieces and leave to rest for about twenty minutes.

Switch on the oven at 195 degrees.

Form into rings (you can stick the ends together with a bit of milk if they're being tricky). Leave for another twenty minutes.

Boil a big pot of water.

CAREFULLY dip the bagels into the water one by one for about a minute. I use a kind of barbecue fork.

Add any toppings – for example, chopped onion, raisins (not together obviously).

Bake for ten minutes, per side, in the oven.

SHORTBREAD

So simple, but so good. Use good quality butter too, but they're delicious anyway. You can put chocolate chips in them but I don't bother myself. This is a good one to do with children, although they find the 'putting in the fridge' bit torture. It is necessary though or they'll go all crumbly.

150 g butter
60 g caster sugar
200 g flour

Line a baking tray and pre-heat the oven to 180 degrees.

Blend the sugar and butter very well and then add the flour till you get a soft paste. Roll this out, no more than 1cm thick, then cut it however you like: with a cutter, or just in little lines to be tidy.

Sprinkle with a little more sugar, then chill in the fridge for at least half an hour. By the way, if you're anything like me I am always grabbing recipes and starting them and not reading them through properly. Then I get to the bit where it says 'now marinate for four hours' when I need dinner ready in the next twenty minutes. So let me highlight that bit in case you are at all like me: **CHILL FOR HALF AN HOUR!** ☺

And then bake for 20 minutes, or until golden brown.

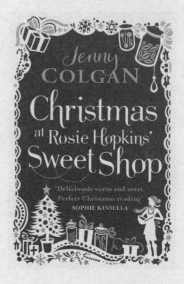

Chapter One

Lipton was quiet underneath the stars. It was quiet as the snow fell through the night; as it settled on the roof of the Isitts' barn and the bell house of the school; as it came in through the cracked upper windows that needed mending at Lipton House; as it cast a hush across the cobbled main street of the village, muting the few cars that passed by. It lay on the roofs of the dentist's and the doctor's surgery; it fell on Manleys, the dated ladieswear boutique, and on the Red Lion, its outdoor tables buried under mounds, its mullioned windows piled high with the stuff.

It fell on the ancient church with the kissing gate, and the graveyard with its repeated local names: Lipton, Isitt, Carr, Cooper, Bell.

It fell on the sleeping sheep, camouflaging them completely (Rosie had made Stephen laugh once, asking where the sheep slept when it got cold. He had looked at her strangely and said, 'In the Wooldorf, of course, where else?' and she had taken a moment or two before she kicked him crossly in the shins). It fell on birds cosy in their nests, their heads under their wings, and settled like a sigh, piled soft and deep in the gullies and crevices of the great towering Derbyshire hills that fringed the little town.

Even now, after a year of living there, Rosie Hopkins couldn't get over how quiet it was in the countryside. There were birds, of course, always, singing their hearts out in the morning. One could usually hear a cock crow, and every now and then from the deeper sections of the woods would come a distant gunshot, as someone headed out to hunt rabbits (you weren't meant to, the woods belonged to the estate, so no one ever owned up, although if you passed Jake the farm-hand's little tied cottage on a Saturday night, the smell of a very rich stew might just greet your nostrils).

But tonight, as Rosie went to mount the little narrow stairs to bed, it felt quieter than ever. There was something different about it. Her foot creaked on the step.

'Are you coming up or what?' came the voice from over-head.

Even though she and Stephen had lived there together now for nearly a year, Rosie still wasn't out of the habit of calling it Lilian's cottage. Her great-aunt, whom she'd come up to look after when Lilian had broken her hip, had moved into a lovely local home, but they still had her over most Sundays, so Rosie felt that, even though legally she had bought the cottage, she rather had to keep it exactly as Lilian liked it. Well, it was slightly that and slightly that Lilian would sniff and raise her eyebrows when they so much as tried to introduce a new picture, so it was easier all round just to keep it as it was. Anyway, Rosie liked it too. The polished

434

wooden floor covered in warm rugs; the fireplace with its horse brasses, the chintzy sofa piled with cushions and floral throws; the old Aga and the old-fashioned butler's sink. It was dated, but in a very soft, worn-in, comfortable way, and when she lit the wood burner (she was terrible with fires; people from miles around would come to scoff and point at her efforts, as if growing up in a house with central heating was something to be ashamed of), she never failed to feel happy and cosy there.

Stephen had the use of Peak House, which was part of his family estate, a bankrupt and crumbling seat that gave Lipton its name. Peak House was a great big scary-looking thing up on the crags. It had a lot more space, but somehow they'd just found themselves more and more at Lilian's cottage. Also, as Rosie was just about eking a living from the sweetshop and Stephen was in teacher training, they were both completely skint and Lilian's cottage was substantially easier to heat.

Stephen may have scoffed a bit at the decor, but he seemed more than happy to lie on the sofa, his sore leg, damaged in a landmine accident in Africa, propped up on Rosie's lap as they watched box sets on Lilian's ancient television. Other nights, when the picture was just too grainy, Stephen would read to her and Rosie would knit, and Stephen would tease her for making the world's longest scarf, and she would tell him to hush, he would be pleased when it turned cold, and if he wasn't quiet she would knit him a pair of long johns and make him wear them, which shut him up pretty fast.

'In a minute!' shouted Rosie up the stairs, glancing round to make sure the door was shut on the wood burner – she was always nearly causing conflagrations. She was struck by the heaviness of the air. They hadn't moved in to Lilian's downstairs bedroom, all of them keeping up the pretence that one day Lilian might want to use it again, so they kept it pristine, the bed made up, her clothes still hanging in the wardrobe. Rosie kept a shrewd nurse's eye on her eighty-seven-year-old great-aunt. Lilian liked to complain about the home, but Rosie could see, in the rosiness of her cheeks (Lilian took great pride in her excellent complexion) and her slight weight gain (this, by contrast, made her utterly furious), that actually, living somewhere with help on hand all the time, and company, was just what Lilian needed. She had lasted a long time by herself in her own home, trying to pretend to the world at large that everything was absolutely fine, when clearly it wasn't. She might complain, but it was clear that it was a weight off her shoulders.

So they continued to sleep in the little attic, adapted years before as a spare bedroom for Lilian's brothers. It was clean and bare, with views on one side of the great craggy Derbyshire fells, and on the other of Lilian's garden, the herb and vegetable patches tended with surprising care by Stephen, the rose bower trimmed from time to time by Mr Isitt, the local dairy farmer.

It was utterly freezing up in the unheated attic. Rosie saw with a smile that Stephen was already in bed, tucked in tightly under the sheets, blankets and thick eiderdown (Lilian thought duvets were a modern intrusion for lazy people; Rosie couldn't deny there was a certain comfort in being tucked in tight with hospital corners, plus it was much harder for your other half to steal the covers).

'Hurry up,' he said.

'Oh good,' said Rosie. 'You've warmed up one side. Now can you shift to the other side, please?'

The shape under the covers was unmoved.

'Not a chance,' it said. 'It's brass monkey bollocks up here.'

'Thank goodness I share my bed with a gentleman,' said Rosie. 'Move! And anyway, that's my side.'

'It is NOT your side. This is the window side, which you insisted, when we were stifling up here in the summer, was making you too hot so you needed the other side.'

'I don't know what you mean,' said Rosie, coming round the far end of the large sleigh bed. 'Now budge.'

'No!'

'Budge!'

'NO!'

Rosie began to wrestle with him, avoiding, as ever, his weaker left leg, until eventually Stephen suggested that if she really needed warming up, he had a plan, and she found that she liked that plan.

Afterwards, now cosy (as long as her feet didn't stray to the far regions of the mattress; if she didn't think it would turn Stephen off for ever, she would have worn bed socks), she felt herself drifting off to sleep, or she would have done if Stephen hadn't been lying so rigid next to her. He was pretending to be asleep, but she wasn't fooled for a second.

Still distracted by the heavy weather, she turned round to face him in the moonlight. Rosie liked to see the moon, and the countryside was so dark they rarely closed the curtains, a novelty she was so keen on it made Stephen laugh, as if it were a house feature. Stephen looked back at her. Rosie had curly black hair that she was always trying to wrestle into straight submission, but he loved it when it curled, as it did now, wild and cloudy around her face. Her eyes were direct and green, her face freckled. Her skin glowed pale, her curvy body lit by the moonlight. He couldn't resist running his hand round her waist to her generous hips. He could never understand for a minute why Rosie worried about her weight, when her body was so voluptuous and lovely.

'Mm,' he said.

'What's up with you?' asked Rosie.

'I'm fine,' said Stephen. 'And don't look at me. That wasn't an "I'm fine" I'm fine. That was an "actually I am TOTALLY fine" I'm fine.'

'That one's even worse.'

'Ssh.'

Rosie glanced towards the window.

'It's weird out there.'

'That's what you said the night you heard the owl.'

'Come on, owls are really scary.'

'As opposed to drive-by shootings in London?'

'Shut it.' Rosie did her proper cockney voice that rarely failed to make him laugh, but she could see in the light, as her fingers traced his strong brow, his thick dark hair flopping on his forehead, his long eyelashes, that he wasn't even smiling.

'It's just kids.'

'I know.'

Stephen had been waiting for a job to come free at the local school for a while. He had only ever taught overseas, so had been considered underqualified and sent off to do his time in various schools, including one in central Derby that had taught him a bit, but nonetheless he was still nervous about tomorrow.

'So what are you worried about?'

'Because I'm not just their new teacher, am I? They all know who I am.'

Stephen was from the local family of landed gentry. Even though he'd rejected everything they stood for, and broken away from his parents – he had now made up with his mother, after his father had died of a heart attack – his every doing was subject to constant speculation in the village. Rosie also got her fair share of snotty gossip for going out with him, as several local worthies had had him in mind for their own daughters, but she kept this from him as much as possible.

'Well that's good,' she argued. 'All the young mums fancy you and all the kids think you're Bruce Wayne.'

'Or they all still think I'm a sulky pretentious teen,' said Stephen sorrowfully.

'Well that's okay too,' said Rosie. 'You'll get on well with the kids.'

She could tell he was still wearing the brooding expression.

'We should definitely have had this conversation before we had sex,' she said. 'Then the relaxing bit could have come later.'

The moonlight caught a glint in his eye.

'Well, maybe ...'

She grinned at him.

'You know, for a wounded war dog. the Right Hon. Lipton, you still have some moves ...'

Just as he moved towards her, however, she leapt up out of bed.

'Snow!' she shouted. 'Look at the snow!'

Stephen turned his head and groaned.

'Oh no,' he said.

'Look at it!' said Rosie, heedless of the cold. 'Just look at it!'

The previous winter in Lipton, after an early flurry, it had simply rained all winter; they had had hardly any snow at all. Now here it was, great big fat flakes falling softly all down the road, quickly covering it with a blanket of white.

'It's settling!' shouted Rosie.

'Of course it's lying,' said Stephen. 'This is the Peak District, not Dubai.'

Nonetheless, with a sigh of resignation, he got up and pulled the eiderdown off the bed and padded across the cold wooden floor to Rosie, wrapping them both up in it. The snow flurried and danced in the air, the stars peeking out between the flakes, the mountains great dark looming silhouettes in the distance.

'I've never seen snow like this,' said Rosie. 'Well, not that's lasted.'

'It's bad,' said Stephen soberly. 'It's very early. Lambing was late this year; they'll need looking out for. And no one can get around. It's treacherous for the old folks; they don't clear the roads up here, you know. People get trapped for weeks. We're barely stocked up, and we're in town.'

Rosie blinked. She'd never thought of snow as a serious matter before. In Hackney it was five minutes of prettiness that bunged up all the trains then degenerated quickly into mucky, splashy roads, dog poo smeared into sleet and big grey slushy puddles. This silent remaking of the world filled her with awe.

'If it blocks the pass road . . . well, that's when we all have to resort to cannibalism,' said Stephen, baring his teeth in the moonlight.

'Well I love it,' she whispered. 'Jake's going to drop us off some wood, he said.'

'Ahem,' said Stephen, coughing.

'What?'

'Well,' said Stephen, 'he'll probably be nicking it from somewhere that belongs to my family in the first place.'

'It's just ridiculous that a family owns a whole wood,' said Rosie.

'Ridiculous or not, I can get Laird to deliver it for nothing,' said Stephen. 'Seeing as it's, you know. Ours.'

'Yeah yeah yeah. Because your great-grandad times a jillion shagged a princess by accident,' said Rosie, whose knowledge of Stephen's ancestry was hazy. 'Whatever.'

'Whatever,' said Stephen, kissing her soft scented shoulder, 'means a warm, cosy house. Unlike this icebox. Come come, my love. Back to bed.'

WELCOME TO ROSIE HOPKINS' SWEETSHOP OF DREAMS

Jenny Colgan

Were you a sherbet lemon or chocolate lime fan? Penny chews or hard-boiled sweeties (you do get more for your money that way)? The jangle of your pocket money ... the rustle of the pink and green striped paper bag ...

Rosie Hopkins thinks leaving her busy London life, and her boyfriend Gerard, to sort out her elderly Aunt Lilian's sweetshop in a small country village is going to be dull. Boy, is she wrong.

Lilian Hopkins has spent her life running Lipton's sweetshop, through wartime and family feuds. As she struggles with the idea that it might finally be the time to settle up, she also wrestles with the secret history hidden behind the jars of beautifully coloured sweets.

'This funny, sweet story is Jenny Colgan at her absolute best'
Heat

CHRISTMAS AT ROSIE HOPKINS' SWEETSHOP

Jenny Colgan

Curl up with Rosie, her friends and her family as they
prepare for a very special Christmas . . .

Rosie Hopkins is looking forward to Christmas in the little
Derbyshire village of Lipton, buried under a thick blanket of
snow. Her sweetshop is festooned with striped candy canes, large
tempting piles of Turkish Delight, crinkling selection boxes
and happy, sticky children. She's going to be spending it
with her boyfriend, Stephen, and her family, who are
flying in from Australia. She can't wait.

But when a tragedy strikes at the heart of their little community,
all of Rosie's plans for the future seem to be blown apart.
Can she build a life in Lipton? And is what's best for the
sweetshop also what's best for Rosie?

'An evocative, sweet treat'
Jojo Moyes

MEET ME AT THE CUPCAKE CAFÉ

Jenny Colgan

Come and meet Issy Randall, proud owner
of The Cupcake Café.

Issy Randall can bake. No, more than that – Issy can
create stunning, mouth-wateringly divine cakes. After a
childhood spent in her beloved Grampa Joe's bakery, she
has undoubtedly inherited his talent.

When she's made redundant from her safe but dull City job,
Issy decides to seize the moment. Armed with recipes
from Grampa, and with her best friends and local bank
manager fighting her corner, The Cupcake Café opens
its doors. But Issy has absolutely no idea what she's
let herself in for. It will take all her courage –
and confectionery – to avert disaster . . .

'Sheer indulgence from start to finish'
Sophie Kinsella

CHRISTMAS AT THE CUPCAKE CAFÉ

Jenny Colgan

Join Issy, Austin, Pearl and Caroline as they prepare
for a very special Christmas ...

Issy Randall, proud owner of the Cupcake Café, is in love
and couldn't be happier. Her new business is thriving and she
is surrounded by close friends, even if her cupcake colleagues
Pearl and Caroline don't seem quite as upbeat about the upcoming
season of snow and merriment. But when her boyfriend Austin is
scouted for a possible move to New York, Issy is forced to face
up to the prospect of a long-distance romance. And when the
Christmas rush at the café – with its increased demand for
her delectable creations – begins to take its toll,
Issy has to decide what she holds most dear.

This December, Issy will have to rely on all her reserves
of courage, good nature and cinnamon to make
sure everyone has a merry Christmas,
one way or another ...

'Light and fun read for the sweet-toothed, with a
clutch of recipes as the icing on top'
Choice

THE LOVELIEST CHOCOLATE SHOP IN PARIS

Jenny Colgan

As dawn breaks over the Pont Neuf, and the cobbled alleyways
of Paris come to life, Anna Trent is already awake and at
work; mixing and stirring the finest, smoothest, richest
chocolate; made entirely by hand, it is sold to the
grandes dames of Paris.

It's a huge shift from the chocolate factory she worked in
at home in the north of England. But when an accident
changed everything, Anna was thrown back in touch
with her French teacher, Claire, who offered her the
chance of a lifetime – to work in Paris with her
former sweetheart, Thierry,
a master chocolatier.

With old wounds about to be uncovered and healed,
Anna is set to discover more about real chocolate –
and herself – than she ever dreamed.

'Gorgeous, glorious, uplifting'
Marian Keyes

WEST END GIRLS

Jenny Colgan

The streets of London are paved with gold ... allegedly.

They may be twin sisters, but Lizzie and Penny Berry are complete
opposites – Penny is blonde, thin and outrageous; Lizzie quiet,
thoughtful and definitely not thin. The one trait they do
share is a desire to DO something with their lives and,
as far as they're concerned, the place to get
noticed is London.

Out of the blue they discover they have a grandmother living
in Chelsea – and when she has to go into hospital, they
find themselves flat-sitting on the King's Road. But,
as they discover, it's not as easy to become It Girls
as they'd imagined, and West End Boys aren't
at all like Hugh Grant ...

'A brilliant novel from the mistress of chick-lit'
Eve

OPERATION SUNSHINE

Jenny Colgan

Evie needs a good holiday. Not just because she's been working all
hours in her job, but also because every holiday she has ever
been on has involved sunburn, arguments and projectile
vomiting – sometimes all three at once. Why can't
she have a normal holiday, like other people seem
to have – some sun, sand, sea and
(hopefully) sex?

So when her employers invite her to attend a conference with
them in the South of France, she can't believe her luck.
It's certainly going to be the holiday of a lifetime –
but not quite in the way Evie imagines!

'Colgan at her warm, down-to-earth best'
Cosmopolitan

DIAMONDS ARE A GIRL'S BEST FRIEND

Jenny Colgan

Sophie Chesterton has been living the high life of glamorous parties, men and new clothes, never thinking about tomorrow. But after one shocking evening, she comes back down to earth with the cruellest of bumps. Facing up to life in the real world for the first time, Sophie quickly realises that when you've hit rock bottom, the only way is up.

Join her as she starts life all over again: from cleaning toilets for a living to the joys of bring-your-own-booze parties; from squeezing out that last piece of lip gloss from the tube to bargaining with bus drivers.

For anyone who's ever been scared of losing it all, this book is here to show you money can't buy you love, and best friends are so much more fun than diamonds . . .

'Jenny Colgan always writes an unputdownable, page-turning bestseller – she's the queen of modern chick-lit'
Louise Bagshawe

THE GOOD, THE BAD AND THE DUMPED

Jenny Colgan

Now, you obviously, would never, ever look up your exes on Facebook. Nooo. And even if you did, you most certainly wouldn't run off trying to track them down, risking your job, family and happiness in the process.
Posy Fairweather, on the other hand . . .

Posy is delighted when Matt proposes – on top of a mountain, in a gale, in full-on romantic mode. But a few days later disaster strikes: he backs out of the engagement. Crushed and humiliated, Posy starts thinking. Why has her love life always ended in total disaster? Determined to discover how she got to this point, Posy resolves to get online and track down her exes. Can she learn from past mistakes? And what if she has let Mr Right slip through her fingers on the way?

'A Jenny Colgan novel is as essential for a week in the sun as Alka Seltzer, aftersun and far too many pairs of sandals'
Heat

Keep in touch with

Jenny

www.jennycolgan.com

For more information on all Jenny's books, latest news and mouth-watering recipes

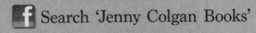
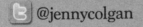